"*Rebekah's Treasure* by Sylvia Bambola is a tale that will capture your attention and heart. Set in war-torn Israel when zealots fought for the honor of the Temple and Jerusalem, when the majesty and might of Rome became a terror and a scourge, one Jewish family's story twists and turns with passion, action, and love. This novel will not only entertain, but satisfy the most avid reader. Well done, Bambola. Well done."

Barbara C. Nelson, author of *Women on a Mission*

"Sylvia Bambola, in her historical novel, *Rebekah's Treasure*, surrounds actual events with an intriguing fictional story and skillfully draws in the reader. Normally not a reader of fiction, myself, I found I was unable to put down this fascinating book until it was finished!"

Cindy Miller, author of *The Home That God Built*

"To read *Rebekah's Treasure*, by Sylvia Bambola, is to become engulfed in an intricate work of art. As your mind joins itself to the story, it will absorb the fibers and finely crafted strands of its tapestry until you are completely captivated. Rich in detail, reading this book is nearly like watching a movie. Bambola has done a remarkable job of deliberately weaving each carefully chosen thread into a story that will alter the way you view the past and the future . . . forever."

Christina Cook Lee, music/media producer and author of *A Quest for Virtue*

"Rebekah's Treasure, a love story that unfolds in the midst of impossible circumstances, captivates the reader from the first page to the last. Drama, suspense, passion, faith—all the elements of a riveting read are found in this novel which follows a family torn apart by Jerusalem's struggle for survival in 70 A.D. The author's exquisite gift for storytelling combined with historically-accurate backdrops, make this book a treasure. I couldn't put it down!"

Joanne Derstine Curphey, Director of Communications at Christian Retreat, columnist for *Today's Seniors of America*, free-lance editor and writer.

"For everyone who enjoys historical fiction, *Rebekah's Treasure* will be right up your alley. Sylvia Bambola has written an extremely well researched story of the fall of Jerusalem. For you who love love-stories, you'll also find this book is for you. If you like mysteries, again this book is for you. I heartily recommend it."

Joe Fouraker, Florida State Faith Fund Coordinator for Gideons International, on Board of Directors of Gospel Crusade, Northwest airlines 747 captain—retired, and history buff

Rebekah's Treasure

Sylvia Bambola

Heritage Publishing House
Bradenton, Florida

Also by Sylvia Bambola

Return to Appleton

Waters of Marah

Tears in a Bottle

Refiner's Fire

A Vessel of Honor

REBEKAH'S TREASURE

Published by Heritage Publishing House

ISBN 13: 978-0-9899707-4-7
ISBN: 0989970744
Library of Congress Control Number: 2013950475

Scriptures taken from Holy Bible, King James Version, Cambridge, 1769

For information:
Heritage Publishing House
1767 Lakewood Ranch Blvd.
Bradenton, FL 34211

dedicated to

VINCENT

in loving memory

Acknowledgements

I can't think of anything more important than family and I thank God for mine. They are surely among the best in the world.

A big "thank you" to my daughter, Gina, for her help in routing out those pesky misspelled words that neither I nor spell-check were able to discover; and also for researching, then creating her maps of ancient Jerusalem, Herod's Temple and the Land of Israel; and this while recovering from major surgery.

Also, "thank you, thank you, thank you" to my son, Cord, who is forever helping me with my computer problems, and never complains or makes me feel I'm an intrusion no matter what hour of the day or night I call and cry "help!".

Appreciation also goes to my church family and friends for their encouragement and help.

You are all such blessings!

"For where your treasure is, there will your heart be also." Luke 12:34

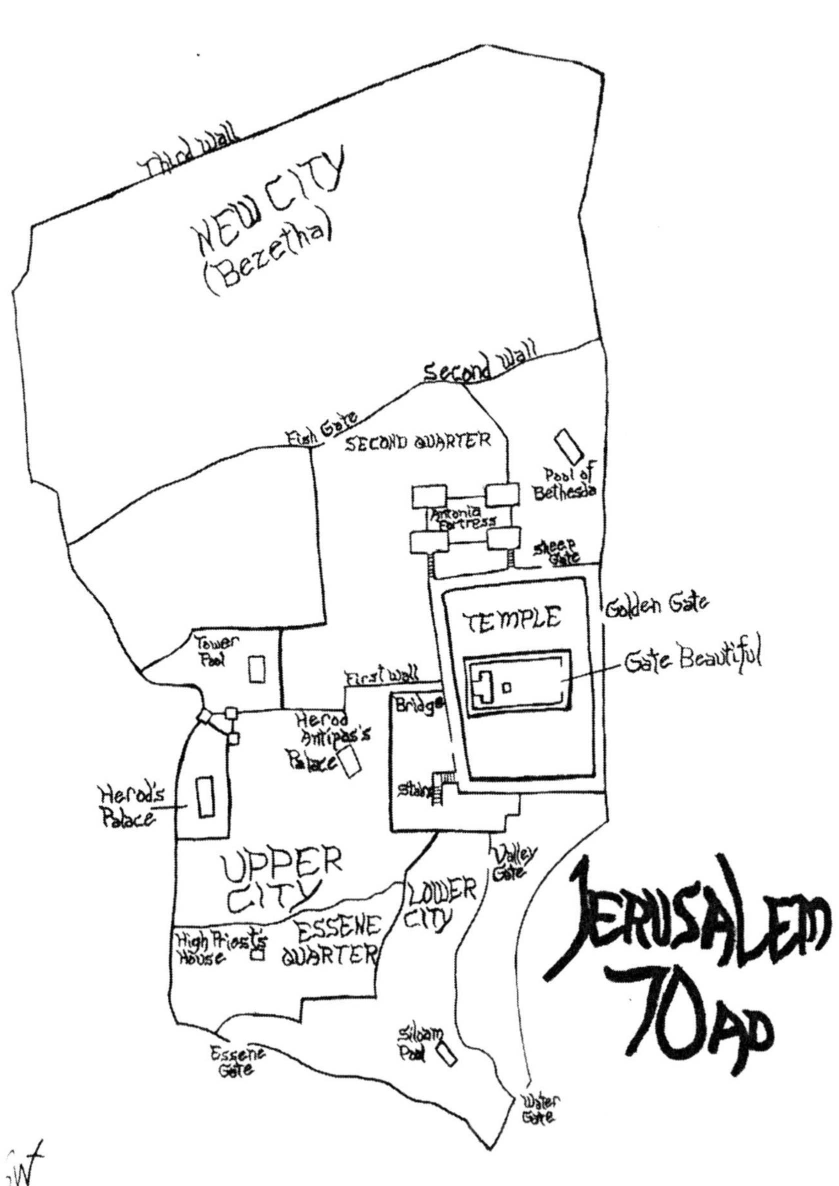
Third Wall
NEW CITY
(Bezetha)
Second Wall
Fish Gate
SECOND QUARTER
Pool of
Bethesda
Antonia
Fortress
sheep
Gate
Golden Gate
TEMPLE
Gate Beautiful
Tower
Pool
First Wall
Bridge
Herod
Antipas's
Palace
Stairs
Herod's
Palace
UPPER
CITY
Valley
Gate
LOWER
CITY
ESSENE
QUARTER
High Priest's
House
JERUSALEM
70 AD
Siloam
Pool
Essene
Gate
Water
Gate
GWT

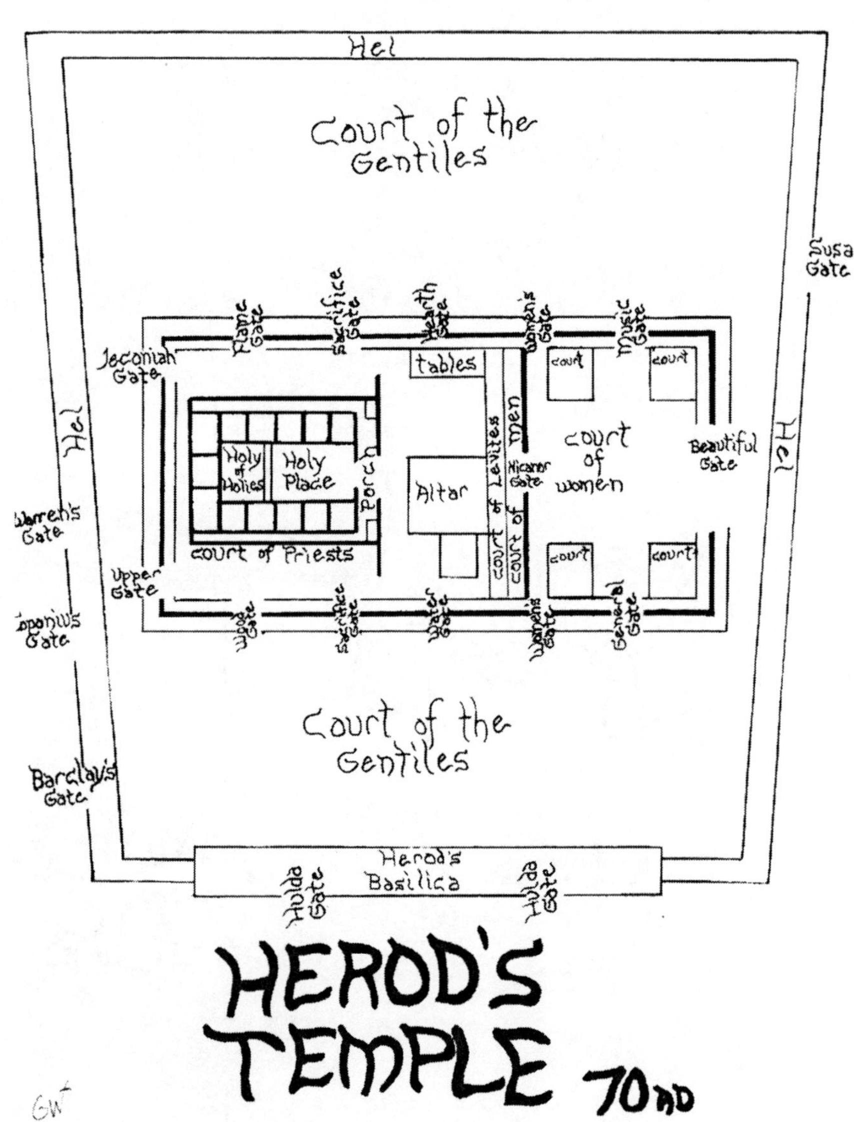
Hel
Court of the Gentiles
Susa Gate
Flame Gate
Sacrifice Gate
Hearth Gate
Women's Gate
Music Gate
Jeconiah Gate
tables
court
court
Hel
Holy of Holies
Holy Place
Porch
Altar
court of Levites
court of men
Nicanor Gate
court of women
Beautiful Gate
Hel
Warren's Gate
court of Priests
Upper Gate
court
court
Wood Gate
Sacrifice Gate
Water Gate
Women's Gate
General Gate
Gate
Court of the Gentiles
Barclay's Gate
Herod's Basilica
Hulda Gate
Hulda Gate
HEROD'S TEMPLE 70 AD

LAND
of
ISRAEL
70 AD
SYRIA
Sidon
Damascus
Tyre
TETRARCHY
OF
PHILIP
Seleucia
Capernaum
Bethsaida
Sea of Galilee
GALILEE
Dor
Nazareth
Megiddo
Caesarea
Pella
Mediterranean
Sea
Samaria
SAMARIA
DECAPOLIS
Jordan River
Joppa
JUDEA
Jericho
Qumran
Philadelphia
Jerusalem
Bethlehem
Hebron
En-Gedi
Dead Sea
Masada
Beersheba
GWT

Prologue

Jerusalem 33 A.D.

"You're not going to be a pest, are you, Rebekah?"

I hug the white limestone cup as I walk toward the long, low table without answering my sister. All the while my small fingers tighten around the plain bowl-like cup that has no handle or stem. "Where will the Master sit?"

"How should I know?" Judith says, stepping around one of our good damask-covered couches and placing bowls of herbs on the table.

"Because no one but the Master can use my cup."

"Oh, stop being a nuisance and just give it to me!"

I hug the cup tighter to my chest. "You needn't be cross. It's not my fault that Anna dropped the tray of goblets this morning. Even Mama called her a clumsy servant."

Judith turns to look at me, "Well . . . forget about Anna."

Her long black hair falls over her face that everyone calls "pretty" and says looks like Mama's. Even so, I see it. That small, rose-shaped birthmark on her right cheek. I know she hates it. She's always fingering it as if wishing she could wipe it away like a spot of dirt. Mama says it's Judith's only flaw. Maybe that's why I like looking at it.

"You know we now only have twelve goblets, and Mama said you must share since there will be thirteen around the table tonight. It's not *my* idea, so stop fussing." Judith tucks one hand under her chin, the way Mama does when telling me the matter is settled. "Stop acting like a baby."

"I'm *not*. It's just that . . . well . . . my cup is pure. Uncle Abner said so. You know he made it just for me in his cave workshop on Mt. Scopus. He said now that I'm six I should have a special cup for Passover and . . . I wanted to be the first to use it, that's all." I glare at my sister. It wasn't easy being the youngest and always having to defend myself.

"So, it's pure, is it? Do you even know what that means?" Judith's look is mocking.

"Yes! It means . . . it means . . . it's *good*." Papa and Uncle Abner were always talking about ritual purity. Gifts or sacrifices to God were *korban*—Holy unto the Lord. How many times had I heard that? Papa, a priest, often bathed in the *mikvah* to "purify" himself. And Uncle Abner, a Pharisee, made "pure" vessels out of stone when he wasn't teaching Torah in the Temple. If anyone knew about purity and what was good, they did.

Judith forces air through the small space between her upper front teeth, making a hissing sound. "Stone doesn't absorb impurities. *That's why* it stays ritually clean."

I walk past her trying to look as though I know what she's talking about, when in truth I don't. I only know ritual purity had something to do with our gleaming gold and stone Temple, and with pleasing the One True God. I wish I understood more because I was sure I never pleased God. I was always getting into trouble, always making Mama or Judith angry. Always dropping things or getting in the way or making messes. But if I were to use a brand new *stone* cup at Passover, now that would please God. And maybe it would make me pure, too. Make me good and acceptable to all of them—Mama, Papa, Judith, and the Holy One.

"Enough talk." Judith's forehead crinkles like a dried fig. "Hand it over."

I swing the cup behind my back and try to keep my chin from quivering.

"You're not going to cry, are you?"

I shake my head, but already I feel tears cluster, like Mama's lentils, across my cheeks. And instead of obeying Judith, I go to the grillwork covering the doorway where a warm breeze carries the sweet smell of linden that Mama said had blossomed early this year. Oh, how I love this big upper room built on our roof; a room used for overnight guests or celebrations or sometimes, like tonight, by people Mama and Papa loved.

Sometimes Mama would even allow me to play here. And sometimes when I got tired of playing and tired of looking out over the huge Upper City, I'd sneak down the outer steps on the wall and run like the wind to the Gate of the Essenes just inside the Lower City. And then . . . as the bad child I am . . . I'd exit the gate into the Hinnom Valley. I don't know why I go to that awful place; why I always disobey Mama by doing it. Way before I was born, or even before Judith was born, children were burned as sacrifices to Molech there. Now it's the place where garbage and animals were burned.

It was the dead animals that drew me, or rather the bits and pieces of those sacrificed as *sin* offerings—crops of birds, entrails, and those butchered carcasses that could not be burned on the Temple altar but had to be burned outside the city gate. Why some animals could not be burned in the Temple and others could, I don't know. But I do know, because Uncle Abner told me, that these animals were punished by men so I and my people would not be punished by God. And though I don't really understand it, sometimes, amid the flies and horrible smell, and the heat that feels as hot as Mama's ovens, and the smoke that makes my eyes water and that covers me with soot, I watch as basketsful of animal parts are thrown into the ravine. And oh, how frightened I get, trying to spot, by some sign from Heaven, the animal that had been sacrificed for *me*. And I'd stand there, my eyes burning, my mind remembering Uncle Abner's stern warning to keep myself "pure." If I didn't . . . *God could do this to me.*

"Well! Give it here!" Judith barks, making me nearly jump out of my skin.

I wipe my eyes with the back of one hand, while clutching the cup with the other. All right . . . if I wasn't to be the first to use it, there was only one who could. The Master was kind; always made time for me, even when his disciples tried to shoo me away. And oh, how tenderly he kissed my forehead! And how he made me laugh when he tousled my hair! And I can't count the times he held me in his arms and called me his "little chick" as though he were a mama hen. Yes . . . I could give up my cup for the Master . . . but it wasn't easy.

"I don't have all day."

Out of the corner of my eye I see Judith impatiently beckoning with her hand. I turn the cup over and stare at the large t carved into its bottom and wonder why Judith couldn't be more like our older brother, Asher. He was never impatient, never unkind. He even had spent hours teaching me to write the Hebrew alphabet; patiently guiding my hand with his over my wax tablet. But it was the last letter in the alphabet that I loved best—the *tav* or rather what Asher called its ancient symbol, the way Moses had written it, as a t and not as an x like the scribes do today.

Asher said all the letters had meaning, too. And he had taken time to explain them one by one. He had learned all this from the rabbis; things I'd never learn, being a mere girl. But he had been so proud of me when I was finally able to form the letters, and even called me a "scribe" when I began carving the *tav* on all my possessions.

"If you don't give it to me now, I'm going to tell Mama!" Judith snarls, planting herself in front of me like a wall.

It was clear. This time, if I didn't obey, Judith would make good her threat and then I'd be in real trouble. Slowly, I extend the cup. No, it wasn't easy being the youngest or having a sister like "Judith the Perfect." Judith would never think of going to the Hinnom Valley. Judith wasn't "impossible" or "headstrong." Judith didn't need to drink from stone cups to please God. Though I try not to, though I even hold my breath until I'm sure I've turned blue, I let out a sob as I give her my treasure.

"I can't be sure where Jesus will sit," Judith says, her voice kind for the first time. "But I suspect he'll take the position of host, and sit in the center."

Through my tears I watch her place the cup on the table and know that later I'll sneak up the wall steps and peek in, just to be sure that it really was Jesus who used it.

Rebekah

Jerusalem 70 A.D.

CHAPTER 1

"You can't stay. It's just too dangerous now."

My husband, Ethan, stands firm, like David before Goliath, and I know I've lost the battle. Maybe if I had phrased it differently. Maybe if I hadn't said those words—*"we are all going to die"*—maybe then he wouldn't be standing before me now with his hand on the hilt of his dagger as though drawing courage. But too late. My tongue has already betrayed me.

"Any day now, that jackal will be here with his siege works, for what's left for him to conquer but Jerusalem?"

"Vespasian? I thought he was in Alexandria."

"Yes, but his son, Titus, continues his push through Judea."

This time the words drive me to the bear of a man I have loved for twenty-six springs. My head finds its familiar resting place on his chest. He smells of sweat and Temple incense. His beating heart thunders in my ear. And amid this thunder, I hear shuffling, and know, without seeing, that the footfalls are made by our sons.

I pull away and glance at the four young men behind Ethan. All are tall and strong and handsome. Any mother would be proud. But when my eyes drift to the blue tassels that trim their tunics, my stomach clenches. I have come to hate that trim. It's the same trim that hangs from Ethan's tunic, "to remind him of the commandments," he says. Does he think I'm simpleminded? Does he think I don't know that Zealots wear blue fringe?

When I look at my sons, I see my little boys in those faces, faces I have kissed and scrubbed and tended. But I also see the fire. Ethan says it can't be helped, this fire which leaps from their eyes, for the blood of the Maccabees runs through their veins.

Ethan is a priest of Hasmonean lineage.

He has told me I should understand this fire, being the daughter of a priest myself, for Rome's authority is in conflict with the Law of God. But I don't understand. To me it's madness. Yes, madness. I will call it by name. For what else would compel men to hurl themselves into a fight they cannot win? My voice has cried out against this fire. God is my witness, it has. I've told Ethan it's one thing to revolt against that dog, Antiochus, King of Syria, as the Maccabees did nearly two hundred years ago, and quite another to disrupt *Pax Romana.*

Oh, why can't he see it's folly to fight the Roman Empire?

"Come now. Get ready," Ethan says with discernable tenderness in his voice.

"No! I won't go!" a voice wails behind me.

Without turning, I know it's Esther. "You'll do as your father says," I respond, forcing my voice to sound stern, for my heart is not in my words.

"I won't leave my husband. I won't leave Daniel! He's already paid the bride price and we have drunk from the same cup. He has only to prepare the bridal chamber. Once it's finished and we . . . well . . . maybe after that if . . ."

I glance at Ethan, and though I try not to, I know my eyes plead. *Can't we stay?*

"There is no 'after' or 'if'," Ethan says, ignoring me, but answering my question too. His strong muscular legs erase the distance between himself and Esther. "You know what Vespasian has done to every Jewish settlement from Galilee to Judea. The man is a beast. Can we expect any better from his son?"

My daughter does not cower beneath the shadow of his massive frame. "It's you who claim that God will deliver Rome into your hands.

That your army will destroy Vespasian's legions. What are you saying now, Papa? That Vespasian will win? That God has abandoned you?" Esther comes alongside me, her hair, soft as flax, frames a flushed face.

Sweet Esther. So headstrong. But she's right. Ethan cannot have it both ways. All these months of blustering in the face of certain Roman retaliation, and now *this*? My arm encircles Esther's shoulder which quivers, I think, with disappointment and anticipation both. But I say nothing. It is for Ethan to say. It is for Ethan to make his case for sending us away.

Ethan knots his broad forehead. "Nothing has changed. God is still on our side. But it remains to us, to us Zealots, to defend Temple and Torah. To return holiness to unholy Jerusalem. Will you make that task more difficult by staying? Must we worry about you and Mama?"

"Oh, this is too much," I blurt. "Are we not living stones, *living stones*, temples of living stones?"

Ethan avoids my eyes. This is the argument he knows all too well, the words he has heard me say over and over. They are Paul the Apostle's words. Words that used to burn in Ethan's heart before this new strange fire took hold. Are not living stones more important than quarried stones? Are not living stones worth fighting for? Worth protecting? I love the Temple. The *Shekinah* once dwelled there. Though the Temple still stands on the mount like a giant pearl, it is a pearl without luster. The Presence . . . the Divine Presence is gone. And the Temple is not alive. It's not made of *living* stones. It does not breathe. Well . . . yes . . . once, once I did see it breathe. I actually saw it shudder, as if in a sigh. Though no one believes me. But that was long ago, the day they say the great curtain covering the entrance to the Holy of Holies was torn from top to bottom.

The day Messiah died.

"Maybe Daniel can come for me early?" Esther says, plaintively. "Maybe he doesn't need to complete the bridal chamber." Her face is a swirl of emotions. Like the young, she lives both as if there's no tomorrow and as if she were never going to die.

Oh, Esther, Esther! Can't you see the city is perishing? Can't you see there's no time for building bridal chambers? Even so, my heart aches for her. I know what it is to yearn for my bridegroom. Wasn't I even younger than Esther when Ethan's father chose me to be Ethan's bride? And hadn't I eagerly counted the days after the *mohar,* the bride price, was paid for Ethan to come and claim me?

"Ask him, just ask Daniel to come for me today." Esther's eyes are large, imploring. "Tell him it's time to take his lawful bride."

But when Ethan shakes his head without even glancing at either of us, and without uttering one kind word of understanding, I feel compelled to intervene. "Ever since Nero cut his own throat, confusion has riddled the Empire. Even Vespasian ordered his army to stand down for a time. Perhaps he'll do so again since Rome still riots and tears herself apart while searching for her new Caesar. Who has not heard how even their shrine of Jupiter on Capitoline Hill lies in ruins? 'The Deliverance of Zion!' How many of our coins have you seen with that inscription? Everyone believes God has stayed the hand of Rome on our behalf. In light of that, what difference can a few more days make? Or perhaps seven days? Enough time for Esther and Daniel to complete their marriage week."

Ethan's eyes narrow. "This is unworthy of you, Rebekah, you who don't believe Zion will be delivered at all. You who have been telling me that God has forsaken Jerusalem and our Temple. That our sin and corruption have forced Him to lift His hand of protection from us. And now when I wish to send you to safety, you want to remain?"

I look away. I can't have it both ways either. "The armies of Simon and John, and even your precious Eleazar have carved up our city like cheese," I say in a near whisper. "All this in an effort to gain control. And now they fight to take each other's slices. Every day our streets run red with their blood, as well as the blood of the innocent citizens they kill. Inside Jerusalem or outside? What is the difference? There's no safety anywhere, except perhaps Masada. If only we had all left with Josiah."

"It's too late to think about what we should have done. Titus's legions camp only twenty miles away. They've finally cut Jerusalem off from the north and utterly destroyed Hebron in the south. Time is running out. While Jerusalem tears herself apart, that jackal is slowly flanking us. You must get out while you can."

This is so far from what I want. In spite of a tongue ever quick to speak my mind, I've failed to say what is really on my heart. I don't fear death—and the stories of rape and pillage and slaughter coming from Galilee, Peraea, Idumaea and, now, Judea, makes me understand how horrible it can be. But what I fear is that I may now have to face it alone. All these months I've believed that when death came, we would face it *together.* My husband, my sons, my daughter, and I.

"But a new Caesar, once chosen, may call off the war. There's always that chance." I throw my final argument into the air as if winnowing wheat to see where the wind takes it.

"A new Caesar has been chosen. Our spy has just brought the news. And, no, Rebekah, he'll not call it off."

"How can you be so sure?"

"Because Legate Vespasian *is* the new Caesar."

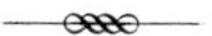

They say he's crazy, this oracle, this son of Ananias. Demon possessed. And though they have flogged him more times than I can count, he still shouts his dark words to every passerby.

But I don't think he's crazy, for I believe him to be a *true* oracle. Even now his words echo in my ears, the words he has been shouting since Sukkot nearly four years ago.

Woe! Woe to thee, Jerusalem!

It's because I don't think he's crazy or demon possessed that my heart is as heavy as lead. I must leave the home I love, the *people* I love. And I must do so knowing Jerusalem is doomed. But how can I leave my husband and sons? My beautiful Upper City? The Women's Court and the Tyropoeon Valley? I cover my face and weep. And when I do, I think of Ethan and my sons, and how they risk their lives every time they slip through the long, dark tunnels beneath the Temple Mount, underground tunnels that snake the city, in order to visit me. I'm a danger to them. A millstone around their necks.

And what of Esther? I picture her soft eyes, large and round as two flatbreads. And so trusting. The Upper City swarms with bandits and cutthroats; and *sicarii*—those fierce assassins—wander the streets, ever ready to plunge their daggers into any who speak of making peace with Rome. What if Esther should fall into one of their hands? I clutch my throat at the thought. No . . . I can no longer think of only what I want. It's Ethan I must think of now; and my sons. My leaving would free them of worry. It would be a blessing to them. And Esther . . . she must be taken to safety. It is foolish to fight it any longer.

Quickly, I slip out of my costly linen tunic and replace it with one of rough homespun, then gather a few things.

I stand in the midst of our sleeping chamber—Ethan's and mine. It's large with walls of plastered Jerusalem limestone, and a floor paved with beautiful tile. It was my mother and father's room when they were alive, and one of many rooms clustered around a paved central courtyard. This house has been in my family for generations, though enlarged over the years, and renovated in both Greek and Roman fashion, so popular since the time of Herod the Great. Aside from the many sleeping chambers and the courtyard, there's a main reception room—with colorful panels, giant frescos and imitation marble borders—several bathrooms with mosaic tile floors, large underground cisterns, two ritual baths, numerous storage rooms, and of course the large upper room which we still use for guests and is still filled with colorful cushions and couches. It remains one of my favorite rooms, a place I often go to pray.

I pray now as I lift my tunic to strap on a leather drawstring pouch. On the bed in front of me lay three of my most prized possessions: an alabaster box filled with costly spikenard from India, my *semadi,* and the cup Uncle Abner made me long ago.

I pick up the *semadi* since it will bc the most useful. The silver coins of the headdress jingle. They are pierced through the center and stitched together, then fastened to padding that covers the forehead and ears, reaching well beyond the shoulders. It is worth a great fortune, and has belonged to the women in my family for generations. Mama gave it to me, and her mother gave it to her. Someday I'll give it to Esther, that is if I don't need it to keep us alive.

A *semadi* is the exclusive property of a woman. No man can ever lay claim to it, not even a husband or son. It should have gone to Judith, but "Judith the Perfect" married a Gentile, a Gentile who raised pigs, of all things, and now lives somewhere in the Decapolis. So, pronouncing her dead, Mama sat *shiva*, despite knowing that the Master taught us there is no longer Greek or Jew, free or slave. We are all one in Him. *One.*

I still miss my sister, and think of her now as I wrap the *semadi* in rough homespun and stuff it into the pouch.

Next I pick up the stone cup, turn it over, and run a finger across the rough carving of the ancient symbol of *tav*. Years ago, the Master drank from it. I saw it with my own eyes, crouched on the steps of the wall. When I think of that night, that's what I remember, that's what stands out. Never what followed. Never the trial, the terrible scourging, the public ridicule, the crucifixion. No. What I remember is the Master in our upper room lifting my cup, *my* cup, and making a covenant. I didn't know then the scope of that covenant. No one did.

My finger lingers on the crude t as I think of my brother, Asher, one of the first of my loved ones to fall during the infighting in Jerusalem. But there were others; neighbors, friends, people I've known all my life. I wrap the cup and slip it into my pouch. It can hold only one thing more. Everything else must remain. I reach for the alabaster box, but stop when I detect a faint scent of spikenard seeping through the porous alabaster. It would be unwise to smell of costly spikenard when passing the sentries. If Ethan's gift had been less precious, saffron or aloe perhaps, I would take it. My heart tumbles at the thought of leaving it behind. Ethan had been so proud of it. And when he gave it to me, oh . . . I can still remember his eyes, liquid and deep—an open well of emotion. And that look was worth more to me than the costly spikenard. Still . . . spikenard fetches even more now, since few were brave enough to enter Jerusalem with such costly cargo. It would surely fetch enough to keep Esther and me in food for months. But no . . . it would be too dangerous.

"Mama! Quickly! We must go!" my son, Aaron, shouts from the courtyard.

In spite of my protest, Ethan has left our oldest son to travel with Esther and me until we reach safety. *Safety.* Is there such a place?

But I do make haste, and tie up the pouch, then position it against my stomach, where it will be more difficult to detect. When I'm satisfied, I pull my rough brown tunic over the pouch, and watch the hem fall across my ankles. Over that, I slip on an outer garment of gray wool, then loosely belt it with a swatch of brown and gray homespun. Finally, I plait my long hair and cover it with a headscarf. From the small table in the corner I retrieve a black jar of burial spices.

"Mama!"

After one last look at the alabaster box on the bed, I dart out the door.

"She tried to escape. To go to Daniel, no doubt," Aaron whispers as we assemble by the door. "If I hadn't been here to stop her, who knows what would have happened."

I squint at Esther who stands by Aaron with her head bowed, surely to avoid my eyes. "Are you crazy!" I say, almost spitting in her ear. "John's men are everywhere, extorting taxes from shop owners and anyone else who looks like he has a shekel to his name. It's dangerous on the streets, especially for a woman alone!"

Aaron nods. "Only this morning, Lamech, one of John of Gischala's generals, the general who's been terrorizing the rich for weeks, beat

Datan, the wool merchant, to death, trying to make him confess where he'd hidden his gold. And yesterday, John's men and Simon bar Giora's Idumaeans—those Edomites who call themselves Jews—battled for hours near King David's Tomb. When it was over, hundreds lay dead. The Upper City is a battlefield with both sides fighting for control."

"And these brutes are always looking for ways to enrich themselves," I add.

"And what a prize you'd be," Aaron says, looking at Esther. "They'd use you to squeeze every shekel from Daniel's considerable fortune."

By the worry in Aaron's eyes I understand how much he fears for our safety. I also understand the great burden that has been placed on his shoulders. I grab Esther and shake her, hoping to make her understand, too. "Give me your word you'll not try to slip away again!"

Esther turns her head.

"Give me your word!"

Silence.

"Don't you understand the danger? If you draw attention to us, if you try to bolt, we could all lose our lives."

For the first time Esther looks at me. "Then leave me behind. I'm not afraid. If anything happens . . . if Jerusalem should fall . . . I want to be with Daniel."

I'm at a loss. If Jerusalem falls, I too want to be with my husband. The thought of leaving him is more than I can bear. How, then, can I fault Esther? In the midst of my silence, Aaron steps forward and takes Esther's chin between his fingers.

"If you love Daniel, you must leave," he says, gently pinching her like he used to when she was little. "Your husband's mind must be clear. Can he fight John of Gischala, Simon bar Giora, the *sicarii*, Vespasian and Titus, *and* worry about you, all at the same time? Worry if you have food? If you're safe? What if this worry causes him to become careless? And what if through carelessness, he gets wounded . . . or killed, how will you feel then?"

"You are cruel to put it so."

"These are cruel times." Aaron releases Esther's chin, his eyes full of compassion.

"You will . . . when you return to the city, tell Daniel how much I loathed leaving him?"

Aaron nods.

"And . . . you'll . . . watch over him?"

Aaron kisses Esther's forehead. "Yes."

"Then it's settled," I say, ignoring my heart which breaks for my Aaron who must now take on another burden; for my Esther, the young bride who has yet to taste the sweetness of lying in her husband's arms; for my beloved Ethan, strong and courageous and too willing to spill his life's blood on a hopeless cause; for my other sons, so eager to be men and follow their father; and for my Jerusalem, the Holy City that has polluted herself. "I have your word, Esther? Your word that you'll come quietly and not cause a disturbance?"

She lowers her eyes, her long lashes cloaking any emotions. "You have my word," she finally says, as though her mouth is full of bitter herbs.

"Hush," I say, but the donkey brays anyway, no doubt to protest carrying the heavy limestone ossuary strapped to its back. We have decided to take the long route through Jerusalem, and head for the Tower Gate. It's safer.

Aaron prods the reluctant donkey along the winding streets. He wears a short brown tunic belted loosely at the waist; over that, a rough homespun robe. Behind his ear is a chip of wood, the sign of a carpenter. It's customary for craftsmen to wear emblems of their trade. Had he chosen to disguise himself as a dyer, he would have worn a strip of colored cloth tied around one arm.

We pass the great stone-paved plaza that borders Herod's palace. It was here crowds gathered while Pilate sat on a raised platform above them and condemned Messiah to death. No Romans are here now. They've long been driven from the city. Instead, the palace and plaza swarm with an assortment of odd-looking men, some in fine leather cuirasses and boots studded with nails, and carrying large swords; others in nothing more than torn tunics and bare feet. It's dangerous here, though far less dangerous than taking the shorter route through the Valley Gate. To get there, one had to cross the Lower City, an area firmly in the hands of John Gischala's men who freely rob whomever they please. At least in the still contested Upper City, John and Simon's forces are too busy fighting each other to bother with us. At least that's what we hope.

When a group of ill-clad rowdies armed with daggers push through a throng of people and head toward us, I question our judgment. A surly-looking man of large proportions leads them. *Gischalites.* John's men. Only Gischalites could look this beastly.

"Now where would you be heading?" asks the leader, his hair a mass of tangles, his metal-trimmed leather cuirass slashed and blood stained. "You're not planning to abandon our fair city now, are you?" He smells of spoiled mutton.

We all tense. The three rebel factions were always on the lookout for Jews fleeing the city. A traitorous act in their view, and punishable by death. Even so, Jerusalem could not be sealed. Many inhabitants had obligations outside her gates. Their shops and fields and vineyards were there. This made the rebels even more watchful for those appearing fearful or too laden with goods. Many an innocent citizen has met his death at the hand of an overly suspicious rebel.

"So where are you going?" the leader presses.

When I see Aaron's hand move beneath his robe to where he conceals a dagger, I thrust the black jar of spices I'm holding into the air, the kind of perfume jug used in burial caves to overcome odor. My chin juts toward the ossuary strapped to the donkey's back. "We're going to my uncle's *kokh.* The year has passed. It's time to place his bones in the ossuary."

The brutish man fingers the delicate rosette carvings that run the length of the stone box, then the lettering beneath them. "'Bones of Abner, son of Eliakim, Pharisee and Servant of the Most High God,'" he reads. "That your uncle? Abner the Pharisee?"

I nod, marveling that this brute can read.

He studies us carefully, noting what is in our hands, how we are dressed. "Why do you bother to advertise your trade? Being so occupied with your dead?" the Gischalite says, gesturing toward the wood tucked behind Aaron's ear.

"A man must make a living. Perhaps *Hashem* will smile on me and cause some passerby to offer me employment for a future day."

The Gischalite pokes the small goatskin flagon strapped across Aaron's shoulder while his eyes sweep over Esther and me to see what else we carry. When he's satisfied we're not taking a long journey, his face becomes thoughtful. "It's wise to gather the bones of one already dead in order to make room for others. These days, people are dying like flies. Who knows when a niche in the family burial cave will be needed?"

The brute rests his hand on the ossuary. "Abner the Pharisee. I've heard of him. A good man. Still . . . you need to open the box."

"Why?" The muscles of Aaron's face tighten as he steps closer to the Gischalite.

The brute smiles, showing a mass of rotten teeth. "A brave lad for a carpenter. But save your courage." He gestures with his hand to where a motley group of men stand watching. "There are too many of us to resist. I *will* see the box. Either open it or my friends will." He chuckles. "But then . . . they'll have to thrash you for their trouble."

When Aaron leans even further, I push the black jar between them, forcing them apart. "There's nothing of value in the box, if that's what you're thinking."

The brute feigns offense. "What? Am I a thief? Would I despoil my own people? You dishonor me. No, no. I'm only looking for contributions, contributions for the cause. If we fighters are to keep you citizens safe from the Romans, shouldn't we be compensated? It's only fair."

I push against Aaron's chest and indicate with the jerk of my head for him to open the ossuary. While he unties it and lowers the box to the ground, I hover near Esther. I'm still afraid she may bolt. If she does, she could disappear into the crowd and not be found. I think Aaron feels as I do, for in no time he has the box open, allows the Gischalite to examine its empty state, then hauls it back onto the donkey where he ties it up in rapid order.

"You were needlessly aggressive," I whisper to Aaron as we head toward the Antonia fortress and Tower Gate. "Must you take such chances?"

Aaron shakes his head. "It wasn't as you think, Mama. If I had shown weakness, the Gischalite would have slit my throat, and most likely yours and Esther's as well. I had to convince him that if he tried anything, it would cost."

It pricks my heart that Aaron should understand such things. It's foolish, to be sure, when such knowledge can save his life. But during all the years of his growing up, he was the son whose heart was most tender toward God, and to Messiah Jesus. And I had hoped he'd become a disciple of John the Apostle in Ephesus. But the war changed everything.

I lament this as we wind through the dusty streets of the Second Quarter. We mingle with a few bleating sheep and cursing men. The sheep are thin, the men shabby. Ragged veiled women and dirty children hover in mud brick doorways. No one smiles. I can feel the fear. Its teeth have sunk deep here. Even those men whose mouths are full of oaths and blasphemies, and whose shoulders are broader than most, lower their eyes when jostled.

No one looks you in the face.

Esther is as sullen as they are. She hasn't formed two words since we began. And more than once I've had to stop because of her lagging. Will she violate her word? The question nags me. She's normally trustworthy. But a woman in love can be foolish.

I fall in beside her, slowing my pace to hers. And I'm so close, our shoulders touch. No matter how much she tries, I won't allow her to break this slender thread, this shackle of the senses that tell me she's still safely beside me.

We walk this way until at last I see the four towers of the Antonia looming ahead. It sits on solid rock, the face of which is covered with smooth flagstone. They say it's like a city inside, full of baths and courtyards and sleeping quarters, but I have no wish to see. It frightens me, even after all this time. Before Herod the Great enlarged it and changed it into an imposing fortress, it was a Hasmonean palace. Perhaps it was a happier place then. But I still think of it as the fortress that housed the Roman garrison and . . . the place where Messiah was scourged and crowned with thorns. A chill runs through me as we pass its double casement walls.

There are more fringed tunics now, for the Antonia is next to the Temple—Eleazar ben Simon's territory; Eleazar, the priest and turncoat aristocrat; Eleazar, the head of the Zealots; Eleazar, the man who now commands my husband's loyalty.

Even here, we must exercise caution. I'm not certain who controls the Tower Gate—Simon's men, I think, for he controls more and more of the city. But whoever does will think nothing of slitting our throats if they believe we're abandoning Jerusalem.

Suddenly, I see Esther walking on tiptoes, straining to see over the tops of the heads around her. And then I know. *Daniel.* She's looking for Daniel! My mouth goes dry. So . . . this is what she's been waiting for. To reach Zealot territory and find her husband. And if she does, she'll bolt.

The area by the Tower Gate is mobbed with people passing in and out. A caravan of ten camels forces us to one side. The noise is deafening. People, animals, all mix together. Ethan told me how it was here. But even seeing it now for myself, it's hard to believe. The change is so great. The city is swollen with refugees who have fled the scourge of the Roman legions. Dirty and ragged, with few possessions, most have settled in the New City where the cloth market and wool-shops are—Simon bar Giora's territory. But there are plenty of refugees here, too, living in flimsy lean-tos and make-shift hovels of canvas or rush mats or twigs. They cram every open space, even between houses—including those clustered along the wall. The stone seats near the gate, where the elders once sat to hear grievances or gossip or news coming from outside, are also taken by refugees who have nowhere else to go. And bordering the streets are the blind and lame holding wooden bowls and begging alms. And the stench! I can hardly breathe.

"We must watch Esther," I whisper to Aaron as we stand beneath the shadow of the Antonia waiting to be inspected by the guards. From outside the nearby gate come the loud cries of lepers who cannot enter the city. "Unclean! Unclean!" they shout from the hovels attached to the massive outside-wall.

The guards at the Tower Gate seem indifferent to the noise, the stench, the sea of ragged, hungry people as they interrogate us. They take their time, pinching and poking, though they stopped short of running their hands over our bodies. Finally, they examine the ossuary and seem disappointed in not finding any contraband. Reluctantly, they pass us through with the wave of a hand. But I think if Aaron were not with us, and if he were not so tall and looked so strong, they would have charged us a "fee."

Just as we are about to step through the gate, Esther shouts, "Daniel! Daniel!"

"Hush!" I say, in a stern voice.

Aaron's head jerks upward. He scans the cluster of rebels peering down at us from one of the four towers. The Antonia is John's territory. Daniel would not be standing on its walls.

"Daniel!" she shouts again.

I yank her hard by the arm. And when a suspicious look clouds the face of one of the guards, I secure my jar in one hand, and opening the other to make a flat palm, I slap Esther's face as hard as I can.

"Shameful behavior! A priest's daughter chasing after a man like a common strumpet!"

"Be gentle, Mother," the guard says with a wink, as we pass through the gate. "She is young."

I don't bother to answer or look back. And God forgive me, I don't even bother to stop and drop a few coins when I see a leaper push his wooden bowl toward me with the stump of what once was a foot. All my might, all my strength, all my attention is focused on two things—getting Esther away from Jerusalem, and getting her away as quickly as possible. I move at a furious pace, my fear pulling me faster and faster into the Kidron Valley while I pull my reluctant daughter, and Aaron pulls the reluctant donkey. Despite the cool breeze, we are all wet with sweat.

"You never had any intention of keeping your word, did you?" I hiss, when we have gone a good distance, my hand still locked onto Esther's arm.

Drops of perspiration run down the sides of Esther's ears, and she strains backward, away from my grasp. "Can't we stop and rest?" she says in a weary voice, the red mark from my hand still visible on her face.

"What did you expect Daniel to do?" Aaron scolds, coming alongside us with the donkey. "Rescue you? Give you refuge? Go against Father and me?" His face is a knot.

"I need to rest," Esther says defiantly, but her chin quivers and tears streak her dust-coated face.

"We'll rest by Absolom's Tomb." I finally let go of her arm, and brush back the stray wisps of hair that stick to my forehead. And though Esther makes a sound with her tongue to tell me she's irritated, she obeys. I push relentlessly, ignoring my daughter's soft whimper when she cuts herself on a jagged rock, ignoring the sob that escapes her lips the further from the city we go, ignoring the breaking of my own heart over the terrible price we are all forced to pay. We trudge along in silent resignation, except for the donkey. He continues his braying, but not so often now. It's as if he, too, is beginning to resign himself. And I allow no more stops until we reach the other side of the Kidron where

Absolom's Tomb rises from the brook bed at the foot of the Mount of Olives.

Esther is the first to find shade and a place to sit. It's a good enough distance from Absolom's ornate tomb and away from the many passing travelers, so Aaron and I follow. While Esther and I sit, Aaron slips the goatskin flagon from his shoulder. It's full of wine mixed with honey and water. It's the only thing he carries that's visible. Under his robe he conceals at least two weapons that I know of, plus food. Esther also carries hidden food. After we drink, Aaron passes out a handful of raisins and a piece of flatbread. So I sit quietly and eat, and watch passersby pile stones against the side of Absolom's tomb in scorn as they curse the traitorous son of David.

I tear large chunks of bread with my teeth and nearly swallow them whole. My haste is not due to hunger as much as my desire to put more distance between us and Jerusalem. In no time only crumbs fill my hand, and after taking a few more sips of our watered wine, I turn to Esther. "Come, it's time to go."

"Oh, Mama, this is hardly the rest you promised!" Esther wails in frustration. But there's a rebuke in her voice, too, as if implying she was not the only one who broke a promise today.

"Mama's right," Aaron says, tucking his half-eaten bread back into the scrip hidden inside his robe. "We must continue. Our journey is long."

In one of the hills north of Absolom's Tomb lies the family burial cave. We'll place Uncle Abner's bones in the ossuary, as we've said. But at dusk, we'll leave the cave and go out under the cover of night to begin our real journey. Our destination is far—nearly as far as the Sea of Galilee. It's to a place I've never desired to go. A place where blended Roman-Greeks study the entrails and livers of birds to determine the will of their gods, and pour libations to Charon, ferryman of the dead. It is the Gentile city of Pella.

It was Ethan who said it must be Pella, and not Ashdod or Jabne—both refuge cities, declared so by Vespasian for those Jews refusing to fight him, and who seek the protection of his Roman army. I think Ethan insisted on Pella because many followers of the Way have gone there, and he knows their presence will be a comfort to me. But his insistence has a ring of foreboding, too. Didn't the oracle tell Christians to flee the coming destruction of Jerusalem? And didn't he tell them to go to Pella?

Has Ethan come to believe destruction *will* come?

I gather my thoughts like crumbs and sweep them aside. "Come, up on your feet," I say, looking down at Esther.

"My feet are as bruised as crushed grapes," she groans. "Have pity and let me rest awhile longer."

I shake my head. We're still too close to Jerusalem. Close enough for Esther to make her escape. Close enough to be overtaken by rebels. "You can rest when we get to Pella." I pull at her arm to force her to rise. How had it come to this? When had the world turned upside down? My heart is like kneaded dough as I look back at my beloved city one last time.

Oh, Jerusalem, Jerusalem, you who slew the prophets, will you now slay my husband and sons?

Ethan

JERUSALEM 70 A.D.

CHAPTER 2

"Ethan? What's the trouble?" Eleazar shouts, rushing to where I stand gazing down upon the body of a lifeless child.

"I never thought it would come to this," I say. Near the small crumpled form lies a woman, the child's mother by the looks of their matching tunics. The woman's face is caked with blood; so is her seamless garment of dyed purple. Her neck is badly bruised, and amid the bruises are numerous cuts. I've seen this before, on other dead bodies of the wealthy, bodies where jewelry had been ripped off necks or arms. What I haven't seen is this happening in the *Temple*. "Have we sunk so low?"

Eleazar ben Simon watches as I stoop and close the little girl's eyelids. "Did you think it would come without cost? Our freedom from Rome?" He stands to the side as though not wanting his garments to touch the dead bodies and make him unclean. It's out of habit, I think, for neither of us has been ritually clean for a very long time.

"Is this how we win freedom? By robbing and killing women and children? And in the Court of Women? *The Court of Women!*" I point to the Corinthian brass gate, so glorious in scope and detail, the gate named Beautiful. "There was a time when a worshiper could pass through that and be safe. Have we become barbarians?"

"Surely the days are evil," Eleazar says, tugging at his beard. He's a strange sight in his white priestly robe and battered leather cuirass, and with a sword belted to his waist. "Men's hearts have turned to stone.

Can we neglect the Law of Moses and it be otherwise? It's not only Romans we must fight, but wickedness among our own people."

"I'm weary of this bloodletting." I brush my fingertips lightly across the child's cheek. I've been fighting at Eleazar's side for four years. Together, we have driven the corrupt priests from the Temple. Priests who enriched themselves by stealing the tithes. Priests who performed daily sacrifices for the Roman Emperor and allowed Roman soldiers to expose themselves in the Temple courts. And then we replaced those corrupt priests by the casting of lots.

"We're all weary, but we must see it through. There's still much to do. As we have restored holiness to the Temple, so we will restore it to Jerusalem," Eleazar says.

"*Holiness*?" My arm sweeps over the two lifeless bodies. "Is this holiness?" Then gesturing beyond the Temple walls, I add, "And how will Jerusalem be restored? The city has been cut into threes with each warring faction surrounding its territory like a girdle around a bloated belly. And in those bellies people are murdered for gain. For filthy lucre, Jews kill Jews. Where is the holiness in that? Surely, this grieves the heart of God."

"Not all. Not all are killing for gain. There is still the righteous remnant. Like always, *Hashem* has preserved the faithful." Eleazar rests his hand on the hilt of his sword. "Many rightly administer His judgment. Those who are called to it, must obey. Didn't Moses, at God's command, order the sons of Levi to slay those who repented not their worship of the golden calf? And didn't three thousand fall in the camp of Israel that day? Slain by the sword? We, too, will cleanse Jerusalem with the sword."

I peer again at the pale, wax-like face of the little girl. Was Eleazar right? Was Jerusalem to be purged by the sword? Was Jew to slaughter Jew? Or . . . was Rebekah right? Had God abandoned His Holy City? Was this slaughter just a sign of His curse upon us?

When I glance up, Eleazar is already walking away. His white robe flaps around him as he shuffles stooped-shouldered. He's nearly swallowed by the throng of incoming worshipers now streaming past me. *The faithful remnant*? If they are, they're a sorry lot, tattered and dirty. Some carry small wicker cages with a pigeon or turtledove inside. Others carry small containers of wheat—hardly the required omer. None have brought animals. Fewer and fewer animals were available for sacrifice. And more bronze *leptas* than silver shekels were being placed in the collection receptacles rimming the Women's Court. Now, amid the sound of *leptas* dropping into one of the thirteen trumpet-shaped containers, I hear Eleazar's voice. He's looking back at me. "There'll be an inquiry. Let your heart be at peace. The guilty will be punished. Oh, yes, the guilty will be punished." Then he heads for the large rounded steps leading up to the Nicanor Gate, the same fifteen steps where, not so long ago, Levites sang the fifteen Songs of Degrees, one on each step. Beyond the Nicanor stands the gold trimmed Temple; so white one can hardly look at it when the sun strikes its stones. Before it, now, plumes the smoke of the morning sacrifice.

With a heavy heart, I gaze at the spot where Eleazar disappeared. I love the man. I've pledged him my sword. And my life, too, if need be. But no inquiry will be held. What are two deaths among so many? And death's hand has yet to exceed its grasp. New refugees flood the city daily. And now pilgrims come, too, for Passover. How will we feed them all with Simon and John's men burning the grain storehouses, and more and more caravans fearing to enter Jerusalem with fresh supplies? How long before hunger becomes the new enemy? And on its heels—panic and more violence? The whole city is in peril.

Eleazar knows it, too. He well understands the problems we face. They burden him and make him close his eyes to the atrocities committed by our fighters. And like the *sicarii*, he punishes, with imprisonment, those who speak out against the rebellion or those who try to escape the city. And he calls these actions "necessary."

I wonder what he'd say if he knew about Rebekah's escape? And about my hand in it? But what was I to do? Is it right that she pay for my fire? And I do burn. My zeal for Jerusalem and the Temple is like molten wax that seeps into the very marrow of my bones. It's this zeal that has forged a bond between Eleazar and me. It's this zeal that has allowed me to fight at his side, even though others who follow The Way have been denied. It's curious that we never speak of Jesus. Curious because, though we fall on opposite sides of the matter, Jesus consumes us both. To Eleazar, He's a "false prophet." But unlike the false prophets who have come before or since, Jesus of Nazareth was the only one who unrolled the sacred scroll of Isaiah in the synagogue and uttered that mouthful of blasphemies, declaring himself *Messiah* and then making himself equal with God; the only one who healed the blind and lame, raised the dead. For Eleazar, such a man had to be discredited, his memory destroyed.

While I do not side with Eleazar in this, I do understand him in part. Many followers of The Way have shown disrespect for our Temple and Law. "Grace, grace," they say. "We live under grace, not the Law." What? Are we to throw out the Law? Are we to pull down the Temple? How can Eleazar abide this? How can any Jew who doesn't understand this grace, abide it? At times, it's even difficult for me.

This "grace" has split our people. It has caused a split in my own heart. I signal two guards, then watch them remove the bodies of the mother and child. Surely, holiness must be restored to our city, to our Temple. In that, Eleazar is right. And Roman rule must be broken. And that meant spilling blood, and, unavoidably, even innocent blood. But I see no alternative. To live outside the law of God is death. To live under Roman rule is slavery. I'll not live as one dead. Nor will I live as a slave.

From nowhere, Rebekah's familiar words fly at me like gnats and deliver their sting. *Rome can't enslave you. You're already a slave to your pride and your hate.*

Was she right? I cannot say. I'm like two cleaved halves of a man. One longs for the peace Jesus promised. The other longs for the Temple and Jerusalem to be as they once were. Did hate push away one and drive the other? If yes, then . . . so be it. Whatever my fate, it lies here, in Jerusalem, with Eleazar, even if that means my death.

Many in the city cling to the slender hope that the Romans will not come. After all, Vespasian has left his headquarters in Alexandria and sailed for Rome to allow the Senate to do what his legions have already done—proclaim him emperor. There he will don the imperial purple and receive his string of seven titles. "Why, then, would he leave Rome to bother with dusty Judea?" many ask. "Didn't the new *Pater Patriae*, the "father" of his country, have enough troubles?" Yes, it was true. Rome was in shambles. What's more, there were rumors that the new emperor's power might be challenged by others who thought themselves more worthy. "No, no," people were saying, "with so many problems facing Vespasian, Jerusalem will be forgotten."

But I don't believe it. Vespasian, the *Pater Patriae*, might forget. But Vespasian, the general who utterly destroyed Joppa out of spite for having to conquer it twice, *never.* He'll return to Jerusalem, to punish the city that, four years ago, massacred the Roman garrison stationed here. And when he does, I only pray that *Hashem* will strengthen my arm for battle.

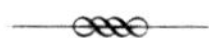

My sword crashes down on one of John Gischala's men, splitting his forehead and sending him crumbling to the paved flooring of the Royal Porch. All around me I hear the sound of metal striking metal and the cries of men falling in battle. My tunic is covered with their blood. Amid a hail of arrows, I spot my three sons and whisper a quick prayer of thanksgiving. *They still stand.* They, too, are covered in blood, but whether theirs or others, I cannot tell.

All morning we've fought John's men. The battle began shortly after the guards removed the bodies of the mother and child. An evil omen—finding those bodies in the Court of Women, as events bear out. We're outnumbered. And John's men are relentless. They seem determined to infiltrate our stronghold and take the Temple today. Even now, the Council House—just outside the Huldah gates—is burning, and the scribes are fleeing with their scrolls. John's men pour like rats through all seven entrances to the Temple platform. The porticos are crammed with them. It seems behind every column there are a half dozen or more flinging spears or wielding swords. And many have found their mark. The floors of the porticos are littered with dead Zealots lying on their backs, staring upward as though studying the elaborately carved ceiling overhead. We are being cut down at an alarming rate. Most of our men have already been pushed back behind the Soreg. That low, ornamental stone wall, with its inscriptions warning strangers not to enter, will not provide a buffer for long.

"Quick, men! To the Gate Beautiful!" I hear Eleazar shout through the din, his white robe now red. "Retreat! Retreat to the Court of Women!"

I beat back two Gischalites, then rush to where my sons are surrounded. "Benjamin! Joseph! Abner! Follow me!" I hack clear a path, and soon we're all retreating into the women's court. Then the four of us stand our ground in front of the gate, along with dozens of other Zealots, restraining John's men, giving time to the rest of our fighters to retreat behind the walls and seal up all the entrances. And when the paving stones beneath our feet are slick with blood and the bodies piled so high we can see no more than five cubits in any direction, we hear the command to enter the gate and close it. And when at last it is bolted, a loud cheer goes up on the other side as our countrymen celebrate their victory over us, for the territory held by us Zealots has been greatly reduced.

We remain barricaded behind the walled Temple area. Throughout the night, lone bowmen have tried to pick us off—a tactic meant to keep us from resting. Then early this morning John began pounding us with his catapults—hurling great stones on our heads while his bowmen shower us with arrows. Several of our men lie dead, scattered over the gouged stone floor. Our fighters, who line the tops of the walls, have inflicted their own damage. It's reported that John continues to sustain heavy causalities, many incurred by our Benjaminite archers—the best bowmen in Israel.

I stand in the Court of Levites, separated from the Court of the Priests by a cubit-high decorative barrier near my feet. On the multi-stair platform above me, clusters of white-robed priests minister around the blazing bronze Altar of Sacrifice. From it, a plume of smoke rises to heaven, and with it, my prayers. Eleazar stands beside me. He has not left the altar since the morning sacrifice. He prays and fasts for our cause. I pray for . . . Rebekah, for Esther, for my sons, for my arm to be strengthened. But I do not pray for God's will to be done, nor for His justice to prevail, for I fear them both. We've been here so long I've grown weary of praying, and shuffle my feat anxiously. I yearn to be with my men on the walls, but Eleazar has asked me to stay by his side. And so I stay . . . and pray . . . and wait.

"The Romans are coming," Eleazar finally says, bending closer to me as if not wanting anyone to hear. "A messenger from Galilee claims they come from every direction. North, along the coast from Caesarea, east from Jericho. The roads are clogged with them."

My heart sinks as I think of Rebekah, Aaron and Esther, and I worry if they're safe.

"These endless months of infighting have sapped our supplies," Eleazar says, signaling with a tap on my shoulder that he's ready to return to the battle. "We're not prepared for a siege." In silence we make our way through the bronze Nicanor gate, then down the semicircular steps that lead to the Court of Women. "The Romans are no more than a day away, and Titus leads them."

"Then we must make peace with John and Simon," I say as we descend the last step. "We must unite if we're to have any chance against his legions."

Eleazar nods as a large stone catapults past us and crashes into the wall of the Parvah, where the hides of sacrificial animals are salted. Overhead, the arrows are so thick they look like a flock of birds.

"Making peace is our only hope. Send an overture. Let's see what that dog, John, says. If we can get him to agree, Simon will surely follow."

From atop the Temple wall, facing west, I watch a cloud of dust swirl above the road from Emmaus. Below that cloud are thousands of Roman soldiers, their mounted officers, their endless mule-pulled artillery and supply wagons. Our spies tell us it's the 15th Legion—from Alexandria, led by Titus. Already, his scouts survey the southern end of Mount Scopus for a campsite. A second cloud follows. It's the 5th Legion—the Macedonica. Their scouts, too, survey Mount Scopus, on the north.

In addition, reports are coming in from the countryside that the 10th Legion is on its way from Jericho. *The 10th*. Can the news be more dire? They will remember how they were sent to punish Jerusalem for the Roman garrison massacre, but sent packing instead. They'll seek revenge for this dishonor. They'll show no mercy, give no quarter. The reports also claim that provisions for the army overflow the storehouses in Ashkelon and Caesarea. It's clear that Titus has prepared for a long campaign.

I inhale the warm air filled with swirling grit and the stench of our rotting dead thrown over the walls to prevent disease from descending upon our city. Behind me, the noise of war continues as it has for two days, with John's men battering our defenses and hurling more arrows, spears and rocks. Does he not have eyes? Does he not see the Romans? Why does he continue to do Titus's work for him by spoiling Jerusalem? And when will that jackal answer my dispatch?

The next day, John does answer. We should have seen it coming, his treachery. But we didn't. It's the season of Passover, a most holy time, and many of us unwisely turned our hearts from the things of war to the things of God. It was agreed that the pilgrims, who have come to Jerusalem for Passover, should be allowed safe passage to the Temple. Throughout the city, they were searched, then passed along by the various rebels controlling the checkpoints. But deceitful men will use any opportunity. And while Eleazar kept his word and ordered the gate to be partially opened for the pilgrims to enter, John did not keep his. Instead, he and a group of his men perpetrated a great deception by disguising themselves as pilgrims. In one wild moment, they rushed the gate, forced it open for their comrades, and with little difficulty, overran us. But before much blood was shed, Eleazar surrendered and a truce was struck. In one bold move, John has become our leader.

May Hashem give him wisdom.

Simon has asked for a truce. But John has refused. Since John has retained me as one of his generals, I have tried to stress the necessity of joining forces. We must put aside our differences for the sake of Jerusalem. Already the 15th and 5th Legions have pitched camp. Vineyards and ancient olive groves have felt their ax. The Romans have no respect for the land. They tear at it like wild beasts until nothing remains. Outside the city walls, houses have been looted and burned to the ground. All structures, all vegetation, have been removed. Nothing is left to testify of the centuries of living that have gone on here. Now, only dirt and dust stand between their camp and a large portion of our western wall. They have removed all obstructions and flattened the land to prepare for their siege works and pending advance.

The city weeps at this sight. I weep, too, for I see the scope of their intended destruction.

The dreaded 10th has arrived. They set up camp, east of us, on the Mount of Olives, while the 15th and 5th fortify theirs by digging ditches and building berms. Siege works have been started by all three camps. And off to one side, a team of legionaries builds a massive battering ram with a tower and catapult. Already they have iron plated the tip of the ram. Scattered piles of green wicker lay in readiness, waiting for the beam housing—which is nearly the height of our walls—to be finished. And then the wicker will be used to cover it, along with layers of leather padded with wet straw. The showdown is not far off. The only consolation is that John has finally accepted Simon's truce. We are, at long last, united. But our infighting has so weakened the city that I can't help but wonder if our unification is too little too late.

Rebekah

PELLA 70A.D.

CHAPTER 3

"This can't be it," I say, peering down into the Jordan Valley where, nestled among the tall green eastern hills, is a large city split in two by a wadi and the bubbling spring that flows through it. Even from this distance, the gutted and charred houses are unmistakable. So are the broken walls, the piles of rubble. "This can't be it," I repeat.

"It can be no other, Mama," Aaron says. His soft beard is caked with the dust of the road, his face blistered from the sun. His eyes, ever on the lookout for danger, squint into the expanse.

Esther leans wearily against the donkey and laughs. "Were you expecting a Hasmonaean palace?"

"Esther!" Aaron's calloused hand jerks his sister's arm. "You mustn't speak so rudely to Mama! Your anger is a mouth looking for someone to bite. If you must be angry, then let it be with Father or me, the ones who forced you to leave Jerusalem."

I wave my hand, gesturing for Aaron to drop the matter. Since leaving the Kings Highway to avoid the Romans, then following along the Jordan Valley through wadis and narrow, dusty footpaths, Esther has been pecking at me like a bird of prey. Then just before Scythopolis and the Jezreel Valley where we crossed the Jordan, the bird of prey became a lioness. I've allowed it because her heart is broken. She's told me she never expects to see Daniel again. She cries in her sleep. Even her appetite is gone. Twice now, I've had to force her to eat. I fear she's losing the will to live. Perhaps anger can revive it.

I turn and look at her. From head to toe she wears the dust of many days. Folds of dirty cloth cover the long oily strands of her hair. Her sandaled feet are cut and bruised. One side of her long, belted tunic is ripped up to the knee. "I didn't expect a palace," I say, barely able to conceal my disappointment. "But surely a city protected by Vespasian, and now Titus, should not be in such disrepair."

Our journey has been difficult. Forsaking the relatively well-kept Roman roads has added days to the trip. It's also allowed us to see the cruel handiwork of Vespasian's legions. Entire towns and villages have been decimated. Whole populations slaughtered. The land stinks from the dead. They're everywhere, bloated, fly-covered, rotting. Many are nailed to trees. And food? There's none to be had, either to buy or glean from abandoned fields. The countryside has been stripped, shaved by the razor of Rome.

Ethan warned me. He told me what the Romans were doing. Even so, I was not prepared for what I saw, nor was I prepared to see the scars of war in a Greek city, even though Ethan had warned me of that, too.

"It must be the work of John of Gischala," Aaron says, holding the donkey's bridle and standing beside me. "Stories of how he looted and burned the Greek cities of the Decapolis have filled the streets of Jerusalem. It made him a hero to many."

"Maybe he'll return and kill us all. A fitting end for traitors who leave their city in her hour of need." Esther's face is red. I think even she knows how far she has overstepped this time.

"At least some followers of The Way will be here," I say, ignoring her. "I take comfort in that."

Aaron looks at me and frowns. "It may be the only comfort to be had. For I doubt the Gentiles will welcome us. They'll still remember what the Jews did here."

Weary, I go and sit beneath a gnarled oak. We're in the midst of a forest of oaks and pines. Esther remains by the donkey, seemingly too tired to walk the few paces to the shade of a tree.

"I'm sorry," she says, her dirt caked fingers combing the short bristly hair of the donkey's mane. "I . . . don't mean to be unkind. You don't deserve it, Mama. Neither do you, Aaron."

I nod in understanding. My heart is broken too. Will I ever see my Ethan again? How I long for him now, for his strength, his comfort. And what of Aaron, so eager to return to Jerusalem? Will he survive the battle that's coming? And my other sons? How will they fare? I wish there was someone I could peck and bite. But there isn't. And for my family's sake, I must sustain my will to live, to survive. Do I understand Esther? Oh, yes. How easy it would be to give up; to give up and just sit beneath this peaceful oak and wait for death.

Aaron strokes Esther's head as if she were a child. A westerly wind pulls at his ringlets. His face is almost beautiful, like how I imagine an angel's face would look. "I'll watch over him," he says softly. "I will watch over your Daniel."

I study them both. He, clumsy and tender, strokes her head. She, too weak to move or answer, leans against the donkey. Their sunken cheeks reveal how little they've eaten. We are all hungry. Only one flatbread stands between us and starvation. If some kind soul in Pella doesn't sell us food, I don't know what we'll do.

As if reading my thoughts, Aaron points to a patchwork of planted fields. "At least there will be something to eat in Pella."

My stomach is as shriveled as an old cow's udder, and grumbles at the mention of food. It will take all my strength to walk the remaining distance to Pella. And Aaron's, too, I think. But Esther is much too weak. I don't know how she'll manage it. And she can't ride. The donkey is nearly dead. He has stumbled three times this last mile. Once, I didn't think he'd get up.

"Give Esther half the bread; you take the other half," I say to Aaron.

Dust floats from Aaron's beard as he shakes his head. A ringlet of hair falls across one eye, partially obscuring his shock at such a suggestion. "How could I do that, Mama? What of you and the donkey? We always divide the flatbread into fours. A quarter for each of us."

"Take the bread, Aaron," I say softly. "The donkey and I will eat in Pella." Again he shakes his head, so I rise and take the scrip from his shoulder then pull out the stale bread. Ignoring the little patches of mold along the edges, I tear it in half and hand one piece to him, the other to Esther. "I don't have the strength to argue."

"*Maranatha*. The Lord is risen," I say to the strangers we pass as we thread our way through the winding street that appears to transverse the center of the city. The street is cobbled and lined with connecting shops, many of which have an upper floor. And though the city seems affluent—for the people are full bodied and show no signs of starvation—and though their dress is neat—some even wearing fine wool tunics belted with leather—John Gischala's handiwork is still visible. Several shops have charred walls. Others, those completely destroyed by fire, remain abandoned, their crumbled walls and caved roofs sitting like skeletons beside the road. Here and there, whole sections of the street have been torn up as though the stones were carried off to make repairs elsewhere. And for its size, the city doesn't appear overly crowded, further evidence of the slaughter that took place here.

I see no friendly faces. And no one answers my "*maranatha*" with the customary, "He is risen, indeed." Many whisper as we pass. Others point to our tattered clothes. Several curse and spit at us. Someone throws a rock, but it sails harmlessly over our heads.

"We're not among friends," I say, when the smell of roast pig wafts from a nearby house and I realize we are in Gentile territory. I'm uneasy, but my uneasiness is overcome by the smell. I would have eaten that whole pig if I had gotten the chance. And I would have done it without once thinking how scandalized Ethan would be.

We must find food. We're nearly faint from hunger. More and more, Aaron leans against the panting donkey, while Esther whimpers and stumbles along behind us. My spirit slumps as we pass one shop after the other that sells only oil lamps and wicks, or spices, metal goods, or assorted fabrics. But it revives when we approach a woman in a doorway, a cook-shop by the looks of it. Wooden bowls of various sizes fill the stone shelf on its outside wall. And the woman, who is cooking on a brazier, periodically leans over and plucks something from a bowl, then drops it into her pot. It's not until we get closer that I see the contents of the bowls: squirming beetle larvae, dead grasshoppers, small reddish-black livers—from chickens or rabbits judging from the size. Another bowl is filled with slices of raw meat; red grainy meat like that from a horse or cow. When I spot a bowl of chickpeas, I hesitate. Aaron frowns and warns me with a shake of his head not to stop. I know he fears this food has been offered to idols. It's not unusual for surplus meat used in idol worship to find its way into the marketplace. But surely not chickpeas. Even so, I follow obediently. Esther follows too, but the distance between us is growing.

When Aaron signals me to walk in the middle of the street and closer to the donkey, I ignore him, then look backward, still thinking of the chickpeas and how I should buy some. We desperately need food.

"Mama! Look out!" Esther suddenly shouts.

But too late. I bump into a table set outside the doorway of a shop, causing dozens of clay statues to tumble to the ground. The shop owner shrieks amid the sound of breaking pottery. "Clumsy Jew! Look what you've done!"

At once a crowd gathers.

I look in horror at all the broken statues lying in a heap on the table. Others lie in pieces on the ground. "I'm . . . I'm sorry . . ."

"You disrespect Isis—the one who gives birth to heaven and earth!" the owner screams. He's a small man with gray eyes that pierce like the tip of a blade. His blond hair, of medium length, is oddly braided. His long aquiline nose looks like the beak of an eagle, while his lips are thin, like the mouth of a fish. On a chain around his neck, he wears the Knot of Isis. His eyes flare as he points to the shattered statues of his goddess.

"Stone her!" someone shouts.

"Stone the abuser of the Queen of Heaven!" says another.

"I'm sorry . . . I didn't mean . . ."

Aaron shoves the donkey between us and the gathering mob. Our backs are against the table of idols. Only the shop owner is behind us. But his hands, like the talons of a hawk, clamp my shoulder.

"How will you atone to the Mother of the Gods for your insult?"

Aaron pulls the dagger from beneath his robe. The look on his face tells me he's about to use it. But before he can, a large, barrel-chested man breaks through the crowd and steps into our midst. He's not dressed like the others, but wears rough homespun, clean though patched in places. There's the most delightful expression on his face, like he's just swallowed a mouthful of prized Jericho dates. His head and face sprout great quantities of bushy gray hair, as do his arms. The man looks ancient. But his eyes . . . oh, my, those eyes are young. They twinkle and dance like sun skidding across a lake, and send sparks wherever they look. When they rest on me—I know all will be well.

"Peace, Argos. Peace," the man says, as bold as you please. He's certainly brave. He carries no weapon, and his size, though great, is not enough to scare such a crowd. But nevertheless, I see fear in Argos' eyes, the kind of fear a lesser man has for a greater.

"I'm sure these strangers meant no harm. No disrespect was intended."

"Leave it alone, Zechariah," Argos warns.

Zechariah laughs, making his whole chest heave up and down. Then he points to someone in the crowd. "Demas, wasn't it you who, only last month, knocked over Argos' table? How many statues did you break then. Eh?"

Demas appears confused. He stammers, turns red, then looks away.

Zechariah's big fingers dip into a pouch belted at his waist. After a moment of fumbling, he pulls out several coins and holds them in the air. "Four *denarii.* Four days wages. Surely, it will take you no more than four days to replace these broken statues."

People murmur and nod. A consensus is building. Clearly, Zechariah's terms meet with approval."

"Take the money, Argos," someone shouts.

"There's a profit in it," says another, "Everyone knows it will take you only two days."

"And just think, only two-hundred and fifty thousand *denarii* more and you can buy yourself a seat in the Roman Senate!" yells someone else.

Now everyone laughs, and the tension is broken.

Though Argos' face shows displeasure, he has little choice but to back down. Reluctantly, he holds out his hand. The coins jingle as Zechariah drops them into his palm. Slowly Argosy closes his fingers around them, his cold gray eyes piercing mine.

"Pay no attention to him," Zechariah says when the people disburse and Argos enters his shop. From where we stand, we hear Argos yelling at some poor soul. Moments later, a young woman, no older than Esther, emerges, carrying a basket. She smiles shyly at me then begins gathering the fragments.

"How can I ever thank you?" I say to Zechariah as I watch the woman work.

"No need."

"Then at least let me repay the *denarii*."

"*Maranatha*," Zechariah says, shaking his head, but I don't know if he's speaking to me or to the young woman by the table. "*Maranatha*," he says again, and this time he's so close his bushy gray beard almost touches my shoulder. At once, Aaron is between us, leaving both the donkey and Esther to walk alone.

"I need no protection from the man who saved our lives," I say, smiling at my son. But Aaron doesn't relinquish his spot.

"*Maranatha*!" Zechariah says, leaning toward Aaron, and laughing. "He is risen."

"You follow The Way?" I whisper, not wishing for those long-faced men who still linger along the street to hear.

"I do. I'm Zechariah, servant of Jesus, the Messiah. I was told of your coming. I've been watching for you all day."

My throat tightens from fear. "How could that be? No one knows our whereabouts."

This time Zechariah laughs so hard his big barrel-chest heaves up and down like a boat caught in a wave. "No one? Surely you don't mean that. Surely you believe *Hashem* knows." He rubs his bulbous nose, then laughs again. "You'll come to my house and eat, and rest. You must be tired."

The man draws me like a moth to flame. But he scares me, too. There's something too free about him, something that makes him take no heed of danger. And that in itself is dangerous.

"I have plenty of food. I've already set a table for us."

Food. The word makes my dry mouth water. It makes my stomach ache and churn. Its promise overcomes my reservation. I look at Aaron, and he nods. Clearly, the promise of food has overcome his as well. And then there's Esther to consider. She limps slowly behind us. She won't last much longer on the streets.

And so we follow this strange, burly man who looks like a bear but walks as nimbly as a cat.

"Is it much further?" I glance anxiously at Zachariah who is carrying Esther now. He's too old for such things, but I won't insult him by saying so. Besides, who else is there to do it? Aaron and I are too weak. We barely carry ourselves.

"We're nearly there," Zachariah says, smiling.

That smile! That perpetual smile. It stays and stays. All through the hostile winding streets of the Gentile sector, then through the wadi, it held, like a melon wedge on the platter of his face. He's been carrying Esther since her collapse near the Roman bathhouse. She looks like a bundle of rags in his large arms.

"And do not trouble yourself about me," he says, as if reading my thoughts. "She's as light as flax."

"God will bless you for your kindness." I huff and puff, and lag behind Aaron and the donkey, both of which breathe heavily, too. It's taken what little strength we had left to cross the wadi into this section of Pella where Zechariah says most of the believers live. Aaron and I are drenched with sweat. I see a few strands of moist hair on Zechariah's forehead, and more around the edges of his beard just above his mouth, but that's all. The man is amazing.

We stumble past house after house. Some are little more than hovels and are clustered together—five or six around a single dirt courtyard sprinkled with animal pens. There are many abandoned houses, too, laying in ruins. Even so, the place throbs with life. Women are cooking over fires or grinding grain for bread. Others tend small herb gardens or children who run and giggle as they herd sheep into pens. Though we are strangers, we are greeted with smiles, while Zechariah is greeted with kind words or blessings shouted into the air.

Finally, Zechariah stops in front of a well-built house. It's unlike many of the others, for it stands alone and has its own courtyard. He tells Aaron to tether the donkey to a nearby tree, and waits by the door, holding Esther. When Aaron is finished, Zechariah bids us enter, but both my son and I hesitate.

"No danger lurks inside," he says with a chuckle, his eyes twinkling.

So we enter. And, oh, how unlike our beautiful house in the Upper City it is! The ceiling is made of massive wooden beams. Stuffed between them are bundles of dried branches, all raw and exposed. Only a small portion is plastered. And the house . . . it has only two rooms. The one by the door is the smallest with a stamped-earth floor. Jars and baskets of various sizes fill the shelves. The second room is nothing but a raised stone platform, full of rush mats, and obviously used for eating and sleeping. A large round tray has been set out with four cups filled with wine. Also there are bowls of figs and goat cheese and almonds. Zechariah was telling the truth. He *had* been expecting us.

Zechariah carries Esther up the three narrow stone steps, then carefully lowers her onto a mat before propping her against the stone wall. She moans and opens her eyes. A glass of wine and a few figs will revive her. After Zechariah says the blessing in a voice that thunders like a Roman kettledrum, I bring the wine to Esther's lips, and holding her head forward, force her to drink. By her second fig, Esther is holding her own head.

Now I turn to my needs and gulp a great mouthful of wine, then bite off a large chunk of cheese, too large, I fear, for propriety's sake. But hunger has no manners. As I eat I wonder at Zechariah. His prayer seems to still linger around us. And when he prayed, I almost felt . . . well, I felt like the heavens had opened and God had inclined His ear toward this house.

No one speaks. We, the three of us, Aaron, Esther and I, all push food down our throats as if we're Philistines. And all the while, Zechariah, his back braced against the whitewashed mudbrick, nibbles a fig and grins at us as if he were the village idiot.

"Tell me how you knew we were coming," I say, when my stomach can't hold another morsel. "Who told you?"

One eyebrow arches upward, like a pigeon's beak. His eyes—large and round rest—on each of us in turn, dispensing love like a baker dispensing warm loaves of bread. "It was the Comforter. He told me."

Of course I know who the Comforter is. He's a tongue of fire, a mighty rushing wind. The One Jesus sent to empower us, to enable us to live as He lived. Who following The Way doesn't know this? But speak? To an ordinary man, not an Apostle? This I wasn't so sure of.

My face must reveal my doubt, for Zechariah laughs, then dismisses the entire matter with a wave of his hand. "You'll find peace here. We're a poor lot, to be sure. Made poorer by John of Gischala, I'm sorry to say. But God provides. We manage to grow enough food to feed ourselves and our guests."

"Then you were here when the rebels came?" Aaron sips his wine and studies Zechariah as though trying to measure the man.

"Oh, no. But I've heard the stories. Part of me understands what that Galilean did. How could anyone not know that the slaughter of the Jews of Caesarea Maritima by the Gentiles would ignite the already smoldering hatred and resentment of our people toward Rome and toward the Gentiles in the Decapolis? It's no surprise then that Jewish rebels retaliated by sweeping through their cities: Philadelphia, Gerasa, Scythopolis, Gadara, Hippos, and of course, Pella. And there was no way to stop them from venting their rage, either. Too many wrongs, too many years, too much hatred. Only . . . in the process they killed many of their own people. Some who survived are still bitter. I've preached the importance of forgiveness, but it's easier to say than do, isn't it? Still, the slaughter of the Gentiles of Pella had one unexpected effect. It provided housing for those of our people who have fled Jerusalem. You see how God can bring good out of any evil?" Zechariah's eyes twinkle as he rubs his bulbous nose.

"You come from Jerusalem?" For the first time Esther sits upright.

"No, Ephesus."

"Why . . . that's where John the Apostle lives!" At once my heart is stirred. "Do you know him?"

Zechariah leans on one arm as he reclines on his mat. "Yes, it's with his blessing that I came here nine months ago to encourage the saints. John and I heard of their many struggles, and we reasoned they were in sore need of God's word. That's why I've brought John's codex with me—so full of the good news, so full of the wondrous deeds of our Jesus."

"His *codex*. Then . . . you're a follower of John?" I glance at Aaron. Oh, how I wish Aaron could have followed the Beloved Apostle. But John was getting on in years. By the looks of things it was doubtful that Aaron would ever get that chance now. "John was a guest at our house, staying many times in our upper room, especially after the Master died. I was young and only spoke to him once. But you actually *know* him."

Zechariah plucks another fig from the bowl. It looks so puny between his large square fingernails. "Yes, yes, and the rest of them, too.

I was among the three thousand who fell under Peter's teaching. Oh, how the Spirit moved that day! There he was, the big clumsy fisherman, speaking to us with such *power*! And there we were, the lot of us, weeping and wailing and crying out to be saved. I tell you, it's a day I'll never forget."

"What has happened to them? We heard that Peter and Paul died in Rome. What of the rest? Do they still live?"

"Some. Jude is in Edessa, Simon in Africa. Matthias, in Cappadocia, or . . . is it Egypt? Philip is reportedly in Hieropolis. The others are dead. Martyred for the faith. Andrew was crucified in Patras in Achaia. They say he was bound to an X-shaped cross rather than nailed, in order to increase his suffering. He hung for two days before death claimed him. I was told Thomas died at the hands of an enraged heathen priest, somewhere in the Far East. A spear, they say, killed him. Nathanael—guileless Nathanael—the reports claim he was beaten, then beheaded by King Astyages in Armenia. And Matthew was martyred in Ethiopia. How? I don't remember."

"And what of John? Is he well?"

Zechariah pours out more wine. "He's well, but aging like us all." He plucks at the hairs of his gray beard and chuckles. "Ephesus has grayed John's hair, too, what there is left of it. The man is nearly bald. I think he's lost one hair for every convert he's made. It has been a struggle, and Satan has put up many obstacles. Oh, how fiercely loyal the Ephesians are to their goddess, Diana! How they love her sacred oak groves. But the slaves love her best, for any one of them can claim sanctuary in her temple." He moves his heavy bulk as though trying to get comfortable, then begins telling us stories of John's efforts to reach these follows of Diana, goddess of the hunt, and of the moon, too.

He talks for hours, until it grows dark, then he tells us we must stay the night. Oh, how this barrel-chested man can talk! And oh, how he made us laugh. Yes, we actually laughed, at least Aaron and I did. Esther didn't utter a peep. She didn't even smile.

—⁂—

"There. There it is! The house I've picked for you and your family—a fine dwelling, don't you think?"

I try to hide my disappointment as Zechariah points to a mudbrick house with a collapsed roof. He hops, first on one foot then another, almost as if dancing. The man can't contain himself for joy.

Aaron's face tightens. "It's nearly destroyed. How can my mother live here?"

"No, no," Zechariah bellows, "the damage is only superficial. I've inspected the dwelling myself. It is strong. True, some stones are charred from fire. And the door is off its hinges, and of course there's the roof. But the rest of the structure is sound. As sound as the Antonia fortress in Jerusalem." He slaps Aaron good naturedly on the back. "And the believers have promised to help you fix what needs fixing . . . that is, when they're not tending the fields or their animals, or maintaining the terraces, or cleaning the cisterns, or doing a dozen other chores." He laughs merrily, completely undaunted by the many obstacles.

Esther makes a clucking noise with her tongue, then wrinkles her face and mumbles something beneath her breath about going back to Jerusalem.

I ignore her.

Zechariah grins at us both, revealing a mouthful of teeth that look like yellowing ivory. "While you women gather branches for the new roof, Aaron and I will fell trees for hewing beams. And I promise you this—I'll over-lay it all with mud plaster. It will not be the crude roof that sits over my head. But what does an old man living alone care about such things? That's not for you, though. You'll have a fine roof. You'll see. In no time the house will be beautiful."

Though he means well, Zechariah's words are not helpful. I don't despise God's provision. The truth is, I'm most grateful, especially considering what I've seen in my travels here. This dwelling was proof of God's continued goodness toward me. I'll not deny that. But no, I won't say this house that stands in ruins before me is beautiful. I'll not speak a falsehood.

"Esther and I will see to the branches after we've unloaded the cart," I say, signaling Esther to come help. Since Zechariah knows where to make purchases without being cheated, I gave him some coins from my *semadi.* And before bringing us here, he crossed the wadi and spent them all. But he has not disappointed. In the laden donkey cart behind us are fine woven baskets filled with chickpeas and lentils and figs, and cooking pots, plus two oil lamps. There are also jars of oil and honey, empty jars for storage, and tools for farming, including the ax needed to fell the trees. "We'll see to these things first," I repeat.

Zechariah nods, pulls the ax and a handsaw from the cart, then gives the ax to Aaron. Before Esther and I even get started, he's off, whistling some tune I've never heard, and heading for the forest. And Aaron has to sprint to catch up, as Esther and I begin unloading the wagon. She carries an empty jar while I carry the basket of lentils to the back of the house where we'll store them, out of everyone's way, until the house has been repaired.

While I walk, my mind is full of thoughts I'm determined to share. I must tell Esther what's on my heart. It's long overdue. "I miss my husband, too," I say softly, as Esther positions the jar in front of me. "I know how you feel."

At once, tears wet Esther's face. "Then how can you bear it? How can you bear being away from Papa?"

It's good to hear Esther speak, even in such a surly tone. "I bear it because I must," I say, pouring lentils into the wide-mouth clay jar. "And so must you. If it's God's will, Papa and Daniel will survive. Let God strengthen you through this. He is more than able."

She brushes away her tears with the edge of the cloth on her head. "The world is upside down. I don't know if I can live . . . if I *want* to live in it without Daniel."

"Don't speak so! It's God who gives the gift of life. Can you say to Him 'I no longer want it'?"

Esther looks at me; her forehead is as furrowed as the fields behind our new house. "You've seen what the Romans do to the men who oppose them. How they're nailed to trees." Her eyes widen. "Suppose Daniel . . . suppose . . . ."

"Hush." I brush my fingers lightly across her lips. "It's not for us to suppose. It's for us to go about the business of living. You're young and strong. When the war is over we will need young and strong women to help rebuild, and to raise up Godly seed for the Lord."

When I see that Esther has stopped her ears to my words, I close my mouth, and in silence we carry our new purchases and stack them neatly at the back of the house. After we finish, I inspect the grounds. The house, a good size, is surrounded by a low wall—important for containing our animals when we get them. In the corner is a large hole. I check it briefly, then wave for Esther to come see.

"Look, a stone-lined pit for storing grain. It needs to be replastered, but otherwise it's in good condition."

"But it's *empty*."

I pat Esther's cheek good-naturedly. "Then we'll fill it. And when we do we'll bake our bread in there." I point to the nearby domed oven, which also appears in good condition.

But Esther has lost interest. She stands gazing out over the wall. At first I think it's because she longs for Jerusalem, but then I realize she's looking at the beautiful limestone hills a little beyond our house. The hills are covered with rock-lined terraces, terraces that are full of gnarled olive trees and lush grape vines. Dotting the slopes are cisterns carved into bedrock. And tucked among them are olive and wine presses. Tall standing grain waves in fields near the hills, and closer to the house are fig trees and several pomegranates. And mingled among them all are well-tilled plots filled with vegetables.

"It's a pleasant land," Esther says wistfully. "We could have made a good life here, Daniel and I."

Her words, mingled with the breeze that carries the scent of wild rosemary, suddenly unlock the secret in both our hearts. "I'm angry with my husband, too, for not coming with us." I put one arm around her thin shoulders. "For choosing to fight for Jerusalem while leaving us defenseless." We stand together for a long time, staring off into the distance; two women who understand a common heartbreak.

As it turns out, the house *is* beautiful—at least I think it is. The roof is repaired, the door back on its hinges. And all the walls, inside and out, have been freshly plastered. There's nothing left to do but pray a blessing over it and move in. Dozens of my neighbors have gathered to hear Zechariah's prayer and to celebrate this happy day.

I glance at some of the people I've come to know during the past weeks: Mary, the wife of Simon the bottlemaker; Leah, the aging widow; Obadiah, the carpenter, and his wife, Tirzah. Hannah and her husband Amos, the cheesemaker. Rina, a young widow, and Ira, a carpenter who specialized in making plows and winnowing forks and other tools for farming. But many others have come too—all followers of The Way, and all have, in generosity of spirit, helped clean, plaster, repair. I've never experienced such love, such outpouring of goodness. They have so little yet give so much.

But my joy is marred by the distracted look on Aaron's face. He'll not be with us long. More and more he looks to the hills. It's only his love for me and his kindness that has kept him here this long. He has not said it, but I fear he'll leave soon.

And Esther, my sweet Esther, burdens my heart, too. Sadness stoops her like an old woman. And she takes no delight in the company of others. Nothing I say helps. I know it's for God to heal, but still I try, with words of encouragement and little acts of kindness. She nods, she smiles—if you can call that stiff upturn of her mouth a smile—then looks at me with dead eyes. Oh, how those eyes haunt me. I see them even in my dreams.

What would I do if there was no Zechariah to cheer me? Or these precious saints, these fellow believers who have gathered in front of my house today? I've prepared a small feast to show my gratitude—a simple fare of leavened bread and cheese and watered wine. But there's another reason, too. Perhaps God will open Esther's eyes. Perhaps He'll cause her to see. *Look, Esther, look. These people have suffered, too.*

I leave Mary, the bottlemaker's wife, who is examining a wine skin, and go in search of Zechariah. I'm anxious for him to say the blessing so the festivities can begin. Suddenly, I hear a voice coming from the side of the house.

"Soon I must leave, for I have sworn an oath." It's my son's voice.

I slip closer and see Zechariah and Aaron standing together. Concealing myself behind a tower of willow baskets, I watch. Zechariah appears to study Aaron. He rubs a finger over his sizable nose and frowns as if making a discovery.

"Then, you haven't come to settle here?" He finally says.

"I made an oath."

"Yes, yes, an oath. To fight in Jerusalem, I suppose."

My heart thumps like a drum as I watch my son. His face is tense.

"I've only stayed these past three weeks to see that my mother and sister are properly settled."

"Of course, of course. And now that they are, you'll be leaving?"

"Yes, tomorrow, at first light."

My breath catches. I had hoped for a few more days. Just a few more days.

"But what I need to know, Zechariah, is that they'll be safe from those Greeks on the other side of the wadi; those Greeks who have no Torah to govern them. Is there justice here for a Jew?"

Zechariah smiles. "Safety? Justice? For a Jew? You don't ask for much, young Aaron." He shrugs. "Still, we can praise *Hashem* for one thing. There will be little interference from Rome. Pella, like the rest of the Decapolis, governs herself. All the leaders are chosen from within. But ever since the Gischalites wiped out the last bunch, Argos has been running things. I guess you could call him the *head* troublemaker." Zechariah holds his large barrel-chest and laughs at his own joke.

Aaron doesn't seem amused. "Argos, the little idol maker?"

Zechariah nods. "Don't let his size fool you. He wields great influence. Many Gentiles believe he has supernatural powers; powers to heal, to interpret dreams and to control the weather. He's forever braiding and unbraiding his hair. Like all his sect, he believes knots have magical powers."

I see Aaron's hand move to the dagger that he carries hidden in his robe. "Then perhaps I should take care of him before I go."

Zechariah appears horrified. "And bring Roman justice down on our heads? The man is a citizen. And so proud of it, too! His wooden *diptych* hangs on the wall of his shop where everyone can see it from the doorway. The hinged boards are always open to reveal the official record." Zechariah rests his large hand on Aaron's shoulder. "Be at peace, young Aaron. Aside from Argos and his sect, the other Gentiles are harmless enough. Oh, they think we're strange, for they believe we eat our own God when we break the bread, but for the most part they leave us alone. They're content to worship the little stone gods they've crammed into niches throughout their homes, honoring them with libations and wafers. But Argos . . . that worshipper of Isis . . . he *is* dangerous. He senses we believers have real power, and this frightens him. Only last month, Amos was badly beaten when Argos and some of his followers found him praying in the field. And the month before, Mary, Simon's wife, was followed and harassed when she crossed the wadi. It made her so fearful, she stayed indoors for days."

"How did that Egyptian abomination come to be worshiped here?" Aaron says.

Zechariah looks stunned. "Surely you know the cult of Isis is widespread. Since Caligula, it has greatly flourished."

"In Jerusalem we don't concern ourselves with idolatry."

"To be sure. But in Ephesus it's all around us. Tiberius tried to destroy this Isis cult that Mark Antony officially established, but Caligula revived it. That mad man rebuilt the *Iseum Campense* and established the Festival of Isis, even donning the clothes of a woman in order to lead the rituals. Now shrines of Isis pepper the hills of Rome. And who has not heard how even Vespasian and his son, Titus, incubate in the *Iseum* to induce an inspired dream or vision?" Zechariah laughs, good-naturedly. "Unless, of course, you are from Jerusalem."

Aaron wrinkles his forehead. He's clearly scandalized. "Years ago the Hasmoneans always purified a pagan settlement before moving into it. Pray well, Zechariah, and beseech God to cleanse this wretched place."

I back away. So . . . in addition to worrying about my family and the Romans, I must also worry about these followers of Isis.

"Fire! Fire!" someone shouts.

Zechariah's prayer of blessing over my house still hangs in the air, and my guests have yet to sip their first cup of wine in celebration. But all is forgotten as we rush to the blazing grain fields. It appears the fire started in the barley fields where the crop has already been harvested, but is quickly spreading to the wheat—the wheat which will ripen in less than two weeks. Some of the men who have run ahead have already stripped off their robes and are using them to beat the flames. I pull off my head covering as I run to join them. The wind is not in our favor. It blusters and snorts around our heads. Already a quarter of the field is destroyed.

Zechariah is beside me, his giant arms slamming his robe, over and over, against the wall of fire. He stands his ground, refusing to give way, all the while saying the name "Argos" under his breath, as if a curse.

For over an hour we beat the flames with our clothes, men, women, children—all who have arms and legs and breath to do so. Some of the older women bring jugs of water from the spring to pour over the smoldering rags in our hands. Cinders and smoke fill the air. Our eyes sting and tear. Our nose and mouth are clogged with soot. We cough, we gag, but we stand and fight. And when it's done, more than half our crop is destroyed, and Simon the bottlemaker's arms have been so badly burned we fear he'll lose one or both of them.

Aaron is gone. He left early this morning. I think of him now as I cover my head with my new square of brown homespun purchased from the widow Leah. Then I fasten the cloth with a plaited cord. From time to time, Leah sells a possession or two in order to live, and someone in the community always buys and always pays more than it's worth. It's a way of helping her out. Torah commands us to care for widows and orphans. There's no shame for either to take alms, but Leah is proud. So this is the system the community has come up with. I've already decided to buy Leah another head covering when I can think of an appropriate excuse for giving her a gift.

"Esther!" I shout as I descend the ladder from the second floor to the broadroom below. We must not be late." I glance into each of the other three rooms on the first floor, but I don't see my daughter. "Esther!"

"You needn't shout, Mama," Esther says, coming in from outside. Her hair is not plaited, but hangs in knotty cascades around her shoulders.

"Quickly, daughter. Prepare yourself. They're gathering even now as we speak."

"I'm not going, Mama. I don't feel well."

I look at Esther's thin, pale face; into her dead eyes. Then I feel her forehead for fever. She's as cool as the spring water in the wadi. "Then you'll not be gathering with the believers?"

Esther shakes her head.

"It will do you good to get out. And they'll pray for you. You need their prayers, Esther."

My daughter stands her ground. "Surely they can pray for me even if I'm not there."

"Yes . . . I . . . suppose." My heart is uneasy. I don't like leaving her. She isolates herself more and more; fellowshipping with no one, and going out only to do her chores. She has even forsaken the normal polite greetings to those she passes. "Well . . . rest then," I say, knowing Esther is ill, but not in body. And it's not rest she needs, but a renewed mind.

It's cramped, and the odor of dung from the nearby sheep wafts overhead. In my hand I clutch my stone cup, the cup which Zechariah has asked me to bring. I was surprised by his request. The cup has always been important to me, but for the first time I'm beginning to understand it might be important to others as well. Zechariah was certainly moved after I told him about it and he examined it. And when he saw the *tav* carved in its bottom, he told me how some rabbis believe that the Israelites applied the lambs' blood on the doorposts and lintels of their homes in Goshen in the form of a *tav*, as a cross. And this, according to Zechariah, foretold of the three crosses at Golgotha; foretold of the sacrifice of our Lord between two thieves.

"Everyone will be here soon," Zechariah says, standing near the gate of the sheep pen. "It's not Solomon's Porch," he adds, with a twinkle in his eye, referring to the place that the followers of The Way favored when meeting in Jerusalem's Temple. "But it's holy ground, nevertheless."

We cluster in his courtyard, the late-morning sun beating on our heads. Clucking hens peck the dirt around my feet, and nearby a donkey brays as one by one the believers trickle in. They wear their poverty as well as their troubles, and appear strained, tired and worried. No one talks about it, but everyone knows there'll be a shortage of wheat because of the recent firing of the fields. And that means nothing to barter with in the Gentile shops.

Zechariah greets everyone by name. I've never known a man so jovial. Oh, how he hugs and kisses the brethren, each in turn! His love, like the seeds in a pomegranate, seems endless.

We unfurl our rush mats and place them on the ground, then take our seat. One by one we begin to pray. Slowly, slowly, slowly, the strain on faces eases; a faint glimmer of hope returns to troubled eyes. After all, didn't the Master promise He would never leave us or forsake us? We have not been abandoned. We have not been forsaken. We are remembering that we're not alone. One by one, prayers of petition become prayers of thanksgiving. Some prayers turn into songs. And though our words are different, we are one voice; one sweet and lilting voice that floats to heaven and fills the air with a fragrance like incense. *We are remembering.* Slowly, slowly, slowly, a faint smile appears on first one face, then another. How long we sing and pray, I cannot say, because time has stopped for me, and so has all my straining and striving, and yes, my worrying, too.

We're still uttering praises when two men carrying a litter and, with it, a foul odor, join our assembly. I know that smell. I've come to know it these past four years of rebel infighting in Jerusalem. It's the smell of a gangrenous body. The praying and singing stop as whispers ripple through the crowd, "Simon. It's Simon the bottlemaker!" People begin standing to get a better look.

What a sad sight he is! I'm on my feet, too, and can see him over the heads of those in front of me if I stand on tiptoes. His arms are black and covered with oozing sores. His eyes are closed and his face, the color of wax. He looks more dead than alive. His presence has caused my spirit to plummet. Just one glance and I have tumbled from the mountain top into the valley. We are all tumbling. I can see it on everyone's face. I think we would have all gone home right then and there, carrying our heavy hearts like the men carrying the litter, if Zechariah had not stepped forward and opened the codex in his hand—the writings of John the Apostle.

His voice is like thunder. "'*In the beginning was the Word, and the Word was with God, and the Word was God . . . .*'"

I close my eyes and listen. The words are like falling dew. Oh, how parched I am! We're all parched—made waste, like our land, by the Romans. There's not one among us who has not felt Rome's heavy hand. But it's the *beginning* we must remember. We must return there, to God, to the beginning.

I tilt back my head and without fully understanding why, open my mouth as though trying to catch the precious drops.

"'. . . *In him was life; and the life was the light of men* . . .'"

Oh, the words, how they comfort! I stand very still. Those around me become still, too. We're all drinking now.

"'. . . *But as many as received him, to them gave he power to become the sons of God* . . . .'"

How long Zechariah reads, I cannot say. But when he's done, when he finally closes the codex, I feel as giddy as a girl and actually laugh. Some others do, too.

"Oh, dear ones, what a glorious treasure we have in earthen vessels," Zechariah say, his face beaming like the sun, his eyes moist with tenderness. "Let us remember what a sacrifice it took to make it so. Let us do as our Lord commanded. Let us break bread together. Let us drink from one cup."

Everyone nods. "Yes, let us remember His sacrifice."

Zechariah extends his hand toward me. "Rebekah has brought us the cup of our Lord's last supper."

I had forgotten the cup, and look down, now, almost surprised to see it there, nestled in my hand. I bring it to Zechariah. He passes it to a man who fills it with wine. Then Zechariah reaches into a basket near his feet, pulls out a large round loaf of flat-bread, and tears off a piece.

"In this way his body was broken for us." He lifts the piece into the air. "Jesus said to do this in remembrance of Him. I remember, Lord. I remember what you did, how you suffered, how your body was broken. I remember how you were beaten and pierced. All for *me*. I remember." With that he puts the piece of bread in his mouth and passes the loaf to the woman next to him. She breaks a piece, eats it, then passes the loaf to another. This is done over and over again. More than once Zechariah has to pluck a fresh loaf from his basket before everyone has broken their piece.

At last, he takes the cup of wine from the hand of the man who's been holding it all this time, and lifts it into the air. "Jesus also took a cup, and he told the twelve it was the cup of the new covenant, a covenant of blood, *His* blood which is shed for the forgiveness of sins. Oh, dear ones, let us remember that Jesus became the lamb, our Passover lamb, and shed his blood so we can apply it to the doorposts and lintels of our hearts, and pass from death into life." He's almost weeping now. "I remember, Lord," he says sipping from the cup.

We all take our turn, sipping the wine then passing the cup. Moments after I've taken my sip there's a stir among the crowd. People's heads press together as they whisper. Then the whispers grow louder, until finally someone shouts, "A miracle! It's a miracle!"

"Praise be to our Lord and Savior," someone else yells. And then everyone seems to shout at once.

"The Lord is in our midst! The Lord is among us!"

"Forgive us oh, Lord, for our unbelief."

"Have mercy on us sinners."

"How great is Messiah, Son of the living God!"

What is happening? I stand on tiptoes but still can't determine the reason for the excitement. People are bent over the litter, obscuring Simon from view. Finally, I reach into the crowd and pull on Mary's tunic. "What is it? What's going on?"

She turns. She's crying and laughing all at once. "It's Simon, my husband. The Lord has healed him. He . . . his skin . . . his skin is as soft and pink as little Joshua's here." She points to the infant in Tirzah's arms.

And so our beleaguered community experienced its first miracle.

The next time we gather at Zechariah's house, two more believers are healed; the widow, Leah, of a cut she gave herself when cooking—I think her eyes are failing. But it shows how God cares even about the little things. Then Ira, who broke his leg falling off a roof. I saw it with my own eyes—the bone sticking through his skin, the leg swollen and purple. All during the time we prayed, he cried and screamed with pain. And then, after Ira drank from the cup, his leg . . . it mended, just like that. The bone disappeared, the skin closed over. He even stood on it, gently at first. After a moment or two, when he realized he had no pain, he began to walk. He walked all around the outside of Zechariah's house. Round and around and around. It made me dizzy. Then he jumped up and down. I thought he'd never stop. But we all cried and laughed and shouted praises to God.

Everyone says it's the cup. But I don't believe it. Jesus drank from hundreds of cups, and ate from just as many bowls. Do these things heal? When I tell people, "no, it's not the cup," they argue that Peter's shadow alone could heal. They remind me of Paul the Apostle's handkerchiefs that healed, too.

Zechariah says the Spirit of God has fallen afresh on us. People are beginning to feel more hopeful. Their spirits are rising. They're beginning to believe it's possible to make a good life here. They're beginning to see that God has *not* abandoned them.

Still, I'm troubled by it all. Too many of our number are looking at a stone cup instead of the Lord. And the Gentiles? News of what's happening here has reached their ears. Argos incites them against us. Anger is rising, and fear, too, fear of what they don't understand. Violence increases. Only yesterday, Ira's winepress was destroyed, and the day before that Caleb, a young shepherd boy, was badly beaten. Everyone knows that both were the work of Argos and his cult. I worry that if this doesn't stop soon, someone will die.

Ethan

JERUSALEM 70 A.D.

CHAPTER 4

Jerusalem, the Holy City, the Navel of the Earth, will soon be under siege—attacked from the north. It's only logical since our other three sides are protected by deep ravines. Foolish to mention the obvious to the men near me, but I do, more to break the silence than anything else. They seem grateful, for at once they nod and voice their agreement.

"Titus will be thorough," adds Eleazar, who stands to my right. "And why not? He can afford to be. Our spies tell me there's no limit to his supplies—leather tents, weaponry, bedding, *food.* The Romans dig trench-and-berm fortifications by day, then play knucklebones and dice, and gorge themselves by night." He curses under his breath. "Look there. Already their campfires glow in the distance. Soon they'll gather for meals of fresh bread, vegetables, meat."

His statement hangs in the air like an accusation. Had John and Simon not burned our grain, the city would not be so desperate, and people wouldn't be breaking into homes stealing bread or fighting in the streets over chunks of moldy cheese and a handful of raisins.

"I ask you, how are we supposed to keep our men fit for battle when they have so little to eat?" Eleazar absently pulls his beard.

Both John and Simon stand nearby, along with their generals, but no one answers. We are staring down from the Phasael, the tower named for Herod the Great's brother, and built on the western ridge of the city near Herod's palace. We can see for miles. It's the largest of the three protective towers Herod built by his palace; and is complete with bulwarks and parapets. It's also honeycombed with lavish quarters. Herod was nothing if not extravagant. Even the other two towers—Hippicus, a water reserve, and Mariamme were laced with opulent apartments.

We are a glum lot. Titus has moved his camp northwest, only eight hundred cubits from our wall. The 15th Apollinaris, the 5th Macedonica, and the 12th—the Fulminata from Syria, which has only recently arrived—share the new campsite. The 10th remains on the Mount of Olives facing our eastern wall.

Four legions are now poised against us.

Titus's move began after he leveled the land. Everything is gone. Even the gullies and caves have been filled. A flat barren wasteland now sits between us. Not one green leaf—not one bush or vine or tree—can be seen. Our spies claim no trees remain standing for ten miles in any direction. All have been cut for Roman siege-works or to heat Roman food or for making the crosses they use to hang us rebels.

And though I grieve this devastation, I also take perverse pleasure in knowing that the Romans are even now reaping what they have sown. A cloud of dust hovers over their large sprawling camp. It swirls in the wind like an army of gnats. It coats their leather tents, their supply wagons and horses, their mules; clings to their hair and bodies, armor and weapons; grits their food. For days I've watched them, eating, breathing, choking on it, but still they worked their pickaxes and mattocks. They've filled baskets by the hundreds with earth, then used the earth to build one massive wall around their camp, another around our city. Their tenacity in the face of such trying conditions is irksome, inspiring and terrifying all at once.

"Titus will try cutting off our supplies," John of Gischala finally says, his eyes riveted on the activities below. "He'll attempt to starve us out."

"He'll try," I say. "But he won't wait for famine to kill us." My hand rests on the hilt of the sword strapped to my waist. "His siege walls are too long. Defending them means spreading his legions too thin. It means making his men easy targets for our raiding parties. He's too good of a general for that. He's also impatient for victory. Already his engineers have heaved lead and line from one of their platforms to measure the distance to our walls for their archers. And look . . . he has started a ramp." Even from here it's clear that the swarming men who keep darting behind screens and sheds and into leather covered passageways are building a ramp.

"Ethan's right. Titus won't wait. He'll bring the fight to us," Eleazar says. "His battering rams are finished, and his wooden towers, too. From them he'll pummel us with stones, arrows, spears."

I glance at the Roman towers. They are covered with hides and iron plates, and sit on massive wooden wheels by which they will be rolled to our walls when the ramp is finished.

Time was running out.

"Yes . . . I believe you're right," John of Gischala says, almost reluctantly. "It does appear that Titus will strike soon. But where? What part of the north wall will he hit?" His question is directed to all the generals, but he looks at me.

"Near the tomb of John the High Priest," I answer quickly. "The ground there is flat, and the wall low and poorly joined. It's our weakest point. If I were Titus, that's where I'd go."

John nods. "Then that's where we'll put the Benjaminite archers."

"Food will be the problem," Eleazar says, "or rather the lack of it."

Food again.

"We must continue the raiding parties to gather all we can while the southern end of the city is still open," Eleazar continues. "Every day, Titus tightens his siege wall around Jerusalem. It will not be much longer before he seals us in."

Before John can answer, a voice shouts from outside the wall, "It is foolish to fight the mighty Roman army! Come, open the gates and Titus will show you mercy!"

I look down and see a man on horseback, galloping toward us. He wears Roman armor and carries a white flag tied to a spear. Two men ride behind him.

"I've come in peace," he shouts, riding so close one of our archers could easily strike him down. "Allow me to speak."

Jeers and hoots are hurled from our walls, along with a large stone, but it drops harmlessly onto the dirt. John sends one of his generals to quiet the men and allow the rider to approach.

"Perhaps Titus wishes to surrender," he says, laughingly, when his general disappears.

But I don't laugh. Titus has not gone to all the trouble of moving his camp to surrender now. It's more likely he wishes to extend the terms of *our* surrender.

When the rider closes in, someone shouts, "Josephus! It's that traitor Josephus!"

My chest tightens with shame. Josephus is a relative, an aristocrat, a Hasmonaean priest, a descendant of the Maccabees, a man who fought for his people in Galilee then switched sides after his capture by the Romans. It is said he predicted Vespasian would become emperor. It is also said he predicts the downfall of Jerusalem. I curse him now, under my breath.

"You miserable fools," he cries, "Why do you insist on fighting Rome? Don't you know God has ordained that everything is to be brought under their rule? *Imperium orbis terrae.* Will you fight against your God? Submit now, and Legate Titus will be merciful. There will be no loss of life, no destruction of the city, no desecration of the Holy Temple. For your sakes, for your wives' and children's sakes, make an end to this rebellion, and all will be well."

The walls erupt with shouts and hoots and curses. Our men are angry wolves desperate to tear the royal eagle and humiliate Titus; desperate to draw Roman blood and avenge all of Judea. I look into Eleazar's troubled eyes and see that which he wishes to hide: his willingness to open the gates to Titus. And I know it's only because he fears for the safety of the Temple. And when John orders one of the bowmen to fire an arrow into the ground near Josephus to show his contempt for Titus's offer, I hear Eleazar sigh, and understand his disappointment, for I feel it too. We both know the ancient law. Once Titus's battering ram strikes its first blow, surrender will be unconditional.

—∞∞—

"The New City has fallen! Bezetha—the New City, has fallen!" people shout as they run past me. Men, women, children—half starved and in rags, pour from the New City, fleeing the advancing Roman army, their eyes wide with terror; tears streaking their dust caked faces. Wounded rebels, limping and groaning and covered with blood, are carried along by the crowd, all trying to escape the slaughter behind them. Even now, anguished shrieks and cries float from Bezetha, along with plumes of smoke and circling birds of prey.

I knew it was coming. We all did. The Romans have been battering our northwestern wall for days while raining arrows and stones upon our heads from their huge iron-clad towers. Not even our firebrands could stop them. The few who dared suggest we surrender have been murdered by John's men. I have said nothing. For my part I'm happy to die for Jerusalem. But something strange has happened. I've been seized by a fear so fierce it sets my teeth on edge. And it came upon me the minute my son, Aaron, was wounded while trying to save Esther's husband, Daniel, who fell early this morning. I've always understood the possibility of losing one of my sons, perhaps all. They are, after all, soldiers, and soldiers die in battle. But I've suddenly learned that knowing something in your head and reconciling it in your heart is a gulf as wide as the Valley of Jezreel.

Even now my insides quiver with this fear, and so I grab Aaron's arm before he can run toward the New City. "Stay here and help the wounded," I bark.

Aaron, holding an oval spiked-boss shield in one hand and a dagger in the other, pulls against my clasp. The bloody cloth wrapped around his head and left eye is loose and ready to fall off. I resist the urge to secure it.

"We cannot let the Romans breach the wall of the Second Quarter," he says. With a fierce jerk he frees himself and pushes through the sea of fleeing people.

"You're needed here," I shout, trying to catch up. How swift he is! Even with his grievous wound. "Come back!" But he pays no heed. The space between us widens. "You'll lose your eye if you continue," I blurt, exposing my fear. I'm running now, and lunging forward I'm able to catch his blood-stained tunic. "You must allow time for it to heal."

The cloth around his head conceals the gash on his forehead and injured left eye. But his right eye looks at me sharply and I see his shock. "You speak like a father."

"I *am* a father!"

"In another lifetime, yes," Aaron says, pulling me to him with his shielded arm. For a brief moment we linger in this tender embrace, his bleeding forehead pressed against mine. "But now you are a soldier," he says backing away. "And so am I."

With that we both run toward the shrieks and cries and billowing smoke of Bezetha to join the rebels that remain there, among them—my other sons.

Titus has once again moved his camp; this time into Bezetha, the New City. It was here that King Sennacherib's Assyrian army set up their camp nearly seven hundred years ago when they came to conquer Jerusalem.

Titus has destroyed homes, leveled more ground. Those who escaped have brought tales of slaughter and looting. All who did not heed the command of our generals to evacuate before Titus's largest battering ram broke through the wall—the ram called "Victor" by our men—have fallen by the sword. Men, women, children, all were slaughtered without mercy. For more than a day, the Romans slashed, looted and burned without restraint. Scores of fresh crosses appeared outside our walls, testifying to the fate of those rebels caught alive. Their corpses are rotted now. Most have fallen away from their crosses and lay in stinking heaps upon the ground. The air reeks from them, and the sky is so full of flies and birds of prey it appears that dark clouds hover overhead.

The Romans are employed in other tasks now. They have already cleared the approach to our wall that surrounds the Second Quarter, and are busily constructing new siege works in addition to repairing their towers and battering rams. They've nearly finished the trench-and-berm perimeter around their new camp. Soon Titus will attempt to breach our wall. If successful, he'll set his sights on the Antonia, and from there . . . the Temple, for the Antonia has direct access to the Temple porticos.

But we have been busy, too. Using the city's underground tunnels and sewers, our raiding parties continue to penetrate Titus's lines, striking work parties and supply columns and carrying off the spoils. It has kept us in food and fresh weaponry. But the cost has been high. Those caught are crucified. But these days, rebels are not the only ones crucified. Ordinary citizens who are found sneaking from the city at night in search of food also meet this fate; at least the men. Women are spared crucifixion but are mistreated in other shameful ways. It makes me grateful that Rebekah and Esther are no longer here. I pray to *Hashem* for their safety.

But as crucifixions increase, so does our resolve. Titus hopes to demoralize us by placing the crosses so near our wall. He thinks it will make us lose heart. But he's wrong. It makes us more resolute than ever. We're all determined to die as men, as soldiers in battle.

But *Hashem* has been merciful. My sons and I still live. And only Aaron has been wounded. His wound, which has been sealed by fire, is nearly healed, but he has lost the sight of his left eye. Still, Aaron is strong and says he's ready to take up arms. I hold my tongue and say nothing. But my gnawing fear persists.

The eerie calm that has hovered uneasily over us this past hour is suddenly broken by Roman trumpet blasts and the banging of drums. All morning we have waited for the legionaries to attack, but they haven't. Only that traitor, Josephus, ventured out and spouted new terms of surrender, shouting out Titus's promise of leniency, which no one believed, at least not the rebels. But that was earlier, and nothing has happened, until now. In numb silence I watch from my place in one of the Antonia towers. The earth rumbles and quakes as thousands upon thousands of feet kick up dirt, forcing clouds of dust to plume overhead. Titus's men march in flawless lines, and according to rank. It takes a minute for me to realize they do not move in battle formation.

"What do you suppose that fox is up to?" Aaron asks. He too is watching the spectacle.

"It's hard to say. But . . . it almost looks like he's preparing for a parade. Unthinkable, isn't it?" I squint into the expanse and notice that the legionaries wear polished tinned bronze helmets and mail shirts. Broadswords, in decorative scabbards, are belted to one side of their waist, a dagger to the other, while in their hands they carry long gleaming javelins. The highly polished metal boss on their wood-and-leather shields is almost blinding in the sun. Many of the soldiers sport medals and armbands. Officers wear red plumed helmets and polished armor. Some ride lavishly decorated horses.

"Aaron, it *is* a parade," I say, barely able to comprehend the foolish sight before me. Then, as if to confirm my words, out comes Titus clad in a gold and red cape. And after he and his generals take their position, the troops begin the long, slow process of passing in review.

The man is insane. My spies tell me that the Roman pay wagons have arrived. Under the guise of dispensing the owed *denarii* to his men, Titus has continued this farce for four days. For four days soldiers by the tens of thousands—privates, decurions, centurions, tribunes and generals—legion by legion, have paraded in front of this madman, saluting and shouting his praises, then collecting their pay.

But Eleazar says Titus is not as mad as I think. He believes the parades—which force us to see this vast, mighty army in full regalia—were meant to intimidate. And they have. Our citizens are terrified. And renewed talk of surrender circulates through the narrow streets of Jerusalem, talk which John's men have tried to silence with their swords. And my heart is grieved that once again, Jews slaughter Jews.

"Hungry, are you? Want a little of this?" a Roman shouts outside our wall just past the range of our archers. He takes a bite of something in his hand—a loaf of bread, I think. His comrades, who stand near him, also taunt us. Some hold up full round wine skins; others, large clusters of grapes. One takes what looks like a piece of cheese and throws it into the dirt, then grinds it beneath his boot, and laughs. He can afford to be contemptuous of such a treasure as fresh cheese—something we haven't seen in weeks. Titus' storehouses are kept full by the endless supply wagons from Syria.

"May *Hashem* have mercy on us," Eleazar says, standing beside me.

We are in one of the Antonia towers viewing the Roman camps. Even at this height the stench is as thick as bark. The city reeks. Famine has struck Jerusalem. Hundreds lay dead on rooftops or in alleyways. People attack each other in the streets, hoping to find food in a scrip. Some kill their own neighbors. Others break into homes and torture the owners trying to force them to reveal hidden supplies. Still others eat bits of straw or leather from scrips or belts, or even their own sandals. Those not having straw or a piece of leather to chew go to their roofs or lock themselves in their houses and wait for death. Bodies by the thousands have been thrown over walls into the ravines, and lie decomposing in the sun. Flies swarm everywhere. Vultures, too.

"We can fight the Romans and even each other and survive, but we cannot fight hunger," Eleazar says.

He looks shorter. I know it's only because of his thinning frame and stooped shoulders, but it pains me to see him this way. "A spy tells me he saw Titus lift his arms toward heaven and call upon God to bear witness that this starvation is not his doing," I say, not bothering to mention that the spy was my son, Abner, who continues to make risky sorties behind enemy lines. I don't mention it because voicing it grips me with fear.

Eleazar laughs unexpectedly—a strange and pleasant sound amid all this unpleasantness. "If Titus is not to blame, who then?"

Rebekah's words swirl through my mind—her pronouncements that God has forsaken us. "Maybe the next time that traitor Josephus promises generous terms of surrender someone should jump from the wall and kill him," I finally say. There was no end to that man making appeals for Titus.

Eleazar strokes his white beard and looks at me sideways. "Then you don't believe him? About the liberality of terms?"

"Oh, I believe. That's why it pains me to hear it. He'll be generous with the civilians. And if I had my way, I'd open the gates and let anyone who wants, surrender." It's the first time I've admitted this. *Will Eleazar think me a traitor?*

"Neither John nor Simon would allow that. They'd kill the people first."

"Perhaps that's why Titus can call upon heaven as a witness to his innocence. We are killing our own people, allowing them to starve to death rather than surrender."

Eleazar touches my shoulder lightly. "You . . . would surrender?"

"Perhaps Titus will be kind to civilians, but no one believes he'll be kind to us rebels. No, my friend, if we surrender, it means crucifixion. And since I have a choice, I choose death by the sword. I will fight."

"Many of our citizens are escaping south, through the Essene Gate, rebels too, only to end up on crosses." Eleazar sighs. "I too believe the time for surrender is past. The Romans have committed too many atrocities. There can be no forgiveness, no peace, no submission to their rule now." He eyes me strangely. "Our path lies in revenge. We *must* avenge this devastation of our Holy City; this supreme insult to *Hashem*." He clasps my shoulders between fingers that are thin and spindly but still strong. "Do you believe this?"

"Yes . . . I . . . suppose."

"Of course you do, that's why you and I will fight to the end."

I feel strangely uncomfortable as I nod, and see, for the first time, something terrible in Eleazar's eyes.

The Second Quarter has fallen. Its outer walls are rubble. We have been firing upon the Romans all day as they build a ramp toward Antonia. They've made great progress but it has cost dearly. Though they are covered in armor, and work beneath wicker screens and sheds, and transport their materials through leather covered passageways, hundreds lay dead. Our Benjaminites are weary from all the arrows they have fired, as are our spearmen and those who work the catapults. Still, the Romans refuse to quit or pull back. And they don't shrink from our firebrands, either. Eleazar is sure Titus has promised them all a promotion if they survive, or the prized meed of valor if they perish. But I believe it's something else altogether. I believe the 10th Legion has inspired the others to partake in their revenge. After all, revenge works both ways.

But we have not been idle. We are planning our own subterfuge. Even now, John and his men are digging tunnels beneath the Antonia to collapse the Roman ramps. They are all congratulating themselves for thinking up this mischief, but I'm not so optimistic. I fear our tunnels won't stop the legionaries for long. The Romans are as men possessed. They fight like demons and stand their ground even in the face of certain death. Their determination to defeat us is terrifying.

Everything is moving swiftly against us. Titus has completed his wall around the city, and has strategically installed watchtowers and small forts along its perimeter. This has effectively closed up the southern end, the last opening through which meager amounts of food and supplies, have, until now, been smuggled. We are completely cut off, sealed, as it were, in our own tomb. Titus has also captured Jerusalem's aqueduct, effectively cutting off our water supply. And inside our city, things are more dire than ever. So dire that in spite of the risk, people are fleeing Jerusalem by the thousands. Even rebels. Simon's Idumaeans left first. Now, even John's men are escaping. Those who stay shout curses into the wind and promise vengeance, but for my part, I fear we are all doomed.

A new forest has sprung up. A forest of crosses. Nearly five hundred a day are being crucified. In the midst of this, Josephus has again urged us to surrender; warning us not to try Titus's patience any further, and threatening grave consequences if we do. He has panicked the city even further. People are jumping from walls only to be captured and gutted by the Syrian and Arab auxiliary units who are searching for swallowed jewels or coins. Inside our city and outside in the ravine, the mountain of dead continues to rise.

And in the quiet of the night I weep.

Hashem, where are you? Will you let the buzzards pick our bones? Will you let the uncircumcised defile Your Temple? Where is Your mighty hand now? The mighty hand that fought for Joshua and David and Gideon?

I'm in deep despair as flames crackle and shoot from the roof of the nearby sixty-cubit-high Temple portico. Smoke curls between its massive columns and carpets the marble paving stones with soot. The smoke is so thick I can hardly breathe. It stings my eyes making it difficult to see. Blood trickles from the wound in my left wrist and drips off my hand. In the other hand I wield a sword whose hilt is so slick with the blood of my enemies it nearly slips from my grasp.

"This way!" Aaron shouts, pointing to the Court of Women with his dagger.

We are surrounded by mail-clad Romans. Everywhere I look I see their red metal-bossed shields. Like a plague of locust they swarm through every opening into the Court of the Gentiles. We are caught up in this plague, and if Aaron and I don't get out soon we'll both die.

It's been days since the Antonia fell, and days since Titus leveled it and used the rubble to make a massive causeway into the Temple to bring up his troops and his battering rams and artillery engines. Now the unthinkable has happened. Titus has penetrated the Temple's outer court.

I hack my way toward Aaron, and see that my other sons, Benjamin, Joseph and Abner are nearby brandishing their own weapons. Men fall on every side and litter the polished marble pavement. Our forces are retreating en mass from the Court of the Gentiles to the safety of the thick, forty-cubit high walls of the Court of Women. An arrow whizzes past and would have pierced my neck had I not stooped to pick up a fallen Roman shield. I loop my injured wrist through its back, then use it and my sword to force my way to my sons. The five of us fight our way up the Temple steps, then to the terrace leading to the eastern gate.

Benjamin is the first to reach safety. Then Joseph and Aaron. I follow, while Abner lags behind. When I reach the terrace I turn and see that Abner is still at the bottommost step, surrounded by three legionaries. His dagger is flashing in all directions. I bound down the stairs toward him, but two Romans prevent me from going the distance. Arms, shields, swords, all clash. I swing blindly, barely able to see through burning, stinging eyes. I know not where my sword strikes. More Romans appear.

I'm totally surrounded. Yet, over shoulders and amid flashing steel, I manage to make out Abner just as he is knocked backwards by a Roman. I see him go down; see a horde of legionaries descend upon his prone body. And while watching, my guard drops and in that second, a legionaries' sword crashes against mine, making it slip from my hand and fly into the air. Now I have only the shield. With my good arm, I swing it wildly from side to side, knocking soldiers off their feet. But no matter how hard I fight to reach Abner, I'm blocked by wave after wave of red shields. And just as I think they'll overwhelm me, I'm yanked backward, out of their reach. When I turn I see Aaron and Benjamin each holding fast to one of my arms. Next to them my son, Joseph, and three Zealots, all wielding their weapons, clear a path for our retreat.

"No!" I scream. "Abner is out there!"

"You can't save him," Aaron says, as he and Benjamin pull me to safety. "You have to let him go."

"Thus says Titus: 'This is your final warning! My benevolence is at an end. I have no wish to desecrate or destroy your Temple,'" Josephus shouts, atop his horse from a safe distance. Engineers have already heaved lead to determine how close he can come. "'Why do you force my hand? Why do you pollute your own Sanctuary with the blood of the slain?'" He makes his horse trot a straight line, careful not to stray closer. "'Why do you not listen to your own rabbi and countryman, and my spokesman, Josephus? He has laid out my terms for the last time. Why not submit to imprisonment rather than see the House of your God destroyed by flames?'"

"We'll have more desertions now," Eleazar says, turning to me.

I nod absently. It's difficult to concentrate. I'm grieving for Abner. I have stood the entire night and part of the morning on the wall of the Court of Women, searching for his body among the slain littering the paving stones of the Court of Gentiles. Sometime before dawn, the Romans gathered their wounded and brought them to safety behind the massive Corinthian columns of the Royal Portico, the one running the length of the outer court's southern wall and the only portico still intact. Could they have brought Abner there by mistake? Impossible to imagine. His fringed tunic, his brown leather breast plate, his bearded face clearly reveal him as a Zealot. From the wall, I've looked a hundred times at the place where he fell. He had to be dead. *But where was his body?*

Someone catapults a boulder causing Josephus's gray steed to rear. When he brings it under control, he shouts his parting words, "Heaven will curse you if you don't surrender now."

Jeers and profanity follow his departure as our men wave their fists and weapons in the air. Their taunts are greeted by Roman heckling. Scores of legionaries lift their shields and javelins threateningly. Some pound swords against their metal boss. A centurion, with arms folded, stands to one side. After a few moments, he raises his hand and silences his men, then points to the fresh crop of crosses planted during the night.

"See to your fate, Jews of Jerusalem. Not even your generals can save you now. They can't even save their own sons." With that he spits on the ground and walks away amid a chorus of curses and taunts.

But I hardly hear over the pounding of my heart as I sprint across the top of the wall, scanning the forest of crosses as I go.

"What's *wrong*?" Eleazar says, wheezing behind me.

I ignore him as I run, searching, searching, searching the anguished swollen faces of those who have been beaten, then crucified. Beads of perspiration dot my forehead as I gulp air through my tightening chest. And then I stop. *No . . . this can't be him.* He is hardly recognizable—stripped naked, his manhood exposed, face swollen and battered, lips split and bleeding, body ripped and bloody from scourging. Flies swarm his wounds. I can almost feel their torment. His head droops against his chest. His arms are stretched. A plaque of wood covers each wrist to keep the nails that pierce them from ripping through the flesh. His legs are pulled up and each heel, also covered with a plaque, is nailed to the cross.

"*Abner*." I choke saying his name. I've never felt such pain. It's as if my heart has been clawed by giant talons. I pull my hair. I curse and pound my fists against the wall. Then I grab the bow from the hand of the rebel near me, pull an arrow from his quiver, and without using a bracer to protect my injured arm, I shoot the arrow at my son.

When it misses its mark I frantically grab for another arrow, but the man backs away, his face twisted in horror. I leap on him like a beast, and am about to wrestle him to the ground when strong, spindly fingers pull me away.

"No need, Ethan. No need," Eleazar says softly. "Abner is already dead."

"You sent for us?" My weary body tenses as I brace for Eleazar's answer and the reason he has summoned us to the Court of the Lepers, the only place not filled to overflowing with exhausted rebels. Many wrongly fear the stain of leprosy is upon it. It is one of four roofless chambers nestled in each corner of the Women's Court. The others, once used for storing wood and oil, are now packed with our men.

It's nearly sunset, and both sides have ceased fighting to seek their own places of refuge. Our men are everywhere, resting, dressing wounds. A few have morsels of food they try to eat without being seen.

My sons stand near me, dirty, blood-stained. Their young faces are drawn; their once strong bodies lean and weak from hunger. I avoid their eyes, for in them I see how much they have aged. *Why did Eleazar want my sons to come, too?* It makes me uneasy.

Eleazar hovers by the large pool once used by lepers as a *mikvah* before presenting themselves to the priests for examination. "You summoned us?" I repeat.

Eleazar puts a claw-like finger to his lips indicating we are to remain silent. The lamp in his hand casts an eerie glow across his face. The glow, his hollow cheeks, his wide, dark eyes, his matted white hair and beard, all make him look mad.

"Follow me," he says softly.

And we do, out the court and up the steps to the Nicanor Gate, then through the court of Men, the Court of Levites, past the Chamber of Hewn Stone where the Sanhedrin once met, past the Altar of Sacrifice which no longer sends the smoke of its offerings to *Hashem.* Instead, it is surrounded by priests who wear armor and carry swords, priests who are prepared to defend the altar with their lives. They take no notice of us.

"I'd like to be among their number when the time comes," Aaron says, lingering by the giant brass laver as he looks back at them. "I will pledge myself to the defense of the altar."

"You *will* pledge yourself to whatever Eleazar instructs," I say, putting an end to the matter. Aaron has more zeal than all of us. Rebekah faults me for this, but I'm blameless. I have only followed Torah's instruction to diligently instruct my children in the ways of God. As Torah commands, I've spoken to them about our great Creator. And I've done this when sitting and walking, when lying down and rising up. I've spoken the holy words of scripture; imparted its wisdom and instruction and admonitions, but not its fire. That came from *Hashem*—a holy fire I dare not quench.

We step into the colonnaded enclosure which contains the living quarters for priests. Slowly, we make our way down its long corridor, careful not to trample any of the hundred reclining bodies that cover the paving stones. They are what's left of John's and Simon's and Eleazar's men; dirty, ragged, hungry, many wounded, many restless in anticipation of tomorrow's battle, but some actually sleep.

I wonder if Eleazar is taking us to one of the thirty-eight rooms built into the three-story walls of the temple and used by the priests. But no, he stops at a room in the corridor, unlatches the door, and bids us enter. We step inside, then Eleazar bars the door. It's difficult to see with only the light from the small oil lamp in Eleazar's hand, but even so, it takes only a second to realize we're in a storeroom. Tables, laden with willow baskets of all sizes, cram the room. The baskets are filled with clay oil lamps, tunics, robes, sandals, and such. One table holds rush mats for sleeping, as well as pots, jars and other sundries. Eleazar's possessions? Or gifts for the Temple priests? Who can say, and I have no desire to ask.

Eleazar walks over to a table containing four finely woven bags, four bulging scrips, and four water skins, which appear full. He quickly lights four oil lamps and indicates we are to take one. "Each bag contains a good tunic and robe and sandals, a hammer, chisel, and small hand shovel. You'll need them. And the scrips are filled with raisins and hard cheese and almonds. You can travel many days on that."

My sons grow restless and whisper among themselves. Aaron actually flits from one end of the table to the other like a nervous sparrow.

"I fear the priest will not take his golden pitcher to the Kidron Valley and fill it with the waters of Siloam during the Feast of Tabernacles this year." Eleazar's dark mad eyes shimmer as he looks around the dim, cramped room. "*Hashem* cannot be pleased with us for stopping the Continual Sacrifice. Ever since the last lamb was slaughtered and the fires died, the battle has not gone well for us. But where are we to find a lamb . . . or even a dove? Our people are starving. Starving people do not bring animal sacrifices to the Temple. They stuff them into their own bellies."

"What is this about, my friend?" I ask, watching Eleazar rake his white hair with spindly fingers.

"One thousand priests were trained as masons in order to build the Holy Place without defilement. And when it was finished, Herod the Great sacrificed three hundred oxen to *Hashem.* Even that dog understood the holiness of our Temple. Now, the Romans will swarm over these sacred grounds and trample its holiness beneath their feet."

"Eleazar. . ." I reach for his shoulder, but he pushes me away. *Has he really gone mad?*

"I give you and your sons one last command," Eleazar says, holding up his lamp to study our faces. "If . . . the Temple falls . . . you must leave Jerusalem so our fight, so our cause can . . . *will* continue."

"If the Temple falls there are still The Upper and Lower City to defend. How can we leave? How can you ask us to desert you and the others?" I say, hardly believing my ears. My sons, too, shake their head in disbelief and mumble their displeasure under their breath.

"It's an order!" Eleazar barks. "You must obey. *Swear* to me you'll do as I've asked."

I look at my sons. They all shake their heads.

"I'll stay here and fight till the end," Aaron says.

Benjamin, taller than his brothers, and the one most resembling Rebekah, clasps Aaron's shoulder. "As will I."

I know my furled forehead reveals my anger at their refusing Eleazar, but I'm proud, too.

"And I'll stay as well," adds Joseph, the follower who always went along with the others.

"You are soldiers," I finally bellow. "You will obey your commander." At once, Joseph hangs his head. Benjamin, in quiet anarchy, pinches his lips and studies one of the bags on the table. Only Aaron remains openly defiant.

"John is our commander," he says, but the words are flat, and ring false. Our loyalty has always been with Eleazar, not John. I stare at Aaron, beating him down with my eyes. Oh how much he reminds me of myself! Foolish, strong headed, and stubbornly faithful. At last he bows his head, and in a shaky voice gives Eleazar his promise, as do each of us.

When the last oath is uttered, Eleazar removes the bags, scrips, and water skins from the table, exposing an object that was hidden beneath them. In the poor light I can't make it out. Eleazar beckons us closer, and as we cluster around the table, the light from our collective lamps reveals a thin flat copper scroll nearly five cubits long. The Temple housed a vast library of scrolls—the Torah, the Psalms, the writings of the prophets—all written with ink on papyrus or animal skins. None was hammered on costly copper. In Roman-Egypt, copper scrolls were used to inventory temple treasures. But I've never heard of us doing so.

I squint down at the scroll and see three sheets of copper riveted together as one. Odd, ill-formed lettering—ancient Hebrew from the looks of it—comprise the hammered text. I bend closer and begin reading, "In Har . . . Harubah . . . in . . . Valley of Achor . . ." It's difficult to read. Some words I can't make out at all. Still I continue, "be . . . beneath the steps . . . east . . . 40 . . . cubits . . . silver and . . . vessels, 17 talents." I frown and look up at Eleazar. "What is this? A treasure map?"

"Yes." Eleazar taps the scroll with a claw-like finger. "Temple treasure. A vast fortune that has, over the years, been dedicated to our God and His Holy Temple. More gold even than the eight-thousand talents Herod used to overlay and decorate the Holy Place. With it you can buy supplies and weapons for a new army."

I blink in disbelief. *Temple treasure?* Even if it were true, what army could I raise? Galilee and Judea were in shambles. The population decimated—slaughtered or taken as slaves. And those who weren't, were demoralized and barely able to eke out an existence in their ruined villages, or as exiles. Who was left to fight Rome?

"There are rebels at Masada," Eleazar says, as if reading my thoughts. "You must take the treasure there. Once it is known you have resources, others will join you. The fight *must* continue!"

This was a fool's errand. But can I tell Eleazar that? I close my eyes. And when I do, I see my son, Abner, hanging on the cross, and my heart is suddenly filled with rage. I have not had time to grieve him as I should. The fighting has kept me from it. Now, I am a swirling caldron of emotions: sorrow, longing, hatred, rage, the craving for revenge. But it is *revenge* that bubbles to the top, like dross over molten metal. It sears, it burns. I've never known its like. Not even my zeal for the Temple compares. I try to fight it. I squeeze my lids closed hoping to drive it back, but I can't. Dark thoughts fill my mind. Bloodshed, pain, dashed hopes, despair, death—these are what shape me now. I never thought it possible to feel such hatred; never thought it possible to want to do such violence. Will I leave Abner unavenged? Surely Rome must pay. Surely Romans must be made to grieve for their sons, too. Eleazar was right. There can be no living in peace with Rome now. No living under Roman rule. My hate gathers strength. It steams and boils, twisting me into a new creature, one sliding down toward its own destruction; sliding toward the burning world of Hades itself.

"I'll continue the fight." My voice is the voice of a stranger. "Yes, I'll continue the fight, but I'll not speak for my sons."

At once my sons surround me and bellow their support. They pledge their weapons. They make oaths. They thump my back and clasp my shoulder. And my heart breaks at the thought that I may be leading them into a pit.

But Eleazar appears pleased. He places his lamp on the table and begins rolling the scroll. When he does, the metal snaps. Without meaning to, he has broken the scroll in two. "No matter," he says, after examining it. "The break is at a rivet line and will not prevent you from reading the words. Guard it well. With your lives, if need be. It cannot fall into the hands of our enemies." He carefully wraps the scrolls in leather, ties them with a leather strap, then tucks the scrolls into his tunic. "Now, I'll show you the hidden passage. Commit it to memory. *All of you.* If one falls in battle, the others will still know the way."

He takes his lamp, ducks into the far corner of the room and pushes against one of the large wall stones. And then, right before our eyes, a section of wall opens revealing a narrow stairway cut into bedrock. He beckons us to enter. When we do, he follows and closes the wall behind him, then inches past us on the narrow steps so he can lead the way.

The steps are steep and many, and empty into a cramped, high-ceiling passageway. It, too, is cut from solid rock. Chisel marks scar the white limestone, and black smudged niches show were workers once placed their oil lamps along the wall. The air is stale. But surprisingly, the tunnel is dry.

We walk a long way. More than once the passage forks. I have the sensation we are traveling downward. As we go, Eleazar points out the variations in the walls—where white limestone gives way to red; the curvature of the floor, the rising or lowering of the ceiling. And he admonishes us to commit them all to memory. Finally, he stops at a spot where the passageway bulges on one side, creating a large landing.

"We are outside the city walls now," Eleazar says, pulling the scrolls from his tunic. He then stands on his toes and tucks the two leather-wrapped rolls into a niche high up on the bulging wall. "If the Temple falls, you must go to the storeroom, change clothes, take your scrips and water and whatever else you need, and come here for the scrolls."

He holds his lamp up to the tunnel opening that yawns before us like a grave and that stretches far beyond the flickering light's reach. "Continue through that passageway. Follow it to the end," he says, leaning against the cold limestone wall. Even in the dim light I see the strain and fatigue on his face. "It leads to the hills of Qumran and empties into one of the caves."

"Such a tunnel exists?" I squint at the long, black passageway in front of me. Jerusalem abounds with tunnels that honeycomb its underbelly: the well known Hezekiah's Tunnel and Solomon's quarries, also cisterns, waterways, plastered ashlar stone drainage channels. Many I've used myself to move about, undetected, especially when Rebekah was still in Jerusalem, but I never knew of this passageway. When I say this out loud, Eleazar nods.

"It is most secret," he says. "Only a few know of it. It was the passage we've been using for the past four years to take the Temple treasure and much of our library out of Jerusalem for safe keeping. We've hidden the sacred scrolls in the Qumran caves. The treasure, we've scattered in over sixty locations."

Eleazar's head slumps against his chest. At first I think he's ill, then realize he's eaten little today, having given his small ration to one of the priests guarding the altar.

"Come, let us go." Eleazar pulls himself upright to begin the long trek back. "Remember," he says, turning to look at us, "you have all sworn an oath. Dying will not be so unwelcome now that I know the fight will continue."

My old injury has reopened. Blood streams from my wrist and also from the new injury to my arm, gained when I stopped a Roman broadsword aimed for my face. All morning we've tried to keep the Romans from pouring into the Court of Women through the gates they've burned, but all to no avail. Now, even the Nicanor Gate is gone, a gate that took twenty men to open and close.

The Court of Women is choked with smoke and embedded with a stench just as thick. The odor is a caldron of burning wood, decaying dead, blood, unwashed soldiers, and bodily waste from men whose bowels have failed from fear.

The taking of the women's court has been costly for both sides. So many have fallen they form a carpet beneath our feet. Now, our men fight furiously to save the Holy Place. Even those priests, who up to now have only tended to the needs of the Temple, have taken up the sword. Hundreds, all in white linen, are stationed around the Altar of Sacrifice. Blood runs, like a stream, between their feet from the dead Romans that are stacked like logs around the base of the altar. Even so, an endless wave of legionaries continues to pour through every opening. And the tide is turning against us. Already, the eight stone tables north of the altar, where animals were once slaughtered for sacrifice, are fast becoming the platforms where priests are slaughtered by Romans. Even now, their death cries rise toward heaven, like incense, against the backdrop of the gleaming gold and white Temple.

I stand near the brass laver. I've killed so many Romans, my arm aches. I stay close to my sons. More than once my sword has saved them. But the circle is tightening. Our men are falling on all sides. I fear we will not be able to hold out much longer.

"Go! Fulfill your oath!" Eleazar says, suddenly coming up alongside me. His face is splattered with blood, his robe stained red. His eyes are wide and dark, like a man foreseeing his own death. "Quickly, there's not much time!" Then he heads for the altar.

I have no stomach for this task. I'm no coward. Yet that is how I feel when I signal my sons with the predetermined gesture to retreat. Then

I fight my way to the colonnaded enclosure and am nearly at the door of the storeroom when I slip on the blood-slick pavement. My weapon flies from my hand as I land on my back. At once a Roman is upon me, thrusting wildly with his broadsword. I quickly roll to avoid the blade and find I've rolled against a Corinthian column. Now, unarmed and unable to move, and with my face less than a cubit from the Roman's hobnailed boots, I'm defenseless. When he raises his boot, I see the nail heads are tipped with blood. And just as he's about to send them straight into my eyes, he topples forward, crashing into the massive stone column, then sliding, dead, to the floor.

Aaron lowers his dagger, and extends his free hand to pull me up. Instantly, my other sons are beside me, fending off attackers until I regain my footing. Then we all rush to the storeroom, enter and bolt the door. Eleazar has prudently kept one lamp lit. We light three others, remove our bloody clothes then replace them with the tunics and robes from each of the bags. Then quickly we gather the scrips and water skins, and a few supplies. Within minutes, we press against the movable stone in the wall and disappear down the narrow stairway.

Rebekah

Pella 70 A.D.

CHAPTER 5

We begin our days before sunrise. We're learning, Esther and I, to do chores our servants once did. She's outside firing the oven while I mix flour, oil and water, then knead it into dough. The dough I form into small flat cakes and place on round clay platters. I've made extra. Zechariah is coming for breakfast.

"The oven is ready," Esther says, entering the room. Her hair falls in oily strings around her face. Dirt smudges her cheeks. Even the bowl of fragrant henna blossoms on the shelf cannot disguise the fact that she hasn't bathed in days.

I pretend not to notice. Lately, I've tried not to find fault for fear of breaking what's left of her spirit. I gesture to the trays of flattened dough and begin cutting a cucumber on my small work table. The bread and cucumbers, along with yogurt made from the milk of our two goats, will comprise our morning meal.

"Do you need help carrying the trays?" I ask, watching my daughter out of the corner of my eye. Her shoulders slump like an old woman's as she drags one foot then the other across the stone floor, and I send up prayers to God. I'm always sending up prayers for Esther. "Do you need help?" I repeat, thinking she didn't hear.

"I can manage." Her voice is barely audible.

She's like one walking in her sleep, and I wonder if she's ever going to wake up. She shuffles out the door with the trays, and I return to work. Before I've finished slicing the second cucumber a voice behind me thunders, "*Maranatha*!" Only one voice can fill a room like that. I turn and there's Zechariah's large frame filling the doorway.

"You're early!"

"Good news begs telling."

"Then tell me for I can surely stand some." I add the cut cucumber to the other slices in the bowl.

"Ah, yes, Esther. Don't worry." Zechariah glances over his shoulder. "We're all praying."

"*This* is your good news?"

Zechariah fingers his beard that puffs like a cloud around his cheeks and chin. "The widow Leah is preparing her bread, too, and has promised to save a loaf for me. How I love her loaves of olives and rosemary. But then, the Evil One knows this." He pats his bulbous stomach.

"Zechariah, *please*. The good news, remember?"

His belly shakes as he chuckles. "You know how to ruin a good story. All right, all right, I'll tell you. We've had another miracle! Yes! Another miracle! Leah says she's been dipping from the same jar of olive oil all week, and it's not diminished a drop! Not one drop! No matter how much she uses, it stays full to the lip. Now what do you think of that?"

I wipe my hands on a rag and frown. "Her eyesight isn't what it used to be. Perhaps it's gotten worse. Or perhaps she's dipping one jar and measuring another."

"Oh, no. I saw it myself. She took a cup of oil from her jar, then another, then another, but still the jar remained full. And there's nothing wrong with *my* eyes!"

I grunt as I gather three wooden bowls for the yogurt.

"You don't believe it?"

"Yes, yes, I believe. It's just that we've had so many miracles lately."

"And what's wrong with that? You should be praising God."

"I do, I *do*. Only, I worry that these miracles have become more dear to us than the Maker of Miracles. When we gather at your house what do people say? 'The cup, we want to know more about the cup.'" When

Zechariah looks puzzled, I shake my head. "Don't you see? They should want to know more about *Jesus*?"

"Well . . . I suppose . . . ."

"And Argos? He grows more troublesome by the day. Mary said she heard him speaking ill of us in the shops. He would turn the whole city against us if he could. His position as healer has been challenged by our miracles; miracles which he believes are due to my cup. We all know him to be a proud man. He cannot be pleased. The other day I passed him on the street and the hatred in his eyes . . . I can't help but think he's plotting some mischief."

Zechariah pats my shoulder like Uncle Abner used to when I was upset. "Don't trouble yourself. This is the work of God. Rejoice in it."

"Yes I know . . . but . . . ."

"Let God do His miracles as long as He wills. There's a plan in it all, Rebekah."

"The bread will soon be ready," Esther says, suddenly entering the room.

And when I turn and see my thin, ragged, sad daughter, I hope, in spite of what I've said, that God will perform just one more miracle.

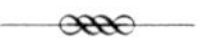

Everyone is looking for Jesus to return. They say all the miracles are a sure sign of His coming. Such miracles, they claim, have not been seen since Jesus walked the earth. I remind them that miracles abounded at the hands of the apostles. Why should it be any different now? But they ignore me. Even Zechariah encourages this belief. "Christ is risen. Christ is coming again!" he says to everyone he passes. He is almost giddy with the thought. After all, wasn't it rumored that his beloved John the Apostle wouldn't die until Jesus returned, and wasn't John getting on in years?

Oh, I know, Jesus *is* coming again, and I wish it were right now, right this minute, but I'm discomforted in knowing that everyone believes

His coming is at hand because of *my* cup. It seems wrong somehow. Besides, have Zechariah and the others forgotten that Jesus said no man knows the day or hour?

Will Zechariah talk about it again at his house today? I hope not. I dress, then fix my hair in preparation of meeting with the other believers. For the past two weeks he has talked of nothing else. "Don't you know that Jesus was crowned king on Passover, the traditional coronation day for Jewish Kings?" he said. "And though his crown was a crown of thorns in order to take even the curse of thorns and thistles from the earth onto himself, it was still a coronation, and soon he'll return as King of Kings."

Amen, so be it. Absently, I secure my plaited hair with a small goathair belt. It's not well done, but my mind is too preoccupied to attend to such details. "Haven't many rabbis, for years, been expecting two Messiahs?" I hear Zechariah's voice drone in my ear. "One, the suffering servant, Messiah ben Joseph; the other, ruler-and-King, Messiah ben David? And anyone who knows the scriptures knows that Jesus, Messiah ben Joseph, has already come. But soon, very soon he'll come again, this time as Messiah ben David."

Yes. Yes. Please come Jesus. I'm weary of this life. It's so hard here. How I long to see your sweet face again, to see you smile, to feel your hand tousle my hair, to look into your eyes and see a well of love that flows into eternity, that will never run dry, that will always refresh and satisfy me, the little girl, yes the little girl still, the one who used to stand by the Hinnom Valley wondering what animal had been sacrificed for her when all along you were that lamb, you were that sacrifice. Oh, what a wonderment! To think you loved me so!

Oh, Zechariah, you are right and I am wrong. You must tell us again how Jesus is coming back. You must tell us over and over again. Never stop telling it. What a blessed hope! And when you tell it today, I pray you look right at Esther, who has promised to join us. And when you look at her maybe, just maybe, she will listen . . . maybe, just maybe, she will hear.

I know I look foolish. My mouth forms a silly upturned arch, grinning at seemingly nothing. But I don't care. I'm walking arm in arm with Esther down the dusty path to Zechariah's. Her hair is neatly plaited and covered with a new linen head covering the color of ripe grapes. Her clean tunic is tied by a finely woven belt of dyed goat hair. Her face, free of shadows and dark broodings, shines.

"*Maranatha*!" says Mary, wife of Simon the bottlemaker, as we pass her house.

Even before I can answer, Esther surprises me by responding. Though her "*Maranatha*" is barely audible, it sends my heart soaring.

"Save us a place," Mary yells, as she waters the stock, "that is, if my Simon ever finishes trimming his beard. And they say women take all day to ready themselves!"

To my greater shock, Esther giggles. When was the last time she giggled? I can't remember. Surely the prayers for Esther, all those prayers of so many faithful saints, are finally being answered. Surely God is pulling her from that dark place where she has been living, and back into the light. I'm so happy I could dance. Instead, I sing Psalms in my head, and before long I'm singing them out loud. Soon, Esther joins me. I can't believe it! I glance at her to make sure it's really so. And yes, she's singing, faintly at first like the mewing of a kitten, then louder and louder. I refuse to spoil the moment with thoughts about tomorrow. *Today*, Esther is awake from her slumber. *Today*, Esther walks with the living. And I rejoice in that. And so we go, the two of us—arm and arm, awash in shimmering sunlight and accompanied by the sweet chirping of sparrows—singing how the Lord is our Shepherd. And we do this all the way to Zechariah's.

Zechariah's courtyard is swollen with the thunderous sound of our voices. Flustered chickens squawk and flap their wings, and run madly in circles. The donkey brays then kicks against the gnarled oak, and a dozen sheep bleat out a ragged rhythm, while we, the small insignificant church of Pella, bellow songs to our God and actually believe He will hear.

"'Oh Lord our Lord, how excellent is thy name in all the earth!'"

We've been singing for hours, Esther too, which surprises me still, for she was never able to carry a tune and has always been self-conscious about it. Her voice now mingles with the host of others. The very air is perfumed with praise. Our hands extend toward heaven, our faces tilt upward as our hearts strive to touch the great I AM; some in petition, some in awe, and some like mine, in sheer gratitude.

Truly, there is nothing too hard for You, Lord.

Mary and Simon stand nearby, and every time Esther sings off key, they look at me and smile. I think they're the only ones who witness my miracle, who know that something wonderful is happening.

When the last Psalm is finished, Zechariah motions for us to be seated, and I'm disappointed. Oh, I tell you, I could have sung all day! Shuffling sounds and whispers float through the air as people squat or unfurl rush mats and sit. I notice, with added delight, that three Gentiles have crossed the wadi to join our service. One is Kyra, the young servant girl from Argos's shop. Leah holds her hand and whispers softly in her ear.

All the while, Zechariah, that large bear of a man, has been tenderly cradling the codex of John in his arms, the very arms that have tenderly cradled us—the weak, fragile church of Pella. But he looks rather somber, I think. His customary smile is missing. And come to think of it, he didn't greet us believers with his usual hug when we first arrived. I suppose my own joy over Esther made me overlook it until now. But no matter, he will read from John's codex then speak to us again about how Jesus is coming soon, and after a while his troubled heart will no longer be troubled. *Speak, Zechariah, speak.* I glance at Esther. *Oh, Lord, let her hear his words.*

But to my surprise, Zechariah hands the codex to a man near him. "I hope you will remember all I've taught you these past two weeks about our precious Lord's soon return. And even if it's not as soon as we think or hope, we must remember that our earthly life is brief, and our hardships nothing when compared to the joys of everlasting life."

I shift uncomfortably on my mat. This is not like Zechariah. His tone is too somber, his mouth too rigid, his eyes darting around too nervously as though wishing to avoid our gaze.

"And," he says with a sigh, "it's important that we continue to do what we did this morning, that is to praise God no matter what the circumstances or even when our hearts are as heavy as an anchor." He thumps his large barrel chest. "Like mine. It's heavy for I know more hard times are upon us. I don't know why God has chosen to test us so sorely, but last night I heard news, news so crushing that it is sure to break the heart of every Jew."

At once the mood changes. People move nervously this way and that. They shift their legs, they cough, they whisper, they adjust their head coverings.

Zechariah opens his palms to heaven as though in prayer. It's only then that I notice tears rolling down his cheeks and onto that wiry gray beard of his. *What has happened?* His lips part but nothing comes out. He tries again. "A visitor . . . a carpenter who escaped from the Lower City, lies sick . . . in my house," he finally manages to say as he lowers his hands and allows them to hang like scrips by his side. "He came last night from Jerusalem and has told me that the New City—Bezetha, the Second Quarter, the Antonia, all have fallen. And the . . . Temple . . . our *Holy Temple* . . . has been . . . *destroyed*."

Groans, then loud cries, erupt throughout our ranks. Men rip their tunics. Women cover their faces and weep.

"Eleazar has fallen by the sword. Simon and John have fled to the Upper City. Thousands upon thousands lie dead inside the city walls. Thousands more outside. Pray! Pray without ceasing. Pray for God's mercy. Pray that Titus will have pity on those still alive."

There's not one among us who doesn't have a friend or relative in Jerusalem. I rip my own tunic. *Oh Ethan, my love! Oh, my sons! My Aaron and Benjamin, Joseph and Abner. Have you all perished, too?* If Eleazar has fallen, surely they have as well, for they would never leave his side. And they would give their last drop of blood to defend the Temple. I double over as though I've been kicked. My heart, so full of joy just moments ago, now pounds out notes of unspeakable pain. We are all weeping and wailing as grief rolls over us—all except Esther. She sits beside me, rocking back and forth, and never utters a sound.

I deposit the last donkey chip into my willow basket. I once abhorred this job, but I'm used to it now—gathering animal droppings for cooking fuel. I've even come to know that donkey dung, if stacked loosely, makes a fine fire, and doesn't smoke as much as the dung of goats or lambs. It's become just another chore, like sweeping our flat rooftop or rolling up the bedding. We have all learned to do things we must, in order to survive.

A gentle wind strokes my face, then plays with my loosely plaited hair. Already the early morning sun burns like a furnace on my bare head. But I don't care. It feels good to be outside; good to labor with my hands. For days I've driven myself, working the fields or my vegetable gardens until I drop with exhaustion. But the work has brought a measure of peace, and helped me stop agonizing over what I cannot know. *Do Ethan and my sons still live?* This is the question my hard work has helped to silence. I've finally placed it in the alabaster box of my heart, sealing it until the Lord opens it with His answer.

But Esther . . . she neither cries nor speaks. And though she has worked as hard as I, the work has failed to purge her pain. I see it on her face. It's always there—in the tight set of her lips; in her dull, blank eyes; in her crinkled forehead. But I refuse to give up, and continue adding more chores to her load. Even now, she's inside crushing grain to mix with milk for our new kids and lambs. Next, I'll send her to till a new garden, the produce of which I plan to give the widow Leah and to our beloved Zechariah.

I'm about to carry my filled basket of dung to the oven when I notice several lambs hovering around my legs. Others bleat loudly nearby. Curious. Esther should have prepared their food by now.

"Esther." I walk to the doorway, then place my basket near the entrance. "Esther?"

The house is strangely quiet, causing me to tread softly across the paving stones. I look in one room then another. In the third, I find my daughter. She sits hunched on a tall stool, her back to me. In front of her is a small table containing a mortar and pestle and some grain. "Esther, the lambs are hungry. What's taking so long?" When she turns, I see a bloody knife in her hand. "*Esther* . . . what . . . has happened? *Esther?*"

She appears not to hear. And those eyes! Dry empty wells. There's nothing there. She doesn't even see me. I grab a clean rag and plunge it into the nearby water jar. Carefully, I remove the knife from her hand before washing the blood that covers her arm from elbow to wrist. *Has she tried to kill herself?*

As I wipe away the blood, I see a dozen small cuts, like rungs of a ladder, on her arm, and my fear turns to anger. Esther has been cutting herself like some heathen mourning her dead. "How could you do this?" My voice is stern.

Esther remains silent.

"You don't even know if Daniel is dead!"

More silence.

"Speak to me!" I shake her roughly trying to force words from her mouth, but the only sound that comes is a long, low wail.

"*Oh Esther.*" I cradle her as she wails and rocks back and forth. And silently, I place her in God's hands for the hundredth time. What else can I do?

"Have you heard that Ira and Rina plan to wed?" Leah says, blowing through the front door of my house like a strong wind.

I look up and smile. I'm sitting on a stool, my foot resting on an overturned willow basket, my tunic tucked between my thighs and belted at the waist. I roll coarse dyed wool back and forth across my bare leg. I'm nearly finished. When I am, I'll spin it on my spindle.

"Well, have you heard?" Leah repeats breathlessly, her head-covering askew, wisps of gray hair curling across her forehead.

"Who has not heard?" I say, continuing my work. "Surely, even the Gentiles on the other side of the wadi know this by now. Our community has talked of nothing else." For the past hour this news has been passed from one house to the next, and eagerly devoured. Our Temple is gone. Jerusalem will surely follow. And we've yet to learn of our loved ones. We're all filled with sadness, but never speak of it. Instead, we speak of Ira and Rina—the widow slightly older than Ira who kindly tended his house when he first broke his leg. It's the sort of distraction we need. And like chickens, we hunt and peck the soil of our lives in search of such morsels.

"Well, good news is worth retelling." Leah moves closer as though examining my work. I'm used to her. She's always stopping by with questions or a bit of news. "What's the wool for?" she says, her eyebrows peaking.

"A rug for Ira and Rina. I only hope I can finish it before the wedding."

"Such a gift! You're very generous, Rebekah. If only my hands . . . well, there was a time . . . ." She sighs, turning her gnarled hands over as if examining them. "My gift is not so generous. I've pledged thirty loaves of my olive-and-rosemary bread for the wedding feast. For that I don't need fingers. I can work the dough with my palms. But fuel for the oven is a problem. My few sheep will be unable to produce enough dung."

"Did I tell you? I've bound too many thistles and acanthus." I continue rolling the wool, not bothering to look up for I'm trying to conceal my smile. I gesture, with a flick of my head toward the bundles. "See for yourself."

"Ahhhhhhh." The sound rolls slowly from Leah's mouth when she sees the pile of bound thistles and spiny acanthus in the corner. "Yes . . . you have a sizable heap." She looks down again at her gnarled hands. "When I was younger . . . when my hands were younger, I could bundle this amount in a day. Now . . . ."

"They are a nuisance. More than once I snagged my tunic and nearly ripped it. You must take some. I've more than enough. It would lessen the pile and prevent me from getting entangled." When she shakes her head I add, "It would be a service to me."

"Well, just one or two bundles . . . maybe three. If I mix them with dung, it will be enough for my bread." She glances at her hands. "I never planned on becoming this useless."

"Useless? Oh, Leah, you are far from useless. Doesn't everyone come to you for prayer? I hear you as I pass your house praying for Tirzah's baby, for Amos the cheesemaker, for our crops to be fruitful, for every need we bring you."

She bends and kisses my forehead. "And I haven't forgotten about your request, either. I've been praying day and night for Esther."

Crash. I roll over, dragging the woolen blanket across my shoulders. *Thud.* My eyelids are as heavy as anvils but I force them open. What . . . was that? I did hear something . . . I think. Or . . . a dream? Have I been dreaming? I listen. All is quiet. I rub my face and pull myself up on one elbow. Then I glance over to where Esther sleeps quietly on a nearby mat. Yes, a dream, nothing more. Of late, my sleep has been fitful and full of images of Ethan and my sons, and Esther, too. Sometimes I wake up wet with sweat or tears. I run my hands across my body. I'm not wet now. Only warm—the soft moist kind that comes from sleeping beneath a cover. I pull the blanket over my shoulders, and just as I close my eyes there's another crash.

This is no dream. *Someone is in the house.*

I crane my neck and listen. Voices. Men's voices! Then footsteps on the paving stones, all heading for the ladder. Perspiration beads my forehead and rims my neck. I glance at Esther. She's still asleep. Thank God she can sleep through anything. But what to do? My mind swims through a murky sea of choices. Only one seems right. I must go downstairs to prevent them from coming up here and hurting Esther. I descend the ladder while sending up desperate prayers. *God, please help me.*

My feet barely touch the stone flooring before two men surround me. One holds an oil lamp, the light of which splashes unevenly across his face, creating shadows beneath his eyes and across both cheeks and make him look like an eerie specter. His hair is twisted into strange knots. *Argos*? Who else can it be? But the other man I don't recognize.

"Why are you in my house?" I say, facing Argos.

"Where's the cup?" he hisses. "Give me the cup and no harm will come to you."

"You have no right to be here."

"I *must* have the cup." His free hand clamps my arm. I can't believe his strength. Is it possible? This little man? He holds me so fiercely I fear he'll snap me like a reed. "Everyone in Pella knows I'm a healer. They know that Isis, the Queen of Heaven, has given me this power. You'll not defame her with these false healings of yours."

The man near Argos moves towards me. For the first time I see the club in his hand. It has strange markings carved on one side. He raises it threateningly, but lowers it when Argos waves him off.

"I'll take the cup to the temple and dedicate it to Isis." Argos's eyes widen as though visualizing the dedication. "And as reward, she'll surely increase my powers."

I back away. I know what temple he speaks of. Zechariah told me about the ancient Canaanite temple, the one that sits across the wadi north of the city, and how Argos had it rebuilt, patterned after the temples in the Nile delta. I close my eyes not wanting to imagine what evil is performed there. "The cup is pure. I cannot give it to you," I hear myself saying, then at once feel Argos's hot breath on my face, smell the stench of his sour vapors.

"I'll destroy your house!"

I open my eyes. He's but a hand's length away, glaring at me like a demon with flaming eyes. When I remain silent, he flicks his hand in the air, and at once his companion, with the end of his club, begins overturning the baskets on the floor and scattering their contents.

"Don't provoke me," Argos hisses, "or you'll lose more than your house. Demas likes nothing better than to employ his club in the smashing of heads."

My knees shake beneath my tunic but I remain silent.

Demas is now working the shelves. His flailing club sends baskets and wooden bowls crashing to the floor. Next he whacks the pouch of salt, bursting it and sending it to the ground, followed by a cone of sugar. When he has emptied the shelf, he looks at the one above it—the one containing the cup, along with three other cups, more wooden bowls, and some spare oil lamps. He raises his club, ready to smash everything, not even considering that one of these four plain cups could be the prize. But just as he extends the club as high as he can and is ready to bring his full fury down upon the shelf, he lets out a shriek.

"My eyes! They burn! Oh, my eyes. Put it out. Put out the fire!" Demas drops his club. "Ohhhhhhhhhh."

"Wash them with water and stop your howling," Argos growls as he glances at the shelf, perplexed.

Demas stumbles to the door, feeling for the large water jar near the entrance. "Yeeeee! It burns! Yeeeee!" he screams, then runs from the house without even stopping to wash.

"What sorcery is this?" Argos says, turning to me. "What have you done?"

"I've done nothing."

Outside, Demas's shrieks and howls are loud enough to wake the neighbors. I hear their sleepy voices calling out. Argos is clearly nervous, and anxious to be off before anyone appears. Even so, he pauses to put his face to mine. "This is not over. I *will* have the cup." With that, he picks up Demas's fallen club and bolts out the door after his companion.

"What's wrong, Mama?" I hear a tired voice say overhead. "What was all that noise?"

When I light a lamp and look up, I see Esther peering over the top of the ladder, and though I know she can't see me clearly in the semidarkness, I smile. "It was God doing another miracle."

Argos, the thief. Argos, the tormenter of women. That's what people call him now. Everyone is outraged over his attempt to steal the Holy Cup, the Cup of the Lord. It was better when it was just *my* cup. It wasn't such a burden then. But its weight is becoming too heavy for me. For the elders, too, I think. It has forced them to act. Headed by Zechariah, a small group of believers have confronted Argos and demanded justice; and, Jepeth, the metalsmith, was paid with contributions from the community to make two bells, one for the upstairs and one for the downstairs of my house, to ring at the first sign of further trouble. And all this without my prior knowledge. But that was weeks ago, and aside from the two bells that are now in my house, nothing good has come of it, for Argos stood his ground before the men of our community and called me a "liar."

Now I look at one of the bells as I ready myself for the wedding. It is not small and delicate like those attached to the hems of the priestly robes my father or Ethan once wore. Rather, it is larger than a man's hand and resembles a cup with a thick-lipped barrel-shaped body and handle. It is made of sand-cast copper, and creates a frightful clamor when rung. I wish I could ring it now as an alarm to God. Would He hear? If He did, I'd say, "What is happening with my Esther? Why aren't You helping her?"

She has refused to go to the wedding. All my scolding, threats, and crying have availed nothing. She is immovable. A mountain of resistance. I blame her father, for she has his temperament. *Oh Ethan, if only you were here! If only you had left Jerusalem with us!* And then I feel the familiar anger. I don't want to be angry. But there it is, bubbling in my stomach like a pit of bitumen. If only Ethan had come with us. If only he had made our sons . . . *my* sons, come too. If only Daniel had come. Then we would all be together. We would all be happy.

What am I to do? *Can you hear me, Lord? My voice is a clanging bell crying for help. Am I a widow? Have I lost my sons? Will I lose my daughter, too? Have pity on me. You are my only help. You are my refuge and strength. In You do I trust.*

Esther watches me from the corner of the room. She sits on a rush mat wearing a threadbare tunic that is mud-caked along the hem. Her hair is a mass of tangles. "It's not too late." I force a smile and point to the beautiful gray garment with thin red stripes that hangs from the wall peg. "I'll wait while you wash and dress."

Both of our tunics are newly purchased from one of the Gentile shops across the wadi. I did it hoping to please Esther, hoping it would pull her from her deep despair. And though I hated taking more coins from my *semadi* and squandering them on such trifles, I even purchased a box of kohl and a small bronze spatula for applying it to our eyes. But best of all, I bought a tiny clay phial of sweet cane perfume. It's been so long since we've scented our bodies.

I adjust the veil over my freshly plaited hair. "You would look so lovely in your new tunic, and with the kohl on your lids you'd . . . ."

"No, Mama. Must I tell you again that I'm *not* going?" Determination and defiance harden her face like plaster. "Can't you understand how impossible it is for me? I, who should have danced at *my* wedding, am forced to wonder if I'm a widow before I'm even a true bride." She leans her head against the cool of the wall as a hot wind blows through the small open window, and with it, the noise of people gathering in the street below. "I rejoice for Ira and Rina, but I don't feel well and would make poor company. I have no wish to cast a shadow over their happiness."

"But Esther . . . ."

"Let it alone, Mama, and go in peace."

"But . . . ."

"*Please*, Mama, let it alone."

My lips pucker like dried figs as I tie a colorful braided cord around my veiled head. It's useless to argue any longer. And after a final glance at my thin, pale daughter I head for the ladder. *Oh why don't you hear me, Lord? I clang and clang and still you don't answer.*

The rug is heavy. It pulls my right shoulder—where it's rolled and draped—downward. I'm surprised I can carry it at all. I'm more surprised that it's finished in time, though it took most of the night to do it. I only hope I can get it to Zechariah's without damage.

The sun beats fiercely overhead. There's little breeze. With each step, the rug feels heavier. As I pass Leah's house she calls my name and waves. I respond with an awkward jerk of my head.

"You look beautiful," she says, coming alongside me.

"You, too." I huff and puff under my burden. She carries her own load—a large tray of bread balanced on her head. Even so, I see she wears the new embroidered headscarf I gave her yesterday as payment for the loaf of olive and rosemary bread she made me, in spite of her insistence that my payment far exceeded the worth of her bread.

"You shouldn't have done it," she says in a near whisper, fingering the scarf with her free hand. But her shining eyes tell me how much it pleases her. Then, appearing embarrassed, she calls to Tirzah who walks ahead carrying baby Joshua, and with a wave "goodbye" bustles toward them leaving the smell of rosemary wafting behind her.

The street is crowded now. Everyone is heading for Zechariah's house for the marriage ceremony and banquet to follow. People scurry past me, dressed in their best tunics and brightest smiles, and laden with gifts.

I walk slowly, falling more and more behind the others as I trudge beneath my load. Dust swirls around me and sticks to the perspiration bathing my face. I'm the last to arrive, and when I do, sweat dampens me from head to toe. My tunic is rumpled, my arms and shoulder nearly numb. It is Zachariah who comes to my aid, may *Hashem* bless him, and takes the rug, then slings it over his own shoulder.

"I heard that Ira asked you to bring the cup," he says, his forehead glistening with sweat as he heaves the heavy rug across one of the many wooden benches placed around the courtyard to hold the gifts. "Did you?"

I wrinkle my face but say nothing.

"I must agree with you this time. I too disapprove of someone wishing to have the cup present only to ensure them 'good fortune.'"

"I love these people, Zechariah. But I cannot let this love keep me from speaking out any longer. This fixation over the cup must stop."

"Be patient with them, Rebekah." Zechariah's face crinkles into that big, generous smile of his, the smile that seems to say there's enough love in his heart to encompass the whole world. "These are dark days. I know they should be looking to Jesus, but desperate times can make people want something tangible, something they can see and touch. Something they can cling to. But they'll come around. You'll see." He pauses to tug on his beard. "And fret not. So will Esther. Give her time. She'll come around, too."

No wedding procession followed the bridegroom to the bride's house. The customary train of friends and family was represented by one—a nephew and sole living relative. Neither did the bridegroom accompany his perfumed, veiled bride back to his house—a neat modest dwelling near the wheat fields. Instead, he walked her—accompanied only by her one living relative, a male cousin half her age—to Zechariah's, where the entire community awaited them.

And the wedding ceremony was neither elaborate nor lengthy, but consisted of the drawing up of a legal agreement, witnessed and signed by Zechariah. Next came the blessing, and a reading from John's codex. But the feast followed tradition. Before the wedding, Ira and some of the men erected a moderately sized wooden frame at one end of Zechariah's courtyard. Then, under Leah's supervision, women covered it with fringed linen curtains to form a canopy, after which they decorated the entrance with palm branches, pink lilies and vines of blue ipomeas. It was under this beautiful canopy that Ira and Rina sat during the feast.

And the food! It made my mouth dance! Even King Solomon, who was no stranger to lavish feasts, would have been pleased. There was Leah's savory bread, Mary's succulent date cakes, Amos's tangy squares of goat cheese covered with herbs, bowls full of olives from our collective groves, roasted pigeons from both Hannah's and Naomi's dovecotes, a huge pot of mutton and lentil stew that Tirzah made, dandelion greens, cucumbers, and melons gathered from everyone's garden—not to mention flagons and flagons of mulled wine. Oh, it was wonderful!

Except for one thing.

All during the ceremony, and for part of the feast, loud, incessant chanting poured from the Temple of Isis just north of us. When even Ira's and Rina's face began to show the strain of this nonstop idolatry, Leah took matters into her own hands and began singing and dancing. Soon others joined in. And before long, women were whirling around in joy; and both voices and instruments masked the heathen clamor.

The temple is quiet now, while we continue our noisy celebration. Mary plays her *tof*, a small hand-held drum, a woman's instrument; Obadiah, the carpenter, plays a *kinnor*, the lyre-like instrument of King David. Two other men play flutes. And Leah continues dancing with the women. I don't know where she gets her strength. It's as if she's young again. Perhaps Ira's and Rina's wedding has brought back memories of her own marriage. She forced me to dance with her once, but I won't again. Let her revel in the past. I can't. I don't want to remember what I have lost. So I sit with Tirzah and her baby, and . . . eat. Even now, I'm shamelessly preparing to devour my third date cake. But I barely swallow the first bite when I hear a gruff voice overhead.

"It's that cup, that accursed cup. You've used it to cast a spell on him!"

I look up and see Argos bathed in sunlight and pointing a shaking finger at me. His hair is arranged in yet another variation of knots. His clean shaven chin juts upward as if trying to give more height to his short stature.

"What has happened?" I say, bewildered.

"Oh, you liar! You sorceress! You know full well what's happened! Demas is blind! Since coming to your house . . . since he . . . it's your doing. And that . . . that . . . cup's. You used it to rob him of his sight."

"Did I lay one finger on him? Did you hear me utter one evil word against him? Even when he overturned my baskets? Even when he smashed my things with his club? Did I say a word?"

"Ah . . . yes! Under your breath. I heard you! You whispered evil incantations and drove him from your house, screaming."

"He was an uninvited guest, an intruder who broke into my home, as did you, and threatened me. But I didn't return evil for evil."

Red streaks flame Argos's neck and cheeks. "Lies! Lies! You would turn the world against me with your lies if you could. I know what you've told the shopkeepers."

"I've told them nothing."

"Then . . . your agents! They've been busy telling everyone how we came in the middle of the night to do you harm. Oh, what falsehood! In front of all these people I call you a liar! Demas and I came only to transact business, to purchase one of your possessions. We would have given you good money. Far more than it's worth. You know it's true! But there you stand, bold faced; daring to accuse us while denying your own wrongdoing!

Denying that you made a man blind. Very well. I won't argue. I will only demand that you give me the cup so I can undo your sorcery."

A dozen men have crossed the wadi with Argos, and now stand behind him, Demas included. The poor, blind Demas stretches his neck this way and that as if trying to catch every word. Two men—his guides by the look of how they hold his arms—flank him, while Demas sniffs the air like a dog, then tries to lay hold of it with an outstretched hand, all the while panic etching his face.

Before I can stop myself, I wave to the guides and tell them to "bring him forward." Oh the boldness! I've never experienced the like. It overpowers me. So does the love I feel for these ill-advised men whose masks of anger can't hide the fear in their eyes. But instead of stepping forward, the men move back, dragging Demas with them. Only Argos remains rooted in place.

"Don't listen to her. She plans more evil," Argos shouts.

"Demas, if you want your sight, come, and we'll pray for you in the name of Jesus." *Why did I say that?* The words just tumbled out as if spoken by another. Will God restore his sight? If He doesn't, what will these men do? But too late. Demas is already straining against those holding him. "Come," I say, feeling a renewed boldness. "Receive your healing."

At once Zechariah forms a circle, a circle of those willing to stand in the gap for this Gentile, among them the newly married Rina and Ira. When it's clear Demas is willing but that his two guides won't bring him, Caleb, the young shepherd boy, and Japeth, the metalsmith, walk past the gauntlet of Argos's hatred to retrieve him.

And then we pray. Each in our own words, each storming heaven with our pleadings and petitions. I don't know how long we prayed. It felt like minutes. But when I open my eyes, the sun is nearly gone and Demas is sprawled flat on his face in the dirt.

"See how God has knocked him to the ground, as though he were a reed," Mary says, gripping my arm. "I felt His power, and thought I would fall, too. That's when I grabbed you. But you never noticed. You were too deep in prayer."

"Is he . . . is he healed?" I say, feeling my former boldness slip away when I notice that, with the exception of Argos, all his companions are now standing within a hand's distance behind us, watching with keen interest. "Is he healed?" I repeat.

Mary shrugs just as someone shouts, "He's stirring. He's waking up."

"Move back. Give him room." Zechariah gestures with his hands, then uses his large frame as a buffer against the crowd. And as we retreat, Demas pulls himself up into a sitting position.

"What . . .? What has happened?" he says, holding his head. "Did someone hit me?" He moans, then rubs his eyes.

It's so quiet I can hear the air passing through my nostrils.

Demas remains sitting in the dirt. It covers his face, his tunic. It floats around him in low, soft clouds. But he appears not to notice.

"Well! Can you see?" someone yells.

Demas looks confused, as if he's forgotten why he came into our circle in the first place. Then a smile splits his face. "Yes! I see! I can see!" In a flash, he's on his feet, dancing and kicking up more dirt and laughing like a madman. "I can see!" And then everyone is laughing, and hugging and kissing and praising God. Even the Gentiles are laughing and lifting their voices in praise to this unknown God; this God who does miracles; this God Who heals the blind. Everyone, that is, except Argos. He stands far off with his arms folded across his chest, and scowls.

"Esther! Wait until you hear the news!" I enter our house and stop. It's so dark. Why didn't Esther light the oil lamps? We always left at least one burning in our front room at night. "Esther!" I crane my neck trying to hear any sound that will tell me which room to enter. But I hear the bleating of sheep through the open door and nothing more. Quickly, I light a lamp. Could she be spinning in one of the side rooms? I rush through the downstairs, checking everywhere, then remember her claim of ill health. So, she was telling the truth. She really wasn't well. Certainly news of Demas's healing will cheer her.

Rushing to the ladder I shout, "Esther!" Still no answer. She must be sleeping. Like Ethan, when he was younger, Esther can sleep through anything. Once, in our house in the Upper City, a servant knocked over his lamp setting fire to one of the rooms, and though there was enough shouting and screaming and running to wake the neighborhood, Esther slept through it all. And didn't she sleep through most of Argos's recent mischief?

My feet fly up the rungs. At the top I see, even in the dim lamp light, that the room is empty. While my bedding is still rolled and placed neatly against the far wall, Esther's is spread across the floor in disarray. Has she spent the day resting? If so, perhaps she felt the need to stretch her legs and breathe fresh air. I'm about to descend the ladder when I notice Esther's new clothes are no longer hanging on the peg. I study our quarters more carefully and see things I missed. Esther's extra pair of sandals that used to be on the shelf is gone; so, too, her scrip and spare blanket. I can hardly breathe as I climb down the ladder and head for the main storeroom. The basket of fresh raisin cakes is overturned and empty, also a small basket of almonds. And the three loaves of bread we made this morning—gone.

Sweat pours from my temples as I race to the small, shelf-lined entrance. I quickly scan it until I find the covered bowl of goat cheese and pluck it off the ledge. Empty! *It can't be true!* I drop the bowl, and still carrying my oil lamp, race outside. I'm like a wild donkey, sprinting to and fro around the house, the animal pens, the area of the grinding wheel, the large cone-shaped oven. And when there's no where else to look, I drop to the dirt, and with my free hand cradle my face and weep.

Esther is gone.

"Another has come," Mary says, stepping into my sheep pen and tugging nervously at the wrapped parcel in her hand. "He's at Zechariah's. But no use going there now. He's half dead. Best you wait until tomorrow, after he's eaten and rested."

I nod and thank her, then continue feeding the lambs their ground grain and milk. *Tomorrow? So long? And will he know? Will he have news of Esther? Of my sons? Of Ethan? Oh, Ethan, my love, my heart, why did you send me here alone? Why didn't you come, too?*

"Leah is still in bed with her back full of pain, even after all this time. I told her not to dance like a madwoman at Ira's and Rina's wedding." Mary shadows me like a mother hen as I move around the pen. "You'd think a woman her age would know better."

"I'll stop by later and check on her," I say, not bothering to lift my head. My mind is full of tomorrow. For weeks, stragglers have wandered into our community—dirty, ragged, starving, and all of them men. These are the fortunate ones; the few who have, by some miracle, escaped from Jerusalem. But the women? The children? What of them? I try not to think about it.

Some of the stragglers have stayed to make a new life with us. Others, after resting and gaining strength, have gone on to Galilee or one of the cities of the Decapolis looking for relatives. But all have been questioned by me. And my questions are always the same, "Have you seen my daughter, Esther? Have you seen my sons? My husband?"

"Well . . . I'm off to Leah's now." Mary peels back the cloth from the two loaves of bread in her hand and lifts them up for me to see. "I've made her *my* special bread, full of cinnamon and raisins. Simon claims he can never get his fill. Tomorrow, I'll make an extra loaf for you."

She's so sweet, so desperate to please, so anxious to divert my thoughts. How selfish of me not to let her. But it's pointless. I'm consumed.

The lambs bleat and push against each other, impatient to get at my bowl. "Thank you, and God speed," I say, turning my thoughts back to tomorrow.

He looks like a skeleton. Never have I seen anyone so thin. There isn't even enough flesh on his cheeks to sag. Instead, they sit like empty bowls beneath dark, vacant eyes. Everything about him reminds me of death: his carriage, his body, his smell. Even his dry, stiff hair falls out in tiny clumps whenever he scratches his head. It's as if the clay is returning to dust right before my eyes.

From the doorway I watch this wisp recline at the platform table and peck his flatbread like a bird. His strength is such that he rests between bites. Zechariah hovers nearby, anxious to serve. Without announcing myself, I slip by my friend, but not before seeing the displeasure on his face. The night has been long. Endless blackness that provided no sleep. Oh, the questions that filled my head! Like buzzing bees. Is it any wonder that at first light I came here? I had to talk to this man, this survivor, this carrier of news from Jerusalem.

"Don't stay long," Zechariah whispers, his face all firmness and reproach.

I nod, and climb the few stone steps to the platform, then slip quietly beside the stranger. Zechariah follows. When he introduces the man as Tobias, the wealthy spice merchant from the Upper City, I bite my lip. I know him. Everyone in Jerusalem knows Tobias. He's one of the richest men in the city, even owning a fleet of ships and a huge caravan of camels to transport his goods. I often wondered why he stayed. Why he didn't abandon Jerusalem when so many of the other merchants did. Some said because he had acquired Roman citizenship and felt he had nothing to fear from the Romans if we lost but everything to gain. Others said it was because his gold was housed in the Temple treasury for safe keeping—a common practice of the rich—and he couldn't bear leaving it behind. If so, neither has done him any good. When last I saw him he was vigorous and three times the size. Can a man change so much? His lip quivers in a slight smile as though reading my thoughts.

Next, Zechariah informs me that Tobias's entire family has died from starvation, and that by all accounts he too should have died. I notice Tobias's swollen belly and wonder if death will claim him yet. The thought makes me rash.

"Did you see my daughter—a recent arrival to Jerusalem?" I blurt. Truly I'm a selfish creature to overlook his poor, wasted state and trouble him with my questions. But I must ask while he's still in this earthly realm.

"My daughter? Did you see her?" I repeat.

"Pray she didn't come." Tobias puts down his bread as though holding it while speaking is too great a task.

"Did you *see* her?" Oh, how shameless I am!

"You ask such a question? When the streets ran red with blood? When the Romans butchered everyone who fell into their hands, not caring if they were citizen or rebel?"

"You know my Esther. We've all been guests at your house. Surely you would recognize her."

"Did anyone have time to see who came and went? We were all trying to stay alive. At the end, we hid in our homes, coming out only to scavenge for food. But they were like men possessed, these Romans. Going from dwelling to dwelling, slashing and burning. For days, I listened to the cries of our people as the sword of Rome cut through the city."

"But you survived. Maybe there were others. Maybe you saw my husband and sons. Maybe you *heard* something, maybe . . . ."

"I survived, yes. The Romans found me lying next to the lifeless bodies of my wife and children. They didn't bother with me, I suppose because they thought I was already dead." Tobias pulls himself up into a sitting position, picks up the nearby cup of hot broth with spindly fingers, then brings it, shaking, to his lips. He sips with his eyes closed.

What was he thinking? What was he seeing? The bodies of his wife? His children? I can almost see them, too.

"When they torched my house, the smoke covered my escape." He placed the cup on the low stone table. "It was as thick as wool. It seemed like the whole Upper City was in flames. Smoke all around. Bedlam. Oh, the bedlam! Titus's men, mad for gold, were searching everywhere for it. Amid the chaos, I managed to pass through the Essene Gate unnoticed.

"I got as far as Titus's abandoned siege walls when I collapsed. How long I was unconscious, I can't say, but when I awoke it was moon bright and the air was still thick with smoke and the cries from the ongoing slaughter." Tobias coveres his eyes. "Oh, that moon! If only it hadn't been so bright. Then I wouldn't have seen the stacks of bodies piled outside the city walls. Titus had been using captives to collect the dead. Nearby, a pit as large as the Pool of Siloam was filled with them—the grave of thousands. Gehenna! Surely, this is Gehenna, I thought." He rakes his head with fingers that look more like bones, and when he's done, clumps of hair fill his palm. He looks at them and laughs. "I'm falling apart."

"Enough. You must rest. And you, Rebekah . . ." Zechariah makes shooing motions with is hand, "you must go home."

To my surprise Tobias shouts, "No! Let her hear my story." He casts his hair to the ground, picks up his flatbread, pecks at it, then places it back on the table. "My stomach can't tolerate much food. It wouldn't stay down. But it doesn't matter. I know I'm dying. But if you're asking, 'why would *Hashem* spare me from death in Jerusalem, only to take my life now?' I'll tell you. It's so I can speak of what I've seen and heard. Someone *must* know what happened to our people, to our Holy City."

A man who walked out of his grave to bring us the story must be heard. And Zechariah understands this. There was no more shooing. No more talk of me going home. Instead, we both sit in silence, waiting for Tobias to continue.

"Before they took the Upper City they took the Temple. After they captured it they brought in their standards." His face contorts. He's seeing it. It's all there fresh and vivid and horrible before his eyes.

"Were they lost? All our men who fought in the Temple?" I hold my breath.

"Surely it must be so. If not in battle, then afterward. Those who were captured were put to the sword or crucified."

"Oh, my *husband* . . . my *sons*. Don't say it, please, unless you're certain."

"It was said that nearly every priest who fought to protect the altar perished that day."

I bite the inside of my mouth to keep from crying out. When Tobias sees Zechariah place a large, gnarled hand on my shoulder as way of comfort, he quickly adds, "But then nothing is sure. How can it be?"

"Tell us about the Temple." Zechariah says. "Others have come from Jerusalem and told us it was destroyed but could tell us little else. What happened?"

Tobias groans like a wounded animal. "When the battle for the Holy Place was over the Romans carried their standards into the Temple, *our* Temple, and set them up opposite the East Gate, then sacrificed all manner of animals before them, even unclean *pigs*. Oh, how we wailed, those of us who watched from Herod's towers in the Upper City, from Phasael or Hippicus or Mariamme. We wailed as the smoke of their sacrifices curled before their heathen standards. We wailed and tore our clothes. The whole city heard us. More than one fell on his sword in despair. The Romans had already looted the sanctuary and carried out whatever they could find. The treasury was emptied. My gold, the gold of other aristocrats, taken. Queen Helena's gold lamp, Agrippa's golden chain, the golden vines over the sanctuary entrance, the Babylonian curtains—all ripped apart and divided by these dogs.

"Titus didn't stop them. This was their due. This was their reward for the months of building siege works and ramps and catapults; for the months of slashing and burning and killing. They cheered their legate.

They saluted him as he partitioned the spoils of war. They were going home rich men. But greed drove them even harder. It was only a matter of time before the Temple itself became a spoil. Fire had melted the gold covering it. Gold ran from the spikes atop the Temple and all along its face and sides. It ran between the stone blocks like drops of rain. When the Romans saw this they began tearing the walls apart, pulling then down, stone by stone, just to scrape away the gold. There's nothing left of our Temple now but rubble."

I cover my eyes and weep as I think of how Jesus foretold this very thing; how He said not one stone would be left upon another. And so it was. Our Temple, and much of our Holy City—gone, all gone. I'm overwhelmed with grief as I weep over this great loss. And I weep, too, for my darling Ethan; for my strong, courageous sons. They were gone too. Surely they were killed along with the other priests defending the altar. And Esther? Was she lost, too? "Oh, *please* Tobias, think. Try to remember if you saw my daughter." It's not my voice that speaks. It's not even reasonable that I should ask this again. But I won't apologize for it.

"Your daughter?" Tobias appears confused. "Yes, you wanted to know about your daughter. She was . . . Sophia's age wasn't she?" Tobias was speaking of his youngest. He had given all his children Greek or Roman names as was the custom of rich Jews. I once disapproved. I find that disapproval so shallow now. "Pray Esther didn't come to Jerusalem. If so, she's surely dead."

"Not surely. No, not surely. You said yourself nothing is sure. Perhaps she lives. Perhaps she was captured. What then? What would the Romans do with her?"

"Was she strong and healthy? Still pleasing to look at?"

"She's thin and worn, but yes, she's still pretty."

"Ahhh . . . then perhaps it would be better if she were dead."

Anger flushes my face. "Such a horrible thing to say!"

"Horrible but true. If she was even half alive and had a pleasing countenance the soldiers would have used her shamelessly. And if she survived that, she'd be sent to the slave markets along the coast."

"Where? What markets?"

Tobias looks at me strangely, his skeleton head tipped to one side. "It's no use. Who can know such a thing? Count her as one dead. Mourn her. Rend your garments. But entertain no hope of ever finding her. You must forget."

"Where would they take her? You are a merchant. You know the Romans. You understand them."

Tobias drops his head against his chest as if it were a heavy boulder he can no longer hold. "Forget her."

"She's all I have left!"

"Is it possible to find one lost grain of sand along the seashore?"

"*Where?*"

Tobias's bird-like chest heaves upward in a shrug. "Caesarea Maritima. Jerusalem is lost; the war nearly over. And before taking on Masada, Titus will most likely deploy his army to Caesarea. To give his troops some rest and pleasure. The brothels will need more women. They will take many of the captured females there."

"Then that's where I'll look."

Tobias waves his bony hand in the air. "No, no! You mustn't. I've seen these places. I know what happens there. Spare yourself, I beg you."

"*She's all I have left.*"

"Then understand this: these girls are forced to see more than a dozen men a day, many of whom are little more than vicious brutes. In no time the girls fall prey to disease, some are even battered to death. Most don't last two years. By the time you find her, if you find her, she'll be dead. And if she's not . . . you'll wish she were."

There are no words to answer. My heart is in shreds. Zechariah's, too, for he weeps loudly, his barrel-chest heaving, his gray head bobbing up and down. But no tears stream from Tobias's eyes. I suppose a person has only a fixed number of tears to cry and he has cried them all. I lean near the drooping skull of a head and whisper, "May God bless and keep you." I do this because Tobias has earned this blessing. The retelling of his story has cost him. And I bless him because, like me, he has lost so much. But most of all, I bless him because he has ended my anguish; my endless opening and closing of that alabaster box in my heart; my wondering if I'm a widow, if I'm a woman without sons. For a brief second, I rest my fingertips on his hand, and we are one—sufferer, survivor, the seed of Israel's future. Then I depart without another word.

"This is folly, Rebekah." Zechariah follows me around my house as I go from one room to the next. "You're acting like a madwoman."

"She's all I have now." I stuff bread and almonds and pouches of raisins into a large woven bag with handles. "I'll not lose her, too. I have lost the others." My throat catches. "My husband . . . my sons."

"Yes . . . grieve them. Stay here and grieve them. Give yourself time to heal. Time to think."

"There is no time. You heard Tobias. You heard what happens to girls like Esther in the brothels. For her sake, I cannot delay. My mind is made up, Zechariah. I'm going to Caesarea with my *semadi,* with my coins, to buy her freedom."

"How do you know you'll find her? Suppose they take her to Rome instead, for the Triumph? The Romans always take captives to Rome after their major campaigns." Zechariah steps in front of me as I try to leave the room. "Suppose she wasn't captured at all." He pulls his beard. "How do you even know she went to Jerusalem?"

"Where else? You saw her, how she dressed, how she behaved. Her mind was filled with Daniel, always Daniel. She thought of nothing else. When it came time for Ira's and Rina's wedding . . . well, I suppose she could bear it no longer."

Zechariah's bushy eyebrows join. His mouth, so well suited to smiles and laughter, tightens. "It's dangerous for a lone woman to travel the roads. The Romans are everywhere. And many of our fellow Jews who survived, first Vespasian, and now, Titus, have turned to banditry in order to live. And they're not above robbing one of their own."

"I must take that chance. Please, Zechariah, don't dissuade me. Give me your blessing and your continued prayers. I need them both. Even so, I'll go without them."

The large man studies me. He sighs, he closes his eyes, he opens them, he shakes his head, then studies me all over again. Finally, he throws up his hands. "If I can't talk you out of it, then I must go, too."

"You . . . would do that?" Oh, how my heart soars. I see God's mercy in this. Surely it shows I follow His path. His will. Or . . . am I just being selfish? "What of the church? How can you leave the others?"

Zechariah's hair looks like a crop of zukkum thorns sticking out all over his head. He could be as prickly as his hair, and as stubborn. But he was also steadfast. He would never shirk any task given him by God. Now I've gone and reminded him of that. And he'll remember his duty and recant his rash words. I brace myself for disappointment, for I'd like nothing better than to have his company.

"My work here is done." His mouth forms that familiar grin. "I came here to strengthen the church, to encourage the believers. With *Hashem's* help, and that of . . . your cup, I've done so. The saints of Pella believe God is with them now. They have new hope, new courage. Simon, the bottlemaker, is a good man. He and Mary will be pleased to open their home to the believers. They don't need me anymore. And I've desired to return to Ephesus for some time now to see John the Apostle again. And to get there I must travel the same road as you. It's only sensible we travel it together. Besides, you're like a daughter to me. Shouldn't a father protect his daughter?"

My eyes tear. "Oh, *Zechariah*! You good, kind, beautiful man. See how God is already preparing my path! Oh, blessings on your head. Blessings! Blessings on that hoary head of yours!"

"Yes, yes, yes," he chuckles. "Only . . . there is one thing I must ask. Bring the cup."

"Take the cup? And not leave it here with Mary and Simon? But why?"

"Since Ira's and Rina's wedding I've known you were right. Our brethren rely too much on it. I fear it may become an idol. Let them focus on Jesus, as they should. Let Him be the object of their devotion."

I nod. "I'll do as you ask," I say, leading Zechariah to the door. "But now you must go and pack. We leave this morning."

All the arrangements have been made. Tirzah will tend the animals; Mary, my gardens. And each will share in the products of both, as will Hannah and Naomi who have promised to keep an eye on the house, and tend it from time to time. The food which can't be carried has been given away: a basket of grain, several melons, leeks, a half dozen chicken eggs. The two bells I've given to Mary. She says she'll use them not only to sound the alarm in times of danger but to call the believers to the weekly meetings.

My *semadi* is safely hidden beneath my tunic, and my two large bags with handles are already tied onto the donkey. I glance one last time around the house, then head for the door. My heart jumps when I see a shadowed figure barring the way. It takes me a second to recognize Kyra, Argos's servant girl. A large bundle, slung over her shoulder, makes her list to one side.

"News has crossed the wadi that you're leaving," Kyra says, standing as still as a plastered statue, though her bundle must be heavy. "I wish to come with you."

No words could have startled me more. She's been attending the meetings at Zechariah's for weeks now, and never expressed any desire to leave Pella. Why would she want to go now? And with a Jewess?

"You must take me with you," she repeats. "*Please.*"

"Impossible." I'm standing next to her now. She's a wisp, barely coming to my shoulder. Her clouded eyes, her thin, sad lips reveal how hard life has been. Even so, determination firms her jaw. "You belong to Argos," I say, trying to look stern. "You wear his collar, the collar of one who's run away before."

"No, it's not true. My parents sold me when I was ten. I was only to serve Argos five years. I've been with him for eight and still he refuses to free me. Last year I tried going home but he caught me, and put this on." Kyra clutches the collar with her free hand. Its rounded strip of fused metal rims her throat like a necklace. From it hangs a metal tag telling all she has once run from her master, Argos.

"If you run again, he'll have the slave hunters track you down. And if they find you, this time he'll surely brand your forehead with an 'F', the mark of a *fugitivus*,"

"I don't care. He's cruel, vicious. If I don't get free of him, he'll kill me for sure."

"He . . . beats you?"

Kyra puts down the bundle then rolls up the long sleeves of her tunic. Large bruises cover both arms; some brownish-yellow and almost healed; others, purple and fresh. "This Jesus Zechariah speaks of is more powerful than Argos. I've seen the miracles. I'll put myself under His protection."

My mind, warring against my heart, scrambles for arguments to dissuade her. She'll make the trip more dangerous. Slave hunters, perhaps even Argos, himself, will pursue us. Yet . . . can I leave her? Can I allow her to suffer more abuse?

Kyra's eyes harden. "Argos doesn't know I'm here, if that's what you're worried about. He's incubating in the Temple of Isis. He'll be there for days, trying to enhance his powers so he can defeat you. He doesn't know you're leaving. By the time he finds out, we'll be far away."

My insides are in an uproar, the war still raging. Even so, I pick up the heavy bundle at her feet, take it outside where the donkey is tied beneath a shade tree, then hoist it upon his back atop the other burdens.

"I can come?" Kyra's large, green eyes widen. "Oh, you won't be sorry. I will cook for you . . . I'll wash your clothes . . . I'll serve you like no other has ever served you before. You'll see. You won't be sorry."

But I'm already sorry as I tie down Kyra's bundle then clasp the donkey's bridle in my hand and motion for her to follow. And all the way to Zechariah's my discomfort builds as I wonder, *what have I done?*

Ethan

QUMRAN 70 A.D.

CHAPTER 6

"We've been here for weeks," Joseph says, in that gravelly, complaining voice of his as he sits on his rush mat and tosses pebbles against the cave wall. "We know every line of the scrolls, *every line*, as well as we know our own names. Why do we wait?" He turns abruptly to his brothers and points to me. "Tell him it's time we go. I've already tried."

Aaron, who is busy sharpening his dagger on a stone, looks up. "It's time, Father."

Benjamin, slumped against the far wall with eyes closed, nods.

I go and squat by the mouth of our large cave. Eleazar did not deceive us. The hewn passageway did lead to a Qumran cave, high in the mountains, though there were moments during our long trek when I doubted him. And here we've stayed, studying the scrolls, committing them to memory, as well as discussing each of the sixty-four treasure locations they mention.

I gaze past the vast expanse of barren cliffs and dusty lowlands to where the Salt Sea shimmers in varying shades of blue. A hot breeze tousles my hair as I revel in the scene before me. There's healing in these cliffs, in this desert wilderness. And I'm loath to leave it. More than my injured wrist and arm have mended. But my sons are restless. It will be impossible to keep them here much longer.

"I had hoped to stay another week," I say, not bothering to turn my head. I'm watching sunlight skip across the sapphire waters. "We could use the rest."

Rebellion erupts behind me.

"Father! We're not children! We're not here to rest."

"Who are we to live in comfort and safety while the Romans ravage our land?"

"We must be quick about finding the treasure, and aid Masada. Who knows when Titus will turn his attention southward?"

And on it goes.

I let them have their say. They're not fathers. How can they understand my father's heart? We've killed many these past four years. Our hands have shed much blood, and such bloodletting takes its toll. Our hearts need healing, though Aaron's the most. Along with his eye, something inside him is damaged. He carries a great inner sadness. Can it be otherwise with such a tender nature?

"It's not right that we shirk our duty," Aaron drones.

His brothers shout their agreement, then talk endlessly about how they are soldiers and men of honor, and how they've made a solemn pledge.

"Peace," I finally say, waving one hand in the air. "It will be as you wish. But first we must find a suitable place for the scrolls." Since the tunnel from Jerusalem leads to this cave, we've decided not to hide the scrolls here. If Eleazar found this passage, others can too. "We'll examine the Essene Yahad again."

"I don't think that's wise, Father," Aaron says, coming over and squatting beside me. Benjamin and Joseph follow.

We're all looking down at the once thriving community of the Essenes which sits on a marl terrace above the wadi. It's a desolate place now. Ruins mostly, and sparse vegetation; a wasteland of crumbling mudbrick. We've visited it many times during the cool of the day. And when I've been there and stood very still and watched the dust swirl through blank windows and open doorways and listened to the wind, I could almost see the community as it once was, alive and thriving with its vast sleeping quarters, its kitchens, potter's kiln, laundry, scriptorium, and large assembly hall. I could almost hear the whirl of a potter's wheel, hear the clinking of pottery, hear the sound of water gurgling along the massive aqueduct after a rainfall—water that came from the hills and was sufficient to fill both cisterns and ritual baths. Now the aqueduct and baths are nothing more than stagnant ponds; the compound, decaying rubble.

"It would be too risky to hide our scrolls in that deserted place," Aaron says. "The Romans could return." Three years ago, during his Judean campaign, Vespasian destroyed Qumran then kept a small force camped here. But the Romans are gone now. Even so, Aaron was right to be cautious.

"I say we put the scrolls in one of the many caves around here," Benjamin offers.

"Yes, one of the caves," Joseph chimes.

"It's the best place, Father." Aaron looks at me thoughtfully as though I've suddenly become the child, and he the parent.

I shrug. "So be it. But let the day cool before you begin your search." I don't delight in the thought of my sons scrambling among the jagged limestone rocks where stones skitter and footing is unsure. "Once we've hidden the scrolls, we'll gather food for our journey. Roots, perhaps, or a quail or two; maybe a hare." Aaron's face contorts. Hares are unclean according to the Law of Moses, and even after all our privations Aaron still concerned himself with ritual purity.

"Will we leave tomorrow?" Aaron says, still frowning.

"If we're ready by then."

"I've found the perfect place," Aaron says breathlessly, appearing suddenly from around a boulder. We've been searching for a suitable cave for hours. "It's a hard climb, but serves our purpose well. Come see."

Benjamin and Joseph scramble behind him, while I try to catch up. Aaron is already far ahead. The climb is steep, and leads us around jagged boulders and along footpaths barely large enough for one. Loose rocks roll beneath our feet and clatter down the cliff side. Here and there, clumps of grass sprout from crevices. Their blades are as sharp as pot shards and nick our ankles as we pass. We breathe grit and dust, while the sun bakes our heads. Despite my warning, my sons have chosen to conduct their search in the heat of the day. It tells me how impatient they are to leave.

Aaron leads us northward, high into the limestone cliffs. We've explored most of the lower marl caves, many of which are manmade, some hewn into the marl terrace as living quarters long ago, others newer, made perhaps by nomads, or rebels fleeing the Romans. Already we're a good distance from the Essene community.

"Here it is," Aaron shouts before lowering himself through a sloping entrance.

We all follow, scrambling into the opening and dropping onto the floor. Loose rocks and dirt follow us in. The musty cave is large, and contains several passageways.

"Look there." Benjamin points to several clay jars clustered near the entrance of a smaller cave. We gather around the jars and watch him remove one of the lids and slip in his hand.

"Is it something to eat?" Joseph says, just as Benjamin pulls out two parchments.

"Do you think only of your stomach?" Benjamin hands one scroll to Aaron, then quickly unrolls the other. "The Psalms." His face shows surprise and pleasure.

Aaron unrolls his. "The Book of the prophet Ezekiel." He glows like a freshly trimmed lamp, and I'm reminded of how much he loved reading scripture with the rabbis.

"This means someone else knows of this cave. It's not a suitable place for our scrolls," I say.

"It is, Father. For you saw how difficult it was to reach," Aaron says. "And you know that Eleazar moved much of the Temple library to Qumran. Surely, this is part of it. He must have scattered the library throughout the many caves here, the same way he scattered the Temple treasure throughout the land of Israel."

Not convinced, I look around and seeing no suitable hiding place I enter the smaller cave that sprouts like a boil along one side. It's darker here. When my eyes finally adjust to the dimness, I notice a ledge at the back.

"Yes, Father, that's where I'd hide it," Aaron says, standing beside me. He's the only one who has followed me in.

And so I pull the scrolls from my tunic, carefully remove the leather covering to keep the rats from eating it and damaging the scrolls, then place them on the stone shelf. "Tomorrow we leave for the Valley of Achor," I say, feeling strangely weary of our mission, a mission we haven't even begun.

"This is a place for madmen and prophets," Joseph says, as we head southwest. "Not soldiers." His skin glistens with sweat, and large wet circles stain his tunic beneath his arms and across his chest. We removed our robes long ago and placed them in one of the bags we carry. Though we left Qumran at first light, the sun is already high overhead. It feels like we are walking in a furnace. More than once we've had to stop and wet our heads.

"Why is there no breeze to comfort us?" Joseph wails. "The wind blows plentifully enough atop the mountains, but down here in the wadi it's as still as death. I feel like I'm breathing through wool."

"This complainer sounds like a girl," Aaron says, winking at Benjamin.

"Perhaps our *sister* needs to be carried." Benjamin suddenly scoops Joseph up, bundles and all, then throws him over his shoulder. He's the only one who could do this, being a head taller and stronger than his brothers. He lets Joseph yelp and thrash awhile before putting him down.

It's good to see my sons jesting together like they used to. It gives me hope that perhaps someday normal life awaits us. And I dare to ponder this life with Rebekah as we continue along the well-worn path through the wilderness of Judea, the path traveled from Qumran to Hyrcania for centuries.

We can't go to the treasure sites around Jerusalem since they're within the watchful eyes of Titus's legions. Instead, we've decided to concentrate on those sites located between the Holy City and Qumran. It's here that the scrolls promise we'll find gold, silver, oil flasks, sprinkling bowls, priestly garments, sacred vessels and texts—a treasure so vast no one man could ever use it, or even transport it safely. The task before us is so daunting that I'm beginning to think it's impossible. But I keep this to myself.

Our first stop will be the Valley of Achor, at the summit of the Hyrcania Fortress—a former palace and military headquarters for both John Hyrcania, the Hasmonean king, and Herod the Great. Now long abandoned and lying in ruins, it will be a safe place to search. According to the scrolls, it is in this remote place that we are to find—in three separate locations—a chest of silver weighing seventeen talents, a hundred gold ingots, and a mix of gold and silver weighing several hundred talents.

Achor was the site of enormous wealth.

To tell the truth, I have no heart for the task. It yearns for Rebekah, instead. How long has it been since I've seen her? I can't remember. But too long. I feel like a pining suitor. Her sweet face fills my nightly dreams. I've even begun smelling spikenard whenever I think of her, at least I imagine I do. And in my mind's eye I see her shimmering auburn hair cascade like silk over her soft, round shoulders.

I love Rebekah's hair, the way it feels between my fingers. I wish I could feel it now. It was her hair that first attracted me to her. She was but ten when its beauty caught my eye. We had been friends for years, playing children's games together, running through the countryside free as the wind. Being three years older I had always imagined myself her brother, the one to protect her from her wild spirit . . . until that day. Even now, I can see her as she was, laughing and challenging me to a race, then laughing as she swiftly left me in the dust, her head scarf slipping to her shoulders, her hair shimmering like copper in the sun. And I still remember the way she looked when I finally caught her, the wind tousling her hair and making it float around her beautiful wide eyes that were so full of life and joy. That was the day I was no longer her brother. That was the day I fell in love.

If only I could go to Pella now. Those weeks inside the cave have blunted my lust for Roman blood, though I've not shared this with my sons. I haven't shared it because it seems disloyal to Abner; and because, though blunted, my lust remains. Thoughts of Abner's crucified body can still rekindle my hatred for the Romans and the desire for revenge, though it's not as easy as it once was. And then there's my promise. Was I rash? Should I have made that oath to Eleazar? I wonder.

"I've never liked this wilderness." It's Joseph again. His head hangs limp against his chest as he trudges over the hard-mud ground. His shoulders sag beneath his bundles.

"Once, I heard the Baptist preach repentance here," I say, stopping to wipe my sweaty brow with the sleeve of my tunic. "It was so crowded I could hardly see him over all the heads, but his voice, how it thundered! He was a storm, speaking words that vibrated, and struck like lightening the hearts of priest and king alike. And oh, how fearless he was! But in the end, it cost him his head." I adjust my wineskin when I feel its strap digging into my shoulder.

"And on the mountain behind us, it's said Messiah withstood the temptations of the Evil One," Aaron adds. "We should bless *Hashem* for this place, for many holy men have been forged here."

"But we're not holy men; merely soldiers," my practical Benjamin says.

"We were . . . to become priests." Aaron's voice is softly, wistful. "But that was long ago . . . long . . . ."

"Long? Did somebody say, 'long'?" Joseph, who walks ahead, turns to look at Aaron and me. "Our food will not last a long journey. I only pray our bones will not end up bleaching in this desert."

I don't know why Joseph speaks as he does. He's no coward. Four years of fighting by his side has proven that. But even as a child he complained about everything. He can wield a sword like few I know but he can't tame his own tongue.

"We could die of hunger," Joseph repeats.

"Stop whining, woman," Benjamin chuckles, adjusting the bundle on his shoulder. "It's still the dry season. There will be plenty of goats around the springs near the Salt Sea should we need food."

And that quiets Joseph. I welcome the silence as we tramp through the rough terrain. The limestone-shale blanket covering the sloping mountainsides, making them appear barren, can also make a man feel utterly desolate. Even so, life can be found here if one cares to look. Most hills on their north sides have enough grasses for shepherds to bring their animals to graze. And along the wadi are additional grasses and even tamarisk bushes in full bloom. But Joseph is right. Only prophets or madmen or shepherds would ever come here to live. The heat, the dust, the falling rocks, the hard-mud pathways—all can kill an inexperienced traveler. And the mountains stretching endlessly over the horizon as far as the eye can see? They can swallow a man as if he were an insect.

"Father, you must slow down or we'll all perish before we reach the ruins."

Joseph, again. But this time no one mocks him. We've walked a good distance and are drenched with sweat. And not only Joseph's shoulders droop, both Aaron's and Benjamin's as well. I gesture to the flat ground in an alcove of boulders just off the path. Joseph is the first to find a spot and sit. He quickly opens his skin of water and drinks. We all do the same, and when we finish, we wet the coverings on our heads.

"We're nearly there," I say, removing some raisins from my pouch. I extend my open palm to my sons. Benjamin and Aaron shake their heads, but Joseph grabs a goodly amount and shoves it into his mouth.

"What?" he says, when he notices his brothers staring. "I'll share with Father when the time comes, you'll see."

"Since when have you ever shared your food with anyone? Willingly, anyway?" Aaron flicks a pebble at Joseph's head but it strikes the boulder behind him. "Benjamin and I have always had to fight you for the last date cake in Mama's basket, even when you had way more than your share."

"Well, if there's anything worth fighting for, it's your mother's date cakes," I say, my thoughts full of Rebekah again.

"There, you see? It's all Mama's fault," Joseph says, still chewing his mouthful of raisins.

We laugh and slap each others' backs; and Benjamin and Joseph wrestle and roll in the dust like fools. I suppose we do this because it's a way of emptying ourselves of the sorrow of these past many years; and because every once in a while a heart must fill itself with joy, or wither. We laugh so hard that tears streak our dust-caked faces. And amid all this foolishness we fail to hear anyone coming until it's too late. All we see is a cloud of dust, and then they're upon us.

"Such a merry group!" A man in costly apparel, his head and faced covered, stands tall over us. But even through the finery I smell his foul odor, an odor not of sweat from honest labor, but from raucous living and overindulgence of every kind. Only his eyes are visible, and there's ill-will in them. He holds a dagger. Behind him stand a dozen others, less exalted-looking but well dressed, too, and we know we've fallen into the hands of bandits.

"We don't usually encounter such joy. We ourselves have little, being an unfortunate lot." The leader gestures with his hand that he means himself and his men.

"Not so unfortunate." I shift my body slightly in order to reach the dagger belted at my waist. "Judging by your clothes."

The leader fingers the edge of his linen robe. "This? It's borrowed. From others. Always we are forced to borrow from others. From men like you who have much to rejoice over. Rich men, yes? For who else has anything to laugh about these days? So I ask you, do you not see virtue in sharing with those less fortunate?"

We're at a disadvantage, sitting in the dirt while they tower over us. And even as my hand gropes for my dagger, I feel a blade at my throat.

"Don't be foolish," the leader says. And then he does something unexpected. He tilts his head as if puzzled, removes his blade and bellows with laughter. "Why . . . I do have something to laugh about, after all. A great joke—us meeting out here like this. Imagine, the mighty general himself sitting on my patch of the world. I didn't recognize you at first. Oh, what a joke! You are the last man in Judea I ever expected to see here. But I've been rude. A thousand pardons!" With that he drops the veil from his face, and even under all the dirt and dust I recognize Lamech, the one who beat the wool merchant to death for his money, and among the first of John Gischala's generals to desert. He extends his hand and helps me to my feet. "A thousand pardons!" he repeats, smiling broadly but there is a menacing look in his eyes. "Of course you'll be my guests. I insist upon showing you my hospitality."

Benjamin and Aaron are already on their feet, their faces grim, their hands moving toward their daggers. I step in front of them. How can we make a stand? Our weapons are not drawn, and Joseph is still on the ground trying to rise. Besides, we carry nothing of value except what's contained in our heads. Lamech may lack honor but he's no fool. He'll not risk harm to himself or his men if there's nothing to be gained.

And so we follow these rogues, not knowing if we're guests or captives.

I shamelessly devour the stolen food. It pricks my conscience, though I try not to think of it as I take another bite.

"Eat, eat!" Lamech bellows as he lounges beside the large bowls set before us. His open robe reveals an ornate dagger tucked into a leather belt at his waist. "Fill your bellies. When was the last time you tasted lamb? Eh?"

Rush mats cover the cave floor where we sit, and large damask-covered pillows cradle our backs. Lamech has already told us how he relieved a merchant of these wares.

"Go on! Fill you bellies," Lamech repeats.

Aaron's face is paved with disgust, but even he takes another bite. We know—that is, Aaron, Benjamin and I—that Lamech robbed one of the shepherds. Only Joseph is unmindful. He eats with utter pleasure, licking the fingers of one hand while dipping the other into one of the large wooden bowls to pull out yet another chunk of meat.

"A good place to live, is it not?" Lamech gestures with his hand, inviting us to inspect the cave with our eyes. His own hard, black eyes watch us as we do.

The cave is cool and spacious and well lit with more than a dozen oil lamps. As far as the eye can see, assorted goods—piles of folded robes, tunics, blankets, rush mats, as well as baskets of lentils, beans, grains and dried fruit line the walls. It's not hard to guess where all this came from, and I see in my minds eye frail, frightened merchants traveling the hostile Judean wilderness on their way to peddle what little goods they had left, only to encounter Lamech and his men. How many have felt the tip of his ornate dagger? The thought makes me want to give Lamech the tip of my own.

"So what do you think?" Lamech presses.

"It's adequate." I know my words will irritate him but I need to test my position. How friendly is he, really? "Yes, adequate," I repeat.

"Ha! It's more than that, my friend. You have failed to see its importance; and you, a supposedly great general! I'll tell you what you should have known; what you failed to notice. It's safe, my friend. *Safe.* And in my business that counts for much. Eh?" He absently fingers the large scar on his cheek and laughs. "No one can see our cave from the road. Even you passed it by without a glance. We watched. I was a general, too, remember? I know something of tactics and logistics, and it serves me well in my new pursuits." His greasy hand taps my shoulder. "And it's spacious, is it not?" His black eyes prick me like darts

I nod.

"Oh, I see you're not impressed. But no matter. We're content for we make an adequate living."

"But a living off others," Aaron says, looking at the chunk of lamb between his fingers.

Lamech snorts with laughter. It sounds like the snorting of a pig. "I remember this son of yours, Ethan. A bit of a hothead and quick to speak his mind." When he pulls his dagger from his belted waist, I reach for mine. Lamech has allowed us to keep our weapons, perhaps to show we are truly guests. Just the same, I don't trust him. But before I can pull my dagger, Lamech plunges his into the bowl of meat, then brings a skewered chunk to his mouth, but not without a sneer.

"Well, young son of Ethan, you may not approve, but can you tell me a better way to make a living? Eh? In these hard times one must gather where he can. Where do you plan to gather?"

My hand remains beneath my robe, resting on the hilt of my dagger. Who knows how Aaron will answer? He's always been more zealous than prudent.

"I'm destined for the priesthood, when I come of age. I'll follow where God leads."

"Ha!" Lamech snorts like a pig again. "A priest, bah! Surely you know the Temple has been destroyed? Or . . . ," Lamech crumples his face, making his large scar look like a worm crawling across his cheek, "or did you leave before the Romans tore it down, stone by stone?"

I hear Aaron gasp. Lamech hears it too, for he leans closer to Aaron who sits on his left. "Then you *didn't* know. So . . . you're deserters like the rest of us. Ha! The great general, a deserter. His sons, too. Now who would have believed that?" He laughs and scratches his head, then pulls some small crawling thing from his hair and squishes it between his greasy, blackened fingers. "That explains your clothes, the clothes of a tradesman. Why you wear no tassels. John Gischala and I used to mock your fringe. Such vanity, those tassels, if you ask me. Still, I must admit we never had your zeal. For us it wasn't about Jerusalem and the Temple. It was about *spoils*. We wanted to be rich men. But you always knew that, didn't you? No matter what John or I said about freeing Holy Jerusalem from the Romans, you *knew*. I hear the Romans have John now; that he hid in the sewers like a girl before surrendering. They'll surely take him to Rome for the triumph, and who knows what will happen to him there. But I feel no pity. He should have left Jerusalem when he had the chance."

Lamech thrusts two dirty fingers into his mouth, then tugs at a piece of meat wedged between his decaying front teeth, but his gaze never leaves Aaron. "Well, young son of Ethan, what has brought you to this wilderness?" He roughly dislodges the meat. "Where is God leading you?" The laughter has gone from his voice. It's obvious that he's deliberately baiting my son.

I pray that *Hashem* subdues Aaron's passion. Already his face shows he's greatly offended over Lamech's assumption that we are deserters.

"Where do you go now?" Lamech repeats.

"Our destination is Masada," Aaron says calmly. "We'll fight with the rebels there." Though Aaron sits tall and straight, revealing the strong well-formed body of a man, his soft curls, hanging limply around his face, makes him look more like a boy. "Masada, along with Machaerus, is our last stronghold against the Romans."

"And Herodium. Some say it's occupied by a small rebel force," Lamech says, eyeing Aaron strangely.

Aaron answers with silence. It's loud, this silence. I want to break it like a clay jar, but I didn't dare. As I tested Lamech, so he is now testing me; seeing if I'll allow my son to speak or if I'll come to his aid, seeing if I have something to hide. And so we sit, eating and staring unfriendly stares, like mountain goats ready to lock horns. But throughout this long silence and under Lamech's relentless gaze, Aaron, my son the Zealot, Aaron, the passionate, remains unruffled, and I'm proud.

"Strange for deserters to go in search of more battles," Lamech finally says. "Stranger still that you didn't take the direct route from Jerusalem, passing Bethlehem and *Herodium*, as most who flee Jerusalem for Masada. Perhaps if you said you were heading to Machaerus, I would think it more natural. But Masada? A queer route you've taken, almost as if you've come by way of . . . Qumran." Lamech wipes his dagger on his sleeve then tucks it back into his belt. "But what is that among disreputable men? Eh?" He laughs his snorting laugh. "We dare not pry into each other's business for we all have something to hide. Don't we?" His eyebrows lift as though expecting some denial, and getting none, he adds, "Well then . . . tomorrow go to Masada if you must. Today, you will eat and rest with me."

"We are grateful for your kindness." My praise is quick in order to keep my sons silent. "And we welcome the rest." I bite into another piece of meat, knowing we'll not get as much rest as Lamech supposes for I'll have us sleep in shifts so that one pair of eyes will always be on our too-gracious host.

We have survived the night without incident, and depart at first light. In a few hours we reach Hyrcania. And after briefly exploring two tunnels at the base of the mountain and finding nothing of worth, we begin the climb. From the base of the mountain the steep winding path to the summit forms a curious M-shape. It takes us a while but when we reach the top we find the ruins of a once great fortress, one among a chain of many that lined the Salt Sea. When we finally navigate the man-made ditch surrounding the fort and gain access to the interior, I point to a nearby tower. "We'll rest in there." And so we enter—glad for the shade—and sit and eat almonds, then drink from our water skins and talk about which treasure we should look for first.

We finally decide to go in search of the chest containing seventeen talents of silver even though this weight of silver cannot be carried to Masada by just the four of us. I've already told my sons that when we find it . . . *if* we find it . . . we'll take only a talent with us to Masada to show them that treasure does exist here, and that it's worth sending their men back with us to help transport the rest.

The scroll tells us this chest of silver is in a cistern and buried at the bottom of a flight of stairs that face east. It will not be easy to find, but I don't bother mentioning this to my sons. Instead I rest my head against the cool mudbrick and close my eyes as I listen to them chatter. Too little sleep last night has left me exhausted. But they are excited, all except Joseph. He continues to complain.

"It's more ruinous that I expected," Joseph says.

I open my eyes and watch him mop his forehead with the rag from his head.

"It will not be easy finding the right steps," he continues.

"At least the scroll tells us we are to look in a cistern," Aaron adds.

"And how many cisterns are there in Hyrcania? Do we even know?" Joseph again. "We could be stumbling around here for days!"

His gravelly voice is beginning to irritate me. It must annoy Benjamin, too, for he says, more sharply than he needs, "At least there's a breeze atop this summit. Be grateful for that!"

"Most of the buildings have toppled." Joseph is persistent. "Bricks and rubble are everywhere. In such a place we could dig for years and never find anything."

"Enough!" I say, springing to my feet. "I would rather labor in the burning sun than endure any more of your complaining. Come, all of you, let's begin."

Aaron chuckles. "See what you've done, my brother? Now Father will work us unmercifully just to prove you wrong, and to silence your disagreeable tongue."

Joseph grumbles about being tired, but even he knows better than to persist in his complaining. Soon we're beneath the blazing sun, eating dust and poking through the ruins.

"Lamech let us off too easily. It troubles me," Aaron says, as we examine the first cistern we come across. It is vaulted and lime-plastered, and a good place to start for it's not goblet shaped but rectangular, exactly the type that would contain a flight of stairs along one of its walls. "I don't think he really believes we're going to Masada." With his small hand shovel, Aaron begins moving rocks and debris which still contain layers of white–lime plaster. After he digs awhile, he looks up and frowns. "All the way here I had the feeling we were being followed, though I saw no signs of it."

"You're beginning to sound like an old woman," Joseph says, shadowing Aaron, and kicking stones and dirt as if he's doing something important all the while his shovel hangs idly in his hand. "Why should he bother with us? He's probably happy to be rid of us after all the food we ate."

"You mean after all the food *you* ate," Benjamin says, helping Aaron move a large pile of rocks to expose what's behind it.

"Lamech is a rogue, a dog who has returned to his own vomit," Aaron says, tossing stones over his shoulder. "Be assured he does nothing out of kindness. His hospitality last night was only a means of seeing if we were birds worth plucking. I say we still need to keep a sharp lookout, in case he really did follow us. He and his men know these hills better than we. It's possible they could have tailed us without our knowing it."

Before I can voice my agreement, Aaron yells, "Look! Here behind the pile of rocks! It's a stairway!"

We all dig now, and soon our faces and clothes are powdered with dirt. But before long we uncover two steps and are quickly disappointed when we see they fail to head east as the steps must, according to the scrolls. And so we leave the relative cool of the cistern for the blistering sunlight.

We walk for hours over loose rocks and hard-mud ground, poking through ruins and rubble, and discover there are six cisterns on this summit, including one lined with benches. We stand before the final one now. The entrance is blocked, and the interior can only be reached by lowering oneself through the hole in the high vaulted ceiling. Though it is as tall as our house in Jerusalem, debris and dirt packed against the outside walls have decreased the distance from the ground to the hole in the rounded ceiling, making outside access easy. But one problem remains: getting safely through the hole and down into the cavernous cistern itself.

"We can tie our robes together; use them to lower one of us through the hole," Joseph says, nibbling an almond. "I'll go, if my brothers are afraid."

Benjamin jabs him with his elbow. "And who was it that jumped out of his skin when he saw that little snake in the last cistern?"

"Little! It was as long as the road from Qumran, and hungrier than me, I'll wager."

We all laugh. But suddenly I stop and crane my neck and listen.

"What's wrong, Father?" Aaron asks.

"Did you hear rocks falling?"

"Rocks have been falling all morning," Joseph says with a chuckle. "Every time we touch something, rocks fall away."

But Aaron doesn't laugh, and neither do I. And by the look on his face I know he's thinking my thoughts. *Has that fox, Lamech, followed us after all?*

Our robes are in knots at my feet. We stand in our tunics, dripping with sweat, while the sun glares overhead. It's the heat of the day, but no one, except me, wants to delay exploring the cistern until it's cooler. The impatience of youth is often like a runaway chariot, best left to curb itself. There are only three of us to dig. At my insistence, Aaron has posted himself as a sentry, high up in one of the towers to keep Lamech from surprising us again. I know Lamech well enough to understand that he's a dog who can't be trusted. At least with Aaron in the tower I feel a measure of peace.

Joseph seems to feel nothing but excitement as he stands grinning and pulling his tunic between his legs. He belts it at the waist. Always first to complain, and first to put himself at risk. He confounds me, this son who is brave and foolish and often annoying. I watch him bend and pick up the knotted robes, then hand the end to Benjamin.

"All the food you stuffed into your mouth last night will make my task the harder," Benjamin grunts.

Joseph laughs, then taking the other end of the makeshift rope, ties it around his waist. Then he climbs up the outside of the partially buried cistern and lowers himself through the jagged opening.

"What do you see?" I shout, helping Benjamin hold the rope.

"It's deep! Very deep. And to my left is a large plastered wall, solid from top to bottom; a separation wall. I've seen this before in other cisterns. There must be another chamber on the other side . . . but how to get in?" His voice sounds muffled as though his mouth is full of dirt. "The wall still looks well mortared except for . . ." his voice trails off.

"Except for what?" I shout.

"Yes . . . I can see it plainly now . . . a hole, a hole near the ceiling, large enough for a man to crawl through. If only I could get a little closer . . . ."

I hear scraping noises and a thud. "Joseph?"

"There, I've lifted myself onto the ledge . . . I can see through the opening, to the other side . . . it's . . . a shaft, yes, a shaft! The opening is just above my shoulders. If you pull on the rope and I use my arms as levers, I think I can raise myself high enough to go through it.

As Benjamin and I pull, I hear another thud, then groaning, then Joseph's voice. "I've done it. . . I'm through." And then nothing.

We wait . . . and wait. Finally, when I can stand it no longer I shout, "Joseph? Are you well?" No answer. I pull on the rope. It's slack. He's untied himself. "Joseph!"

"Be calm, Father," Benjamin says softly. "He's not as foolish as you think. He'll not take unnecessary risks."

And so we wait, my mind conjuring up dreadful scenes of what may be happening: Joseph has fallen and broken a leg; a plummeting rock has crushed his skull; the shaft is full of water and he has drowned. I'm getting old. I'm beginning to think like a woman—cautious and fretful. *Oh, be careful, Joseph!*

It will take two of us to safely pull my son from the cistern, so I can't go in. If only Aaron were here I'd send him after his brother. And just when my patience is at an end and I'm about to call Aaron from the tower, I hear a muffled voice say through the hole in the roof, "It was dark down there!" The rope jerks and I know it's Joseph tying himself once again. "Only the hand of *Hashem* kept me from falling into that well," he yells to us.

Benjamin and I pull Joseph up. "What's this about a well?" I say, relieved to see my son, but afraid to show it. It's not always easy for a father to let his son be a man.

Joseph laughs as he slides off the top of the rounded cistern and lands on his feet beside me. "Oh, yes, there's a well at the end of the shaft, but between the shaft and the well are stairs, stairs facing *east*!"

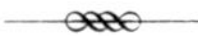

My sons won't sleep. The young can be foolish in more than matters of love. The sun has long set, and we're sitting on the first floor of the northwest tower, one of four towers positioned at each corner of the fortress perimeter. A sliver of moon stabs a broken piece of wall. It's the only light we have.

"What can we use?" Benjamin says. "If we are to dig beneath the steps as the scroll says, we must actually dig inside the well for there is nothing in that space except the well. And Joseph says it's too dark. What, then, do we use for light?"

"First we must be certain there's no water in it. We can't dig if there's water." Aaron says.

"I already told you the well is dry." Joseph's voice is strained by both annoyance and fatigue.

"How can you be so sure?" Aaron persists. "If it was as dark as you say, then there's no way to know."

"It only became dark at the end of the shaft. The light from the hole in the cistern reached at least that far."

"My point exactly!" Aaron says, sitting cross-legged on the floor, rigidly leaning into our circle.

"Let Joseph explain," I say, putting my hand on Aaron's broad shoulder and feeling pleased that my words and touch make him relax against the mudbrick wall.

"As I was saying," Joseph continues, a bit too cocky, "at the point where it became dark, I dropped to my knees and felt my way forward. That's when I found the flight of steps and crawled over each one until I felt *nothing* but air. All the steps, except for the last, were free of debris. That last one was so cluttered with broken bricks and dirt I nearly lost my balance and toppled into the well. Only *Hashem's* hand prevented it."

We all praise *Hashem*'s name, then Joseph continues. "After making sure the step was sound, I pushed the debris to one side, then carefully felt around. Below the last step my fingers felt a thick lip of stone; below that a wall—stone lined and plastered, and with tufts of dried plants clinging to the cracks. I could reach no further, but I already knew that what my fingers probed was the inside of an old well." Joseph pulls a clump of dried vegetation from his tunic and hands it to me. "See? I brought this to show you." He watches as I examine it. "Then to test if the well was dry or not, I tossed in a brick and heard no splash, just the clatter of the brick hitting the sides of the well as it fell."

"So it's a dry well. That still doesn't answer the question of light," Benjamin says. "We can't dig inside the well without light. We'll need torches."

"Why don't we just peel back the roof?" Joseph's voice suddenly sounds drowsy. It's obvious he wants to be done with this business. But his idea is met with derision as both Aaron and Benjamin laugh.

"Now wait. Your brother might have something," I say. "If we break into the roof just above the hole in the separation wall we might let enough light into the well for us to be able to dig. It's worth a try."

"But Father, we have only those small hammers and chisels and hand shovels Eleazar put in our bags," my practical Benjamin says. "The mortar in this cistern is still strong and calls for the work of a pickax. It will be difficult to break the roof with our meager tools. Better to make torches; cut strips from our robes and . . . ."

"Without pitch they'll burn too quickly and it could take a long time to dig through the well. You must consider that, and while you do, I'm going to sleep." I struggle to my feet, then walk along the wall of the tower searching for a place to stretch out for the night. My son's voices still dip and rise as I kick away broken bricks from my chosen ground, then spread my robe for a bed. And even as I drift off to sleep, I hear them arguing.

"Come on, hit it harder!" Aaron shouts.

Benjamin raises his wet glistening arms and brings the small hammer he's holding crashing down on the slowly crumbling mortar of the cistern roof. "It's almost there," he says, perspiration dripping from the drenched rag around his head.

All my sons are drenched from taking their turn at breaking the roof. They have been at if for hours. Since there are still no signs that we were followed, I've not taken the precaution of posting a guard. The work is strenuous and we need every hand. Late last night, my sons finally determined the best plan for bringing light into the well was to open the roof, so now they labor at chiseling out the edges of a large circle. The idea is that the weight of the bricks will do the bulk of the work for them. Their hope is that once the circle is partially chiseled and loosened, the weight of the sagging circle will cause it to pull away from the rest of the cistern ceiling.

I think it's a good plan.

"Watch out now!" Joseph warns. "It's ready to go!"

Suddenly, the walls of the cistern groan as the weight of the loosened section becomes too great, and bricks and mortar pull away from each other. Then bricks crash and skitter on the way down where they end in a thunderous heap at the bottom.

Amid the noise and swirling grit, Benjamin rolls down the outside of the sloping roof just in time to keep from being sucked in with the falling bricks. The roof did not give way in a neat circle as planned, but pulled other sections with it, sections not solidly held by mortar, including the area where Benjamin had been standing only moments before.

We're all laughing as we watch dust mushroom upward through the hole; laughing because we're grateful no one was hurt. And when Benjamin, powdered white from head to toe in lime dust, hands me the hammer still clutched tightly in his hand, we laugh all the harder.

"Surely I should have reached the chest by now," Joseph complains, scooping more dirt with his shovel, and dropping it onto his robe, the one we've been using to haul dirt from the bottom of the well and out through the shaft."

"We'll go one cubit more," I say. "And I'll dig it."

"No Father, I'll do it. But if I don't reach the chest by then we must try a different site."

"Agreed," I say, standing on the last step which juts out slightly over the lip of the well and just above the dirt ramp we've built to haul away the debris.

The opening in the roof has supplied all the light we need. It floods the shaft and well. We have each taken our turn digging, then hauling dirt up through the shaft. But we've dug so deep Joseph is beginning to work in shadows. Already, my mind has declared this effort a waste and I'm thinking of where to dig next. Perhaps that tower facing the aqueduct? Weren't there stairs in the corner, jutting out from beneath the debris? But were they facing east? I wasn't sure.

I watch Joseph work. His sweat has mingled with dirt and now he's coated in what looks like a thin layer of mud. With every scoop of his shovel, he moves more slowly. I'm about to tell him to stop when he yells, "I've hit something." Quickly, he brushes away the loose dirt and uncovers a flat, hard surface. I peer from the bottom step that overhangs the rim of the well and see that it is wooden . . . and bound with rusted hammered-metal straps. A chest? I look again. Yes! A chest!

"Pull up my robe," Joseph yells. "It's nearly full and in the way."

And so I pull up the heavy bundle of dirt, dragging it first up the dirt ramp, then up the steps, then up the shaft where I finally pour it through the hole in the separation wall and into the cistern below. By the time I return, Joseph has uncovered the chest, broken the straps with his shovel and opened the top to reveal a mound of tarnished coins. With a shout I scramble back up the shaft to where I can see Aaron's face peering through the opening in the cistern roof. "We've found it!" I shout. "We've found the chest of silver!"

"How much do you think it's worth?" Aaron says, staring down at the mound of coins atop one of the robes by our feet. We're all sweaty and grimy and exhausted from hauling the talent of silver from the well. "All the treasure buried here? What could it be worth?" Aaron repeats.

"It's hard to say." I plunge my dagger into the mound, nearly burying the hilt."

"I'm sure we could have carried more." Aaron frowns. "You should have let Joseph bring up another robe full."

"We'll have a hard enough time with this. We'll cut up one of the robes, make four bundles and transport the silver that way. Believe me, after an hour of carrying it on your back you'll begin complaining about how heavy it is."

"Then let me lighten your load."

The voice startles me, and when I turn there is Lamech and his men surrounding us, their weapons drawn. But the men hardly give us a glance. They all gape, wide-eyed, at the silver. Only Lamech looks at me, his lips curved like a melon wedge.

"You were as quiet as snakes," I say, my dagger now pointed at him. "I congratulate you."

Lamech inclines his head in a mock-bow. "A necessary skill in our trade." With the point of his own dagger he calmly begins cleaning a thumbnail. "I knew you were up to something. The great general would not be wandering the Judean wilderness, going so far out of his way for nothing. And I was right, eh?"

My sons have all scrambled to retrieve their daggers and now stand battle ready. Lamech pays them no heed. It's obvious his superior force gives him confidence.

"But tell me this," his eyes are now riveted on the coins, "why should such a trove be buried way out here in these ruins? Eh?" He juts his chin towards me but seems unable to make his eyes follow. They linger on the mound of silver then flicker, in a back and forth struggle. "There were rumors that Eleazar ben Simon removed the Temple treasure to keep it from Roman hands. Is this it?" I can't hold his gaze. The pull of the silver is too strong. It owns him now. He runs his thumb slowly over the scar on his cheek. "If it is, then there must be *more*."

"The silver is my concern, mine and my son's," I say fiercely. "We're acting on Eleazar's orders. It's for the rebels at Masada." Better to admit the truth, at least in part. It was my only chance of keeping Lamech unbalanced, and possibly dissuaded about more treasure.

"So, you're not deserters?"

"Hardly," Aaron answers before I can, his mouth curled with disdain. "We're rebels still, soldiers ready to fight the Romans."

Lamech chuckles. "Ah, young son of Ethan, such waste of talent and zeal." He motions to his men as he stands ready with his blade. "Throw in with us," he says, looking at me. "We'll divide our spoils equally, you and me. The roads of the Judean wilderness contain enough plunder for all. A man of your skill would do well. Come, live a life of ease." The coins draw him once more. "You never did say if the rumors are true; if there was more treasure. But no matter." He gestures toward the mound. "This is answer enough. Eleazar would not hide just a portion of the Temple wealth and leave the rest in Jerusalem for the Romans to plunder. And I'll wager you know where it all is, too. Oh, think of it, Ethan, we could be rich men! You and your sons could live like kings. We could all live like kings."

Aaron bristles, then lunges forward. I restrain him only by pressing my arm firmly across his chest. "Do you really think that's possible, Lamech? Us joining you?"

Lamech, cutthroat and killer of defenseless wool merchants; Lamech, wearer of fine clothes who snorts and smells like a pig . . . laughs. "I suppose not. We could never tame this son of yours." He twists the gleaming dagger in his hand. "But that leaves us with a problem. We seek different roads." He points to the silver. "And both of us want to take that on the road with us. So what is to be done?"

"The matter is already settled. It goes with us to Masada." Aaron raises his weapon. My other sons do the same.

Lamech points to his men. "You're outnumbered. Don't shed your blood over these coins. Go to Masada. Go and fight the Romans if you must. We'll let you depart in peace. But the coins remain here."

Already his men are fanning out, trying to encircle us. There are ten to our four. Still, the advantage is ours. This is our territory. We've gotten to know the fortress well. But before I can tell my sons to scatter, Joseph lunges at the two men closest to him, killing one with a quick flick of his blade, then the other, but not before a dagger is thrust into his inner thigh, bringing him to his knees.

It all happens before the rest of us can even move a muscle. Now, the sight of Joseph crumpled on the ground throws me into action. I flash my dagger to and fro in a wide arch, driving Lamech and his remaining men backward. "It's foolish to continue this," I say. "We know the ground here. We can hide in places you'd never find. The sun will set soon. You can't move the treasure off the summit tonight. You have lost two men already. By morning you'll all be dead. We will kill you, one by one, in the darkness."

Lamech raises one hand in the air. "Ethan, Ethan. Is this the way friends behave? All this talk of killing. Such a waste. But surely you don't suggest I leave empty-handed? As you said, I've lost two men. Perhaps they were worthless dogs who fought like women," he spits on the ground, "but they were *my* dogs. You have so much." He eyes the mound of silver. "You can afford to be generous."

"Perhaps," I say, lowering my dagger. "But not too generous. Your dogs injured my son. Give us your scrips of food and your water skins, then descend the summit. For that, and your two lost men, I'll allow you to leave with a small bag of coins and your lives."

"Even now the sun hangs red in the sky. You expect me to travel that steep, winding path at night? Without food or water? All the way back to my wadi? You take me for a fool?" Lamech growls.

"Then come," I gesture with my dagger, "and I'll send you to Hades instead." My sons have fanned out. Even Joseph is back on his feet. Blood covers his leg.

Lamech's men don't move. They fear us. Lamech, too, for I see it in his eyes. My sons are known for their bravery. Their exploits are numerous and renowned. They've often vanquished forces far greater than themselves.

"Well, speak up. What will it be? A bag of silver to share with your men or . . . this?" I hold up my dagger. "Come. It grows dark. Let's conclude our business, one way or the other."

For a moment the only sound I hear is the wind blowing atop the summit. Finally, Lamech laughs and slips his dagger into his belted waist. "A good bargain, if I say so myself. I accept your terms, Ethan. Two worthless men, five bags of food, five skins of water, for one bag of silver. Yes, a good bargain." He points to the scrips and water skins on the ground behind him, then tosses me a small empty leather pouch.

I give the bag to Aaron who quickly fills it with coins. And when I toss it back, Lamech signals for his men to leave.

"One more thing," I say, causing Lamech to stop. "If you follow us again I'll kill you."

Lamech shakes his head. "Such unfriendly talk. So unnecessary among friends." He raises the bag of coins into the air. "I will think of you often, my friend," he says, smiling with his mouth, but his eyes are hard as pebbles. "I'll not forget you."

If only Joseph would complain instead of lying listless on his rush mat, unable even to lift his head, it would give me hope. But his life is draining away. Though Aaron has dressed the wound—a deep gash the length of my hand—the bleeding continues and there's no way to stop it since the wound is by the groin. I've seen injuries like this on the battlefield where men have bled out. I feel helpless and angry, and sick with fear that Joseph will die. And how can my heart bear that?

"They're nearly down the summit," Benjamin says, looking out a window. We are in the north tower, which gives us a good view of Lamech and his men as they make their descent down the winding sloping path. "They've stopped by the old aqueduct . . . oh . . . they are beginning again . . . now . . . now they're mere shadows in the distance. They'll not return tonight."

"But sooner or later they will," I say, watching Joseph drift into sleep or unconsciousness, I know not which. "Perhaps Lamech will recruit more men. Either way, he'll be back. And he must not find us here."

"What of the rest of the coins still in the chest? Joseph has covered it over with dirt, but if Lamech comes back, surely he'll search out this cistern where he knows we have been working. He and his men may even dig throughout the ruins. What if he finds the gold ingots under the monument or the talents buried in the courtyard cistern?"

It's Aaron, Aaron the son who is always mindful of his duty even when his own heart is heavy with grief, for I see on his face that his fear for Joseph mirrors mine.

"We must leave them, and hope some of the men of Masada will return with us before Lamech does. But now, we must see to Joseph."

"And have my brothers call me a girl?" Joseph says, as if waking from the dead. His voice is but a vapor in my ears. "You must not take me into account, Father." He lifts his hand but when he can't reach mine he lets his drop. Even in the fading light I see him grimace from the effort. And I see the look in his eyes, too, though I wish I hadn't. Because he *knows*. He tries to tell me but I'm a coward and look away. "Do not consider me, Father," he repeats. "Do your duty."

"My duty is to get you to Masada." I bend over Joseph and touch his bandaged thigh with my finger tips. Already the newly wound rag is soaked with blood. "When you are safe and properly tended, your brothers and I will come back here with more men. But rest now." Joseph closes his eyes. "Rest while we prepare your litter, for soon we leave."

"Tonight, Father?" Benjamin says, turning from the window. "It's dangerous to make the descent in the dark."

"But more dangerous to stay," I say.

And when Benjamin glances past my shoulder to where Joseph is lying and sees the great quantity of blood covering the fresh bandage, he nods in understanding.

"Let me carry him," I say, squinting down at the prone body on the pallet. A bed of rush mats atop Aaron's spread robe provides support for Joseph's back. But already the robe, which is knotted at the four corners for ease of carrying, is beginning to wear. Aaron holds the end by Joseph's head. Benjamin carries the other, only the robe isn't long enough and one of Joseph's legs folds at the knee and dangles off the edge. The other leg, the injured one, juts straight out like a log, being tightly wrapped in one of the rush mats. In addition, I've folded my robe under his thigh to lift the leg. I'm praying to *Hashem* that these efforts will keep the wound from spurting blood.

"Come, it's my turn," I repeat. "Let me do my share."

"We can switch after we reach the wadi and the road is better," Aaron answers in a labored voice.

"When we reach the wadi we'll *all* stop for a rest," I say. "There's no need for you to bear so much of the load." But Aaron ignores me and continues the descent.

The trek downhill is treacherous. We don't travel the path that Lamech and his men took for fear they may still be close by. Rather, we descend the opposite side of the summit where the path is less defined, the terrain more inhospitable. And only moonlight guides us. Everything seems to conspire to make our journey maddeningly slow. And this eats at my gut. I'm desperate to get Joseph to Masada, for surely there must be at least one physician there to help him.

Throughout all the jostling and stumbling over rocks, Joseph has not uttered a word. Only an occasional groan tells me he's still alive. But he's heavy. So are our bundles and the bags of silver we carry, and they all take their toll, sapping our strength as we try to safely maneuver the steep incline. I've already relieved Benjamin. But Aaron has yet to rest. He pants like a dog beside me.

"Let me take him," I say again, and to my surprise Aaron tells Benjamin to stop, and amid a level spot near a jagged limestone protrusion, he gives me first one knotted end of the litter, then the other.

"An unencumbered man can walk to Masada from Hyrcania in a day," Aaron whispers beside me, then takes great gulps of air as though trying to catch his breath. "With Joseph injured we'll be fortunate to do it in two."

"Yes, that's what I calculate."

"But in another day, he'll bleed out. His wound is grievous, Father, and even if we travel day and night, I fear it will be too late."

I'm silent for a moment. "Scout ahead and find a better patch of level ground," I finally tell Aaron. "I'll stop the bleeding."

"How?"

"By packing the wound."

"But we have nothing, Father. No oil or wine, no clean wool," Aaron's voice shakes, "only our filthy rags. You'll poison what blood he has left."

"Find me the ground!" I hiss. And so Aaron, my obedient Aaron, disappears into the night amid the sound of skittering rocks. And before long, I hear his voice say, "Over here."

After Benjamin and I rest the litter on the level ground that Aaron has found, I feel Joseph's leg. The rag around his wound is sticky and wet. "Give me your robe, Benjamin." Without a word, Benjamin pulls his robe from his sack and hands it to me.

"Uncover his wound." Again, Benjamin obeys, while I tear his dirty robe into strips. "Hold him down, both of you." I kneel beside Joseph and reach toward the bloody gash. My hand stops in mid air and trembles in the moonlight as I pray to *Hashem*. Then I force open Joseph's wound and begin jamming in the dirty strips of cloth, one by one, until I can fit no more. Throughout it all, Joseph screams—piercing, anguished, pleading screams. And between the screams, he begs us to let him die. I'll never forget those screams or his words, or that they came because of my hand. He tries to roll off the litter, but his efforts are feeble and easily restrained by Aaron and Benjamin. By the time I'm done, Joseph is unconscious and my cheeks are streaked with tears.

The sun has risen. I feel its fingers poking my eyelids, forcing them to open against my will, and when they do, everything is a blur. I know we're in the wadi, cradled in the arms of a limestone niche, one of many along the base of the bordering mountains. The climb down the summit took everything we had. And because Joseph's bleeding has stopped, I ordered a brief rest just before sunrise. I think we all would have collapsed if I hadn't.

My open eyes burn and feel as though they're filled with grit the size of boulders. I squeeze my lids then wipe the corners with dirty fingers. Now they are more painful than ever. I'm covered in dirt. It coats my hair, lines my nostrils and mouth; powders my torso and limbs. In desperation, I sit up and feel for my water skin. And when I find it I use some of the precious water to wash my hands, then my eyes until I can finally see the outlines of my sons sleeping beside me, and see that it is Benjamin who snores so loudly.

"Aaron, wake up." I shake him, for he's the closest. "We must be on our way." Aaron opens his sleepy eyes and yawns. Benjamin stops snoring and sits upright. Joseph doesn't move. His head is turned away. I struggle to my feet and go to his litter.

"Joseph." I bend to examine his leg. His dressing is nearly dry, and for that I praise *Hashem.* Then I probe a little harder, to make sure.

"Don't press, Father, it hurts too much," Joseph says, in a thin, tired voice as he turns and squints up at me.

"Next time don't be in such a rush to pick a fight." I smile, trying to keep the worry from my face. He's as white as lime dust, even his lips. Only his eyes have any color at all. And they look more like black stones pressed deep into a lump of dough.

"I only followed . . . Aaron's lead." His voice is so low I bend closer and put my ear near his mouth in order to hear. "He was ready to strike, only I . . . beat him to it."

"Don't talk. Save your strength."

He takes my hand which is resting on his hip. His fingers are cold. "I want you . . . to know that no matter what happens . . . it's alright."

"We'll follow the wadi along the Salt Sea until we reach Masada," I say, trying to gather courage. "There'll be plenty of mountain goats near the springs. If time permits, perhaps Benjamin will kill one for you. The fresh meat and hot broth will do you good."

"Benjamin? His bow can't . . . hit the side of a . . . mountain," Joseph says, trying to force a smile when Benjamin suddenly kneels beside me. "Best you send . . . Aaron." And as we lift the litter to resume our journey, Benjamin jeers his brother and laughs. But it's a sad laugh, one sounding more like a sob.

"Just . . . leave me . . . Father," Joseph says, his deeply sunken eyes sending me a pleading look.

"That would be unthinkable." I kneel beside him, and note the foul odor of his leg.

"They will bury . . . me." Joseph makes a feeble motion with his chin in the direction of the nearby woman who squats on a mat and sews the edges of a large animal skin around the two long wooden poles her husband, Bahij, made for her. I'm paying them to make a new litter for Joseph. Aaron's ripped robe was discarded long ago. And my robe, the last one left, has already begun to tear. It would never have lasted all the way to Masada.

"Let me . . . stay here . . . and die," Joseph says.

"No one is going to die. Soon you will be well again. You'll see." I motion for the woman to hurry and silently praise *Hashem* for this great gift of a new litter. But she pays no attention. She's covered from head to toe in folds of dark cloth. Only her eyes and dry leathery hands are visible. It's difficult to determine her age, but I think she's old. Even so, her hands move swiftly, expertly, as she works to secure the skin. And again I praise *Hashem.*

"You would . . . make . . . better time . . . without me," Joseph says, his words sounding like gasps. "What if Lamech . . . is on our trail?" With each succeeding word, Joseph's voice fades. "You must get . . . the . . . silver . . . to . . . Masada."

"Be still, Joseph. And don't speak. God has not brought us to these tent dwellers for nothing."

Joseph looks away.

We're resting beneath a large tent of skins. It provides shade, but the air is heavy and foul. Bahij, a tall, leathery man with bushy gray hair, stands nearby, observing the woman and us. His arms are folded and his grinning mouth reveals few teeth. We're in the company of shepherds, nomads who move with the seasons in order to graze their flock. In the rainy winter months the sheep are driven higher up along the north side of the mountains; in summer they are kept nearer the springs. Their son, even now, is close by with the herd.

When the woman makes her last stitch, I leave Joseph's side and walk to where Bahij stands. I thank him as I press several coins into his hand. Then my sons and I lift Joseph onto the new litter, strap him down with the goat hair rope I also purchased from the couple. Finally, we carry him outside. And as we do, he pleads with his eyes, one last time, for me to leave him.

"If you weren't always stuffing your face you wouldn't be as heavy as three mountain goats," Benjamin banters as he carries the foot of the litter.

"Joseph, tell him he would tire carrying a rabbit," Aaron says, holding the litter at the head.

And between them, Joseph remains silent.

"Perhaps we should drag him on the ground like a sheave of wheat." In jest, Benjamin slightly dips the sturdy pallet. And Aaron responds by saying that maybe Benjamin should be the one dragged on the ground.

And on it goes; my sons bantering back and forth, hoping to rouse Joseph, to keep him clinging to life until help can be found. And I bless them for it as I walk silently beside them. We've already passed En Gedi. If we keep this pace we should make Masada before nightfall. My one concern is, will Joseph live to see it?

"Joseph, you must drink." He burns with fever, and quakes in my arms. I cup his head while Aaron puts the goat skin bag of water to his mouth. For hours we've been walking the hard-mud ground, keeping a furious pace. If only we had time to kill that goat—to make fresh broth for Joseph to drink. But there is none. Even if there was, we are worn to the bone and have no strength for a hunt. We've taken refuge from the sun in a low lying cave. But I'm determined to push on to Masada. It is Joseph's only chance.

"You must drink," I repeat, still cupping his head while Aaron slowly squeezes the bag trying to force droplets of water between Joseph's dry, cracked lips, but most of it just dribbles down his chin.

"The smell is worse," Aaron whispers, bending closer to me. As soldiers, we know what that means.

Benjamin tears a strip off what's left of my robe, has Aaron wet it, then places the wet rag across Joseph's forehead. "It won't bring the fever down but maybe it will make him more comfortable."

I release Joseph, then rise to my feet. "We must press on to Masada."

"We must rest or we'll never see Masada." Benjamin looks at me with a frown. "You know I'm right, Father. Let us take a few minutes to regain our strength."

I struggle with Benjamin's words, then finally clasp his shoulder and nod. He speaks wisdom. We've driven ourselves most of the day; resting little, hardly eating. It's doubtful we could make Masada in our condition. But Benjamin has always been the practical one.

"We'll rest," I say grudgingly. "But only for a short while." I stretch out on the dirt floor nearby and pillow my head with my arm. But I don't close my eyes. I'm listening to Joseph's slow, ragged breathing.

"Will we take the Serpent's Path?" Benjamin says as we stand at the base of a massive mountain of rock and look up at the steep winding trail before us. There are only three ways up the summit to the flat rock-top of Masada: this one, the Serpent's Path, on the eastern side, and two on the western; and the Serpent's Path is the most treacherous.

"There's no time to walk around the mountain; not if we wish to make the climb before nightfall. And it would be suicide in the dark, especially carrying Joseph. It's the Serpent's Path or nothing." I examine the sky where the sun glows red and its fingers already dip below the horizon. "We must hurry."

Benjamin, who has just taken his turn at the foot of the litter, nods. "I only pray we have the strength. We are nearly done in, Father."

We've been walking for hours. Our faces are blistered; our feet cracked and swollen and bleeding. We are worn to the bone, and the steep uphill climb looks so formidable I'm almost ready to order a short rest when I hear Aaron's voice.

"Joseph is unconscious. I can't rouse him."

I bend over the litter and peer at Joseph's pale, lifeless face. His dried, cracked lips are bleeding, and when I put my hand to his nostrils, I feel little air. "Every minute counts, now," I say, as the wind blows dust in our faces. But when I see Benjamin and Aaron so haggard, I add, "We can't rest, but we can lighten our load. Leave everything but the coins."

And so we shed our scrips and water skins and other bundles, and lay the large bags of silver between Joseph's legs, leaving us with only our tunics and the daggers at our waist, and Joseph's litter between us.

Then we begin the slow torturous climb up the narrow, stony trail; Benjamin at the foot of the litter, I, at the head—for before Aaron's sandal even touched the Serpent's Path, he became faint, and would have dropped the litter if I hadn't been by his side. He now walks behind us, barely keeping up. And as we ascend the steep mountain, we drop great beads of sweat and the last of our strength until we can barely put one foot in front of the other. It's as if we're climbing to the top of the world. Even the sight of Herod's Hanging Palace—the massive three-tiered villa built into the distant cliff-face—doesn't revive me. We move like swamp turtles, swallowing dust as the wind whips our faces. I pray to *Hashem* to give me the strength to take one more step, then another, then another. And when I think even *Hashem's* hand can't move me any further, I hear a voice ringing out from atop the far-off fortress wall.

"State your business or I'll have my archers drop you where you stand."

We grind to a halt, all panting for air. My muscles quiver as I tighten sweaty palms around the poles of the heavy litter that is becoming slippery in my hands. But my mouth is as dry as the Negev, and I can't speak.

"I said, state your business!" the voice rings out again.

I swallow hard, then run my dry tongue over parched, cracked lips. "I am Ethan, General under the command of Eleazar ben Simon, here on official business."

"Ethan? The Hasmonaean priest? Son of Reuben? Is that *you*?"

"It is."

"You mean to tell me I was summoned to this wall just to witness the assent of that loutish braggart who stole Rebekah, niece of Abner the Pharisee, the Jewel of Jerusalem, right from under my nose?" The sternness has gone from the voice.

I squint up at the speck of a man atop the wall. He's surrounded by a cluster of armed soldiers. In the fading light, and from this distance, I can't see his face, but the voice I recognize. "Josiah?" At once my ears are filled with exploding laughter, and I know it's my boyhood friend, a Zealot also, the one who pleaded with me to follow him to Masada two years ago after becoming sickened by all the infighting in Jerusalem.

"Josiah, send your men to help carry Joseph. He's injured," I say, not wanting to waste any more time on meaningless banter. And before long, a swarm of men descend upon us, taking the litter from me and Benjamin, while others help Aaron navigate the remaining harsh terrain.

When at last we gain entrance into the fortress, I'm ushered into the upper tier of the Northern Palace, the palace that once was Herod's living quarters. And then I'm directed to a large, lavish room. I carry two sacks of silver, the size of small boulders, by their necks. Benjamin follows, carrying two others. Aaron is not with us for he's gone to help tend Joseph.

It's cool here, with thick stone walls covered in clean bright plaster and painted frescos. I'm no longer accustomed to such splendor or cleanliness. The rebels have not reduced this palace to ruins like those in Jerusalem did to Herod's palace there. I feel strangely out of place as I track dirt across the gleaming black and white tiled floor to where Josiah stands on a columned semi-circular balcony. To one side, a simply dressed leathery-faced man of uncertain age sits on a long stone bench. I know him. He's Eleazar ben Ya'ir, commander of Masada.

Josiah laughs when he sees us. "Have you crawled here all the way from Jerusalem? Never have I seen such dirty men! Or smelled riper ones, either."

Benjamin and I extend our greetings, then Josiah begins the questioning while Eleazar remains silent on his bench. "What is this business you spoke of?" Josiah says, his face furrowed, his voice authoritative. Two years heading security in this wilderness outpost has made him more serious than I remember, though there's still ample evidence of a more genial nature. "What is your mission?"

By way of answer, I plop my heavy sacks on the bench beside Eleazar. Benjamin does the same. Then I untie one, plunge in my hand, and pull out a fistful of coins. "For the rebellion. Eleazar ben Simon commissioned us to bring this to you. To fortify your defenses; to purchase arms and supplies." When I open my palm to display the coins, a few fall from my hand and skitter across the floor.

Josiah's eyebrows arch as he looks at the four large, bulging sacks, but he doesn't move from his place by the column. "It's a welcome gift. It will go far in filling our storehouses with food and weaponry. An easy matter too, for we have contacts in Damascus, and our men are expert in navigating the tunnels."

I nod. I know the tunnels of which Josiah speaks. They snake the interior of the Judean hills, and were dug by merchants who used them for years; merchants who preferred to smuggle their goods in and out of the countryside rather than pay Roman taxes.

"I'm grateful to you and to Eleazar ben Simon," Josiah says, folding his arms and leaning against the column. "We've heard how all the priests perished defending the altar. It's a great loss. Eleazar ben Simon will be missed."

"But it pleased him to know his last command would be fulfilled."

"So . . . the rumors of Eleazar hiding the Temple treasure are true?" Josiah eyes me carefully.

"They are."

"Then we can expect more contributions in the future?"

"I made a vow and hope to fulfill it. If you give me men to keep away the bandits that roam the area, we'll go back to Hyrcania and retrieve what remains there." Then I quickly tell him about Lamech.

"Done. You can have however many men you require, and I'll personally command them. Only . . . when your vow is fulfilled I hope you and Rebekah and your sons will join us in the safety of our fortress. Many Jerusalem survivors have already come with their families."

Josiah pushes himself off the column and finally bends over the stone bench to pick up one of the bags. He holds it for a second as if calculating its weight, then puts it down. "I see Abner isn't with you." He frowns as if suddenly understanding the obvious. "I grieve your loss. He was a dutiful son; a noble fighter for Israel. But in this war, we've all lost those we love. Still . . . I was greatly distressed about Esther."

"Esther? What about Esther?"

Josiah is clearly surprised. "You didn't know? I saw her myself, roped to the other captives."

It's as if sand clogs my throat. "Where . . .when?" I sputter.

"When my men and I disguised ourselves as nomads and journeyed to the outskirts of Titus's siege walls trying to rescue those fleeing Jerusalem. We heard how bad it was, and that the end was near. Eleazar and I thought it worth the risk. We knew about the scarcity of food in the city. And we knew that many who managed to flee would die if left unaided." Josiah shakes his head. "Even so, scores died on the way here; a cruel end after their brave efforts. We saw the Romans slaughter the old and infirm, men and woman alike, and the very young, leaving only those who could be auctioned as slaves or used in the arenas. Esther was among them."

"*Impossible*." My head reels. "She's in Pella with Rebekah."

"I tell you I saw her. I've known Esther all my life. It's no mistake. It *was* her."

Benjamin places his hand on my shoulder. "We'll find her, Father."

"Don't torment yourselves with that thought," Josiah says. "Thousands of women were taken. And they'll be sold throughout the Empire."

"But first they'll either be sold to slavers along the way to Caesarea Maritima or made to board ships at the Caesarean port," I say, setting my jaw. "Either way, they'll travel the Via Maris, the Way of the Sea. And we'll travel it with them."

"Careful, Ethan, you're speaking like a fool. When the Romans see you and your sons, they might just add you to their string of captives." Josiah points to Benjamin. "And this strong, broad son of yours would make fine sport for them in the arena."

"Not if we go as slavers ourselves."

Josiah throws up his hands. "Most of the slavers are Greeks. You could never pass for a Greek."

"Not a Greek; a Syrian from Damascus. No one would think it odd that a Syrian looks for slaves."

Eleazar ben Ya'ir rises to his feet. "What you propose is folly, but I don't fault you, nor will I try to dissuade you. Rather, let us make a bargain. Josiah will accompany you to Hyrcania, and from the gold and silver gained there, he'll give you a tenth, to go and purchase your daughter, if possible, and as many other of our people that you can. And when you have, you may bring them here, to this refuge."

My heart is elated. "A good bargain," I say. "And as soon as Joseph is well, I'll leave for Hyrcania."

Eleazar frowns. "You can't wait. Titus has razed Jerusalem, leaving only Herod's three towers standing. Now that jackal, after resting his troops, will turn his attention on us, and we must be ready. Go—you and your sons, and bathe; not in the public bathhouse but the private one in the Western Palace, and enjoy the cold plunge bath and the heat of the caldarium. I will send someone to scrape and oil your skin. Clean clothes will be brought, as well as food. Then eat and rest yourselves. At first light, you must go with Josiah."

When I hesitate, Josiah puts his hand on my shoulder. "Do not fear. Joseph will be well cared for. We have no physician, but even now, a skilled midwife, who understands the healing arts, attends him."

My heart is not in this. How can I go off digging for gold when my son lies so near death?

Seeing I'm still unmoved, Josiah leans closer and adds, "I make this pledge, a runner will be sent to bring you news if Joseph's condition worsens. Now, will you go with me tomorrow?"

I should stay with my son. If he dies, I wish to hear his last words, to feel his hand in mine, to kiss him as a father should. But I'm a soldier, a man of war. What else can I say but, "yes."

I'm kneeling beside Joseph's bed. His skin is strangely lucent like the uncooked white of an egg. His chest moves in small, rapid jerks as he struggles to pull air into his lungs. He has been bathed from head to toe, and lies beneath a blanket, unclothed. His injured leg protrudes. The filthy packing has been removed, the wound bathed with wine. But oh, how it smells! The gash has become an ugly festering sore, oozing puss, and black in color. And the leg? Dead as the leopard whose hide we used for Joseph's litter, for mortification has already set in. I know the leg must come off, but I try not to think about it now.

I'm told the midwife has not left his side, not even while Aaron and Benjamin and I slept. Even now she's shuffling about in that quiet way of hers—small and hunched and wrinkled—brewing herbs that smell strangely like hyssop and vinegar.

We're in the Western Palace. The administration wing, the service wing, the royal quarters, the storerooms, all have been converted into living quarters for the several hundred families billeted here. The remaining inhabitants of Masada are scattered throughout the three-tiered Northern Palace, as well as the rooms inside the casement wall of the cliff face.

I feel Joseph's burning brow. Already his clean wool blanket is damp with sweat. "Joseph. Your brothers and I are leaving for Hyrcania."

Joseph's lashes flutter, then his eyes open. His badly cracked lips are covered with the midwife's salve. "I . . . wish . . . I was . . . going." His voice is as thin as a moth's wing.

"Don't talk." I touch my fingers lightly to his mouth. "I just wanted you to know we are going to finish the job."

"But this time we're bringing a sizable army," Benjamin blurts, kneeling beside me. "Josiah is leading one hundred men. Lamech and his thugs won't bother us this time."

"And there will be plenty of hands to carry the treasure back to Masada," Aaron adds, he too now crouches by the bed. "Before you know it, we'll be here telling you all about the things we've found."

"You're in good hands," I say, frowning at the midwife who's waving at us, trying to get us to leave. "You're in good hands," I repeat, rising to my feet. But it's not the midwife I'm referring to. It's *Hashem.* For only His hand can snatch Joseph from the jaws of death now.

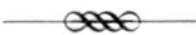

After I've directed some of Josiah's men to bring up the rest of the silver coins from the chest in the well, my sons and I and a few other men dig in the cistern of the columned courtyard, the third location mentioned in the scrolls. We nearly missed it, since all but two of the columns are utterly destroyed, and even these are nearly covered with rubble. But it was Aaron who discovered the site after tripping over the edge of a column stump.

A deep layer of sediment covers the floor of the cistern. We dig, using the large, new shovels we've carried from Masada, and in no time expose the still partially plastered floor. In one section we uncover a trench running parallel to the joints between the wall and floor where quarter-round molding seals the two. Josiah's rebels, using pickaxes and shovels, break through the hardened floor of the trench and before long, uncover a huge stone box, the size of an Egyptian sarcophagus, carved right into bedrock. The cover takes six men to lift, and no one is prepared for what lays inside. It's filled to the top with disc-shaped gold and silver ingots, coins, gold bracelets and neck chains. Astonishment covers our faces. Only Josiah is calm, and displays his former good nature by looking down at the vast treasure and quipping, "Not bad for a day's work."

The following morning at first light, Benjamin finds an elaborate sepulcher, nearly intact, on a small hill southwest of the fortress, and at once I declare it to be the site of the second location described in the scrolls. The sepulcher is built like a room of stone above the ground, square in shape and having several steps that lead into another, smaller room, one hewn out of solid stone and lined with three stone benches to hold the dead, though I see no dead on them. Even so, my sons and I are reluctant to desecrate the tomb. Not Josiah. Without so much as a flick of an eyelash, he orders his men to enter it and lay their pickaxes to its base. I don't think less of him. His concern is for the living. Does my reluctance show that mine is for those dead and dying . . . for my Abner and Joseph? Well . . . so be it.

After an hour of hacking and displacing dirt, part of the foundation gives way, making the stone chamber above, topple to one side, causing the dozen soldiers inside to scramble through the partial opening that remained. It takes another hour to clear the debris and shore up the leaning sepulcher before anyone can go back inside. But shortly afterward, we're rewarded when one of the men spots a niche in the wall, partially uncovered by the previous collapse, and from which protrudes a large cedar chest. And when the heavy box is loosened, then pulled from its hiding place and opened, we see it is full of gold ingots. One hundred in all. Josiah had one of his men count them.

During this time a minor incident occurs. Of the hundred men Josiah brought to Hyrcania, only twenty are used as diggers, the rest are posted as sentries around the summit. And Josiah's strategy pays off, for when two men try to breach the perimeter, his archers quickly make an end to them. Later when I investigate, I recognize the dead men as belonging to Lamech. Spies? To discover our activities? Was Lamech nearby? Who can say? But with such overwhelming strength on our side, I hardly consider the matter. I'm eager to conclude my business here and be off in search of Esther.

According to the copper scroll, there is one more treasure site in the Valley of Achor. I've not told Josiah this because my sons and I differ on the scroll's translation. The hammered letters are difficult to read. Aaron and Benjamin, and even Joseph believe the scroll indicates we are to dig in the middle of "two buildings," while I think it reads "two chambers." It could take weeks, even months to explore all the possible sites, time we cannot spare if we hope to recover Esther. I've instructed my sons to remain silent, as well, but have promised them and myself we will return, and right this wrong.

So we use the remainder of the day to stuff bags with treasure, bags without number and small enough to be carried back to Masada by Josiah's men tomorrow, though it is evident they will have to make many trips back and forth to carry it all. But four bags, larger and more bulbous than the rest, are set aside for me. I don't take inventory of their contents. Is it exactly the tithe Eleazar promised? Or just Josiah fitting what he can into this number of bags and claiming it a tenth? It doesn't matter. They hold a king's ransom. Enough to buy thousands of slaves in the marketplace.

Now it's nearing sunset, and my sons and I are just settling down for the meal of herb-cheese and raisins provided for us when one of the sentries shouts, "A runner comes!" and my heart stops. *Joseph!* He must have worsened!

I jump to my feet and dash to where the sentry stands peering northward at the shadowed path, and see a cloud of dust and a small figure sprinting towards us. He's a speck, this runner, insignificant-looking amid the great expanse of the Judean wilderness. Behind him, mountains tower toward heaven, mountains almost white in the sunlight. Surely, someone so inconsequential can bring no harm.

How difficult it is to wait! I would run to meet him but years of living the disciplined life of a soldier prevent me. My sons have gathered by my side. Josiah, too. We all wait, and silently watch the runner. Finally, the nameless man reaches the summit. His tunic is drawn between his legs and tied at the waist to enhance his speed. His sandaled feet are encrusted with blood and dirt. His sweat makes his skin glisten like an oiled wrestler.

"As ordered, I bring you news of a change." The runner doesn't look at me but speaks directly to Josiah. "Joseph, son of Ethan, has died of his wound."

He speaks like I'm not even here! I suppose it's an unfortunate occupation to be a messenger of bad news, but right now I could break his teeth or bloody his face. "Tell me . . . was he conscious before he died?" I say between tight lips. "Did he speak?"

The runner looks confused. Obviously this was not part of his duty, to commit to memory the words of a dying man. "I don't know," he finally says. "I only know the midwife said his blood was too poisoned, and she couldn't save him."

Josiah dismisses him, and at once my sons and I fall on each other's necks and weep. The pain in my heart is unbearable. It's as though a thousand daggers thrust and cut. It will kill me, this grief. Even with the arms of my sons around me, I cannot bear it. The daggers carve a hole, making my heart an empty basin that must be filled or I'll die. And so I fill it with every morsel of rancor and enmity my mind can conjure. I'm a man who hates the world. A man filled with loathing and hostility; no longer my brother's keeper. Oh, how my hand desires to shed blood! To see the blood of my enemies pooled at my feet.

"He was a fine man. A good son. A brave soldier." I hear Josiah say.

"It would be better if the Romans had killed him," I finally respond, almost in a croak. "There's honor in that. It would ease the pain. But to be killed by one of our own people! How can I bear that, Josiah? It makes me want to slice the world into pieces."

"I understand. But consider this: today we killed two of those bandits. Two paid for the life of one."

"But not *Lamech*," I spit. "Lamech, who beats wool merchants to death for their money. Lamech, who robs his own starving countrymen. Lamech, who cared nothing for our Holy City, our Holy Temple. Lamech, who killed my son for *gain*." I wipe my wet cheeks with the back of my hand. "All the wealth in the world is not worth Joseph's life."

Josiah's strong hand grasps my arm. "Whatever you ask, I'll do. My men are at your command. What is it you wish?"

"Lamech's blood on my dagger." And even as I say it, I see Aaron's face fall, and Benjamin's too.

"Shedding his blood will not bring Joseph back. What of your oath to Eleazar? What of Esther?" Aaron says.

I stare at him, my eyes hard. "I haven't forgotten either. But first I must kill this snake."

It takes most of the next day to catch up with the snake who has made his way back to his hole. From my place of concealment I watch him lounge at the mouth of his cave alongside his men. Our overwhelming strength at Hyrcania obviously made him abandon all hope of despoiling us. Josiah, and fifty of his men, have come with me and my sons. The rest have gone to Masada with some of the treasure. So we have fifty to subdue Lamech's ten or twelve. I don't feel shame or pity that my enemy is so outnumbered. I feel only hate.

Without waiting to formulate a battle plan, I let out a loud cry and charge toward the cave, surprising Lamech's men and mine. The bandits drop bread and cups and rush inside, and I right behind them with my dagger waving. I slash and thrust like a wild man, plunging my blade into one rogue after another. When Josiah's men finally join me, they make a quick end to the rest, and within minutes the floor is littered with bodies, though not one is ours. How many I killed, I cannot say. It's all a blur. I only know I feel profound disappointment that my dagger, dripping with blood, has no other foe to strike.

I stand in the middle of the cave, my chest heaving for want of air, and watch Josiah's men collect bodies, then lay them in a row for the diggers. They are, after all, Jews, reason enough to honor them with a burial.

"Ten dead, in all," reports one of the men when at last all the bodies have been collected.

"That's it then," Josiah says, clasping my shoulder. "You have avenged your son."

I nod, and am about to leave, then I stop. "I will see him. I will see this jackal before I go." And so I walk down the line of bodies, examining each face until at last I reach the end and realize Lamech is not among them. "He's not here!" I shout, hardly believing my own words. "He's not among the dead!"

At once a dozen men scour the cave, my sons among them.

"There's an opening in the back, Father," Aaron says, coming up to me, his face strained. "It was concealed by baskets and rush mats." Aaron holds his dagger in his hand. "I'll go in."

"It's for me to go . . . for me to . . . ."

"No Father." Aaron bars my way, and the look in his one good eye stops me. There's no hatred in it. Only a wistful sadness that makes me feel diminished somehow. I watch him and Benjamin disappear into the opening. And then I wait. And for the first time in many months I think of Jesus. He promised us a kingdom. Why, then, didn't He drive out the Romans and set it up? Why has He allowed His people, the Jews, to suffer so? Was it all a lie? That promise of His? No . . . not a lie. I was only a boy but I heard Him speak. I saw Him die, saw the sky blacken, felt the earth shake. And I saw His wounds, too, after He came out of the tomb. After he rose from the dead. Yes . . . I *saw* them. So it wasn't a lie. But oh, how far we are from that kingdom now, that kingdom of love and forgiveness and peace and joy that He spoke so much about. *Where was it?* For one fleeting second I yearn for Jesus and His peace. Then I remember Lamech, and the Master fades from my thoughts.

"Let me see his blood on your dagger," I say, when at long last my sons reappear.

"You'll not find it, Father," Aaron says, looking at me with pity. "The opening leads to a narrow tunnel which ends as a small cave on the north side of the mountain, a cave with an egress. The coward has escaped; deserted his men in order to save himself."

"Give me the word, my friend, and I'll order my men to scour the hills," Josiah says, his eyes blazing.

I look at my Aaron. His face, even after all these years of fighting and bloodshed, is still like the face of an angel with its delicate contours framed by soft matted curls. His one damaged eye attests to his ferocity as a warrior; but the other, the eye that probes and pierces me so deeply, is hopeful and kind, but sorrowful, too. And I know he is praying that I'll rise to the higher calling. And though my heart desires to shed more blood, I bow to his better instincts.

"We'll not waste time looking for one rogue." I wipe my dagger on the sleeve of my tunic and slip it into the belt at my waist. "We'll return to Hyrcania, and in the morning, you, Josiah, must go to Masada with the rest of the treasure, with wealth enough to supply your army for years to come, while I and my sons must head north."

"We search for Esther?" Benjamin asks.

"We search for Esther," I say, watching Aaron offer prayers of thanksgiving to *Hashem*.

Rebekah

On the road to Caesarea 70 A.D.

CHAPTER 7

"She didn't even know murex snails were found in Dor."

"Yes, Zechariah, you told me . . . a dozen times."

"But wouldn't she know that? Coming from Dor as she claims? After all, it's big business there, and the Tyrian dye from these snails is famous. All the imperial families of the Empire have worn its purple." Zechariah glances back at Kyra who trails behind. "And when I mentioned Dor's temples to Zeus and Astarte, and purposely described them wrong, she didn't correct me. I'm telling you, I have a bad feeling, Rebekah. It's like an anchor in my chest. It always lodges there just before trouble comes. And I'm never wrong."

"What could I do? Leave her behind at the mercy of Argos? She asked . . . she *pleaded*. What could I do?" I say this for the hundredth time. Oh, how Zechariah frets when he suspects an ill omen is looming. He's been complaining about Kyra since we left Pella and we're already far from the Decapolis, having passed Scythopolis nearly three days ago.

"And why did she want to take us out of our way and spend the night in Megiddo? Can you answer me that? She was so insistent, too. Getting all red-faced; looking like she was going to burst into tears. It's almost as if she were meeting someone there. But would she tell me when I asked? No. She wouldn't even tell you, but only talked about having a sore foot as if neither of us had sore feet from this journey. And what does that have to do with Megiddo, anyway? So what am I to think? Can my thoughts of her be good? I'm telling you, she's trouble. Mark my words, Argos will come for her. He's not one to give up anything easily."

I sigh, but don't answer. In a way I feel guilty. I know Zechariah doesn't speak out of a spiteful nature, for his heart of love is as big as Mount Carmel. The truth is, he's burdened for my safety. I've heard him praying far into the night while I was busy with my own prayers for Esther. Soon we must stop and make camp, and that adds to his worry for I know his concern is greatest during the dark hours. But now that we're west of Megiddo, having passed it without stopping and without incident and with only a mild complaint from Kyra, I hope his mind will be more at ease.

We're still south of the Mount Carmel ridge, on the Caesarea-Scythopolis highway, scattering pebbles with our sandals, causing them to skitter across the dusty road. The large stone markers that tell us the distance we've traveled also tell us they were built by the 10th legion under the command of Marcus Ulpius Traianus only a year ago. It's hardly the Via Appia, the main thoroughfare of Rome, and one, they say, that's built of smooth, tightly-fitting paving stones. Rather, our road is lined with kerb stones and paved with pebbles and sand and little else.

Though trees and shrubs have been cleared on both sides of the road to deter any ambush by rebels, I'm happy to see that Roman axes have not decimated the hills. Lush trees still flourish there, nourished by the rains carried to these parts on the pinions of the westerly Mediterranean winds.

I glance around at the many caravans that clog the dirt path running parallel to our road. The path is made of smooth earth; built by the Romans for their horses since it is kinder to hooves than the pebbled road. The path is heavily traveled by caravans coming from the Decapolis with their wares.

"It's more crowded than usual," Zechariah says, mopping his sweaty brow. "Merchants everywhere must have heard that Titus is marching his army back to Caesarea; an army with booty enough to spend on the most lavish goods."

Two Midianites push by, each wearing an undergarment belted by a wide leather strap, and over that a sheepskin cloak, loose and ill-fitting, with the wool facing outward. They're wild looking and rough, like most Midianites, and I wonder if they could be slave hunters. I'm relieved when they pass without glancing our way. But it's evident that Zechariah's fears have become mine.

We travel slowly. Kyra holds us back. She meanders like a mindless child while one traveler after another passes us by. Another large caravan overtakes us, all laden with goods. For Titus? Or for shipment to other parts of the Empire out of Sebastos, Caesarea's man-made harbor?

As the camel drivers laugh and talk and encourage their animals to move faster, I leave the road and follow behind on the dirt path gathering camel chips for my cooking fires. And while I do, I study the men, searching for any who might be the slave hunters we fear. Finally, I laugh at myself for allowing Zechariah's words to disquiet me, then praise God that in two days we'll be in Caesarea.

"She's left the road again," Zechariah grumbles, as he glances over his shoulder.

I turn and see Kyra seated a good distance away, near an oak; not a great oak of Bashan with an impressive trunk and full, rounded top, but a small bushy, prickly-looking tree that hardly invites company. At once I'm irritated by this delay until I see her metal collar glinting in the sun. We've yet to find a way to remove it without injuring her. Now it reminds me of her sad, dangerous state, and I feel pity.

"That makes a dozen times she's stopped today. If I had a more suspicious nature, I'd say she's deliberately trying to slow us down."

"*More* suspicious? Zechariah, you're a bundle of suspicion. You've not stopped speaking of Kyra since we left Pella. Though I understand your concern, I must confess you weary me with your words."

Zechariah thumps his chest with a fist, causing the dust on his tunic to float upward. "In here, I'm uneasy. I tell you, when God stirs me this way, I know trouble is coming." He looks at me sideways, pulling at his beard. "I feel sorry for her, too, Rebekah, but I must be cautious, for both our sakes. And though I hate speaking of this for fear of worrying you, I must tell you that last night I caught Kyra going through one of your bags. When I confronted her she mumbled something about mistaking your bag for hers in the dark. But how was that possible? When yours is made from rushes, and hers from homespun?"

I pull the donkey off the path, allowing the remainder of the caravan to pass, then double back and head for Kyra. Zechariah follows, his face as soft as cheese, and so sweet I feel sorry for being cross. "Forgive my impatience. You're right to be cautious," I say as we walk. And he just smiles.

"Why have you stopped?" I ask Kyra when we reach her.

"Ooooh," she moans, rubbing her bare foot, her dusty sandal lying beside her.

She lifts her leg slightly to show me her sole, while her large green eyes avoid looking at my face. "A pebble was lodged in my sandal, and cut my flesh."

I see only blood-tinged dirt. Without a word, I hand the donkey's bridle to Zechariah, take up one of the water skins, wet a clean rag, then squat in the dirt.

Kyra recoils when I touch the rag to her wound. "No . . . you mustn't. I can do it myself."

I ignore her, and holding her foot firmly by the heel, carefully wipe away the grit. Oh, the faces she makes! First a frown, then a soft bewildered look, and finally her cheeks turn the color of pomegranates before her chin juts out defiantly. I think it odd, all this emotion, until I see that the wound has not been made by the grinding of a pebble. Rather, it's long and thin, with clean edges like the cut from a blade or other sharp object.

Has Kyra inflicted this wound upon herself?

She looks at me as though reading my thoughts. And the longer I take, the more uneasy she becomes, until finally, before I can even apply the olive oil, she pulls her foot from my hands.

"This is unseemly. I'm a slave and should tend myself." With that, she replaces her sandal and springs to her feet.

And we're off again, with Zechariah leading the donkey back to the path while Kyra and I follow. And as we trudge along the gritty hills heading for the Plain of Sharon, I feel a heaviness in my chest. Weighed down by an anchor like Zechariah? Hardly. But though I'm still not convinced Zechariah is right about Kyra, I've decided to watch her more closely.

I stir the bubbling pot of barley as Zechariah pounds three posts into the ground then stretches and secures his robe over them as a tent for Kyra and me. He'll sleep under the stars. The air is still hot and sticky, though it's nearly sunset, and I wonder if I might be better off sleeping beneath the stars as well. I'm grimy from the dust of the road and my own sweat. It will be uncomfortable beneath an airless canopy.

Kyra is close by, rubbing oil into the bottom of her foot. Her limping brought us to a stop earlier than we intended. That foot of hers is more swollen than the first time I saw it. Redder, too. Without proper tending, it could become a problem.

When she sees me watching, she smiles. "You've been so kind all through the trip. You and Zechariah, both. You haven't even let me wash your clothes or cook. And now you insist on *serving* me. And who am I but a worthless slave?" She replaces her sandal, then rises to her feet and limps to where my pot is simmering over a slow-burning dung fire. "At least let me tend the barley while you refresh yourself. I've had worse injuries than this and still managed my chores." She holds out her hand, and reluctantly I give her my wooden spoon.

"It's nearly ready," I say, then go to the tent, and using water from my water bottle and a rag, I wash my face and hands.

"Soon there will be an end to these hills." Zechariah comes over and sits beside me on the rush mat. "I won't lie. I dislike traveling. It will be nice sleeping beneath a roof again."

I nod as I watch Kyra. "Her wound, Zechariah . . . is not a wound one gets from a pebble. She might have . . . she could have . . . ."

"Inflicted it herself? Yes, I suspected as much. But why? Why would she deliberately want to slow us down? Unless she's waiting for someone to catch up. Argos perhaps?"

"It can't be Argos. You should have seen the fear in her eyes when she begged me to let her come. She's terrified of him. This is her chance to be free. It hardly seems reasonable that she would deliberately ruin it. There must be some other explanation."

Kyra's shadow suddenly falls over me. I look up and see her holding two steaming wooden bowls. "I hope you don't mind, but I've added raisins and a bit of cinnamon to conceal the blandness of the barley. I think you'll like it."

I thank her and take the bowl, along with a piece of flatbread. Did she overhear? Her face, blank as parchment, tells me nothing. When she returns to the barley pot I ask Zechariah what he thinks. But before he can answer, she's back with her own bowl and takes a seat beside me on the mat.

"I'll miss you both when we part in Caesarea," Kyra says, blowing on her steaming pottage. "I can't remember when I was treated with such kindness."

I actually believe her. I actually think there are tears in her eyes. I actually feel sorry for thinking ill of her. "Are there any in Dor you still call 'friend?'" I say hopefully, for the thought of this desolate, young woman all alone fills me with sadness.

"Dor? Yes . . . there should still be a cousin or two."

"No parents?" Zechariah asks.

I think he feels sorry, too.

Kyra scoops barley with her flatbread. Her movements are slow, deliberate, as though she's thinking of an answer.

"Have you no parents still living?" I repeat Zechariah's question.

"Why should I speak of those who sold me as if I were one of their goats?" Kyra shrugs as though trying to convey contempt but all she conveys is a wounded spirit, for her eyes rim with tears. "To me they are dead."

"You're angry," I say, "without even knowing their reasons? Perhaps they were poor, and in debt?"

Kyra wipes the tears from her cheeks and looks away.

"Will you not try to forgive them? As Jesus taught? You've heard Zechariah speak of this many times." Without thinking, I brush the stray wisps of her hair from one of her damp cheeks, then let my fingers linger. "Begin your new life now, by extending this forgiveness. What better way to celebrate your freedom?"

Oh, those green eyes! How they stare at me. Full of sadness and anger both. But her cheek remains turned toward my caress, like a starving little bird grateful for any meager kernel a cruel world was willing to dispense.

"For some there is no freedom, there is no forgiveness, there is only suffering," she finally says, pulling away.

Camels groan behind us. And donkeys bray. All around, in little pockets, are other travelers who have stopped for the night and set up camp. Laughter and voices fill the air. But we are silent, Zechariah and I. What can we say to Kyra's sad comment? Can we say "Come to Jesus and He will heal you? He'll take your heart of stone and plow it with His love, creating deep, rich furrows in which He'll plant a beautiful new garden?" No. She has heard all this before at Zechariah's house. So, instead, we sit close to one another, quietly eating our barley, and watching the great orange and red sun slip behind the horizon.

But Kyra's words haunt me. They remind me that somewhere along the Via Maris, the highway that runs along the coastline of the Mediterranean Sea, my Esther is among strangers, and frightened, too. And I'm crushed by the thought.

Strange rustling sounds awaken me. They're so close I'm sure a thief has entered out midst. Kyra and I sleep under Zechariah's tent. Zechariah, himself, is nearby. I see his great bulk curled on the ground just outside. But I see another form further away, bending over our bundles. I resist the urge to cry out. Instead, I prop myself up on one elbow, and when I do, I notice Kyra is not beside me. Where could she be?

I squint into the darkness at the moving shadow. It's smaller that I first thought; merely a wisp. Something drops to the ground and the thief turns slightly to pick it up. And then, by moonlight, I see Kyra's face.

I rise to my feet and, quiet as a cat, tip-toe to where my bags and baskets sit in a heap, then lunge for her arm. "What are you doing! Those are *my* bags."

She shrieks like an owl, waking up those around us. At once, curses fill the air, and for a moment I fear one of the camel drivers will come over, for I see him rise to his feet. But when Zechariah hurries to my side the moment passes.

"What is this? What's happening?" Zechariah looks at my over-turned bag, then how I grip Kyra's arm, and he pulls her from me. "Tell me what you are searching for!" he says, shaking her fiercely. "Don't lie, or so help me I'll leave you to these camel drivers."

Kyra begins to whimper. Again, curses fill the air. And then Zechariah does something unexpected. The big ox actually lifts Kyra into the air by cupping his hands beneath her arms, and after carrying her to a spot a good distance from all the sleepy drivers, puts her down. I follow behind, carrying my bag with me.

"Speak!" he hisses. "And I want the truth."

Kyra sobs into her hands, and I see Zechariah falter. That heart of his, that big tender heart that loves the world and everyone in it, is unraveling before my eyes, undone by a young woman's tears.

So I step forward and place my palm beneath Kyra's chin to lift her face. "Why were you going through my things?" My own heart is greatly moved, and gentles my voice, perhaps because I'm remembering how Esther used to cry this way. "What were you looking for?"

Does she sense my love? I think not, because when she tilts her tear-smudged face towards me, she trembles with fear. "What were you looking for?" I repeat.

"Your cup," she says, jutting her chin defiantly, but expecting me to strike her, too, for she flinches when I move my hand.

"Tell us what mischief you're up to." Zechariah crowds closer, having collected himself, but my fingers, which brush his shoulder lightly, keep him in check.

"Here," I say, fumbling in my striped rush bag and pulling out the stone cup. "Here it is." Zechariah gasps. So does Kyra. "Now what do you want to do with it?"

Kyra is clearly frightened by the cup for she steps backward. "I . . . wanted to pray to it . . . for healing . . . for the healing of my foot."

Zechariah shakes his head. "Why do you persist in lying? Tell us the truth and we will help you. Has Argos put you up to this? Were you to steal the cup for him?"

"No! I swear!" Kyra drops to her knees in front of us. "I only wanted to heal my foot . . . so I wouldn't slow you down. I know you speak against me, Zechariah. I've heard you. But you speak falsely. I mean no harm. I'm just a worthless slave trying to reclaim her life . . . just a worthless slave."

I kneel in the dirt beside Kyra, the cup in my hand.

"You don't believe me. Do you?" Kyra says, looking at me imploringly. "Even by moonlight I see how your lips are tightly pinched. Like Zechariah, you think I'm lying." She begins weeping again.

"Be still," I say, placing the cup and my bag on the ground beside me. After making her sit, I take her injured foot between my hands. And then I pray, softly, fervently. I pray prayers I know Kyra doesn't understand, prayers for the healing of her spirit and soul, as well as her body. As I pray, heat flows from my palms into Kyra's foot, and startles her. She stops crying. Her breathing becomes heavy, almost like the panting of a frightened animal. Behind me, Zechariah prays, too.

When I'm finished, I release Kyra, scoop the cup from the ground and rise to my feet. As I do, I hear her shout, "It's gone! My wound is gone!" I feel her hand tug on mine. "You didn't believe me, yet you prayed. You still asked your cup to heal me."

"No. I asked my God to heal you."

"But . . . why?"

"Because my God wishes you to be healed. In every way."

"I don't understand this, but I do understand why Argos wants your cup. It's more powerful than his knots or incantations. But he would never use it as you do. He would not be kind or generous. He would only use it to enhance his own power; to increase his reputation and wealth."

"It's not the cup, Kyra. The cup is only stone." But by the way she shakes her head, I know she doesn't believe me.

We're nearing the edge of the rocky Samarian hills. To the right is the Carmel Ridge; ahead, the Plain of Sharon with its lovely flowers, oak forests, and swamps. We still trail the same caravans we've been following since passing Scythopolis. The noisy chatter of the drivers and the steady plodding of their camels give me comfort.

Since Kyra's healing, Zechariah, too, seems more at ease. I won't say he trusts her any more than before. But he's at peace. I think he believes God has some purpose for her being here since He took the trouble to heal her. In any event, I welcome the peace. Though we still fear the slave hunters, the presence of such a large caravan gives us a feeling of protection, however false that might be.

"I've decided to stay in Caesarea until you've found your daughter." Zechariah's bushy gray beard flutters in the meager breeze. "Once you two are reunited and safely joined to a caravan heading for the Decapolis, I'll push on to Ephesus."

My heart swells with gratitude. *Dear sweet, faithful Zechariah.* "Thank you," I mumble. I'm so grateful, not only for his continued protection but for his absolute faith that I'll find Esther.

"I'll be better company, now that my mind is no longer troubled about Kyra." He speaks freely for Kyra trails far behind. She's been trailing behind all day, though her foot is healed. The one consolation is she doesn't stop beside the road anymore.

"Perhaps we've both let our thoughts run wild," I say with a chuckle.

Before he can answer, I hear Kyra scream. When I turn, I see a man, his back toward me, beating her with his fists.

"Why didn't you do as I said?" the man shouts, striking her again and again. "I told you to meet me in Megiddo!"

It's Argos's voice. No mistaking it. I drop the donkey's bridle and race toward Kyra. Argos has her on the ground now, kicking her in the chest and ribs, while three large men, unknown to me but obviously companions of Argos, stand nearby, watching.

"Stop!" I scream. "Stop! You'll kill her."

One of Argos's friends grabs me and holds me in place. "This is not your affair," he growls. "Argos has every right to chastise his slave."

"Zechariah!" I scream. But there's no need to yell. Zechariah is already by my side, facing the man who has me by my wrists. And with one good thump of his fist, he knocks the man backward. The other two approach, but when they see Zechariah's great size and fierce expression, they back away.

"I waited all night for you to bring the cup! While you spent the time resting, I wore myself out pacing!" The veins on Argos's neck look like squirming asps, as his fists and feet rain blow after blow. I hear the sickening sound of bones snapping.

Kyra offers no struggle. It's as if she's been expecting this, waiting for it; as though it was her fate to be here on this dusty road and abused in such a manner. A crowd has gathered. Two of the camel drivers have pulled daggers from someplace inside their robes, but their faces show confusion, and they stand idly by holding their weapons as though not knowing what to do.

"What's happening?" people murmur all around us.

I hear Kyra whimper; see Argos raise his sandaled foot for one final blow. But before he can slam his foot into her neck I jump on his back and claw his face with my nails. Zechariah, who has been busy keeping the three men at bay, shouts for me to stop. But I don't. And after Argos finally casts me, like a bag of grain, onto the dirt next to Kyra's motionless body, he turns to the crowd. Then leaning over Kyra, he pulls her limp body up by the metal band around her neck and shows them the tag.

"My runaway slave. Worthless slime. I'm done with her!" He lets her drop backward onto the dirt with a thud, then points to me. "I could have you arrested for your interference!"

But the sight of the small, battered body with blood oozing from lips and ears and eyes, has horrified the throng of onlookers. And even Argos, in his rage, sees this and understands that the crowd is against him. He lowers his trembling finger, and throwing back his chin adds, "Yes, I could arrest you. But I choose to let the matter drop." With his hands, he wipes the blood from his cheeks, the blood drawn by my nails, and glares at me. Then he and his three companions head toward the Plain of Sharon.

I kneel by Kyra's side and cradle her head in my arms. Blood streaks her face and tunic. She looks so small, so helpless, so broken.

"The ferryman . . . comes . . . but I have no coin," Kyra says in a ragged voice. Her lips are swollen. "How will I cross the River Styx?"

"Hush. Don't speak." I take the rag from Zechariah, the one he has wet from his water skin. But when I begin washing the blood from Kyra's face, she winces so pitifully I stop.

"*Please,*" Kyra peers at me through eyes nearly swollen shut, "one last kindness. When I die . . . place a coin in my mouth . . . for the ferryman . . . for Charon."

It's useless to tell Kyra she's not going to die. The lie would be an offense. Her breath is fitful and shallow. Most of her ribs are surely broken. Blood still trickles from her nose and mouth. She's like a mist evaporating before my eyes. Over my shoulder I hear Zechariah praying.

"You don't need the ferryman," I say, softly. "You can fly to the afterworld. Zechariah has told you many times before, if you commit yourself to Jesus, if you put your hand in His, He will take you."

"But I . . . lied. I betrayed you. Argos promised . . . he promised me freedom. I came only to steal your cup. That was my one purpose." Kyra sinks deeper into my arms. "Forgive me. You . . . have been so kind. But Argos, he . . . . " Her hand slides limply onto the dirt. "If only . . . Jesus would forgive . . . if only it could be His hand that takes me . . . ."

"Jesus will forgive you if you ask Him. He will forgive you everything if you ask."

She raises her bloody hand to touch mine. Where she gets the strength, I know not. "You mustn't . . . say that . . . if it's not true. Please . . . don't deceive me."

"I'm not deceiving you." I stroke her head softly. I think Kyra smiles, though her lips are so swollen it's hard to know for sure. She mumbles something I don't understand, but I hear the words "forgive me, Jesus". And then I hear her say, "Argos . . . beware of Argos . . . he will try . . . oh, yes, I see Him now." I turn, thinking Argos is behind me, and see only Zechariah and a few lingering camel drivers, and realize it's not Argos she sees, but Jesus. And this time I'm sure there's a smile on her poor swollen lips as she takes her last breath, and I imagine that I see her spirit fly into Jesus' arms like a little caged bird that has been set free.

Caesarea has been described to me many times. It is the capital of Judea, the seat of the Roman *praefecti*, and the abode of the Roman governor. But looking upon it now for the first time makes my heart race and my throat become as dry as linen. It's the largest city in Judea. But it wasn't always this imposing. When it was called Strato's Tower and controlled by the Phoenicians, it was barely a mud puddle. But leave it to Herod to change everything in a grand way. He loved all things Greek and Roman, and his lust for power was legendary. That was his downfall. It made the Jews hate him. I doubt he was ever content with who he was: an Edomite who tried to pass as a Jew; a king never anointed with holy oil.

Many call Herod the Great a master builder, for he built lavish cities all across our land. I call him a demon. His intent was always to Romanize us Jews. Just look at what he did to Strato's Tower. Made it mirror decadent Rome with its massive harbor, its marketplace, palaces, theatre, amphitheatre, its public baths, its temple to Augustus Caesar. For good measure, he even changed the name to Caesarea in order to ingratiate himself to the Emperor. But for all his accomplishments, I don't think he ever obtained peace. How could he with so much blood on his hands, having murdered the babies of Bethlehem as well as so many of his own relatives, including two sons and a wife. Emperor Augustus once said it was better to be Herod's pig than a member of his family. Still, many of his accomplishments live on, and most are huge and impressive, like Caesarea.

"It's . . . daunting, isn't it?" I say to Zechariah in a near whisper as I look at Caesarea's famous grain fields and orchards that stretch before us. Behind them, and on this side of Caesarea's massive walls, I see the white stone top of the giant amphitheatre through a clump of trees. It's a massive structure said to seat fifteen-thousand people. And its floor of crushed chalk has hosted chariot races, wrestling matches, gymnastic tournaments, and even gladiatorial events.

I can't imagine such contemptible activities. Though to be honest, the entire city is contemptible to me—a byword for violence and cruelty, for it was here that the rebellion against Rome began several years ago after its Gentiles massacred a good portion of the Jewish population, then desecrated their synagogue.

"It's a fearful place," I say, still reluctant to continue my journey. "We must pray for God's protection and favor, for how else are we ever to find Esther in such a place?"

Zechariah places his hand on my shoulder. "For days we've prayed without ceasing. Now it's time to trust God."

Zechariah knows the city. For that I'm grateful. He also knows some in the Jewish Quarter, at least what's left of it. The man we seek is Achim, the tentmaker. He's a Jew who follows the Messiah. His house is in the northern part of the city near the aqueduct. That is, if he's still there. Zechariah isn't sure. It's been almost a year since Zechariah has been here.

Amid the city noises I hear our donkey's hooves clatter along the giant paving stones of the busy street. I'm told all the streets in Caesarea are paved with stone slabs and are laid out in the Roman grid system with major roads running north and south, and east and west, and with the forum or Public Square in the center; useful information for navigating those parts of the city Zechariah knows least.

We are in the Jewish quarter now, having entered Caesarea by the north gate, and are moving south along the aqueduct. Surprisingly, the quarter teems with life. Merchants hawk their wares in croaking voices. Children laugh and chase each other into alleys. Men argue in doorways. And women, or their servants, rush home with fresh fish or sacks of ground grain and other foodstuffs in anticipation of preparing their evening meal. It hardly looks like a street that once ran red with the blood of twenty-thousand Jews.

Our first stop is Achim's house. We quickly learn he's no longer there, and the new tenant doesn't know his whereabouts. And so we begin stopping at every open doorway we encounter.

"I can tell you about Achim," an old woman says before we even approach her door. She's sitting on a small wooden stool, dressed in a fine striped linen tunic. A similar fabric loosely covers her plaited gray hair. Her face crinkles in a wide grin, revealing few teeth. She points to a basket of grain by her feet. "Come, I'll tell you of Achim, and feed your donkey as well." Without waiting for an answer, she tosses a handful of oats outside her door. And so we oblige her and unbridle the donkey, then refresh ourselves by drinking from our water skins.

"Last time I was here, Achim lived in that house over there." Zechariah wipes his mouth with the back of his hand before pointing to a modest mudbrick house further up the street.

"Yes, that was his house. But he's gone now." The old woman studies us as she tosses another handful of oats onto the street. "You from Jerusalem?"

"From Pella," Zechariah answers. I know him well enough to sense his caution rising, and some impatience, too. "But about Achim. Is he still in the city?"

"No. He's been gone about six months now. And I say, 'good riddance.' He spent too much time talking about a dead Messiah. No one wants to hear about another Messiah. We've grown a bushel full of them lately. Like weeds, they've popped up all over our land. The Romans don't like that. And who wants any more trouble with the Romans, or the other Gentiles here, for that matter?" She dabs her perspiring forehead with the edge of her headscarf. "You're not one of them, are you? A follower of this Jesus Achim talked about?"

"We are," Zechariah says, without flinching.

"Did you hear what they've been doing with your kind in Rome? They're covering them with pitch and using them as torches to light the arena for the gladiatorial games." Her smile is gone and her eyes probe us.

I want to tell her "yes, under Claudius and Nero, not Vespasian," but why defend Vespasian? His Judean campaign proved him to be just as cruel. So, instead, I bridle the donkey. "Thank you for your kindness," I say, pulling my animal forward.

"You'll need a place to stay the night," the old woman says with a crooked smile, "and I have rooms . . . for a price."

"Our business takes us elsewhere," I answer quickly. The woman makes me uneasy. What does she mean by feeding our donkey then telling us about how believers were made into torches? I glance at Zechariah as I lead the donkey away. He seems perfectly at ease, and I'm left wondering why.

"If only that Centurion Cor . . . Cornellus . . . ."

"Cornelius," Zachariah says, correcting me.

"Yes, if only he and his family were still here. They would help us," I say, happy to be leaving the house of that strange woman.

Zechariah shrugs. "It's been years since he and his family were baptized by Peter the Apostle. The last time I was here I could find neither him nor his relatives."

"But surely Caesarea has a Gentile church? Surely Cornelius left a remnant of believers behind?"

"Yes, Peter broke that barrier, and Paul, too. And I've heard the church was a strong one even though some Jewish believers refused to fellowship with them. But where to look? The revolt has soured many Gentiles toward us Jews. And the followers of Jesus, even Gentile followers, are not highly regarded by the Romans. Making inquires could be dangerous. We must be cautious, and first formulate a plan."

By the time we reach the end of the Jewish Quarter we're still without a plan, though Zechariah surprises me with a strange suggestion. "Our long journey has wearied us both. Come. Let's return to that women's house and pass a restful evening. Tonight we'll pray and ask God what He would have us do."

"But . . . Zechariah . . . you heard the woman . . . how strangely she spoke. Surely, you don't mean you want to lodge beneath *her* roof?"

Zechariah chuckles. "Yes, I believe that's just where the Lord would have us go."

And so we head back to the house near the north gate.

Her name is Hannah, and she smiles when we ask for lodgings. By way of answer, she takes the reins of the donkey from my hand, then leads us around to the back of the house and into a small outer courtyard where she feeds and waters my animal before bringing us inside.

Her dwelling is tidy and clean, and made of plastered mudbrick, with several rooms built around a central courtyard. Though it is modest, being neither overly spacious nor lavishly furnished, compared to my house in Pella it's a luxurious mansion.

She brings us into a large room with a tiled floor where a waist-high work area, all made of masonry, contains both an oven for baking bread and a fire pit for cooking. She gestures for us to sit at a well-made wooden table. It's evident that Hannah is a woman of some means.

"I have a pot of lentils cooking." She grins and gestures to the many spaces in her mouth. "I fear that's all I can manage to eat these days, other than cheese. Even so, the lentils must be very soft. You won't mind that, will you?"

"I'm grateful to share whatever food you have. Of course we'll pay well for both it and our lodging," I add, eager to relieve her of any worry that she has invited worthless strangers into her house.

Zechariah, who sits beside me, nods.

"We can discuss that later," Hannah eyes us strangely as she stirs her lentils. "But first tell me, have you come from the Via Maris?"

"No. We traveled the Caesarea-Scythopolis Highway," Zechariah says.

"Ah, yes, of course, you coming from Pella, from the east, like you said. Then you missed all the congestion. I hear the Via Maris is clogged with Titus's legions." She makes a strange spitting sound. "Clogged with soldiers, and thousands of captives from Jerusalem." Hannah's back is to us as she hovers over the steaming pot, but she turns her head to the side and watches us out of the corner of her eye.

"When will . . . they arrive?" I say, hardly able to control the tremor in my voice.

"In three, maybe four days. At least that's what I've heard."

My stomach rolls into a fist. Can Esther really be so near?

"Might be longer, though." Hannah puts down her wooden spoon, then walks over and takes the stool next to mine. She sits close, too close, and I begin to feel we've made a mistake in coming here. After all, what do we know about her? She could be mad, or even a spy for the Romans.

"That pig, Titus!" Hannah suddenly blurts, then begins spitting on the floor. She actually spits on her tile floor! "He's been squandering his captives in lavish blood sports. They say he's stopping in every arena along the Via Maris." She gazes at us intently. "Too many captives drive down the price. Titus knows he'll get little for the slavers. So what better way to use his human booty?"

"But . . . I heard he was bringing the captives here, to Caesarea," I say. "Some destined for Rome, others for auction in the marketplace; especially the women. With the army returning, surely they'll want more women for the brothels?"

"If they're young enough, yes." Hannah tents her fingers. Her yellow, cracked nails, the deeply creased skin of her hands, all betray her advanced age. But her gray eyes, those piercing gray eyes reveal a keen, vibrant mind. "Ah," she finally says, after a long silence. "You have someone you're hoping to find. Someone captured in Jerusalem."

I cover my face with my hands. The anxiety of the trip, the death of Kyra, and now this devastating news that Esther might have already been killed in the arena, all conspire to reduce me to a quivering heap as I bend over the table and sob.

I feel Hannah's leathery hand patting my arm. "Yes, I understand. I understand. For I, too, search."

When I sit up, she quickly tells us how her son went to Jerusalem for Passover, in spite of her warnings and pleadings; then became trapped inside the city like so many other pilgrims. "I don't know if he lives. How could I know for sure? But something inside me," she thumps her chest, "something in here tells me he does." She suddenly clasps my hands like a madwoman and throws back her head and laughs. "Oh, how I've prayed to *Hashem*, imploring him night and day; asking Him that if my son still lives, to bring him back here to Caesarea."

When she jumps from the chair, her scarf slips from her head and rings her shoulders, revealing thick gray hair bound in one neat plait. "And what else do you think I've been praying for?" She waves her hands in the air. "Never mind, I'll tell you. Money! Money enough to buy my son from the slave block. I'm a widow. My husband left behind this house and the possessions in it, but only one bagful of shekels. After so many years, that bag is nearly empty. We had our son late in life. And after my husband died I had to raise Judah alone. He was only a boy of eight and unable to provide for me, so the bag of shekels kept us both. He is a man now, a good son who supports me, but even so I fear there are not enough shekels left for the slavers. But see, *Hashem* has sent you!

"I tested you, with talk of this dead Jesus, with talk of human torches. And still you spoke out fearlessly. My son—he believes as you do—he says this Jesus isn't dead. But never mind that now." She points to Zechariah. "I knew you were the one. 'Now there's an honest man,' I said to myself. 'He can be trusted.'" Hannah is skipping around the room now. "See how good *Hashem* is! He has answered one prayer. He has sent me an honest man, someone I can trust to share my house and food, and to pay me for it; to give me the money I need to buy my son's freedom. And if *Hashem* answered this prayer, surely He'll answer the other."

As I sit and watch Hannah leap around the room like a young girl, clapping her hands in glee, my heart is greatly moved and I determine then and there to help her. Should she need more money, she can have some of the coins from my *semadi*.

Finally, when she has tired herself out, Hannah returns to the table. She leans over and takes both Zechariah's hand and mine in hers. "Until Titus comes," she makes a spitting sound again, but this time I'm not so horrified, "until that pig comes, you'll stay with me. And we'll pray to *Hashem* and make our plans, for I've not forgotten your sorrow either." She squeezes my hand. Then she closes her eyes as if suddenly remembering something. And when she opens them, those wonderful vibrant gray eyes are fierce. "It's only fair I tell you of an added danger. We, my son and I, are from the tribe of Judah, from the house of David. And it's rumored that Vespasian has ordered the slaying of all the descendants of the royal house, in order to cut off David's bloodline forever.

Ethan

Pella/Caesarea Maritima 70 A.D.

CHAPTER 8

My heart races as I look down into the Jordan Valley and settle my gaze on the city nestled among emerald hills. I picture Rebekah, and imagine her arms around me, her sweet lips covering my face with kisses, her beautiful hair blowing in the breeze. Will she weep? Will she laugh in disbelief? What will she say? Surely she will bless *Hashem* and praise the name of Yeshua.

And what will *I* say? My throat tightens. How will I tell her about Abner and Joseph? How can I relive these sorrows or inflict them on her? I've prayed about this for days but am no closer to a remedy, as if there is one. And my dilemma is compounded by my prayer that Esther has not gone to Jerusalem as Josiah claims, when I already know in my heart that she has.

"There, to the left of the wadi, is where the believers live." Aaron points to a section of Pella whose houses are smaller, more rundown than their counterparts on the other side. "I know a way to bypass the Gentiles. It will avoid trouble."

We didn't travel along the coast on the Via Maris as originally planned. Benjamin talked me out of it. Too many Romans, as Josiah warned. And the closer we got to Jerusalem, the thicker they became. Without disguises, we were in danger of being recognized. So we skirted the ruins of the Holy City, and traveled the isolated footpaths of the Judean wilderness instead.

Now Aaron leads us down the slope toward Pella. He's told me much about this city, about the believers here. It was this telling, this description of Rebekah and Esther safe among friends that provided my one comfort these many months.

But the war seems far away now as I listen to the bleating of sheep, see the fig trees laden with ripened fruit, smell the aroma of freshly baked bread. And my heart soars as it beats out Rebekah's name.

"How will you tell Mama about Abner and Joseph?" Benjamin says in that calm, practical way of his, causing my soaring heart to plummet to the ground. And a shrug is the only answer I can manage

---

"Rebekah!" I shout when we near the small mudbrick house Aaron has lead us to. My breath catches when a woman appears from around the back, her hands caked with dirt. "Rebekah?" I squint against the harsh sun, but even in the glare I can tell the woman is a stranger, someone I've never seen before.

She studies us for a moment, then throws up her arms in delight. "Aaron!" She wipes her hands on her tunic, smearing dirt down each side, then scurries to meet us. "Oh, Aaron, we thought you were lost! But God has answered our prayers!" She enfolds Aaron in her arms. "You are one of many friends and relatives He has preserved. Sons, husbands, brothers, uncles, all have been returning to us in small numbers. You are the latest miracle."

"Where . . . is she?" I stammer like a young bridegroom when the woman releases my son. Before she can answer, Aaron introduces her as Mary, wife of Simon the bottlemaker.

"Rebekah's not here," Mary says, peering kindly at my face. "I and others have been tending her gardens and watching the house." She makes a sweeping motion with her hand. "You'll find everything in good order."

"But where is she? Not sick . . . she hasn't sickened and . . . ?" The word sticks in my throat. *Died.* That was the word I couldn't say. I've seen too much death. Now it's always the first thing that comes to mind.

"Oh, forgive me. Here I'm going on as if you knew her whereabouts. Rebekah has gone to Caesarea by the sea."

"Caesarea! Now why would she go to Caesarea?" Without meaning to, I sound like a General interrogating an underling.

"Rebekah hoped . . . that is . . . she thought she'd find Esther among Titus's captives. She planned to purchase her daughter's freedom."

I fling curses into the air like pebbles, trying to assail both my disappointment and fear. Mary's face reddens. I've embarrassed her. My sons, too.

"*Father*," Aaron says softly.

Benjamin puts his hand on my shoulder to steady me.

"How could she put herself in such danger?" My voice still sounds like a blasting trumpet. I, who once commanded armies, am now unable to command my own emotions. "She knows how dangerous the roads are! Why didn't she wait for us?"

Benjamin tightens his grip on my shoulder. "Father, she could hardly know we were coming."

Mary, the bottlemaker's wife, bobs her head up and down like a quail. "Yes, that's right. She thought you were dead, all of you. Oh, how she grieved! But for Esther's sake she gathered her strength and courage. The thought of losing her daughter, too, was more than she could bear."

The woman's words are like darts in my heart. For the first time I'm forced to consider what life has been like for Rebekah; the uncertainty, the fear, the agony of not knowing what was happening to me, to her sons. The loneliness, the feelings of abandonment. And anger? Was there anger, too? Hadn't she pleaded for us all to leave Jerusalem? *Together*? She never wanted to go alone, even preferring death in Jerusalem to separation. I knew that. I've always known it. But how could I allow my sweet Rebekah and Esther to perish in such a manner?

Still, Rebekah has a keen mind. I've always been able to trust her judgment. "It's not like her to behave so foolishly," I hear myself bark. "She knows better than to travel alone."

Mary's cheeks are as red as pomegranates as she rubs her hands along the sides of her tunic. "She wasn't alone. Zechariah went with her."

"*Zechariah*?" I don't know whether to feel relief that she has a protector or anger that she is alone with another man.

"He is . . . was the elder of our church," Mary quickly adds. "He's a godly man who came here from Ephesus, straight from John the Apostle."

My mind is a grinding wheel, crushing emotions and thoughts together like kernels of wheat. Rebekah believes I'm dead, and has gone off with another man—a godly man, says this bottlemaker's wife. I've seen so-called godly men before. Didn't Eleazar ben Simon drive them out by the hundreds from the Temple?

But it was *I* who sent her away. Can I now blame her if she has made a new life? Can I blame her if she now has found love with another? *Oh, Rebekah, do you love another?*

Maybe if I had come to Pella sooner . . . maybe then Esther wouldn't have gone to Jerusalem . . . maybe Rebekah wouldn't be with this man. What kept me? Revenge, as Rebekah claimed? Or duty to *Hashem* and His Temple? *Living stones. We are temples of living stones.* I give my head a shake to dislodge Rebekah's accusing words.

"How long ago did she leave?" Aaron's face is taut.

"Less than a week." Mary turns to me, her fingers picking at her tunic nervously. "But I think you misunderstand. Rebekah and Kyra *both* went with Zechariah."

Benjamin, my level headed son, laughs. "There is no misunderstanding. We are grateful for Zechariah's protection. And Kyra's too, whoever she might be."

I know what he's doing. He's clever, this son of mine, and he understands me well.

Mary quickly explains who Kyra is, and ends by telling us that Argos has also left the city. Then her brows knot. "He made a great display of leaving with three men, spewing outrage and anger, and vowing he would reclaim his runaway slave. But word is, he actually ordered Kyra to escape in order to pursue Rebekah's cup."

"Her cup?" Now I am perplexed. Rebekah has always had a high regard for her cup for reasons I well understand and respect, but why would it be worth anything to someone else?

"Her cup has brought many miracles to Pella," Mary says. "Argos is sick with jealousy, and desires it for himself. The believers here have all been praying much for Rebekah's safety. Zachariah's and Kyra's, too. But now that you've come, surely you and your sons will be God's strong arm, and protect them."

I bless her for her kindness. And as she exits through the gate in the stone wall, I'm already planning what we must do.

My hand tightens around the hilt of my dagger as I lean against the small open window of Rebekah's upstairs loft. I've been watching the same shadow pass back and forth outside our gate since just before sunrise. Age keeps me from sleeping as soundly as my sons who still lie snoring on the floor. I've resisted waking them. The journey here was long and tiring, and tomorrow we leave for Caesarea. But the shadow outside disquiets me, so finally I nudge my sons awake. If trouble is coming we must be prepared.

When they stretch and yawn and open their eyes, I press one finger against my lips and show them the dagger in my hand. Quickly and quietly they rise, then secure their own weapons.

I return again to the window. It's light enough now to determine that the shadow is a tall, broad man in a Greekish-looking tunic. What could a Greek be doing here? I'm still wondering about this as one by one my sons and I descend the ladder. After Aaron and Benjamin conceal themselves along the wall, I open the door.

"You there," I shout. "What is the meaning of your presence?" Instead of the man fleeing, like I expected, he opens the gate and steps into our courtyard.

"Are you Ethan, husband of Rebekah the Jewess?" The man yells, clearly hesitant about coming closer.

"And if I am, what business is it of yours?"

"I . . . that is . . . must we shout at one another? May I approach?"

"If you come in peace."

The man raises his hands above his head, then slowly turns around making a complete circle. "I carry no weapon. My mission is one of good will."

I signal for Aaron and Benjamin to show themselves. The three of us must be a sight: Benjamin, tall and broad, still holding his dagger; Aaron, with a patch over one eye, frowning; and me with my scarred bare arms glistening with sweat as I sheath my own weapon; all crowded together in the doorway.

For an instant the man looks like he's going to bolt. But then he walks forward with arms still held high above his head as though wanting to make sure we understand he's unarmed. When he's nearly upon us, he stops, looks us over, puts down his arms, smiles, then says the strangest thing: "I've been sent by God."

"You are a Gentile." Aaron's voice is edgy. "What would you know of our God? And why would he send *you*?"

"My name is Demas, and what I know of your God can fill a large scroll. To begin with, I know He heals because He has healed me."

He's young, this Demas, perhaps only a year or two older than my sons, but he's no warrior. Though he is muscular enough, his soft hands and perfumed clothes tell me he is someone unaccustomed to hardship or much labor. And how can you trust a man who has not known either? My first instinct is to let him feel the flat of my dagger across his back, then send him on his way, but before I can, Benjamin steps forward, and taking the man by the arm pushes us aside and ushers him into the house.

"Come join us for breakfast." Benjamin smiles, looking so like Rebekah. And before I can utter an objection, he shoves the Greek onto a small stool near the wall, then sits on the floor beside him.

What can I do? Dishonor my son by retracting the hospitality he has just offered? So I position myself on the floor next to Benjamin, but keep one hand on my belted dagger. Aaron follows, his face showing displeasure. Benjamin has already placed a basket in the middle of our circle. It's filled with the raisins and cheese Mary, the bottlemaker's wife, brought us yesterday just before sundown.

"Now tell me," Benjamin says, chomping on a handful of raisins, "why does a Gentile think that the God of Abraham, Isaac and Jacob has sent him?"

"I . . . don't know." Demas frowns and smiles at the same time. "I only know that last night your Jesus, who has also become mine, revealed to me that I was to offer you my services."

"And what services are those?" I say.

"I wasn't told. I thought you'd know."

"Perhaps it's best to begin by telling us your trade," Benjamin says. "Then we can determine your usefulness."

I think my son's suggestion wise until I hear Demas's answer.

"I am . . . rather I *was* the head beekeeper in the Temple of Isis. Her priests are forever making ambrosia, the elixir of the goddess. There was much need for my honey."

"Isis! That abomination?" Aaron nearly spits out the words.

"How is it that a Greek without a shaved head is a beekeeper?" I say, pointing to Demas's short curly locks and ignoring Aaron's outburst. No beekeeper worth his name would approach a hive with scented hair for fear of agitating the bees. And Demas's oiled hair smelled strongly of lilies.

"I used to shave my head in spring and again in late autumn when we harvested the honey. The rest of the time my servants would oversee the hives."

"Well, Greeks *are* considered clever beekeepers," Benjamin says, smiling.

Demas shakes his head. "Egyptians are the true masters. My father was Greek. But my mother was an Egyptian from Lower-Egypt—where the best beekeepers in the world reside; among them, my mother's family. From them I learned how to cover baskets with mud to make hives, how to make elixirs, ointments and medicines from the honey, how to render the wax for amulets, writing tablets, sealants. It's a profitable business." He gestures toward his expensive tunic and sighs. "But I no longer keep bees for Isis. Not since my healing. I suppose you can say I'm a man without employment."

"And this is all you have to recommend yourself?" I glare at our guest in disbelief. "Do you take us for fools? Why would we need someone who collects honey for idols?"

"Used to collect, *used* to collect honey. No more." Demas is surprisingly calm.

Benjamin laughs. "You have courage, to sit with men who have no sense of humor and tell such a tale. What else but courage can you offer us?"

"I know Argos, your enemy. We were friends once. Perhaps God has sent me to help you fight against him. He's powerful. You must understand that it's not the slave girl, Kyra, he's after, but your wife's cup. He'll not rest until he gets it. And he may make trouble by accusing Rebekah of harboring his runaway slave."

"How do you know this?" Aaron says, thrusting himself a bit too close to Demas.

"We used to spend hours talking about how best to use Kyra to get to Rebekah. We even sent Kyra to Zechariah's weekly gatherings hoping to gain Rebekah's confidence. But all that was before I came to Jesus. He changed everything."

How do you trust such a man? Perhaps he does know Jesus. Or perhaps he's laying a trap. Aaron certainly believes he is. I can tell by his thin, tight lips, by the way he studies Demas's every move, and how his hand, even now, holds the hilt of his dagger beneath his robe. Benjamin is less suspicious. Always calm and logical, I know he's quietly sifting Demas's words to discern truth from lie. While I, myself, am not sure what to think.

"You've given us little reason to believe we need your services. I see no value in a beekeeper," I finally say. When Demas's face falls I quickly add, "Don't misunderstand. I have no wish to insult you. Beekeeping is, in itself, an honorable profession."

Demas rises to his feet. "Then God speed. But be warned. Argos will fight you, both with the powers given him by Isis, which are formidable, and his knowledge of the rules of *Jus Gentium* concerning slaves, which is vast."

Benjamin rises too. "And how does an idol maker know so much about the laws of slavery?"

Demas smiles sheepishly. "Because I taught him."

"You?" Benjamin looks puzzled.

"My father was a slave dealer. He trained me in the business, believing I would follow in his footsteps. But I had no stomach for it, so I chose the trade of my mother's relatives, instead. He wasn't pleased."

Benjamin smiles at me, then gestures for Demas to retake his seat. "Perhaps I'm beginning to understand why God has sent you, after all."

Aaron tells me he doesn't trust Demas. It's difficult for Aaron to trust anyone these days. His tender heart has been seared by years of war. I only pray *Hashem* will heal it.

Benjamin, on the other hand, tells me only a fool or someone telling the truth would come up with such a story. And who fears a fool?

I'm inclined to believe Demas, though I must confess trust came easier after I spoke to Mary and her husband, Simon. "Oh, yes, Demas is a follower of Jesus," Simon said. While Mary talked about how Demas received "both his physical and spiritual sight."

I admit it irritates me a bit. Not that I don't believe what happened to Demas is real, it's that I *do*. And that begs this question: Why would God heal the eyes of a heathen, a former worshiper of Isis, and *not* heal my Aaron's eye—a man of virtue, one of the Chosen, a Jew not only faithful to Jesus, but to Torah and Temple as well? It's a thorny question that pricks my heart.

I still grapple with it as we cross the wadi to join Demas and purchase supplies for our trip to Caesarea. When we meet him, he is as calm and pleasant as he was yesterday. We waste no time but at once set about making our purchases. First we buy enormous amounts of date cakes and raisins and flat breads from street vendors. Next, I ask Demas to take us to a seller of *shirwals,* Syrian tunics, and *kaffias.* He looks at me strangely, but asks no questions. This makes Aaron even more suspicious, for I see it on his face. After all, what normal man would not question the purchase of Syrian garb by a Jew?

Demas points to a shop at the end of the stone-paved street. "Markos sells Greek and Roman togas, *stolas,* a few *pallas,* a good collection of tunics, and of course loin cloths. But he also carries clothing for the rich Syrian merchants who sometimes pass this way, or used to." He tactfully avoids my eyes. "With the war, well . . . few have graced our city." Was he thinking of John of Gischala and what his men did to the Decapolis and the rich who traveled between these cities?

"Perhaps Markos has some of this clothing left." Demas's face suddenly brightens. "If he does, he'll be happy to be rid of them for who knows when another rich Syrian will come along? You should get them for a good price."

So we enter the shop and are greeted by Markos, the owner. He is a small hunched man with skin the color of saffron and who wheezes loudly as he stands anxiously by our side. When Demas tells him what we want, he leads us to the back wall where on a stone shelf are stacks of assorted folded garments. He unfurls them one by one, praising the quality of the stitching, the amount of gold thread, the red, black or blue embroidery around the neck, the perfection of the appliqués along the chest. He offers each garment for our inspection, begs us to handle them and even try them on. Most of the tunics, which fall to the ankle and are heavily decorated, are white cotton with long sleeves, decidedly unsuitable for Romans and Greeks since they consider long sleeves effeminate.

My sons and I choose several, causing Markos great distress over the speed with which we make our choices. He frowns and shakes his head and continues to extol the virtues of his other garments and insists we examine them further. Politeness prevails and we listen, but when he sees we're not going to change our minds, he finally packs the remaining tunics away and pulls down his *abayas*. Since the weather is still warm, we choose lightweight cloaks of fine cream-colored Syrian cotton, though we also pick one or two heavier cloaks for the cooler evenings. Again, Markos provides endless commentary, happily praising each embroidered shoulder seam and neckline, and pointing out that one of the cloaks in my pile of chosen garments is stitched with spun-gold thread.

Next we select scarves or *kaffias* for our heads. Many are silk with long fringe, others plain Syrian cotton. To hold them in place we add several fine braided *agals*, or head ropes. Last of all we each select two pairs of Markos's best leather sandals.

The little merchant is overjoyed that such good fortune has come his way, for we have nearly emptied his stone shelf and hardly haggled over price. But if we're to succeed in our charade, we'll need a generous wardrobe befitting men of our supposed stature. Besides, I don't begrudge him his profit.

"You'll need clothes for the journey, too," I say to Demas.

"Then I am to go?" He looks surprised.

I smile and point to the many shelves containing Greekish clothes. "Pick out some tunics and sandals, perhaps a *pallium* or two, and whatever else you need."

"A *pallium*? The cloak of the wealthy?" Demas's eyebrows raise.

Markos dances gleefully around his shop as he realizes even greater profits are to be his. "Here, over here," he gestures, leading Demas to a section of shelves containing carefully folded garments. "Here are my finest wares. Wools from Laodicea and Attica, and all weighted with lead along the hem in order to drape a man properly."

Demas shakes his head. "Perhaps something less costly."

As Demas turns, I bar his way. "Choose from this lot," I say, much to Markos's delight. And so Demas plucks several tunics and belts and togas and *palliums* and sandals from the shelf of costly wear, and before we're done we each have a large bundle to carry.

Poor hunched Markos is so grateful he bows repeatedly and articulates his appreciation all the way to the door. And even after we're a good way into the street he continues to profess his gratitude.

"So when do we leave?" Demas asks once Markos's shop is far behind. Sweat beads his forehead, and he breathes heavily beneath his large bundle in stark contrast to my sons who barely show any strain.

"If you can secure the camels I've commissioned you to buy, we'll leave tomorrow at first light."

"You and your sons will go as rich merchants? From Damascus?"

I nod.

"And I as a Greek . . . slaver?" It's clear Demas has guessed our plans.

"It's as you say."

Demas wrinkles his forehead. "I thought I was done with that business." He sighs. "Even so, if Jesus, the restorer of my sight, wishes this, how can I refuse? But this brutal, heartless business will try my soul. It doesn't please me to enter it again. It once made me brutal and heartless, too, until . . . well . . . until I met Him. But you already know all that. Surely, Mary and Simon have not spared any details, not even the part of how I broke into Rebekah's house and tried to rob her of the cup." There's a twinkle in his eyes. "They told me you spoke to them. But I don't fault you for making inquiries about me."

"Then understand this," Aaron says, suddenly coming up from behind and staring fiercely at Demas, "though we'll be dressing like rich, soft fools on this journey, we are far from soft or foolish. Four years of fighting in Jerusalem have hardened us. I can kill a man with one flick of my dagger. And I would do it in an instant if I thought he was plotting any treachery against me or my family."

Oh, my Aaron. I want to enfold him in my arms and hold him there until every memory of killing has faded from him. But it would take a lifetime of holding, and he is a man, and such a thing would be unthinkable, so instead I ask *Hashem* to hold him.

Our trip is a blur of dusty roads, sore haunches and backs, sun baked bodies, the odor of unwashed men, groaning camels, cursing camel drivers, and sleepless nights ripe with thoughts of Rebekah.

Does she love another? My mind can hardly comprehend it. Sweet Rebekah, wife of my youth. Still young and beautiful to me. Oh, yes, beautiful. And how she loved me! Once. She loved me once. I've never played the coward, but I feel cowardly now. If *Hashem* is kind and allows me to find her, how will I bear it if she spurns me? If she no longer wants me? Fear invades my being, me the general who has fought fiercely in a hundred battles. What has come over me? It must be age. I'm beginning to feel old. Even so, didn't I have to fight for Rebekah once? After Josiah's father initiated the *shiddukhin*, the match, between Rebekah and his son? Didn't I fight them all? Even my own father who had already picked out a young maiden from Jericho for me? Someone I had never seen but who came from a wealthy priestly family? Yes, I fought them all because I *loved* her. And because she *loved* me. And I knew of her love because my wild, sweet, matchless Rebekah had defied custom and whispered it in my ear one starry night when we sat together on the narrow steps outside her upper room. It was this love of hers that made me brave and persistent in the face of both family opposition and the pressure of a tradition dating back centuries—the tradition that the father of the groom picks the bride.

But can I fight for her now, not knowing if she still loves me? The ache in my heart tells me I can do no other. I picture her now as she looked that night on the outer steps, so young, hardly fifteen, and so beautiful. And how she laughed when I told her my father was away in Jericho initiating a match for me. And how her hair shimmered in the moonlight as she bent closer to me, smelling of lavender and telling me such a thing could never happen. And when I asked "why," she simply said, without hesitation and with a hint of merriment in her voice, "because *I* love you!"

Oh, Rebekah. Is it possible you now love another?

"Make way! Make way!" Demas shouts, walking beside his camel, and leading it and two others laden with goods through the crowded north gate of Caesarea. As he goes, he pushes aside other travelers who lead their own camels. A dog with matted fur and flies buzzing around his eyes nips at Demas's heels. And behind Demas and the three camels and the yapping dog come my sons and I, riding atop our beasts like we were the three magi. We're perfumed and decked in our finest cloaks, and we all wear gold chains and rings.

Benjamin appears to enjoy the charade. I suppose because we have no choice but to disguise ourselves and he's simply making the best of it. He nods his head condescendingly at those who stare up at him in awe from the street. Aaron, on the other hand, appears embarrassed and hardly lifts his eyes.

And I? I scout the lay of the land, looking for hidden dangers, measuring the people, searching for potential snares. My vigilance ends when I realize we're in the Jewish Quarter. Then I remember we're masquerading as Syrians and must appear to be contemptuous of the poor Jews around us. It's difficult, for I feel only love and compassion. When I recall how Titus's Syrian auxiliary gutted fleeing Jewish refugees for the gold they believed they had swallowed I'm able to produce the desired contempt, but it's for the Syrians.

An old Jew carrying a talith scurries past, obviously on his way to the partially rebuilt synagogue. I picture him drawing the fringed cloth over his head and shoulders, then stooping and swaying in prayer. What will he pray for, I wonder? From what I've seen so far, there's much need here.

Two children run in front of my camel, laughing and chasing a small spinning clay disk, and in spite of myself, I smile. It's good to see such abandonment, such carefree joy. It's been a long time since I've heard the laughter of children.

Our gaudy little caravan travels south through the streets of Caesarea, and in no time exits the Jewish Quarter. Now, columns of pink Aswan granite line the paved streets. The houses are larger, too; and silks and expensive wools, rather than homespun, clothe the people. All the buildings look white, being made of either limestone or marble, and gleam in the sun. It's a grand city, this Caesarea; a city of fountains and statues, vaulted warehouses and temples, and cook shops oozing with aromas of roasting meats. Even Benjamin is impressed. Aaron hardly looks.

Demas points west to a massive columned building which can be seen even from our vantage point several streets away. "The Temple of Augustus. See how it towers above all else? Use it as a guide and you'll not get lost." He looks at me and chuckles. "Herod always knew how to curry favor with the powerful. He made certain his tribute to Caesar would stand out among the other structures in the city by building it on a raised platform."

"Are we going there now?" I ask, seeing Demas turn in the direction of the temple and feeling disquieted.

"No, to the market place and docks beyond. Both are excellent places to gather information. I'll seek news about Titus and his captives there."

What would we have done without Demas? I see *Hashem's* hand in this for Demas is the only one who has ever been to Caesarea, and being a Greek he'll know just how to glean information here. I glance at Aaron. For the first time since leaving Pella I see no rancor on his face. Perhaps he's come to appreciate Demas, too.

When we pass the square near the idolatrous temple of Augustus Caesar and enter the teeming market place, Demas instructs us to stay with the camels while he makes inquires. Then he disappears into the crowd. An hour later he returns, proving his worth yet again.

"I've secured a house. I learned of a man who is fond of gambling and whose luck has not been good lately. He needs money to pay his creditors and is willing to rent to us."

"Well done," I say. And to my surprise even Aaron mumbles his praise. "And Titus? What of him?"

Demas strokes his clean shaven chin and studies me. "He and his men and the Jerusalem captives are camped just outside the southern wall of the city. The paymaster has told the slave dealers to assemble tomorrow." He shakes his head when he sees my excitement. "Steady, Ethan. Remember, Titus has lost many captives along the way. Thousands have been purchased by those slave dealers who make it their practice to follow the army and buy up the best of the lot. The remaining prisoners have been culled even further: some to the arenas, some through starvation and the rigors of the journey, others by their own hand."

Demas grips my shoulder when he sees the look on my face. "Yes, it is so. Many unwilling to face their unhappy future take their own lives. I've seen it so often. But those who are left will be put up for sale tomorrow." He looks at me and sighs. "You must understand that it will be a miracle if your daughter is among them."

The gentle trickling of the large marble fountain is a restful backdrop to my prayers. So is the peaceful atrium. I've been praying here for hours, waiting for the sun to rise. Who can sleep? Not even my pleasant shuttered quarters with its array of colored silk pillows, and couch of imported swan's down could stop my mind from twisting and turning. Would I find Esther? Has she been sold? Is she dead? And Rebekah? *What if*. . . .

Even now my mind buzzes like a hive of bees. And I have no answers, only more tormenting questions. I've tried losing myself in prayer, and found a measure of peace. It's from this womb I now pull myself.

Through the open roof of the atrium come the first pale streaks of daybreak. Rising from my seat built against the low stone wall, I walk across the polished marble floor to the shallow fountain pool. Bending, I wet my hands, then splash my face to freshen my eyes.

I'm fully dressed and wearing my splendid gold-embroidered cloak. Aaron says we look like peacocks in these Syrian garments, and he says it with great disdain. I allow him his grumblings, for I know he too carries the same fears for his sister and mother that I do. My heart has grown even more tender towards him for he looks like a boy with his shaven face. We are all clean shaven now. We scraped away our beards when we first began this charade. I miss mine. Will Esther recognize me? Will Rebekah?

The house is quiet, and I assume everyone is still asleep. So when I rise from the pool I'm surprised to see Aaron standing beside one of the nearby marble columns. He, too, is dressed for the day.

"Father," he says, in a steady voice. Though he's boyishly handsome in his elegant flowing cloak and fine silk *kaffia*, his voice is the voice of a man. "Whatever happens today, you must accept it as the will of God."

I nod, trying to appear calm. But inside, my heart flogs itself against my chest, and my dry mouth resumes its silent prayers.

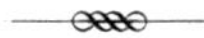

The smell of vomit, human waste and filthy bodies fills the air, alerting me that the captives are being assembled somewhere nearby. Legionaries stroll among us. Some keep order. Others look as if they're waiting to claim, when the slave dealers are finished, their gift from Titus—two or three captives apiece. A dozen slave dealers and their minions have gathered, and stand in clusters, laughing and talking. A few of the more enterprising are craning their necks to glimpse the flesh about to be peddled.

Demas has his orders. He's to purchase up to a thousand males and another thousand females. I can afford five times that many, but how can we get them all safely to Masada? The care and feeding of that amount would be an impossible task so I must restrain myself. It has already been announced that the males are to be sold first. This will delay finding Esther, and I have difficulty remaining patient. I glance around anxiously.

From where I stand I see the nearby theater built by Herod the Great whose construction greatly offended the Jews. It is said that inside are depictions of Roman victories and all manner of pagan trophies. But who knows for sure? I only repeat what I've heard. But this I know, it was here Herod Agrippa died nearly forty years ago, when dressed in a shimmering silver robe, he was hailed a god then struck down by the angel of the Lord for this blasphemy. If only that angel would strike Titus's camp now, a camp that is so close by!

I'm uncomfortable here among so many Romans. "Vale" I hear them say to each other—their customary word of departure or benediction for strength and health. But I wish them no such good will. They swarm like repulsive flies. My sons, too, appear distressed, but we do what we must. It's Esther and Rebekah we think of now, and the many poor souls we hope to snatch from Titus's hand. The great Titus himself is not to be seen. Word is, he's already entered Caesarea and is living in Herod's palace in comfort and luxury.

"Look, the spear," Demas says, pointing to the Roman lance stuck into the ground, marking the place where the captives will be sold. Already soldiers are herding the men, strung together at the neck by a coarse rope, to a spot near us.

The stench is unbearable. I resist the urge to cover my face. And oh, how wretched they look! Their once virile young bodies are now wasted and filthy, and covered in rags. Many, so weakened by their ordeal they can barely stand upright, are prodded by spear tips every time the *quaestor*, Titus's paymaster, barks an order.

At once, Demas goes to work, quickly walking the line and discreetly marking the arms of many he passes. Meanwhile, the dozen other slavers busily mark their wax tablets as they inspect the captives. Those who stop and ask questions are obviously seeking captives with education or skills. Others, looking to purchase slaves for the silver mines near Cartagena or the copper mines of Cyprus, eye the strongest, the healthiest.

But all are unaware of Demas who carries a leather pouch of limestone powder open at the neck, or that he's been dipping his finger into the pouch and marking the upper arms of his choices. It was his father's own system.

The line of captives stretches endlessly like a long tattered ribbon swaying in the breeze. Even my untrained eye can tell many of them are sick, some near death. I watch Demas move quickly until he is so far away he disappears from view. I wait for what seems like hours, then suddenly he appears out of nowhere and stands before the *quaestor*, announcing he has marked his choices and is ready to make an offer.

This causes a great stir among the other buyers, for they have yet to complete their own inspection. At once their curses and shouts fill the air as they run from their place along the line to bring their formal protest to the ears of the *quaestor*. Angry shouts soon turn into pushing and shoving. The dealer from Cyprus pulls a dagger, but immediately two of the *quaestor's* slaves, both broad, savage-looking men, subdue him. It's apparent to the dealers that they've been outsmarted.

"I'll give you seventy-five *drachmas* apiece," Demas says to the *quaestor* who seems barely able to conceal his admiration for Demas's craftiness. "It's a good price. I'm sure these thieves," he indicates with a flick of his head that he means the other buyers, "weren't even going to offer you fifty."

"Done," the *quaestor* says quickly as if confirming Demas's accusation. He then orders several of his many personal slaves to go and cull the men from the line.

The other buyers are still cursing and complaining when Demas comes over to us. His face is wedged with a smile, his eyes sparkle with mischief. "We've done well. I've purchased the strongest. But when they bring the women, it won't be so easy. The dealers will be ready for me."

"Remember, don't look too eager. When you see Esther, don't go to her at once." I lean close to Demas in order to whisper in his ear. "But don't lose her, either. You must not let another slaver get her. You *can't* let that happen."

"Peace, Ethan, peace," Demas says, looking at me with compassion. "We've gone over this a dozen times. I know what to do. My father taught me well. If Esther is here, I'll get her."

I compress my lips to keep from speaking further. All this waiting makes it difficult to keep my fears contained. And Demas knows his business. He has proven it all morning, first by his keen eyes at picking those who appear strong, then in his agility in making his purchase before the others, and finally in paying some of the *quaestor's* slaves to billet and feed the newly acquired captives. We're fortunate that Titus's *quaestor* allows his slaves *peculium*, so they can hire themselves out, though Demas tells me they give their master a portion. Demas has hired thirty such slaves to oversee our new acquisitions—nine hundred and thirty seven males.

Even so, I've sent Aaron and Benjamin with them, to watch that the *quaestor's* slaves don't pocket the gold meant to feed the captives. I've also asked my sons to determine the true condition of these captives, as well as to identify any capable of leading the others and becoming captains over them.

Now, to the next task. Word has come that soon the women will be here. My palms sweat while my mouth feels dry as flax. The waiting taxes me so greatly I begin to pace. At once, Demas pulls my arm and brings me to a stop.

"It's unseemly for a rich man to appear so nervous," he whispers.

And so I force myself to stand in place beneath the boughs of an oak. The only consolation is that it shelters me from the hot noonday sun. Then I close my eyes and pray. *Oh, Lord, please let Esther be among the women.*

"I'd like to buy one of your slaves."

I blink, and there standing in front of me is an elderly woman dressed in a fine striped linen tunic that falls to her ankles. Her head is covered by an equally fine shawl, though her gray hair is still partially visible along the edges. The cloth and style of her garment tell me she's a Jewess. In her hand she carries a small sack that jingles when she moves.

"What . . . did you say?" I ask, squinting at her in surprise.

"I said I want to buy one of your slaves." I hear a gulping sound when she swallows. "A widow needs a strong young man for the heavy work around her house." Her eyes dart from side to side as she wets her lips with her tongue. She is clearly nervous. "I'm not as strong as I used to be." She pushes her dark leathery-looking lips upward forcing a smile, and when she does she reveals few teeth.

"Talk to my slave dealer," I say gruffly, not wanting to appear sympathetic to a Jewess and compromise my mission. "Demas!" I shout. Just then, the women are marched forward, and the *quaestor* orders the sale to begin. When I try to step closer, the old woman bars my way.

"I have money." She jingles the pouch. "I know what you paid and I can promise you a good profit."

"Not now!" I dismiss her with a wave of my hand, then move around her so I can get to the captives. Like the men, the women are roped together at the neck. None look older than twenty. All the other females, the old and the very young, have been slaughtered long ago. I watch the women fold their arms around themselves like shields; see their heads droop forward. Filthy rags cover their thin, frail bodies, bodies that huddle together like sheep trying to hide from the eyes around them. Some weep softly. But most are silent, like sad little statues. Several thrusts of a Roman spear separates them, and soon they form a long continuous line that seems to stretch forever.

Demas is already walking the line. But as he predicted, the dealers are prepared. Two have purchased kohl from one of the shops to mark their choices. Another carries a basket of mud and a rag-covered stick for the same purpose. Others carry bags of henna. But Demas has outsmarted them again. He has given the *quaestor* a handful of coins to blind his eyes, then hired another two dozen of his slaves to impede the dealers. As Demas makes his way down the line, the *quaestor's* slaves bump and jostle the other dealers, ask them questions or simply bar their way. After nearly an hour of this, one frustrated dealer points to Demas and shrieks, "You have no honor!"

Without turning his head, Demas laughs and continues walking. Finally, when he's done, he brushes past me on the way to settle with the *quaestor.* "She's not among them," he whispers.

His words are like a blade in my heart. I can hardly breathe.

"I ask your pardon."

I turn to the voice and see the old Jewess by my side with her bag of coins.

"Now that your dealer has finished his business, will you allow me to see him?"

Her face is so pleading, so tender and sad, I don't have the heart to turn her away. Was she searching for a loved one, too? I dare not ask. I throw out my chest and point a jeweled finger at Demas. "Can't you see my man is still busy with the *quaestor*? And he has yet to separate and quarter our slaves. Come back in three hours. You may see him then and make your purchase."

She grabs my hand and kisses it with her leathery-looking lips that are actually surprisingly soft. "May the God of Heaven bless you! You won't be sorry. I promise you a generous profit."

I watch her as she scurries to a large oak behind me. Then watch her speak excitedly to a waiting couple: a burly man with gray hair and a gray bushy beard, and a younger woman, trim of figure and whose face is partially covered by a veil. The two women hug, and when they do the younger woman's veil falls away and my heart catches. *Rebekah!* Can it be? It looks so like her. The same high cheeks and dark eyes, the same height and build. I quickly draw my *kaffia* across my face and look again. Yes, it *is* Rebekah!

Oh, how I long to go to her, to declare myself. I don't even care that she's with another man; a man old enough to be her father, and a weeper besides, for he's crying large glistening tears. It's enough that she's alive and well. I take a step toward her, then stop. No. Too dangerous. I must wait for a safer opportunity. I head for Demas and pull him aside. Then I instruct him to sell the old Jewess any slave she wants. When I point her out as she stands beneath the oak with the others, his eyes grow wide.

"Yes," I say in acknowledgement. "It's Rebekah. You must avoid her at all cost, but find out where the old woman lives."

Rebekah

CAESAREA 70 A.D.

CHAPTER 9

"In three hours my son will be free!" Hannah's hand shakes as it clutches mine. Her eyes brim with tears as we praise God together. But our rejoicing is cut short when Hannah's face darkens, or is that the shadow of the oak tree falling across her brow? "He wouldn't deceive me, would he? This slave dealer? But no, he said, 'come back in three hours.' He wouldn't lie?"

"No. Why would he?" I draw the old woman closer, allowing her to lean into me as though she could extract strength from my lesser age. "It *must* be true." *Oh let it be, Lord. Let it be true.*

"But Rebekah, he's so thin, my son. Walking bones. Oh, I mustn't think of that now. He's alive. What more can I ask? But *so* thin." A breeze flutters her scarf and the three of us, Hannah, Zechariah, and I huddle together, for courage I think, because all around us are Roman soldiers who swear and shout and laugh as they inspect the remainder of the women slaves who have not been sold and will now be divided among them.

"Ah, well, three hours," Hannah says nervously. "Only three hours. What is three hours after all this time?" She stiffens. "Suppose the dealer wants more than I have?"

I wrap Hannah in my arms and slip several coins into her hand. "He will be glad for the profit, and glad he has one less slave to feed."

A mother's love makes Hannah slide the money into her leather pouch. Pride colors her face and makes her look away. "Oh, what a selfish creature I am!" she says, suddenly throwing back her head. "I've been going on and on, never once thinking of you. What news of your daughter? Did you see her?"

My arms drop and I shake my head. When I do, I notice Zechariah silently weeping beside me.

"Tomorrow, we'll visit the marketplace," Zechariah says, wiping his eyes with the back of his hand. "The more enterprising slavers purchase captives nearer the battlefield for almost nothing, then sell them for a handsome profit on the slave block."

Hannah nods. "Don't give up. We'll go to the block every day if we have to." Her eyes are filled with pity.

"You mustn't think of me now. You've found your son. Let him fill your thoughts. And when it's time to claim him, you must go with her, Zechariah." I smile at the large, rugged man whose heart breaks so easily for others. And rejoices, too. "That gold bedecked slaver will think twice about cheating Hannah if you're there."

Zechariah nods, then leans closer as he looks around at the milling soldiers. "Return to the house. It's senseless for you to wait here with all these Romans about. I'll care for Hannah. But it will ease me to know you are safely away." His large fingers brush my shoulder. "And fear not. You'll find Esther." He thumps his chest. "I know. I know it in here."

All the days I've spent at Hannah's waiting for Titus to reach Caesarea has given me time to think. At first my thoughts were full of Esther—dark, despairing thoughts. She is, after all, the last of my family—all I have left. *Was she dead, too*? That was the question my mind asked over and over again. And this: Was I to be left alone, with *no one*? Then I heard it, the answer, soft like a whisper, as though it were carried by the wind. *"But you have Me."* That's all. Just those words, *"But you have Me."*

"Who? Who do I have?" My voice was a shout; loud and rancorous and full of self-pity. And for a time it drowned out the whisper. I felt as if I was the only one in the world who had suffered. As if I was the only one in the world who cried herself to sleep.

As if I was the only one in the world . . . .

And then it was clear. Like the giant statue of Agrippa's daughter that dominated the public square of Caesarea, so *I* dominated my thoughts; an idol of my own making. Oh, the tears that flowed then! Tears as briny as the Sea of Salt. But amid the tears, I heard that gentle voice.

"I will never leave you or forsake you. I love you with an everlasting love."

"Oh, Jesus," I whispered, falling on my knees. "Forgive me for not remembering."

Now, entering Hannah's house—the fresh disappointment of not finding Esther still stinging my heart—I fall on my knees once more. I am heartbroken. The prospect of rescuing Esther is as dim as the caves of Mount Carmel, and there is only One who can comfort me. I bow in deep agony, and when I do, there comes that voice, soft as a sparrow's breath.

"Weeping may endure for a night, but joy comes in the morning."

We're going to feast like kings! Lamb stew bubbles on Hannah's stove, pluming aromas I've not smelled in a very long time. It's in honor of her son's homecoming that I'm making it, for meat is rarely eaten except during the feasts of the Lord or on special occasions such as weddings or the entertaining of important guests. I've also prepared *shefot,* a cream poured into tube-like wooden vessels and sprinkled with sugar. And two large barley loaves seasoned with cumin and fennel are baking in the oven. In addition, I've purchased fig cakes and cheese and pistachio nuts from the nearby shops. I'm nearly overcome with anticipation of seeing the happy look on Hannah's face when she arrives.

As I wait, I busy myself washing leeks and radishes, and wonder how long before Hannah walks in the door with her son. All this preparation helps diminish my sorrow over Esther. Though I have received no promises, no assurances from the Lord regarding my daughter, I'm determined to walk by faith. God has promised me joy. When the joy is to come, well, I must leave that to Him. So instead, I picture Hannah's happy face, feel *her* joy at finding her son. But I grow impatient. I've been cooking for hours. *When will they come*?

I scamper around the kitchen making final preparations by setting four wooden bowls on the polished table. And just as I place the last one, I hear a commotion outside and rush to the door to open it. The street is full of people weeping, shouting, laughing. Arms wave like wheat in the air, and bodies press around a central figure. The house is raised a good hand's length higher than the street and I'm able to make out the top of Zechariah's wiry, gray head. Surely Hannah is with him; her son, too, though I can see neither. Everyone is talking at once.

"Welcome home, Judah!"

"God has been merciful!"

"Blessed be the name of the Lord!"

"*Hashem* has answered our prayers!"

I lean against the doorpost, my heart filled with gratitude as I listen to all the well- wishes. They seem to go on forever, but I don't grow weary of hearing them, for I'm caught up in the moment, this sublime moment when good has triumphed over evil, proving it's possible, even in these dark days. And I'm overcome with joy.

The crowd slowly dissipates. I hear a young man, surely Judah's friend by the way he is greeted, offer to prepare the *mikvah*, then see him head toward the back of the house where the entrance to the lower level and baths are located. Finally, only Hannah and her son and Zechariah are left standing outside the door.

When Hannah sees me, when her eyes light upon me for the first time, she giggles like a girl, then beckons me to come. I do, and she introduces me to Judah. She's right to worry. I see rags and bones and little else. And his face? Oh, how gaunt it is, and the color of sifted flour! And all the while his body smells like an open sore. But what I see in his eyes makes me take heart. Mini goblets of horror, yes. Judah surely has seen terrible things. It colors him with darkness. But there's strength, too, and determination, and gratitude, and a light, a small stubborn light that refuses to be extinguished.

I enfold him in my arms as if he were my own son, and weep at his neck. But when we part, my fingers feel the deep hollows around his protruding ribs. *Be Merciful, Lord. Heal him. Do not let Hannah lose him now.*

"Such a wonderful smell!" Judah says when we enter the house. Then he closes his eyes and sniffs. "Can it really be lamb stew?"

"It is! And in your honor. There are other good things, too: flat bread and cheese and *shefot*, and fig cakes and . . . ."

"First he must bathe, then dress in his new tunic." Hannah's eyes are full of love, and they are looking at me. "Then he'll have some of your fine supper. But only a little. You can't bring back a shriveled stomach all at once. Judah must eat only a small portion at a time until he's used to real food again."

Her son laughs and pushes oily, matted hair from his forehead. "For weeks I've been ordered about by the Romans. Now that I'm home, it appears I'm to be ordered about by my mother!"

"I like your Judah," I say to Hannah when he leaves and heads for the stairs to the lower rooms of the *mikvah*. "He has a sense of humor."

"At least the Romans haven't taken that from him." Hannah rubs her face with her gnarled hands. "But he's thin and weak. You see. You have eyes. He pretends he's well, but if it hadn't been for Zechariah's strong arms to gird him . . . well, we might not have gotten here."

I lead Hannah to the table. "Sit," I say, pulling out a stool and gently helping her onto it. "And be at peace. God will surely restore your son. Would He bring him so far otherwise?" I take a fig cake and place it in her hand. "You haven't eaten since this morning. This will strengthen you until Judah is ready to join us." Then I go and pull the two loaves of bread from the oven, and at once fill the room with a pleasing yeasty aroma. Finally, I dip two cups into the large clay water jar by the door and give one to Hannah, the other to Zechariah, who up to now has done nothing but stand nearby and grin from ear to ear. "Now tell me how it went with the slave dealer."

Hannah takes a bite of her cake, chews for a moment, then swallows. It seems to revive her for she sits straighter on her stool. "That jackal made me wait for hours. And after he finished his business with the *quaestor* he disappeared. No one knew where he went. He just vanished. Finally, he sent one of the *quaestor's* slaves to me. He didn't even come himself. In fact, I never saw him again.

"And the slave he sent! What a slovenly lout! With green eyes like a cat, and so much hair on his arms he looked as though he was covered in fleece. He took little interest in me or his task. Just told me to pick out anyone I wanted, and then, without examining Judah, fixed the price at one hundred *drachmas*. One hundred *drachmas*! I expected him to demand six times that amount. I could hardly believe my good fortune.

"But when I paid him, he asked me where I lived. Said he needed it for his records. I thought it strange. But I was frightened and didn't want anything to go wrong, so I told him. But after I left him, I began to worry. Suppose he went back and the slave dealer was dissatisfied with the price? Suppose he sends his men to my house? And takes Judah away? Those were my thoughts. Are my thoughts still."

"Perhaps it was the sight of Zechariah that made him so generous," I say, handing my large friend, who has finally taken a nearby stool, his own fig cake. His brow is crinkled. "What troubles you, Zechariah?"

"I don't know . . . an aging man's imagination, perhaps. But just before the dealer disappeared, I got a good look at him and . . . well, he looked like Demas!"

"Demas? You mean Demas from Pella? That Demas?"

Zechariah shrugs. "I know. It sounds mad. Forget my saying it. I'm sure I was mistaken. Demas is a beekeeper, not a slaver."

"Let's not indulge in worry," I say, taking a bite of my own cake and sitting on the stool next to Hannah. "God has been good to us. He has returned Hannah's son. Let's rejoice in that." And just as we all begin to relax, there's a knock on the door.

"Ah, another well-wisher no doubt." Hannah rises from her stool.

I listen to Hannah's sandals scrape across the stone floor, hear the door open, hear her strained voice say, "What . . . do you want? Why have you come?" I hear a man's voice, low and gruff, but not his words. When Hannah begins to cry, Zechariah and I leap from our stools. By the time we get to the door, Hannah has already closed it. Her face is drained, and in her hand she holds a wax tablet.

"What's wrong? What has happened?" My arm encircles her shoulder.

Instead of answering, she hands me the tablet inscribed with a crudely drawn map of the Cardo Maximus, the main street of the city running north and south, and directions to a house in the Greek Sector. "I don't understand," I say, squinting down at the tablet.

Hannah takes Zechariah's arm, no doubt to steady herself. "That . . . accursed slave dealer! His master is displeased, he said. Displeased with the price I paid for Judah. Said his master claims I cheated him, and demands I bring Judah back to his house, along with five-hundred *drachmas*. Or face arrest." She pauses, and looks at me strangely. "He said I was to bring you as witness to the sale. He was very insistent about it, too. 'Bring the other woman who lives in this house, as witness. And don't bother coming without her.' Those were his words. But why? Why would he say that?" She presses a gnarled palm against her cheek. "It makes no sense."

"It could be a trick." Zechariah rubs the side of his bulbous nose. "Perhaps the Romans have found out that you and your son are from the House of David."

"Then why insist I come, too?" I shake my head. "No. There's something more to this."

"I've told no one who you are," Hannah says. "The Romans have spies everywhere, even in our poor little Quarter. I didn't want anyone knowing that you, Rebekah, are . . . were the wife of a priest and rebel. Or that you, Zechariah, are a friend of that menace in Ephesus, the one you call John the Apostle. I didn't want to bring trouble down on your heads. But perhaps they've found out. Or perhaps they think you are my relatives, making you descendants of the House of David, as well."

Without a word, Zechariah leaves the room then returns with his dagger strapped to his waist. "We'll smuggle Judah out of the city. It will be easy enough with your house so close to the North Gate. By the time that slave dealer knows we're gone, it will be too late.'

Hannah shakes her head. "Judah can't survive such an ordeal. He's too weak. Oh, I don't know what to do! Am I to lose him again?"

"Lose who?" a voice says behind us.

I turn, and there is Judah, bathed and smiling. He's a handsome young man with brown wavy hair and dimpled chin. But the way he wears the new linen tunic Hannah purchased—belted at the waist—reveals how thin he truly is, though his broad shoulders testify he was once a powerful man and makes me understand why a slaver would purchase him. And there, there in Judah's eyes is a shimmering light.

We all stare without saying a word, forcing Judah to repeat his question. "Who will you lose again?"

It's foolish to keep such a thing from him so I quickly tell what happened. Judah says nothing. But that light dims a bit.

"Go to your friends in the Greek sector, those followers of Jesus," Hannah says, her voice desperate. "You'll be safe there until you're well enough to travel. Then we'll smuggle you out of the city. Oh, *please* you must go."

"And leave you to face the Romans alone? What kind of son would do that?" His voice is laced with fatigue, but there's resolve in it, too.

"We're like chickens running around without heads," I say, frowning. "We say, 'maybe it's this, maybe it's that,' but we don't know anything. Before we act foolishly, we must understand the trouble."

Zechariah leans forward in his stool. "Surely you don't mean for us to surrender? Like sheep to wolves?" He fingers the hilt of his dagger.

"What will your one blade do against the Roman army? For it's a simple matter for Titus to send the full weight of his forces against us if he chooses. No. Let's use our heads."

"What do you propose?" There's reluctance in Zechariah's voice.

"You and I will go alone." My eyebrows arch as I look at Zechariah. "If you're willing, that is." When he nods, I turn to Hannah. "We'll act as your agents. I have enough gold from my *semadi* to turn the head or heart of the most jaded slaver. If we're not back in two hours, then Hannah, you and Judah must either seek refuge among the followers of the Way or escape through the North Gate. I see no alternative. Fortify yourselves with food, then pack in case you must leave."

Hannah's gnarled fingers clasp her throat. "What you propose is too dangerous. I can't ask you to do it."

"You didn't ask. And my mind is made up. Perhaps Esther is beyond our saving, but Judah isn't. Zechariah and I will tell this slave master that Judah is too ill to come; that already he appears a defective slave and we have a good mind to return him for our money." When I see the look of horror on Hannah's face I laugh. "Don't worry, after I give this jackal a piece of my mind and a few of my coins he'll be happy to be rid of us."

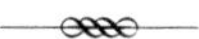

I wear a costly white wool tunic the hem of which reaches my ankles and is decorated with thin black stripes. The same fabric covers my plaited hair. Over the tunic I wear a belted black robe edged in red. Tucked inside is a bag of gold coins. These are my best clothes. I wear them for a reason—to appear before the slaver as a woman not easily dismissed. And nothing accomplishes that so effortlessly as a show of wealth.

Zechariah has not bothered to change, but wears his dusty, worn clothing. He says it will make him look more intimidating. He's right, for in his rough homespun he appears almost as wild as I remember the desert prophet, John the Baptist, to have looked.

We walk the stone-slab sidewalks of Caesarea's wealthy sector as we head for the slave dealer's house. We've passed this way before on the way to the auction of Titus's captives so I'm unimpressed by the large gleaming stone houses, and hardly look at them as we pass. Neither

Zechariah nor I speak. He's praying, for he has that far away look he always gets. I'm praying, too. And considering I don't know what danger awaits, I'm surprisingly calm.

Zechariah carries the wax tablet, the one with the crude directions, and from time to time indicates we are to turn here or go there. At last we come to an imposing house whose doorway is trimmed in ornately carved marble. In the middle of the lintel is a large face of some unknown goddess surrounded by clusters of grapes and curling vines. Already, I don't like the place, and by the look on Zechariah's face, he doesn't either. Without saying a word, Zechariah knocks.

A tall, broad, finely-dressed man opens the massive wooden door.

"*Demas*?" I say in disbelief, for the resemblance is striking.

At once the man smiles. "Your eyes do not deceive you. I am Demas from Pella." He quickly ushers us in.

"But . . . but . . . ." My thoughts are as jumbled as stew, and words will not form.

Demas laughs as he closes the door behind us, then greets Zechariah and me with a kiss. "Don't ask questions. Soon you will know all." His eyebrows arch when he sees our strained faces. "Fear not, for it's a happy business. But brace yourself, Rebekah."

My mind is whirling now, like the winds off the Judean mountain tops. *What can this mean?* A pebble, caught in the sole of one of my sandals, makes a scraping noise as I cross the beautiful mosaic floor. I stay close to Zechariah. Without a word we follow Demas down the hall to a large sun-streaked atrium. Everywhere I look there is marble: on the floors, over doorways, around the ceilings. And columns—columns too numerous to count. The walls themselves are plastered, and brightly painted with birds and flowers. With so much wealth, have I any hope of impressing the slaver with mine? I begin to fear he'll be unreasonable. And when I see the outline of three men standing in the shadow of a large column, my heart pounds. Even so, there's something familiar about them: their stance, their build, the shape of their heads.

When we reach the marble fountain, Demas stops and points. That's all, just points. I grasp Zechariah's arm as my eyes follow Demas's finger to the shadowed men, and when one steps into the shaft of light pouring through the open roof, my knees buckle. Had I not been holding onto Zechariah I would have surely crashed to the floor.

"I'm sorry I had to bring you here like this. Without warning," the man says. "Forgive me. But it would have been dangerous to expose ourselves at the house where you are staying, or dangerous even to send you word that I was here. I'm told there are Roman spies everywhere."

"*Ethan?*" I blink. Surely I'm seeing things. This can't be my Ethan. His face is clean shaven and looks strange to me, but that voice . . . . The man steps closer, then stops. His eyes rest on my hand, the one clutching Zechariah's arm. Oh, I know those eyes, those shoulders, those arms!

At once I release Zechariah and rush to my husband. "*Oh, Ethan*! I thought you were dead!" Then I wrap him in my arms and kiss his face. There's no end to my kisses. I'm laughing and crying, all at the same time, and praising God. "*Oh, Ethan,*" I say again, when I pull away. "I never thought . . . I never thought I'd see you again." I can barely speak I'm so overcome. "Oh, my love, it's really you." I struggle to get the words out as my arms encircle his neck and my kissing begins anew. Now he's laughing and crying, too, and holding me close and kissing my cheeks, my neck, my lips.

"Then you still love me," he whispers in my ear, as if there was ever any doubt; as if I could ever love another. "I wasn't sure . . . I only hoped . . . ."

I don't know how long we go on like this. Time has stopped, and for me there's no one else in the room. We just hold each other and kiss and laugh and cry. Finally, when I'm fully convinced my husband is flesh and blood, and really here in my arms, my eyes drift to the two men still hovering beside the marble column.

I shriek when at last I recognize Aaron and Benjamin. Then it all begins anew, this time with the four of us hugging and kissing and weeping on each other's necks. Oh, I could have stayed in my family's arms the whole night long—this family which I thought was lost. I feel such joy. Oh, yes! For me morning has come and joy washes over me—wave after wave of pure joy.

Until . . . .

I notice the patch over Aaron's eye. See that two sons are missing. "Abner and Joseph?" My voice is a vapor.

"Gone," Ethan says, pulling me closer to him; encircling me with his strong arms that infuse me with strength. I can do nothing but lay my head on his chest and weep. Sorrow pours from me like an overflowing cistern. And as we had just come together in joy, so now we all embrace in grief, and mourn our great loss. We nearly wear ourselves out with crying, but at last we part. And when I look into their faces, I feel a new wave of joy. Yes, I've lost two sons, but God has spared two others as well as my husband. I am blessed, and I'll not take this great blessing lightly. I think my sons and Ethan feel the same way, for they smile as though reading my thoughts.

Then Ethan tucks me under one arm. "I've prepared a feast. Come, let's eat." He glances at Zachariah who, like Demas, has been standing quietly behind us. I'm surprised to see his eyes and mouth harden when I introduce Zachariah. And as Demas leads us into a large room, I quickly tell Ethan and my sons all Zechariah has done for me. By the time we enter the area where a long, low table sits, surrounded by elegant pillowed couches, Ethan is smiling.

The table is laden with roasted lamb, fish, quail, figs and bread, and so many other good things I can scarcely believe it. I haven't seen such food in years.

Ethan points to a couch at the end, and I take my seat, then he beside me. Everyone else settles on one of the other couches. And after Ethan offers thanks and praise to God for this feast and the miracle of our reunion, we begin dipping bread into the many bowls before us.

We are all mouths now, and talk for hours. Ethan, Aaron and Benjamin speak about Jerusalem. How they lived. What they saw. The final battle for the Temple. The copper scroll. They save, for last, the details of how Abner and Joseph died, and even how Aaron lost his eye trying to save Daniel. And then they tell me why they're here, in Caesarea. It's hard to hear, to take it all in. Even so, I'm sure they haven't told me the worst of it. It's in their eyes, especially Aaron's. I know there are things seen and done which they'll never share with me.

When they finish, Zechariah and I tell our stories. We talk and laugh and cry for hours on end. And when it seems we stop and take our first breath, I notice the oil lamps are lit, and from where I sit, see that the roofless atrium is as black as onyx.

I jump to my feet. "Judah! I've forgotten about Judah!"

"Have they left the city, do you think?"

Zechariah, who holds my elbow, doesn't answer. We are nearing the Jewish Quarter. I want to run, but fear of drawing unwanted attention stops me; that, and Zechariah's tight grip.

"How could I have been so selfish? To while away the hours in feasting and talking? Oh, how frightened Hannah and Judah must be!"

"It's useless to flog yourself with words," Zechariah says softly. "What's done, is done. And I'm as much to blame. All thoughts of Judah flew from my head, as well."

"But Zechariah, he's so weak. So . . . ."

"Hush." Zechariah's voice is stern. "Someone might hear. You never know who lurks in the shadows."

And so we continue in silence until we reach Hannah's. My hand is on the latch first. When I discover it's unlocked, I burst through the door. Zechariah's heavy breathing tells me he's close behind. And as he comes alongside me, he unsheathes his dagger.

The house is quiet, and except for a small flickering light coming from the kitchen, it's dark as well. We head toward the light. And there, sitting on a stool holding her own dagger with two hands, is Hannah. She flashes it wildly in the air, then stops when she recognizes us.

"The way you burst through the door, I thought you were the Romans." Her hands shake as she places the dagger on the table. "I left it unlocked so those beasts wouldn't break it down and destroy the house. I was afraid . . . I thought . . . ."

"I know." I bend and kiss her head, and notice she's trying to stop her hands from shaking by clutching the sides of her tunic. Her eyes are still wide with panic. "It's my fault. My fault," I say, feeling downcast and sorrowful at causing Hannah such anxiety. "I should have come sooner. Only . . . the most wonderful thing has happened." I quickly tell her about the events of the evening. Suddenly, she is our Hannah again, laughing and clapping and wiggling on her stool like a girl.

"But oh, how worried I was when I realized I had forgotten about Judah! I imagined all sorts of terrible things. He's so weak. Any journey now would be difficult for him. I'm so glad you and Judah didn't leave."

"But Judah did leave. I made him go to the Greek Quarter to hide with the followers of the Way. A rich couple there leads the Gentile church; a couple known for their kindness. Judah didn't want to go, but I cried and fussed until he did."

"And you stayed behind?" Zechariah says. "Why?"

"I thought if the Romans came and found me, it would satisfy them, and they wouldn't bother looking for Judah. What's one more sick captive to them?"

"You're very brave," I whisper.

Hannah shrugs. "I'm old. Too old to leave my home. What better way to use what's left of my life than in trying to save my son?"

I laugh and cover her face with kisses, then pull a wooden tablet from my robe. "Here. It's official. The bill of sale for Judah. Now you have nothing to worry about. And tomorrow, we'll bring him home."

Vendors hawking their wares sound like squawking birds as Zechariah and I enter the marketplace. We head for the long, large block of stone that serves as a platform. Even from this distance and over the throng of bodies, I see that as yet there are no slaves on the block for auction. The marketplace is so crowded I must squeeze between two portly women to keep up with Zechariah. We stop when the wall of bodies becomes too tight to breach. I stand on my toes in hopes of glimpsing Ethan and my sons. For safety's sake, we cannot be seen together. But oh, how difficult that is! To be forced apart after only just being reunited.

My heart catches when I see Ethan's broad frame. He stands in front, well positioned to see the entire stone block which runs along one section of the market. I envision the enterprising Demas securing Ethan's place with a bribe to the *aediles*, the Market Manager, who oversees the public auctions. My sons flank Ethan, and talk with heads together. How strange they look with their shaven faces, their elaborate robes and silk head coverings, their long gold chains that gleam around their necks. If I didn't know who they were I'd never recognize them.

Zechariah leans closer to me. "We should have been at Hannah's by now with Judah. She's sure to worry."

"Yes. But I must stay. You go and fetch him. After last night, it would be too cruel to make her worry again."

"I won't leave you. Suppose there's trouble? Then Ethan and your sons would be forced to expose themselves by coming to your rescue."

"Oh, Zechariah, *please*. You go. I cannot. Surely it was God's mercy that brought me here. If I hadn't overheard those two men talking about coming to buy women for their brothels, I wouldn't know about this slave dealer from Jerusalem and his auction today."

"I won't leave," Zechariah repeats. And by his firm expression I know it's pointless to argue, so I sigh and pull him by the arm hoping to get closer to the block. But it's no use. People press us on all sides. Most are Greeks or Romans. Only a handful of Jews are peppered among them, and I wonder if they're also searching for loved ones.

Suddenly, the Market Manager appears. He's a stout man. Even from my vantage point his double chin is clearly visible. He wears a toga, the symbol of Roman citizenship. Its purple stripe along the edge, and the eagle-capped ivory baton in his hand, testify to his office as *Curule Aedile.* So do his two accompanying lictors, who each carry a thick bundle of leather-bound birch rods symbolizing their authority to arrest and punish.

The massive folds of the white linen toga make the Manager look like a draped barrel. He carries his baton upright, while the stubby fingers of his other hand hold a tablet, no doubt for calculating the taxes due him from the sales. He sits on a tufted litter shouldered by eight slaves. They carry him to a curved backless chair beneath a canopy. After he's settled, he signals for the auction to begin.

The crowd stirs as a dozen young women are forced to mount the block and walk its length. They are freshly bathed and scented, with hair cascading over their shoulders. For clothing, they wear only a loosely draped cloak. Around each of their necks hangs the customary scroll prescribed by law that describes any sickness or defects. Though they look in need of nourishment, they are all pretty.

The Market Manager sends one of his lictors to examine the feet of each woman. Two have chalked soles. One is a Nubian from Egypt, the other, with hair the color of gold, is perhaps from Germania. The rest, judging from their complexion, hair, and eyes, appear to be Judeans. The Manager notates this on his tablet, obviously to tally the import taxes, for all imported slaves must have their feet chalked, a practice common in Rome but not here in the East. I suspect it is merely a way for the Market Manager to enrich himself.

That done, the slaver invites all interested parties to inspect the women. At once, men rush the block and pull off the women's cloaks. Now they stand naked and at the mercy of prying eyes and probing hands. I look away. Esther is not among them, and it breaks my heart to think she had or will have to endure this.

Bids are shouted into the air. Men push against each other. Everyone talks at once. I'm on my toes searching for Ethan. He stands away from the block. The look on his face, the jut of his chin, the way he cocks his head to the left tells me he's appalled by what he sees. Only Demas is walking the line, or trying to. He roughly pushes aside those in his way. Men curse him and wave their fists. I know Demas is only playing his part, for we've all had time to see that Esther is not here.

When the bidding ends, the crowd thins. Some people wander toward the nearby docks. There were always new ships arriving with goods from all over the Empire being unloaded on the quays running along the edge of Herod's magnificent semicircle harbor: cargos of hippopotamus teeth or elephant tusks for inlaying furniture or making combs or knife handles, spices and perfumes, silks, expensive cedar wood, and exotic foods.

Zechariah and I remain where we are. Ethan, too, for I see him more easily now. But soon more people will pour into the plaza, for we've heard that women will be forced to walk the block throughout the day. It's useless for Zechariah to stay, and cruel to leave Hannah needlessly worrying for hours. I'm about to insist that Zechariah go for Judah, when suddenly there's the most awful shriek behind me.

"Eeeee! By the gods! There she is! The idolater. The defamer of Isis! The one who stole the sacred cup from her temple!"

I turn around and see Argos, the scratches, the ones I made with my fingernails, still visible on his face.

"Who will help me obtain justice for the Queen of Heaven, the Mother of the Gods, the one who gave birth to both heaven and earth?"

People gather around. Many eye me with raised brows, not certain if I'm the offender Argos describes. Zechariah rises up like a bear, spreading his large frame, arms and all, between Argos and me.

"We must leave," I whisper, "before Ethan exposes himself to danger." But I'm also thinking of Zechariah. Nothing good can come of a Jew fighting a Greek.

Before I can make my escape, Argos darts around Zechariah and grabs my arm. "Look how the thief seeks to flee! Good citizens of Caesarea, what's to be done? Have you no laws to protect your gods?

In this, the seat of Roman justice, should such a malicious act go unpunished?"

I jerk free of Argos, but three men, the same men I encountered on the road, bar my way. My heart catches when I see Ethan's broad frame making his way toward us.

Stay back, my love. Oh, please stay back.

Zechariah's fists are clenched as though ready to hurl them squarely at Argos's face. Are we all to be undone by this mad follower of Isis? My mouth forms a disjointed prayer while Zechariah raises his arm as though ready to strike. We're all doomed now. I close my eyes.

"What's the meaning of this?" says a shrill voice that seems to come from overhead.

I open my eyes, and there to the side is the Market Manager, his double chin quivering, his eagle-headed baton waving, his tablet balancing on his amply draped lap as he sits on his raised, tufted litter held aloft by glistening slaves. But his two lictors stand between Argos and me, just as if God had plucked them out of the air and placed them there Himself.

"Well, speak up!" the Market Manager bellows. When no one utters a word, he shakes his head sternly. "I won't have my market disrupted by troublemakers. We're here to conduct commerce. And you," he points a jeweled, sausage-like finger at me, "are obstructing it." He gestures for his bearers to lower the litter, then pulls his squat body upright, nearly dropping his tablet. The crowd has already moved aside for the lowering of the litter, then to make a path for the Manager to walk through. Though he's as round as a barrel, he's hardly as sturdy, for he leans on one of the bearers as he walks. He takes several steps, then stops in front of me. "Well! What have you to say for yourself?"

"I . . . have done nothing wrong, my lord. This man lies." I glance at Argos, and when I do I see Ethan and my sons rapidly closing the distance between us. They are near. Too near. My head throbs.

The Market Manager turns to Argos. "Can you prove your claim?"

"Well . . . that is . . . ." Argos's face turns as purple as the stripe on the Market Manager's toga.

"Can neither of you speak without stammering? Tell me plain and true what goes on here." The Manager looks at me for an answer as he signals for his litter. Strain and fatigue mar his face as if he's thoroughly wearied by the whole affair.

"My lord," I say, "I've never stepped foot in the Temple of Isis. I am a Jewess and as I'm sure you know, a Jew would never, could never do such a thing."

"A Jew? Ah, yes. I'm well aware of your aversion for other gods."

The litter is brought closer, then lowered. And when the Manager hikes up the great folds of his tunic to take his seat on it, I see his shriveled leg.

"Oh, yes, I know how it is with you Jews," he says. "But that is hardly proof you don't have his cup." The round puffy face frowns. "Perhaps I should bring this matter before the Procurator and let him decide who is right and who is wrong."

"I do have a cup," I quickly say. "But the cup is mine. And Argos desires it because he believes it can heal." I see the Manager's eyes flash and know I have pricked something inside him. "But it is God who heals, not the cup. I've tried telling Argos that."

"A god who heals? There are many gods. Surely they all heal? But I suppose you are referring to only yours?" The Manager's eyes fasten on me. His tablet lies discarded among the folds on his lap as he fingers the ivory baton. "That's it, isn't it? You mean only *your* god can heal."

A murmur spreads throughout the crowd as people wait expectantly for something to happen. I'm surrounded by those who worship all manner of gods, and who appear ready to fiercely defend their worship. Many press closer to hear my answer.

"If you wish, I will pray and ask my God to heal you," I say in a near whisper.

"Heal me? Of what?" The Manager raises his baton, and I fear he is about to order my arrest.

I lower my eyes, waiting for his command, but all I hear is laughter. When I look up, that double chin is heaving up and down, the baton is on his lap alongside the tablet, and his hands are pressing against his round, quivering belly. Surely, he means to mock my God. But when his laughter subsides, his eyes tell me something altogether different, and I see how desperately he wants to believe.

"I have no wish to offend the gods, not even yours," he says, with a smirk on his face. "Pray if you like, but make it quick. I've business to conduct."

And so I place my trembling hands on the hem of his toga and ask the God of Abraham, Isaac, and Jacob to heal him in the name of Jesus. It's over before anyone knows what's happened. I see the Manager move his leg this way and that beneath the folds of his garment, then see the look of disdain on his face. "I am as I always was," he says, ordering his slaves, with a flick of a hand, to hoist the litter. "It seems your god is as deaf as ours." He takes up his baton as the slaves carry him away. "You'll cause no more disturbances in my market," he shouts back at me. "If you do, I'll have you arrested." With that, his bearers carry him back to his curved seat beneath the canopy.

As soon as the Manager is settled in his chair, Argos and his thugs waste no time surrounding Zechariah and me. Two of them hold daggers. Now our predicament is worse than before. The Manager's disappointment over my seemingly fruitless prayer has embittered him towards me. He'll surely make good his threat if any trouble begins.

"No one will help you now," Argos says, grinning like a madman. "We will all go to your house, and there you'll hand over your cup."

What happens next occurs to fast I can hardly comprehend it. But suddenly, five Galatians with blond hair and sky-blue eyes, and as quiet as death, appear in our midst; large men, and fierce, too, with bodies like gladiators. Without raising a sweat or their voices, they knock Argos's three men to the ground. Then two Galatians take Argos by each arm and pull him to the side to make way for an elegant looking woman to enter our midst. Her white muslin *stola* nearly touches the ground and is richly bordered in red. Over one shoulder is draped a red *palla,* fastened by a large emerald pin. Her wrists and fingers are covered with gold and precious gems. Three necklaces ring her throat: two gold; one, a mix of pearls and emeralds. Her elaborately braided hair is piled high atop her head and covered with a thin gold-spun net. And over that is draped a sheer white silk veil. It's been a long time since I've seen anyone so wonderfully arrayed.

"Come with me," she says quietly, then turns before I can say a word.

Ethan and my sons are now only a few cubits away, and fearing they'll do something rash, I turn on my heels and follow the strange woman. Several steps later, I hazard a backward glance, and am relieved to see only Zechariah trudging behind.

"We've been searching for you," the woman says over her shoulder as she leads us down a stone-paved street toward the largest houses in the city. "Ever since Judah came to us we've been searching. We were ready to give up, thinking you dead. But praise our Lord and Savior, we've found you."

The woman is agile and slender. She moves quickly along the columned streets, heading south. It's as if there are wings on her heels. She doesn't even bother looking back to see if we keep up. I worry about Zechariah. He's beginning to show the wear of the past several weeks. They've sapped his great strength, and he huffs and puffs behind me.

Finally, the woman stops in front of an enormous house, larger even than the other grand houses around it. Its front double door is carved cedar; the doorpost and lintels, carved marble. Before her hand can touch the door, it's opened by a man, stooped and far past his prime. She says something to him in a low, pleasant voice, then ushers us into a large sunny atrium. The fountain, an imposing marble statue of a girl holding a jug from which water pours into a pool at her feet, dominates the center.

The strange, elegant woman beckons us to sit on a nearby cushioned bench, and Zechariah looks grateful as he lowers his bulky frame onto the colorful damask pillows. For the first time I wonder what has happened to her Galatians. "Your men? Are they . . . ." I stop in mid sentence for she is laughing. She laughs and laughs, and just as I begin to feel uncomfortable and wonder if it was wise for us to come, she brushes back her veil to reveal her full face.

"Well? Don't you recognize me?"

I stare at the lovely face with its high cheekbones and almond shaped eyes the color of carob. "Who . . . are you?" I stammer in bewilderment.

When she smiles I see it; the small space between her upper front teeth and the barely noticeable rosette-shaped mark on her cheek, which she points to with her jewel-bedecked finger.

"*Judith?*" I rise, but my legs, which feel like dough, can't hold me and I drop back onto the pillows. "Judith? Is that you?"

She laughs. Oh, how she laughs. Then she dances around the room, and finally she comes to where I'm still sitting dumbfounded, and scoops me up in her arms.

"Rebekah! My darling sister! It's so good to see you. I knew you right away. It almost cost us dearly for I nearly gave myself away. How I wanted to hold you and kiss you and tell you who I was. I never dreamed you were the 'Rebekah' Judah spoke of—the 'Rebekah' brave enough to risk death to save one half-starved young man and an old woman. But I should have known. You were always brave. Always standing up to me and Mama."

"Then *you* are the rich follower of the Way Hannah spoke of, the one who heads the Gentile Church here in Caesarea?"

"Yes, my husband and I both. We do what we can for the believers. Many are poor, and some, like my Galatians, we have saved from the arena. God has been good to us. And while He has not blessed us with children, He has blessed us with great wealth. Titus's legions love roast pork with their *garum.* My husband has grown rich selling pigs to his army." She laughs as she pulls me up off the bench. "You'll meet him later, and I'll enjoy getting to know yours better, too," she smiles at Zechariah. "But first we have over twenty years of catching up to do."

We're all sitting here in Judith's house with her and her husband—Apollonios, my husband and sons, Zechariah, Demas, Hannah, and Judah. We've been here all afternoon and most of the evening, laughing, talking, catching up on the missed years as well as eating foods I've never eaten before, and which Hannah refused because they were "unclean."

Judith was kind about it and had the cook make Hannah a special dinner of minced beef soaked in wine. The rest of us, even the normally ritually observant Aaron and Ethan, ate roasted hare stuffed with chicken livers, baked dormice filled with pine nuts, and pork sausages. There were also platters of apples and pears and apricots, almonds drizzled with honey, the best date cakes I've ever tasted, as well as the finest Egyptian-wheat pastries filled with fruit and nuts. It was a feast befitting this great reunion of so many formerly disconnected souls. Oh, I tell you, I felt God smile upon us! I felt His pleasure! We were a family again, all of us. And how we laughed over Judith mistaking Zechariah for my husband, though Ethan didn't seem to think it was funny.

We have all eaten until I fear we'll burst. All but Judah. Hannah continues to watch him like a hawk, and reminds him at every turn that his stomach is as shriveled as a dried date.

Soon, many followers of the Way will come, both great and small, rich and poor. For all are welcome here in Judith's and Apollonios' house. And Judith has promised to ask the believers to pray for Esther. Though Ethan, my sons, and Demas stayed until the last of the slave girls were auctioned, Esther was not among them. Judith says God has done many miracles in Caesarea for His people, and she's sure He'll do one for us. That's when I tell her He already has. After all, wasn't this reunion a miracle?

My sister is here in Caesarea! I can scarcely take it in. And she and her Gentile husband head the church. Oh, how God's ways are different from ours! How high they are! The man my parents spurned and deprived of knowing and loving, the *pig farmer* they called him—and the only name they ever used when speaking of their son-in-law—has turned out to be a kind and generous and mighty man of God—the head and not the tail.

I would feel sad over the waste of it all if I were not so full of joy. I can't feel sad about anything, not today, tonight, this moment. My head spins like a child's clay disk. It reels with the knowledge that my husband and two sons sit by my side, that the sister my family mourned as dead is restored to me, that we have good friends in Zechariah, Demas, Hannah and Judah. And that we're all together.

My head leans on Ethan's shoulder as I listen to my sister tell of the wondrous things God has been doing in their lives, and I feel incredibly blessed. Oh, yes, weeping endures for a night but joy *does* come in the morning.

"We might have found her," Judith says three days later. "But don't get your hopes up. One of my spies claims there's a young woman named Esther recently brought here with other girls from Jerusalem by a slaver who follows the army. He's been selling his girls to every brothel along the Via Maris."

My breath catches. "Oh Judith, a brothel?"

My sister shakes her head. "Though the slave dealer swore she was as healthy as a camel, the brothels wouldn't take her because they thought she looked diseased. Even with the kohl on her eyes, and the alkanet and ocher on her lips, they said she looked sickly."

"Then where is she?" I can hardly get the words out.

"In the house of Cassius Plotius Flavillus."

"Who?"

"The Market Manager." Judith ignores my groan. "The slave who runs his kitchen purchased her for a few *drachmas*. Said the dealer was happy to be rid of her. She now carries wood for their fires."

"Oh, this is terrible!"

"Surely it's better than a brothel," Judith says, looking puzzled. "And Cassius Flavillus is not unkind to his servants. It could be worse, Rebekah."

"You don't understand. The Manager holds me in contempt. He'll not be disposed to show me any kindness." I quickly tell her how I prayed for his leg just before she and her Galatians arrived at the marketplace.

When I'm done, Judith tucks one hand under her chin, just like she used to when signaling the matter was settled. "Don't think about that now. Let's first determine if she really is *our* Esther. Tomorrow, I'll send someone to the house to make inquires."

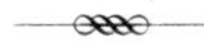

An aging servant—for none in Judith's house are slaves but all are free and are paid wages—leads a lanky, middle-aged woman to the atrium where Judith and I sit talking by the fountain. We've been expecting her. All morning I've torn my nerves to shreds waiting. She is related to the head kitchen slave at the house of the Market Manager, and was once a slave there herself until she purchased her freedom. She's also a follower of the Way. For these reasons Judith chose her to make the inquiries.

"Come, Joanna," Judith says, in a pleasant voice. "Sit here." She pats the cushioned bench where we also sit. "Tell us what you've learned."

Joanna rearranges the deep lines on her cheeks when she smiles. It's not difficult to see by her face that she's had a hard life. She takes a seat beside Judith, but as she does she slides one hand to the waist of her tunic to conceal the patched fabric. "I brought my cousin the date cakes and honey jars like you asked, with your compliments and good wishes. And just as I said, nothing loosens Quintus's tongue like honey." She giggles, sounding almost childlike. "I couldn't get him to stop talking after that."

I feel my impatience rise. "Did you see her? Did you see the wood carrier? The one they call Esther?"

"Oh I did, indeed," Joanna says, sounding very pleased with herself. "A scrawny thing. As pale as chalk. But Quintus said she works well enough."

"And . . . what does she look like? Describe her. *Please.*" I'm barely able to contain myself.

"She was pretty, at least she would be if she had some meat on her bones. But she had other qualities. Long eyelashes for one; the longest I've ever seen. And eyes as big as flatbreads. Only . . . ."

"Yes?" I say leaning closer.

"Only, her eyes looked dead, like there was nothing behind them, no spark, no life. And she walked as one sleeping. But I've seen plenty like her. Poor girl. No telling what she's been through. All things considered, she's well off. Quintus is not a cruel man. He doesn't follow the Way, but he's not a cruel man. She could have done worse. Now, if she had been sold to a brothel, for instance, that would . . . ."

"Yes. Yes, we quite understand." Judith rises to her feet, then pulls a few coins from a silk pouch attached to the belt of her *stola* and hands them to Joanna.

"Oh, no, no. Not necessary, no, not necessary at all. I was happy to do you this service."

Judith presses the coins into Joanna's hand. "Your husband is still recovering from his injury. It may be some time before he's able to go back to work. Allow me this blessing."

Joanna frowns. "Who knew a camel could do such damage! My husband's foot has been as swollen as a melon since that beast stepped on him. He can barely walk. But God willing, he'll soon return to the market with his water skin slung on his shoulder and his wooden cup in hand, offering drinks to thirsty passersby for the usual fee." Her fingers curl slowly around the coins. "Jesus *did* say it was more blessed to give than receive. So I won't deny you your blessing." With that she kisses my sister and turns to go.

"I almost forgot," Joanna says, spinning around to face me. "It seems the Market Manager has been scouring the city for you."

"For me?" I place a finger on my chest in disbelief.

"I didn't give you away. But someone who saw Judith come to your aid in the marketplace has told him about it. He's sure to send his men here. No one knows why he wants to see you, but his slaves claim he's obsessed with the matter." Her world-weary face furrows as she picks nervously at her long tunic. "I don't know what you've done, but Cassius Flavillus is not a man you want as an enemy. You must take care."

Judith smiles. "I'm sure it's nothing. A misunderstanding only. Be at peace." With that she ushers Joanna out of the room.

"Perhaps you should leave the city," Judith says when she returns. "It's evident Cassius Flavillus is as angry as you thought. It's not wise to stay."

"And leave Esther?"

"I can see to her. I'll think of some way to get her back."

"And when Cassius's men come? What then? Shall I leave you to face his displeasure?"

"My husband's wealth has made him powerful. Cassius would not dare to trouble us without cause. And what are we guilty of, anyway? Having you as a guest in my house?"

"You may be rich and powerful, but you're also a follower of Jesus. You know how suspicious the Romans are of believers, and how they hold them in contempt. I've hurt Cassius's pride. Might he not try to humble you if he believes you've had some hand at thwarting his attempt to find me?

"But it's not only you I think of. What of Ethan and my sons? If Cassius is as intent on finding me as Joanna said, then no one I love is safe. Not Ethan or Aaron or Benjamin. Even now, they await word from me regarding Esther. If they find out I've fled and they follow, that will endanger them as well. And what of all the captives they have purchased and their plans to free them? And then there's Zechariah. It would be a simple matter to find him at Hannah's. Oh, Judith, surely you must understand that everyone I've been seen with will be in danger if I run. And I'll not secure my freedom at the cost of all of yours."

Judith sits down beside me, takes my hand, then presses it between hers. "You are the only family I have left. Mama, Papa, brother Asher, Uncle Abner, gone, all gone. I don't want to lose you now, not after our sweet reunion." She puts an arm around my shoulder and presses her cheek to mine. "But you've always been stubborn so I know it's useless to try dissuading you. So tell me, what will you do and how can I help?"

"I must trust the Lord and go to this Cassius to learn of my offense. And you must pray."

Before I can test my courage and go to the Market Manager's house, his two lictors come to Judith's and take me away.

I walk between them now, on the Decumanus Maximus, a wide street flanked on each side by a majestic marble colonnade and walkway. We head toward a large house near the market. To my right is the ever imposing Temple of Augustus, to my left, jutting into the sea is the daunting palace of Herod the Great, now occupied by the Romans.

My guides speak not a word. And since they're strong, rough-looking men who seem neither to want nor encourage conversation, I remain silent as well. They each carry their bundle of white birch rods tied by red leather straps. The one consolation is that no bronze ax head is tied to them as well, for they do not have the power to execute since Caesarea is governed by a Procurator.

The sidewalks are full, and people stare and whisper as we pass. But few look me in the face. We finally stop at a house just outside the market, a house that sits beneath the shadow of the massive Temple of Augustus.

A tall, stern-looking man with the flat face of an owl opens the door when one of the lictors knocks. "Follow me," he says gruffly. I obey, and notice my guides follow too, as though discouraging any escape. And it's not until I'm ushered into a large room where the Market Manager lays sprawled on a couch eating an early evening meal, that they depart.

The long, low table is covered with bowls of fruit, bread, various meats, and a jug of wine. The Manager continues eating a fig without a word or even glancing my way. He makes me stand so long my legs tire and I'm forced to shift my weight. My mind races with scenarios of the worst kind, thoughts of imprisonment, torture, even death. I suppose it was his intention that I ponder my fate.

"Well," he finally says, wiping his hands on a large cloth. "I see my men have found you at last." He rolls his barrel-shaped body around so he can face me. His fleshy lids puff over his eyes, making it almost appear as though he's asleep. "You have caused me great inconvenience." He studies me through the slits of his eyes. "I've been searching for you for days. I've bribed, threatened, cajoled. I've upset my entire household. How, I wonder, shall I repay you for all this trouble?"

"I . . . would have come sooner, my lord, had I known my presence was required. Forgive my ignorance."

"Yes, well, sooner or later they all beg. But it won't help you. I've made up my mind. And I'm determined to follow it."

"What have I done, sir?"

"*Done*?" his voice thunders like a gong. "Can you be so ignorant, woman, that you don't know?" He kneads his doughy cheeks between his fingers, his eyes fierce.

My heart pounds as I think of Esther in this house, as I think of Ethan and my sons, and my mind forms desperate prayers. "Whatever my offense, perhaps I can make it right. At least let me try. Allow me to change it or . . . ."

"Change it! No! Never! I won't allow it!" With that he laughs, then claps his chubby hands in glee while I stare dumbfounded. "'Make it right,' she says. Ha!" He suddenly leaps off the couch and dances around the room, jumping and stomping until finally I realize he's no longer lame.

"Your leg . . . is healed," I stammer.

He lifts his robe slightly so I can see that the once shriveled leg is as round and firm as his other one. "It took two days. But hour by hour it became plumper and stronger and fuller. Oh, the wonder of it! Such a thing I've never seen. And *you* did it!"

"Not I, sir, but my God."

"Ah, yes . . . this Hebrew God of yours. But I'm told you were found in the house of one who follows the Way."

"Yes, for I also follow the Way," I say quickly, not willing for him to know of my family connection to Judith, though I don't know why.

The Market Manager frowns. "I've heard of this man-God of yours, the one crucified by Pontius Pilate. A strange religion. But I won't quarrel with you. If you say your God healed my leg, so be it. I'll honor him by making sacrifices in our temple."

"Oh . . . you mustn't do that."

"Doesn't this God of yours like sacrifices?"

"Only if it's your own heart."

The Manager smiles. "Ah, you play with words. It's not my heart he would have as a bloody offering on the altar, is it?"

I shake my head. "No, my lord, it's your love He wants."

"Love a god? You don't love the gods. You fear them, honor them, pay homage to them with the obligatory sacrifices, but love them? Such an idea! I'll hear no more of it." He returns to the table and sits down, then quickly reaches for a honey cake and takes a bite. He chews awhile, knotting his brow as though in thought. "Still . . . I feel obligated to do something." He shoves the last of the cake into his mouth. "And so I'll reward you directly. Name what you wish and you shall have it."

"*Whatever* I wish?"

The Manager brushes crumbs off his toga and laughs. "Can a simple woman like you desire much? Let us see. Name the desire, and allow me the pleasure of fulfilling it."

"I desire one of your kitchen slaves, Esther the wood carrier. She's nothing in your household."

"But something to you?" The Manager eyes me curiously.

"Yes, a great deal." Perhaps I shouldn't have answered truthfully, for I see him hesitate. Will he change his mind? But my fear is groundless, for suddenly he slaps the table and laughs.

"I'm glad this wood carrier is important to you, for it makes my gift all the greater. Take her, she's yours." He calls the steward of his house and tells him to give me a scroll, stamped with his seal, freeing the slave girl, Esther. And with a wave of his hand dismisses us both.

My heart pounds as I follow the steward into the kitchen, carrying the stamped scroll in my hand. The kitchen is a large, bright space with two wooden tables in the center and assorted metal spoons and pots hanging on one wall. And the stone cooking area is three times the size of Hannah's. A fire crackles in the curved hearth, and a pot bubbles on the stone counter above it. A man stands alongside it, holding a large wooden spoon in his hand.

"Call the slave, Esther," the steward says to the cook. And without a word, Joanna's cousin, Quintus, leaves his pot and disappears. I hear his raspy voice call my daughter's name. Within minutes he returns, followed by a thin, dirt-smudged young woman with stringy hair, her tunic covered in wood shavings.

"Go with this Jewess. You are hers now," the steward barks. "But see that you take nothing but the tunic on your back! For all else belongs to the master."

The thin woman nods, then looks shyly at me. And when she does, I nearly burst into tears. Her face is drawn but pretty. Her eyes are indeed as large as flat breads, and her eyelashes as long as rushes, but she is *not* my Esther.

"Come," I say, trying to swallow the lump in my throat as I lead the stranger out of the Market Manager's house.

Ethan

Caesarea Maritima to Judean Desert 70 A.D.

CHAPTER 10

Fear is a strange thing. It always finds you out. And what I've feared has finally come to pass. Someone has recognized us. Even now, that little weasel Rebekah calls "Argos" stalks us as we walk through the marketplace. Though he walks along the shops—his shadow clinging to the walls like mold—I've seen him. He's been hanging around for days, especially around Demas. I know Argos recognizes him; perhaps Aaron, too, though without his beard Argos may yet be fooled. I'm only glad Rebekah has kept her promise and stayed away, for if Argos were to see any of us together it would end our charade, and perhaps our lives, for that weasel would surely inform the Romans.

He still bears the scratches my normally gentle Rebekah gave him. Benjamin says we should give him more than scratches. He has suggested we kill the Greek since so much is at stake. But I've cautioned against it. Now I wonder if I've made a mistake.

"Demas! Is that you?" Argos suddenly cries, breaking his silence and stepping from the shadows of the shop walls then scurrying, like a rodent, among the crowd. The knots on his head blow in the breeze making him look like he wears a cluster of writhing serpents. Now he moves with the boldness and determination of a legionnaire; the pride, too, for he walks as if expecting people to make way. Surprisingly, several do; frightened by the knots, perhaps, since Isis has many followers in Caesarea.

My hand moves to the dagger hidden beneath my robe as I look around for his companions. *Hashem* has blessed us for he is alone. It will be easier to take him down, if it comes to that.

"Demas!" he shouts again, darting and weaving among the crowd.

Demas continues walking alongside the block as though he doesn't hear. I know that Demas, too, has feared this encounter for we have discussed it. Demas has walked the block for weeks looking for Esther, and in the process buys several slaves every day to avoid suspicion. Even now, he's inspecting a strong, broad man with a thick crop of silky brown hair that hangs across his forehead like a stallion's mane. And judging by the defiant look on the slave's face, he's just as wild. But the muscular slave looks oddly out of place among the emaciated men on either side of him.

"Demas?" Argos calls out yet again.

Demas continues to pretend he doesn't hear.

But my sons hear. Aaron draws his *kaffia* across his face. Then he and Benjamin push forward. With a wave of my hand, I caution them to stay back, while I myself bob and weave through the crowd hoping to head Argos off. This man can undo us all.

And then it happens. Argos breaks free of the crowd and heads for Demas. When he reaches him, he yanks Demas's arm, making him turn. "Eeeew! It *is* you! Oh, I knew it! But . . . what are you doing here!" Argos's voice is loud, angry, as though he bears Demas a grudge.

Demas's face is the color of ash. His lips part, but before he can say a word, I'm beside him. "Is this the cook you promised?" I say. "Judging from his size, he knows how to keep his belly full." Demas's eyes widen in confusion, for I'm talking nonsense, trying to throw Argos off. And though it seems I've thrown off Demas instead, there are too many watching to stop now.

"He seems a good match for a gaggle of squawking women," I bellow, "someone who can handle them from here to Damascus. And I *must* have someone to handle them for the sake of peace. You know two women over one fire is a recipe for strife unless there is a man to oversee them. And don't we have twenty such contentious women in our camp?"

"I cook," the broad man on the block says suddenly, as if I were talking to him. "And I can handle women."

"Oh?" I say, relieved I don't have to continue my babbling. Then I eye the silky-haired slave, wondering why such a fine specimen of manhood has not been purchased already. I gesture for him to bend down so I can read the wooden placard that hangs around his neck. "It says you're a runner. That you've run from your previous master. But he didn't brand you. Why?"

The broad-shouldered slave smiles. "He tried. When I knocked the teeth out of four of his best men and flattened the noses of three others, he stopped trying, and sold me to this one." The large man gestures with his chin to a thin slaver who has been standing nearby, listening.

"So you're a brawler." My interest is peaked.

"I've had my share of fights in the minor circuses, before being purchased by a fat magistrate as his bodyguard."

In spite of myself, I chuckle. "And then the magistrate found himself in need of protection from *you*?"

The slave's smile deepens. "He would have had me killed if he hadn't wanted to recover at least part of the large sum he laid out for me."

"Enough talk, Thracian," the slaver says with a quivering voice, as though fearful of both the large man and the possibility I'll lose interest.

I brush the dealer away with the wave of my hand, my eyes still on the slave. "I'm not a gambler. I've no desire to risk my money either. How do I know you won't run?"

"You don't." The Thracian's hands are bound together in front. He brings them up and pushes his flowing hair away from his eyes. "But you see my worth. I'm strong. I can work hard."

"I'll make you a bargain of him," the nervous slaver blurts. He steps in front of Argos who has, all the while, been listening with a perplexed expression. "You can purchase him cheap. He's an ill mannered Thracian, but with a firm hand, he can be tamed, I'm sure of it."

"Offer eight-hundred *drachmas*," I say to Demas without looking at the slave or the dealer, "and not one *drachma* more."

"Done!" the slaver says quickly. "The Thracian is worth three . . . maybe four times that, but yes, I'll let you rob me. It is done."

I turn and push past Argos. The little Greek is now beside himself, having been so ignored. He waves his arms, then jumps up and down. "Something is wrong here. There is mischief afoot. I sense mischief afoot!" He looks at me and points to Demas. "This man is not what he seems!"

I draw my dagger. "Go away," I hiss. "Can't you see we are conducting business?"

"I won't be dismissed," Argos says, white with rage. "You can't dismiss me! I know this man. He's a beekeeper! Something's wrong here."

Now we are drawing an even larger crowd. People stare and whisper. The owner of the Thracian wrings his hands. Several other slavers eye Demas suspiciously. And despite my orders, Aaron and Benjamin move closer.

When Demas twists around to count out the eight-hundred *drachmas,* Argos shrieks, "Don't turn your back on me! I know who you are. Don't think I don't know!" It's evident Argos is bent on making trouble—Argos, who is used to having his way; Argos, who is used to people listening when he speaks.

I'm about to shove the little Greek aside when someone shouts, "Make way, make way." And when I see two lictors with their birch rods coming toward us, I quickly sheathe my dagger.

The lictors look fierce and greatly agitated as they move along the path cleared for them. When they get closer I see, for the first time, that the jewel-bedecked Market Manager is walking behind them.

The Market Manager's flabby face quivers with displeasure as he clutches his ivory baton. "What is the meaning of . . . ." He stops when he sees Argos. "Oh, it's *you.* Is it your intent to make a habit of disrupting my market? Well! What do you have to say for yourself this time?" The Manager doesn't even try to hide his contempt. His face is a storm as he waves his baton in the air, and for an instant I think he's actually going to crack Argos over the head with it. Was he thinking of Rebekah? Was he remembering how his leg was healed?

Argos's silence is like a spark that sets the Manager's face on fire; his cheeks burn like coals. "Are you deaf?" he shrieks. "Answer me, or by Jupiter I'll send you straight to prison."

Argos takes a deep breath as though gathering courage. "I know this man," he says, pointing to Demas. "A beekeeper for Isis, posing as a slave dealer. I tell you, something is wrong."

The Market Manager's eyebrows, looking like feathers, arch upward. "A beekeeper? Hardly. I've done business with him. A keen eye, he has, for flesh; and a shrewd negotiator, too. I see no fault in him."

"I tell you he's a fraud, and up to no good!"

"*You* tell me? Who are you to tell me anything?" The Manager's doughy cheeks shake as he pinches his lips together. "This is my market. *I* do the telling. Now for the last time, state your grievance."

"Perhaps . . . I've overstepped," Argos says, dropping his voice as well as his chin as though finally sensing the Manager's ill will. "Perhaps I've been too zealous. But as a good citizen of Rome, I merely wanted to point out that something could be wrong here." Oh, how contrite and submissive he is now! The man could be a play actor in the court of Caesar.

The Market Manager looks at him sideways, studies him a moment, then nods, as though taking him more seriously. Whether it's because of Argos's tone or because he has revealed himself to be a Roman citizen I cannot say, but Argos has the Manager's attention now. I tense. If he is believed, we are all doomed.

"You claim he's a fraud," the Manager says, turning his gaze to Demas. "Very well. We shall see. I will test him."

"But sir, his father was . . . ."

"Silence!" The Manager waves his eagle-topped baton in the air, causing the many rings on his chubby fingers to glint in the harsh sun light. "You, slave dealer, tell me, what can a master do if a slave is injured or killed by another?"

Demas, tall and broad, with one soft hand cupped beneath his chin, smiles. "Under *lex aquilia*, he could sue for damages or charge the killer with a capital offense."

"And if the slave is despoiled by another? And falls into evil ways? What then?"

"The master has a *praetorian action in duplo* against the offender, and the offender must pay twice the assessed damage."

"And what if the slave incurs a *naturalis obligation*? What is the master's responsibility?"

"None sir, unless the slave was employed as his representative, in which case the master could be liable to an *actio institoria*."

The Manager throws up his hands. "Enough! This man is no fraud!"

"Yes . . . he knows the law," Argos says, looking wild, desperate. "I tried to tell you his father was a slaver. But *he* is a beekeeper." Argos is so bent on proving his point that he again seems heedless of the Manager's growing impatience. His enmity toward Demas must be great, indeed, for him to be so reckless. "He would never return to the trade of a slaver," Argos stammers. "He told me so himself! I *know* something's not right here!"

"First you accuse someone of stealing a cup without proof. Now you proclaim this man a fraud when it's obviously not so, as my testing proved." He signals his lictors. "Take this madman away." Then he adds, "For my part I'd throw you straight into prison. But since you are a citizen, you are entitled to a trial. The Procurator will deal with you."

"No!" Argos shrieks. "I've done nothing wrong!"

One of the lictors grabs his arm, but Argos pulls away, then narrowly dodges the second lictor. And then he does something foolish. He bolts. He actually tries to run away, but he doesn't get far for his path is littered with people.

"Stop him!" The Market Managers shouts. With that, one of the lictors takes his long bundle of white birch rods and swings it at Argos's head. But it hits him in the neck instead and drops him in his tracks, but not before I hear the sound of bones cracking.

Even before Argos hits the ground I know he's dead, that his neck has been broken. He lands face down on the paving stones, his knotted hair fanning out around his head.

"Look what this worthless goat has made me do!" the Manager says, hardly glancing at the prone body. "Now I'll have to waste endless hours explaining this to the Procurator." He waves his hand in disgust. "Remove him." Then turning to Demas he says, "Now, what was your offer for this slave? Eight-hundred *drachmas*, I believe you said?" He points to the broad man on the block. "Of course you know he's an import, which means you'll have to pay me an extra tax."

That jackal, Titus, has begun gladiatorial games in the amphitheater, forcing many of the unsold captives into the arena to be slaughtered for sport. He claims it is in honor of his brother Domitian's birthday. They say so far two thousand captives have been killed in the games. The city has gone mad for blood. It's too dangerous to stay. Soldiers and even citizens swarm the streets looking for sport, and for trouble. I fear they'll find both if they meet up with Aaron or Benjamin.

And we've been here too long as it is. Some of the slave dealers have begun whispering, wondering among themselves why such wealthy Syrians stay; wondering why such an expert slaver as Demas stays. Do we know something they don't? Have we heard some news they haven't? Others have begun asking Demas outright why we're still here. After all, hasn't all the good flesh been purchased? Even the lowest, most disreputable of the slavers have begun leaving. But can we tell them we are still hoping to find Esther? Or that the longer our captives rest, the more likely they will survive the harsh journey to Masada?

Even so, we have done more than just search for Esther. Demas has discharged the *quaestor's* slaves. And my sons have been busy organizing our captives according to their home towns, then dividing them into groups of fifty with a captain over each group. Only the captains know of our true plans, plans to either free the captives near their villages or take those who wish, on to Masada.

The captains also oversee the camp, which includes keeping order and seeing everyone is fed, as well as seeing that the sick are tended. This leaves Demas free to purchase camels, wagons, tunics, food, and all the other supplies needed to relocate our large entourage.

But in light of the current mood of the city, we can no longer delay the inevitable. My sons and I agree, in two days we must depart. By then, Demas will be finished making his purchases. Now all I have to do is tell Rebekah. I dread it for I know she'll resist. She still holds out hope that Esther will be found. I, myself, have no such hope.

"I'm only glad the lictor killed Argos before we had to," I say, dipping my bread into a bowl of lamb stew. "He was bent on making trouble."

Benjamin, sitting on a nearby couch, chuckles. Demas only nods. But there's something sad about Demas's face, the way his eyebrows fold together, the way his eyes mist.

"It was his hatred for me. That's what got the better of him. He just couldn't let it go, couldn't forgive me for forsaking Isis. I tried to explain. I even hoped that he, too, would follow Jesus some day, but . . . ." Demas's voice trails off.

"I'm sorry about your friend," Judith says, her face soft as lamb's wool. "I, too, have many friends who follow other gods. I talk to them, I pray for them, but in the end they must decide for themselves who they will serve."

Judith's large room erupts with conversation as her husband, Apollonios, voices his opinion. Then Zechariah, Judah, Hannah, and my sons, all take their turn. Only Rebekah is silent, and sits beside me nibbling a date cake and watching Apollonios and Judith eat fried, milk-fed snails. They are the only ones who will eat them.

We are all lounging on couches around the grand table Judith has set for us. And for hours I've tried to lift Rebekah's spirits, but failed.

I'm still remembering that look on her face when I told her we were leaving Caesarea, how it reminded me of someone hearing their loved one had just died. But she didn't weep. I think it would have been better if she had.

"A fine feast you've set before us," I say to Judith as I dip again into the stew. "I will remember it when I'm eating gruel on the highway." Everyone laughs, except Rebekah.

"I couldn't let you leave without us all coming together one last time." There is a trace of sadness in Judith's voice.

"You still plan on leaving tomorrow?" Hannah asks.

I avoid Rebekah's eyes. "Yes, at first light."

"I only wish you were coming Hannah," Rebekah says, finally breaking her long silence. "When Titus has had his fill of blood in the amphitheatre, he'll turn his attention to the descendants of King David. Already there's talk . . . ."

"I'm too old. Could I survive such a journey, then begin all over again in a new place? I think not. My life is in God's hands; my days measured out according to His good pleasure. But my son must go. We've been arguing about it for days. Tell him, Rebekah, that he must go."

Rebekah places her unfinished cake on the table. "It's the only sensible thing, Judah. Why stay in the center of Titus's stronghold and put yourself in danger? The believers in Pella will hide you. You can begin a new life there. Perhaps Titus will not think to look for David's descendants among the followers of the Way. It will certainly be safer than staying here."

"Did you hear what she said, Judah?" Hannah says. "*Safer.* It will be safer. And if you won't do it for your sake, then do it for Esther's."

Judah blushes. Everyone knows he and Esther—the wood carrier who has been staying in Hannah's house and is, even now, convalescing there—have become fond of one another.

"Yes, it would be difficult for Esther if anything happens to me," Judah says thoughtfully. "Where would she go? What would she do? Her entire family has perished. But I can't think of that now. Esther is still regaining her strength, as am I. Maybe in another week we'll be fit to travel. Still . . . can a son leave his mother?"

"Jesus left his," Zechariah says, fingering his wiry, gray beard. There's a smile on his face, but his eyes are full of compassion as though feeling the young man's struggle. "And while your mission is different from His, you still have one. Our land and people have been decimated. The ax has been laid to the tree. But can we allow our race to die? God forbid! No, we must plant new seeds. You, and others like you, must survive. You owe it to your tribe, your nation, to the land God has given you, to God Himself. You must ensure the future of Israel. You must produce fruit. You must have offspring."

That man, bulbous and covered with gray hair, has such an effect on people. His few words seem to comfort Judah, while they agitate me. Why do I find him so offensive?

"I'll pray about it," Judah says, but I see by his mouth, the way it has softened, the way it no longer looks like a rigid, dead snake lying across his face, that in his mind's eye he's already on his way to Pella.

"I, too, will be going to Pella when I wish to visit my sister," Judith says, leaning from her couch to ours, and taking Rebekah's hand. "For now that I've found you, I'll not lose you again. That is, if I'm welcome."

"Always," Rebekah says, squeezing Judith's hand.

"No," I say, without thinking. Now all eyes are on me. "What I mean is, we won't be going to Pella. I . . . haven't had a chance to tell Rebekah this but we're heading for Masada."

"*Masada?*" Rebekah's jaw drops. And the look in her eyes! It's as if some light has gone out, as if my words have snuffed out all those little candles of hope she's been igniting these past several weeks; hope of us all being together—living normal lives. She shakes her head as she looks at me. "Even now . . . even after all this, after all we've gone through, you'll not give up the fight? *Even now*?" she whispers. But I suspect, by the look on everyone's face, they hear it too. And for the rest of the evening Rebekah doesn't say another word.

I sit high atop my grazing camel. Next to me, Aaron and Benjamin straddle their own camel. The breeze blowing off the Mediterranean plays with our silk *kaffias* and embroidered robes that smell of jasmine. Light from the newly risen sun dances on the jewels around our necks and fingers. Behind us is a string of twenty camels loaded with goods. Behind them are eight wagons piled high, and hitched to oxen. And behind them, over eighteen hundred souls. Last of all is Demas, who pulls up the rear.

We have all stopped just outside the north gate. From between the trees I see the amphitheatre only several cubits away. In a few hours the roar of the crowd will be heard for miles as more captives are slaughtered for sport. We'll be safely away by then.

I watch Rebekah, who stands nearby saying goodbye to that irritant, Zechariah. He has come unexpectedly. We all thought he was sailing for Ephesus this morning. For my part, I was disappointed to see him waiting outside the gate. I'm close enough to him to spot the tiny gray hairs protruding from his nostrils, and wonder if Rebekah finds him as repulsive as I do. But no, there she is smiling at him. Smiling! At me she hasn't smiled since learning we head for Masada.

"Do you think you could bear parting with the cup?" Zechariah rubs his bulbous nose. "I would like to take it to John the Apostle. If you wish, I could bring it back to Pella in a year or two when I come for a visit, and leave it with Mary. This war with Rome must come to an end sooner or later, and then perhaps you can return to your friends in Pella where it will be waiting for you."

Rebekah shakes her head. "I've had my sister's Galatians destroy the cup, pound it into pieces with hammer and chisel, then bury the pieces. There will always be men like Argos who would try to steal it for evil purposes, and there'll always be those believers who would make of it an idol."

Zechariah frowns, then finally nods. "I understand. Yes . . . you did right. Besides, your treasure is within you, where our Lord resides. It's in all who believe. We don't need His cup." He smiles and pats her arm. "I'll pray for your safety. And for your patience. God is in control, Rebekah. He'll lead you where He will. Have faith."

All the while I've been listening, and now I feel the veins of my neck throb. Oh, but that man is arrogant! Does he think he's the one to comfort my wife? Does he think that his are the words she'll hearken to? Does he think he can take my place?

I watch them hug and say good-bye, and know that in a way he already has, and I burn with jealousy. But I'm not jealous of him as a man. He's not a lover, a suitor. In a sense, he's far worse. He is her friend, her confidant, her counselor. *He* was there when I was not. *He* cared for and protected Rebekah these many months. It was *his* words that comforted, guided, cautioned. And there will forever be a part of Rebekah's life that belongs to him and not me. Things they shared, dangers thwarted, things I'll never understand. If only I had . . . if only . . . but I'm a man of honor. Could I have forsaken honor and left Jerusalem with her, like a coward? And now? Am I to forget my pledge to Eleazar? How is that possible? Must I choose between honor and my wife? Was I to keep one at the expense of the other?

I watch in numb silence as Zechariah, a good man, a man I both admire and loathe, turns and heads back to the north gate, and to the ship that he claims will soon depart for Ephesus. Then I watch Rebekah walk toward the cook's wagon. Her coarse head covering slips to her shoulders, exposing beautiful plaited auburn hair. It glistens in the sun, as if on fire. Suddenly, the wind catches the loose tendrils and swirls them around her head. How young and wild and carefree she looks! As beautiful as when we first wed! And for an instance my yearning is so great I would willingly give up my honor and everything else just to hold her in my arms and hear her sweet voice tell me she loves me, for I sorely need to hear it now.

"Have you spoken to the captain?" I say to Benjamin, who rides his camel beside me on the dirt path.

Benjamin nods. "All morning he's been instructing his fifty. They'll be ready."

Suddenly, curses fill the air as yet another caravan tries to pass. "Move aside!" the drivers growl. One driver actually raises his stick to strike my camel but when he sees the size of my sons and me, our fierce countenance, and the large daggers belted at our waists, he swats his own camel instead, and makes a wide arc around us. Others follow, swinging around us amid a swirl of dust.

Our party stretches along the Caesarea-Scythopolis Highway for as far as the eye can see. First the camels. They walk the soft dirt path paralleling the paved road, led by my sons and me. Then the wagons—one of which carries Rebekah—clatter over the hot paving stones. Following them trudge hundreds of men, roped together and wearing filthy, ripped tunics. And behind the men come the women, also roped and tattered and dirty—all to perpetuate our charade. Last comes poor Demas who eats the dust of us all without complaint, though my sons have offered to spell him numerous times.

We head east, toward the King's Highway—the main road to Damascus, and have already passed Megiddo. Our plan is simple. We deliberately move slowly to frustrate the other caravans and make them pass us. That way, no one is around us long enough to notice that every day our numbers decrease. Already our party is down by nearly five hundred. Each night we lose about seventy-five souls. Daily, the excitement grows among the captives as they wonder if their group will be the next to taste freedom.

So far our plan is working.

In the glow of the camp fires, I watch Rebekah move swiftly among the silent group of men, nearly fifty in all, who are freshly washed, and dressed in new tunics. She hands each a small pouch of food filled with raisins and nuts and a few date cakes. Another group of about twenty women, also washed and dressed in new tunics, wait patiently nearby for their rations.

In the distance a coyote howls as a gust of wind swirls dust around our faces. It's unusually dark. Clouds have partially obscured the moon—a bad night for travel.

"You don't have to go. You can wait until tomorrow," I say to the captain of the fifty, but my eyes are still on Rebekah.

"My men are anxious. The women, too. No one wants to postpone the departure. All are willing to take their chances. And the men have promised to help the women when they get to the rough terrain. And . . . if anything happens, we won't betray you. We've all sworn an oath."

"Well, then, have them eat and rest. In another few hours you can be on your way."

Our sprawling camp has sentries posted at various intervals, sentries hand-picked by Aaron for their combat experience. Even so, as usual, numerous travelers have made their own camps along the highway. It would not be safe for the captives to break camp and disappear into the countryside until deep into the night. If they were seen and caught, it could go badly for us all.

"You should rest, too," I say to the captain, my heart twisting strangely within me as I think of him facing a future alone. He's a tanner by trade who escaped Galilee and sought the safety of Jerusalem after Vespasian annihilated his family. Though he fought against the Romans while in the city, he somehow convinced them he had not, and was spared crucifixion with the other rebels. "God speed," I say, firmly clasping his arm.

He unexpectedly holds fast to mine. "What you have done for us . . . for all of the many souls you have rescued, can never be repaid. I pray *Hashem's* blessing on your head." Then he releases me and slaps my back good-naturedly. "Your wife is very beautiful. You are a fortunate man."

I follow his eyes. They are on Rebekah. "I . . . that is . . . she's only one of my many cooks." For safety's sake, I've kept Rebekah's identity a secret. This way, if our charade is discovered by the Romans, she won't be in danger.

The captain chuckles. "Anyone with eyes can tell she's more to you than a cook. Even your sons speak differently to her than the others. Many of us have guessed your secret." He leans closer. "I would give anything to have what you have. I lost mine . . . I lost them all." His voice is low. "But you still have sons and a wife. I pray *Hashem* gives you many happy years together."

Hours later, when the wind picks up and scatters some of the overhead clouds, the captain and his band of seventy creep from camp and disappear into the night. As I watch them go, I remember the captain's words. And unable to resist any longer, I leave my place beside my snoring sons and walk the long line of sleeping captives until I reach the wagons that have been moved to last position, wagons guarded by Demas and the large Thracian cook, Skaris.

As I stumble in the darkness, grinding my knee into the dirt, I tell myself this is foolishness. What am I doing? I'm mad to be here, searching the grounds for Rebekah in this dim moonlight. Demas stirs, so does Skaris. How would I explain myself if they awoke? I peer into the darkness, hardly able to make anyone out. And just as I'm about to give up, I spot the familiar form of my Rebekah sleeping near the twenty other women who help with the cooking. I move carefully around the prone bodies. When I reach her, I kneel down, and bending over, I kiss her cheek. "I love you," I whisper, and before anyone can awake, I force myself to rise and silently steal back to my pallet.

"We're nearing Pella," Aaron says, straddling his dusty camel and fanning himself with an empty leather scrip. "Our group is ready. Everything has been divided: food, clothing, weapons."

"I still don't like the idea of you leaving us," I say, my camel clomping beside his.

"You know I must. Your group numbers less than two-hundred, while ours is nearly twice that, far too many for Demas to manage alone. Besides, you'll have Benjamin to help you, and Skaris, too."

The blistering sun beats relentlessly overhead. I mop my face with the edge of my *kaffia* and nod. Of the over eighteen-hundred captives, less than six-hundred remain. But only one-hundred and ninety—mostly men—have chosen to go to Masada with me. The remaining captives will go with Demas and Aaron. They'll pass Pella, then head west skirting Gerasa. But they won't continue beyond that to the King's Highway. Most will head north to Gilead and return to their shattered villages.

"I know you must go with Demas," I finally say. "But I don't have to like it. There will be more Romans the nearer to the King's Highway you get. If anything goes wrong . . . if you should be questioned or stopped . . . ."

Aaron laughs. "Wait for us in En Gedi. You and Mama and the others could use the rest. By the time you get there and have your first nap, we should be on our way to you. And while you're enjoying the shade and fresh springs, and eating your date cakes, Demas and I will be eating dust in the Judean Desert. But don't worry, Father, we'll be careful . . . nothing will go wrong."

Rebekah won't look at me. Tears wash her eyes as she watches Aaron and Demas, their wagons and camels, and the nearly four-hundred souls they lead, head in the direction of Pella. I can see the city from here nestled among fields and trees, and with a spring running through it. Though scarred by war, there is something inviting about it.

Demas needs fresh supplies, but won't stop in Pella. It is, after all, predominately Gentile, and a city where he is known. Other than the believers, who would help him if they learned he was trying to resettle hundreds of Titus's captives? Hundreds of *Jewish* captives. Besides, it would be dangerous to expose our plans in this manner. The news of it could get back to the Roman legions. So they'll bypass the city and head straight for Gerasa while we, Benjamin and I and Rebekah and Skaris and nearly two-hundred emaciated souls, head to the Jordan Valley, then on toward the Judean Desert and En Gedi.

They have taken all the wagons; we, most of the camels. Our course will not be a smooth Roman road. Rather, we'll travel footpaths and narrow rocky trails, and hide in caves along the way.

My mind is already considering the many dangers when Rebekah suddenly turns and walks in my direction. She holds a new tunic, the same type of tunic she's been giving to all those who have made their escape. She hands it to me. Her eyes look away but not before I see fresh tears well up. My heart is heavy as I take the garment. I know I have disappointed her and it nearly chokes me with grief. Shielded by my camel, I remove my *kaffia* and Syrian robe, and slip on the tunic. From now on, I'll no longer be dressed as a slave master. Who would believe a Syrian slaver would wander the Jordan Valley with his slaves, going in the opposite direction of Damascus? Even now, Benjamin and the broad Thracian, Skaris, are unyoking the captives, giving them water to wash and a new tunic along with a small bag of food. When they are ready, they'll leave in small groups and head for Masada on their own, for a large company of travelers would be too easy for the Roman patrols to spot.

"We don't have enough tunics for everyone," Rebekah says softly, lifting her eyes and looking at me for the first time. "We are nearly fifty short, but Demas could find no more."

Demas has been purchasing supplies in every little shop and bazaar along the way. But there were only so many goods each merchant had to sell. He had gotten us this far on dried fruits and nuts and grain for pottage. He even managed to keep our water skins full by stopping at every watering hole and well along the way. And he had purchased enough clothing for most of the captives. As far as I was concerned, the man was a wonder.

"I told him to leave us short on this end," Rebekah says softly. "It will be easier for our people to fade into the interior than for his. We have the hills to hide us. He . . . and Aaron must contend with the heavily trafficked areas of the Decapolis and Kings Highway. Still, I made sure there was one for you and Benjamin." Her eyes drift back to Pella, and a sigh, as soft as the breeze, escapes her lips.

I know what she's thinking. It's in Pella she wants us to make our home, *all* of us, she and I and Aaron and Benjamin. And for the second time, I'm breaking her heart.

"You do know I love you," I whisper. But she doesn't answer.

There are only twenty in our group when we reach En Gedi. Rebekah, Benjamin and I, Skaris, fourteen other men, and two women. We avoid the oasis, for the deserted Jewish village and date-palm groves are too near it. I have no wish to encounter any Romans who may be grazing dates there. And some say a few poor Jews still eke out a living on the Roman-owned lands. But I have no wish to see them either. Nor to visit yet another place where Jew has slaughtered Jew, for it was here that many *sicarii* from Masada came and massacred the people in the village, then plundered their food supply. Josiah said it happened before he came to Masada. But it's well known that even now many of the *sicarii* that co-mingle with the Zealots at Masada come periodically to despoil the surrounding land and its people. Nothing changes. The *sicarii* are still scoundrels, and not even honorable men like Josiah can rein them in.

So instead, we climb the steep ravine heading for the spring—the "fountain of the young goat" as it's called. We're surrounded on either side by what looks like high rock walls. Above our heads, huge cave openings gape at us like watchful eyes, and I'm reminded that it was in one of these caves David hid from King Saul. The ravine itself is littered with trees and shrubs which help keep down the dust as well as provide some shade. We won't climb all the way to the spring but will stop at the pool just ahead. Though I've never drank from it, I'm told the water is warm and sweet.

I hear Rebekah gasp, and see a badger on a rock ledge above, standing as stiff as the dead carrion we've seen along the road. But the badger is very much alive, and stands this way hoping no one sees him. Skaris picks up a rock and tosses it, making the animal bolt, clearing the way for Rebekah to pass.

He has proven invaluable this Thracian who knows Jesus; strong as an ox, carrying and lifting and kindling fires. He's especially useful now, carrying a heavy basket of kettles and pots. We are all carrying baskets full of supplies, but none heavier, I'll wager, than Skaris's. We've let go of the camels. The climb is too steep. Instead, we sold them to a Bedouin family in the Judean Desert just below.

We're all straining under our bundles, and a few of the weaker captives have fallen beneath their load more than once in the oppressive desert heat.

"Perhaps we should rest, Father," Benjamin says, sweat pouring down his face, his shoulder bent beneath a large basket of grain.

I shake my head, "I'm sure it's just ahead, for I hear the noise of water." And no sooner than my words are out, we see it—a sparkling waterfall tumbling from the limestone cliffs above and splashing into a large shimmering pool. Around it, and between some of the crevices in the massive walls, grow moringa and tamarisk trees, ferns and giant reeds and capers. But one side is nothing but solid rock where a ledge, the height of my knees, leads to a long though shallow-looking cave—the perfect place to make camp. Twenty would easily be comfortable here.

"This must be paradise!" Rebekah says, smiling and looking around.

It's good to see her smile. It's the first time she's smiled since leaving Caesarea.

She lowers her basket to the ground, then makes a dash to the pool, giggling all the way as if she were a girl. When she gets there, she plunges in her hand and begins to drink. Most of the others follow. Soon, everyone is drinking, then splashing each other in jest. When everyone has had their fill of both, the women, with Skaris's help, begin setting up camp.

"We'll camp here while we wait for Demas and Aaron," I say to Benjamin who stands beside me, grinning at all the activity. He has yet to touch the water. I think he's waiting for me to go first thereby proving himself more manly. It's something Joseph would have done, not Benjamin, though lately, nothing is as it once was.

"It's a good spot, Father. And we could use the rest."

I nod. The journey has been long and hard, and also dangerous. Titus has left the 10th legion behind in Jerusalem, and we nearly encountered one of their patrols.

"Have you appointed the sentries?" I ask.

"Yes, but most of the men are done in. I don't know how effective they will be." Benjamin gestures with his chin to a group of men who still wear tattered rags and look woefully thin. "We'll be no match for the Romans if they come." Then he looks at me and laughs. "Must I drink first?"

I smile, then dart toward the pool and jump in, clothes and all, feeling both free and foolish. And at that moment, Rebekah turns and our eyes meet. My heart skips a beat as she breaks into a wide smile. Perhaps even Rebekah is changing. Perhaps she's beginning to believe life in Masada won't be so bad.

Rebekah is sitting on the low stone ledge with the only other two women in our camp. Her head is thrown back in laughter, her hair loose and flowing as one of the women drags a camel's hair brush through Rebekah's long tresses, tresses that glisten in the sun in varying shades of red and brown. She looks so beautiful my heart aches with desire. I've missed her. We've had little time together since our reunion in Caesarea. And none alone. But that is about to change.

"May *Hashem* bless you this day," I say, approaching the ladies with one hand behind my back to conceal the small sprig of yellow acacia flowers I picked from a tree nearer the wadi.

The women smile shyly. Only Rebekah answers. "And may He bless you, as well."

"I've come to walk with my wife," I say, bringing my hand around and presenting the flowers to Rebekah. Everyone knows our secret. We are past pretending. I smile when I see her eyes twinkle. She's always loved acacias. The other women giggle as Rebekah rises to her feet and takes the flowers.

"Don't hurry back," they say, shooing her away. "We can manage making the gruel without you."

And so Rebekah takes my arm as I lead her up the steep ravine where Benjamin said he discovered another smaller pool and waterfall when checking out the area.

Birds chirp overhead as we climb. A hyrax scampers among the undergrowth causing a small lizard to take to the rocks. And though the way is rough, Rebekah never lets go of her flowers.

"It's good to be here, like this, with you," she says, smiling and brushing her chin against my shoulder. Her eyes are moist with joy.

We walk a ways until finally we come upon the spot Benjamin described. The pool and waterfall are indeed smaller, but unlike our campsite, the surrounding rocks and cliffs dwarf everything, rising above us to dizzying heights. I gesture toward a nearby rock that is flat and shaded by lush greenery. We sit and remove our sandals, then dangle our feet in the water.

"I've asked Benjamin and Skaris to keep the others away so we can have time together."

She blushes, but I see by her smile and eyes that she is pleased. "That is good. It will give me a chance to tell you what has been on my heart these many days; how I've grappled with the issue of Masada and . . . ."

"Rebekah, I don't want to argue. Must we talk of that now?"

She presses her fingers to my lips. "Yes, let me speak, because I want you to know that though I don't want to go, though I hate the thought of leaving Pella and living on that slab of a mountain top, the thought of life without you is even more intolerable. And so I'll follow you wherever you wish. I'll go where you go because I *love* you."

And then she's in my arms, and my face is buried in her long auburn hair that still hangs loosely around her shoulders. It's been so long since I've held her like this. I feel young again, and vigorous. She is the bride of my youth, full of passion and sweetness, and as we kiss, I hear the clattering hoofs of a wild goat, hear rocks skitter and fall, and I look around. Something has startled the animal. I glance at the vegetation above the falls. Did it just rustle? Or was it my imagination? I should go and see if all is well. But as I'm about to rise, the sweet look on Rebekah's face holds me captive, and I find it impossible to leave. Yet, as I kiss her once more, I have the uncomfortable feeling we are being watched.

Rebekah

Judean Desert 70 A.D.

CHAPTER 11

Long before they arrived, our sentries informed us they were coming. I know I shouldn't have done it, embarrassed Aaron and Demas that way, but I couldn't help myself. I suppose too much loss kills hope because, truthfully, I never expected to see Aaron and Demas again. How could I when they were walking into the jaws of danger? They could be stopped. Questioned. Their deception discovered. A captive might be caught, then betray them under torture. See how much could go wrong?

Even my prayer ran toward the melancholy. I didn't pray, "Lord, protect Aaron and Demas," but, "Lord, if it's your will to take Aaron and Demas, give me the grace to endure it." So I've been preparing myself for the worst. Is it any wonder then that when Aaron and Demas entered our camp I was upon them both, showering them with kisses?

It is Ethan who finally pulls me away.

"I'm *so* happy to see you," I say, all tears and smiles and breathless joy even after Ethan restrains me by gripping my arm. "*So* happy!"

"That is evident, Mama," Aaron says, tucking his head as though feeling like a child.

Demas smiles and says nothing. I think he enjoys the fuss. With no relatives among our number, who was there to shower him with affection? In a way, he reminds me of a wool rag absorbing my love as if it were scented water.

"So, tell us how it went," Ethan says, leading my son and Demas to the low cave ledge and the large rush mats spread out in welcome.

A smaller mat in the center contains bowls of raisins, nuts, and fresh pottage, along with cups of sweet spring water.

Aaron sits beside Ethan; Demas beside him. I take the seat where I can best see my son. Aaron looks thinner, older. In just ten days? How is that possible? A dusty patch covers one eye, but the other reveals so much. He's weary and troubled, and I see a new hardness in his face. He smiles, but his forehead is crinkled. *Oh, Aaron, Aaron, where is that sweet boy who so loved the Lord? The boy with a heart as gentle as a dove's?*

"Well, brother, did you have to kill many Romans?" Benjamin asks, suddenly joining us.

Aaron laughs. It sounds cold, hollow. "Only twenty."

"Single handedly, I suppose," Benjamin quips, dipping his hand into the bowl of almonds.

Demas answers for him with a nod. But there's no smile on his face. It is dark, somber.

"Then tell us about it, my brother. Don't keep us in suspense."

Aaron picks up the cup of water. "First allow me to wash the dust from my throat." He drains the cup then places it back on the mat.

"Eat something, too," Ethan says, but Aaron doesn't even look at the food.

"There's little to tell." Aaron appears nervous, and shifts his legs. "Just past Gerasa we ran into a party of soldiers transporting a handful of Greekish-looking prisoners, I assume for trial in Caesarea. Over three hundred captives had already left us by then. The remaining seventy or so were to strike out on their own that night. It was already dusk. A few minutes more and we would have made camp.

"We had sold all but two wagons. That was our downfall, because the two overflowed with goods. One of the soldiers saw the pile of new tunics in one of them as he passed. He grew curious and stopped, then began asking questions. At first the questioning went well. But as it progressed it was clear he was growing suspicious. 'Who was your slave master?' he asked Demas. 'Where in Damascus do you head? Have you ever heard of Adad the Syrian who specializes in eunuchs? Who in Damascus was buying your slaves? And why would any Syrian want these worthless dregs from Jerusalem?' And on it went.

"Demas gave his answers. But when the soldier asked his final question, when he asked why any Syrian slaver would buy new tunics for this Jewish filth, Demas gave no reply, so I spoke up. 'What did he mean by asking so many questions? What right did he have to block our path? We were honest men of business. Was he looking for a bribe? For coins to line his pocket?' He was obviously offended by my remarks, for he called the others over, and before I knew it, they were inspecting our wagons, rifling our supplies, taking things for themselves, and threatening to bring us in for questioning.

"There we were with over sixty men and nearly ten women, all roped together, filthy, ragged, plus a wagon full of new tunics, which purpose we couldn't adequately explain. So what could I do but pull my dagger and attack? I killed five before the others even blinked. Then the rest swarmed like angry hornets. Soon their bodies were also sprawled across the roadway. Not a Roman soldier was left alive. Up to this point, *Hashem* had smiled on us. This normally well-traveled road was deserted so no one saw the carnage or that it was I who killed the Romans. But how long would that last? We were at a bend and not easily seen, but soon any number of travelers could appear and see their bodies and my blood-covered garments.

"So what was to be done but cut the ropes of the captives, give them each a tunic and some food, and urge them to make a hasty departure? Demas and I also grabbed a tunic, food, a water skin, then left the wagons and headed south toward the Jordan where we hid in caves by day and traveled by night. What happened to the other seventy I cannot say. I only pray that *Hashem* has led them to safety."

When I look at the normally confident Demas I don't like what I see. His face is tense, his brow furrowed. Aaron has not told us everything. There was something more, and I was determined to find out what it was.

"You have something on your mind?" Demas asks, looking at me sideways.

I nod. It's taken me two days, but I've finally gotten him alone. The sun has barely risen and I've asked Demas to walk with me. He's obliging, this broad Greek, agreeing to come without even asking why; so unlike the Demas who smashed my jars and foodstuffs with his club.

We have followed the waterfall downward, and are now lower than our campsite even though Ethan has insisted no one stray from it. He said he's been hearing strange noises, and fears that Roman patrols are wandering about. I say my husband is weary from too much war for our sentries have seen no signs of any soldiers.

It's beautiful here, lush foliage everywhere, and water cascading across boulders and into one small pool after another that forms a glistening chain beneath the sun. I stop and lean against a huge limestone boulder shaded by supple ferns and giant reeds.

"Tell me what happened the day you and Aaron fought the Romans." Demas's lips tighten. I've caught him off guard, that much is certain.

"I . . . didn't fight the Romans. I'm ashamed to say I left it all to Aaron." Demas's face flushes as he looks at me sideways. "It seems I'm only brave when it comes to confronting women or having to use a club on pottery and shelving. But Aaron . . . I've never seen such a skilled warrior. And good thing too, since all I can manage with a dagger is to slice up a sausage or two when hungry."

"But you watched, you *saw*. Tell me about it."

Demas absently picks the fern. "It was my fault. It should never have happened. Aaron warned me we shouldn't stray so close to the Kings Highway, that we should turn and go west. But I insisted we go just a little further north to this village I knew that made the best roast piglet I've ever eaten, all stuffed with vegetables and thrush and sausages. I couldn't stop talking about it or telling Aaron how it would be worth the extra walk. I even convinced him to try it. And that wasn't easy since he claimed, after eating those sausages at your sister's, he was through with pork. But I suppose after weeks of eating gruel and nuts and dried fruit, the thought of eating this delicacy was irresistible. Now I feel only shame for risking all our lives, though at the time I justified it because I also planned to purchase fresh supplies.

"We were almost at the village when we ran into the Romans. I didn't answer the questions nearly as well as Aaron would have you believe. I stammered and bumbled my way through them, only adding to their suspicions. Aaron knew it, too. A fight was inevitable. It was the only way Aaron could get us all safely away, for surely death or imprisonment would have been our fate if he had not."

"Perhaps you can't do what Aaron can, but Ethan told me how valuable you have been; how skilled you are at the auction block, at gathering supplies and making sure there was plenty for all. Ethan said a thousand things would have gone wrong if it weren't for you. You've done well for us all."

"I can bargain for slaves, buy and sell merchandise, but when it mattered, when Aaron needed me, I did nothing. I just stood there."

"Everyone knows you're not a warrior, Demas. Why do you fault yourself for that?"

"Because of that look on Aaron's face. I'll never forget it; his eyes . . . wild like a wounded animal's. And afterward, he wept. Like a little child. Sometimes in my dreams I can still hear him."

My heart thumps. "Make sense, Demas, for pity's sake. What is it that you are holding back?"

Demas sighs and closes his eyes. "An official, in a covered litter, was traveling with the Roman guards, I suppose under their protection. The litter's thick red curtains were drawn so we didn't know until later that a child traveled with him, a young girl of perhaps four or five. When the fighting began the six slaves carrying the litter nearly dropped it in their haste to run away. Before it even hit the ground, they were slipping the poles from the straps on their shoulders. That's when the little girl jumped out in fright. Aaron was in a deadly clash with one of the soldiers, and as he swung his dagger backward, it caught the little girl in the neck, killing her."

"Aaron never mentioned . . . he never said . . . ."

"No, he wouldn't."

Now I understand the new hardness on Aaron's face, his aged and troubled look. Perhaps to other seasoned warriors, killing an innocent child would give them only a moment's pause. So many children were dying these days. One could not weep over them all. But for Aaron . . . my tender Aaron . . . it was an act that was bound to leave a deep wound in his heart.

"Thank you for telling me," I say, feeling my own heart weighed down. And just as I'm about to ask him not to let Aaron know we spoke, I hear a spine-chilling sound.

"Eeeeeee! Eeeeeee!"

It comes from below. Demas and I quickly follow it to the lower level pool, scrambling over rocks and boulders, and nicking our ankles on the thick, sharp vegetation.

"Eeeeeee! Eeeeeee!

The cry is louder now. What could it be? A wounded animal? A dying traveler? An escaped captive? It could even be a trap. I suddenly remember Ethan's warning not to stray from camp. Perhaps we're foolish to follow the sound. But we're nearly there; too close to turn back now. I slip and scrape my leg as I slide down the incline, nearly missing a pile of wild goat droppings.

"Grrrrrrr! Eeeeeee!" The cries are hideous, and full of anguish. No human could make such sounds. It had to be an animal.

"Careful, Demas," I caution as he maneuvers around a white limestone boulder, and I behind him. And then we see it . . . more beast than human, wearing a tattered dirt-covered tunic, with a face nearly obscured by dirt and long, wild, tangled hair. Its hand is buried in a crevice as though tightly wedged, until I see the swarm of bees, and know that the creature has found a hive and is after honey.

"Let go!" Demas shouts. "Let go of the comb! They'll keep stinging if you don't."

The creature groans in pain as bees sting its grimy arms and legs, its face. Other bees get caught in the wild tangle of hair, and sting the scalp. Dark eyes blink behind the matted hair when it sees us. Its mouth parts and emits what I can only describe as a growl. To scare us away? Still, the hand remains jammed in the crevice.

Without another word, Demas bends and picks up a thin, flat rock. I wonder if he plans to use it as a weapon, but no, with it he scoops up a clump of goat dung, sets it aside, then quickly peels a piece of bark off the trunk of a dead balsam. He picks up a nearby stick, lays the thin bark over the dung and after pressing the tip of the stick against the bark begins twirling it rapidly between his palms, grinding the point through the bark. The heat of the motion suddenly ignites the dung.

What was he doing?

As the dung begins to smoke, Demas, carrying it on the stone plate, moves toward the creature that is now hissing and spitting and making clawing motions with its free hand. Its fingernails look long and menacing. A madman for sure.

"Watch his claws!" I shout, and as I do the creature turns to the side and I see the small mounds on its chest. "Oh, Demas, it's a woman!"

Demas moves slowly, ignoring the hissing and growling. Oh, what a poor mad creature this is; spitting and grunting and crying out with pain as bees swoop and sting. "The smoke will calm the bees," Demas says, speaking softly. "Then you can claim your honeycomb."

The madwoman suddenly makes barking sounds, almost like a dog, then spits again. I shrink back behind the reeds, keeping my distance.

"No one will harm you," Demas says, stepping past the giant reeds to get to the crevice. "And no one will take your honey."

The woman thrashes about, whether in pain or madness I cannot say. She even lunges for Demas, barely missing his shoulder with her claws, all the while keeping her hand wedged between the crevice. Demas stops, just out of her reach, and calmly blows smoke toward the woman; blowing, blowing, blowing until little by little the bees fly away.

"Now," he says, his voice gentle, "if you let me blow smoke into the fissure, the bees that guard the hive will become calm, too."

The woman doesn't answer, but when Demas moves closer with his smoldering dung, she doesn't hiss or growl or try to claw him. "Bees won't harm you if you know how to handle them," he says, blowing smoke as he walks. "And it's surprisingly easy. My mother was a bee-keeper. Do you know what she used to do? She used to call to the young queen bees with a reed flute. If they answered, she knew she needed to separate them and put each queen into her own hive. So you see how manageable they are?"

The woman just stands like a pillar of dirt, her hand in the crevice, not moving a muscle as though both Demas's voice and his smoke has calmed her as well.

"If you let me break off the front piece of the comb, I think I can get the rest out."

She doesn't respond at first. Then slowly she removes her hand, steps away and allows Demas access to the crevice. I hold my breath for I fear when his back is turned, this madwoman will attack him. But no, Demas places his smoldering dung near the large crack, spends some time blowing smoke into the opening, then reaches in. After twisting his arm this way and that, he finally pulls out a large comb dripping with honey, then smiles and hands it to the woman.

She grabs it without a word and begins devouring it as if she hasn't eaten in days. She rips it with her teeth, swallowing large chunks at a time. But she has earned her spoil. Even from my partially hidden spot, I see the large welts on her hands, arms, legs and neck.

I watch as honey drips from her chin and down her wrists. She grunts as she eats, then makes sloshing sounds as she again tears into the comb.

She is such a sad sight that I'm overcome with pity. I rip the hem of my tunic, then, leaving my hiding place, step out and quietly kneel at the pool to wet my rag. "Come child," I say, when she has finished eating. "Sit by the water and let me bathe your bee stings."

Her body becomes rigid. I can't see her face beneath the tangle of hair, but her partially visible eyes are wide and staring. For a moment I think she's going to bolt. But then she cocks her head and walks slowly toward me. I remain by the pool, not knowing what to expect. Will she claw me? Bite me like a savage? I should run. But how can I leave this poor creature in such a state? I point to a flattened area near the water line. "Sit here while I wash you."

She doesn't sit, but remains standing, then stares at me for a long time, those eyes peering between matted strands of dark hair. "Mama?" she finally says, bringing shaking hands up to her face and brushing hair from her eyes. "Mama, it's me. Esther."

What joy we all feel! Even my Ethan, normally so strong and composed, weeps when Demas and I return with Esther between us. And the hugging and kissing that goes on! Aaron especially is overwhelmed. He holds his sister for such a long time I begin to wonder if he's ever going to let her go. How tenaciously he clings. Perhaps it's not only Esther he's trying to hold onto, but the past, the way things were, how life once was for us all. Even the other two women who are strangers to my daughter join in the weeping and kissing and rejoicing.

But Esther doesn't weep. She stands like a stalk of wheat, allowing us to make fools of ourselves with hardly a response.

It takes me hours to scrub Esther's dirt caked body and hair, then another hour to untangle the nest of knots on her head, and while I do, the other women take Ethan's ornately embroidered Syrian tunic, since we have no others, and cut it down for Esther.

It's nearly noon by the time we're finished, and Esther is once again recognizable. Her clean hair is plaited. The fine white Syrian tunic with its ample folds of material is belted at her thin waist by a piece of fabric cut from the hem. Her eyes, dominating her pale, drawn face, seem enormous, but she looks nearly as she used to, and yet so different. Suffering has aged her.

She remains silent while I direct her to a mat, then place a bowl of date cakes before her. She looks around nervously, and hesitates before taking one, as if frightened to do so. She squirms in place, seeming uncomfortable, and avoids my eyes by shielding hers with her long lashes as she fixes her gaze downward.

Then Demas comes and sits beside her. What an affect he has! Suddenly, Esther lifts her eyes, her face relaxes, her squirming stops. He is like a soothing balm.

"You should eat," he says, pointing to the cake in her hand.

Without a word, she brings it to her mouth and takes a large chunk, then nearly swallows it whole. She looks again at Demas as she takes another bite. This time the bite is smaller, and she chews more slowly.

"That's right. You don't need to worry. There's plenty of food here," he says, smiling kindly.

She slowly eats the rest, then takes the cup of spring water Demas offers her, and drinks. Finally, she wipes her mouth with the back of her hand. "What did you say your name was?" Her voice is almost childlike.

"Demas. I'm from Pella, but I don't think we've ever met."

Esther shakes her head. "I would have remembered."

"She won't talk. Not to any of us. Not even to *me,*" I say to Demas. Ethan stands beside me, his big scarred arms folded behind his back, his face a cloud of worry.

"I've seen this with other captives; captives who have been nearly starved to death, mistreated, and often humiliated and shamed. Some are driven mad by it all. Others commit suicide. Those who don't, often become hardened, callused. Some, like Esther, become sullen and withdrawn."

"But we are her parents," I protest. "We love her. She knows that. She's safe now."

"Be patient," Demas says, frowning. "She's like a tightly closed bud and won't flower all at once."

"Mama." The soft, childlike voice weaves between my dreams. "Mama. Mama." Now it evaporates my misty sleep and forces me to open my eyes. I'm on a rush mat near the other women on the stone ledge. Esther has chosen a spot further away. "Mama," I hear her say again.

I leave my mat and creep closer, feeling my way in the dark, trying not to wake the others. I'm glad the men are at the far end of the ledge. I hear my sons snoring.

"Mama!" the voice becomes louder.

"Here I am," I say, reaching my daughter's thin curled frame. I'm on my knees, and stroking her face softly. Then, as though she was no heavier than a handful of wool, I gently lift her and cradle her in my arms. "I'm here, Esther," I repeat, not knowing if she's asleep or awake. This is not the first time she has called out in the night.

"Oh, Mama," she says in a choking voice and clutching me tightly. "Oh, Mama."

"Yes," I say softly. "I'm here."

"Why did I ever leave Pella? Why didn't I listen? Why am I so foolish and headstrong?"

"Because you take after your father," I say, laughing softly, trying to make light of a heavy thing for Esther's sake. But my heart pounds wildly. Esther is actually talking, and she's talking to *me*.

"But if I'm really like Papa, shouldn't I have his courage, too?" She sounds as if she's choking over the words. "But instead of having courage, I'm so cowardly."

"You were brave enough to rush into the mouth of danger in search of your husband. Brave enough to stand up to two strangers when you thought they were going to steal your honey."

Esther groans. "I was nearly mad from hunger. I think I would have tried to kill Demas if he had taken that honey from me. Oh, what would have happened to me if you hadn't come along? What would have I become?"

"God is gracious, and in my finding you, has answered my prayers. But He alone knows how much you could have endured."

"Does he? Does He really? There were times I felt He had abandoned me, Mama; abandoned all our race. I felt as forsaken as our Holy Jerusalem. It burned, you know, our beautiful Jerusalem. I wish I hadn't seen it. Even now, I can't dig that memory out of my head. Oh, the sounds! The screams! It was horrible. The Romans killed without mercy; slaughtered men, woman and children. Only the young and healthy they kept alive, both to sell and for their own amusement. My lips can't even speak of all they did. Of their cruelty, their depravity. In the face of all this horror . . . this terror, why should I weep because two drunken legionnaires took me away from the other roped women and . . . defiled me?"

"Oh, *Esther*," I say softly, pulling her closer.

"Don't lament, Mama. What does one woman matter? I saw many women defiled. Why should I be any different? But the drunken pigs passed out before they retied me, and in the dark I made my escape."

I hold her for a long time, and weep softly. Then, I hear her cry, too, just little sniffling sounds at first that gradually turn to sobs so deep they shake her entire body. We stay like this for a long time, holding each other until we are weary from crying. And then in the quiet, I hear her soft voice.

"Do you think anyone can ever love me again . . . after . . . after what happened?"

"I love you," I say, and at once understand that wasn't the answer Esther wanted to hear.

I trudge up the steep ravine to the small waterfall and pool just above our campsite. It's our trysting place, Ethan's and mine. In spite of the difficult climb, I hum as I go, for my joy won't be contained. We haven't been here in days, not since Esther's return. I've not wanted to leave her. But she's blooming even faster than Demas expected, due mostly to his kind attentions and his knowledge of how to handle such a wounded soul. They've become inseparable. And this morning I actually heard Esther laughing at something he said.

Ethan has decided to stay in En Gedi a few days more, to allow Esther time to regain her strength for the trip to Masada. I'm not complaining. I welcome the chance to stay longer; to be all together as a family and to have more time with Ethan. When we reach Masada, it will all come to an end. Ethan and my sons will be busy once again with matters of war. Josiah will surely want their help in preparing the fortress for the Roman attack that is certain to come.

So I climb cheerfully, wishing to savor the moment, thinking of Ethan, thinking of his arms around me and his voice whispering words of love in my ear. We were to come here together at noon, when the sun climbed the sky. He's sure to be angry that I came alone. Ethan's a soldier, seeing danger everywhere. Even now, he's scouring the hillside for trouble, he and my sons and that bear of a man, Skaris. But how could Ethan understand a wife's desire to come and prepare herself, her desire to bathe and scent her body and hair before seeing the man she loves? All morning I've been steeping, in water and oil, the crushed dried acacia flowers Ethan brought me awhile ago. Now I carry the crude perfume in a small bowl-shaped rock, trying not to spill the precious contents as I maneuver the rough terrain. I only hope that after Esther tells Ethan I'm here, he'll not be too angry to appreciate it.

I hear the small waterfall splashing merrily ahead and picture Ethan's face when he arrives. At first it will be crinkled with annoyance. Yes, as wrinkled as a raisin. But then he'll smile and fall into my arms.

And what will we talk about? Esther, for one. And Demas's growing attention. Should I worry? Could their growing affection lead to something more? And if so, would Ethan object to a Gentile as a husband for Esther? I must ask him for I see how Demas and Esther are beginning to look at one another.

I enter our secret refuge of shimmering pool and greenery. I love it here. There will be nothing like this at Masada. I look up at the sky and see that the sun is already overhead. I must hurry if I'm to be ready for Ethan. I carefully place my perfume near a clump of reeds, then unbraid my hair. But just as I'm about to remove my tunic to bathe, I hear a rustling sound behind me, and then a voice.

"I was beginning to think my little quail was never going to fall into my trap," a man says, snorting with laughter.

Whirling around, I stand and blink stupidly. I don't recognize him. His clothes appear costly, but he smells like rotting fish. His mouth arcs in a wide grin, revealing decaying, brown teeth. His eyes are cruel and hard. A large scar covers one cheek.

"Who are you!" I demand, trying to sound braver than I feel. My hand reaches for a large stone, but the man is swift and grabs my arm.

"She has courage, this wife of Ethan, eh?" He looks up at the ledge above the falls. I follow his gaze and see a half dozen men standing there, then notice what looks like an opening barely visible through the dense vegetation.

"That's right," Lamech says, grinning. "There's a cave up there."

"Hurry and bring her here before Ethan comes," one of the men shouts. There's fear in his voice.

The scarred man laughs as he cups my face with the dirt encrusted fingers of his free hand. "Yes, Ethan will surely be here soon, for I've seen how he loves to sport with his wife." When I knock his hand away, he quickly pulls an ornate dagger from his belted waist. "Careful, woman. I'm not a tolerant man."

"Don't kill her, Lamech!" one of the men shouts in panic. "We'll never get the treasure then."

The scarred man grins and gently brushes the tip of his dagger across my neck. "Just a little more pressure, that's all it would take. Remember that. If you give me trouble, any trouble at all, I'll slit your throat." With that he grabs my arm and pulls me to a path so obscured by dense vegetation I never noticed it before.

And as I'm yanked and jerked up the steep incline, I chide myself for coming here alone, for not listening to Ethan, and I burn with anger. But I don't know what angers me most: that I have fallen into the hands of this pig, or that all this time he and his men have been watching Ethan and me make love.

I'm sweaty and bruised and cut from my forced rapid climb. But I'm hardly settled on the ledge above the waterfall, when I see Ethan.

"Rebekah," he calls, as he looks around the pool.

Lamech yanks me to my feet. Then grabbing me by the hair on the back of my head, he forces my chin upward and lays the blade of his dagger against my throat.

"She's up here, Ethan, with me," Lamech shouts over the noise of the splattering falls. "And if you don't want to see her die, you'll make no trouble and listen to me carefully."

At once, Ethan's own dagger flashes in his hand. "If you hurt her, I'll not spare any of you. We've both seen how the Romans can kill a man slowly, until he begs for death. Mark my words, Lamech, I'll reserve such a treatment for you."

Lamech snorts with laughter. "I have no wish to hurt your wife. I have no interest in her except to get your attention. But it's not even you I want. It's the treasure. You cheated me, Ethan, and now you must make amends."

Ethan unties the money pouch at his waist. "Here, take what I have on me and let Rebekah go."

Perspiration drips from Lamech's face. "I spotted you when your party was only two days from here. My men and I were working the trail, looking for suitable plunder, but never expected to find such a prize! And you, the big general, not knowing you were being followed! Ha! No wonder Jerusalem fell to the Romans." Sweat drips into Lamech's eyes making him squint, and I wonder if he sweats from fear or the heat.

"But do you think I'd bother to follow you all the way here for the meager coins in your pouch? Or stay day and night lying in wait in the cave behind me with men who smell like goats and have the brains of Sodom apples?" He ignores his men when they grumble.

"Yes, I see what useless fodder you've recruited," Ethan says with a sneer.

"Well, what could I do, eh? After you and your Masada Zealots killed all my other men I was forced to glean where I could. But never mind. It's pointless to bring up *all* your transgressions."

Ethan ties the pouch back onto his belt. "You know the Zealots took most of the treasure to Masada. If you want it so badly go get it."

"Ah, Ethan, Ethan, why be difficult? I've heard the rumors. We both know that vast temple treasure is buried all over our land. But you never wanted to share. Well, now I think you will."

"There's plenty of treasure in the tombs—Absalom's, David's, Queen Helena's. There, I've told you what you wanted to know. You don't need me now. Dig where I said and you'll find enough treasure to satisfy even your greed."

Lamech laughs. "And all under the watchful eyes of the 10th Legion, eh?"

"That's where most of the treasure is."

"But not all, not all, Ethan, eh?"

When my husband doesn't answer, Lamech nicks me with his blade, drawing blood. I bite my lip not to cry out and give Lamech any pleasure, or give Ethan any grief. Blood drips down my neck onto the blade, then down my tunic. Lamech holds the bloody dagger in the air. "A little deeper, Ethan, and I could have killed her. What say you now?"

"No, not all the treasure is in Jerusalem. There's still some in the Valley of Achor."

"Achor?" Lamech brightens. "How much treasure?"

"Two pots of silver coins."

"Pots? Small pots, large pots? What?"

"I don't know. But they'll have to do. Because that's all the treasure you and your men will get."

Lamech, still holding me tightly by the hair, yanks my head back hard, exposing my bloody neck. "You're in no position to dictate terms. Don't think I won't kill your wife if you don't give me what I want."

Ethan shakes his head. "You won't kill her. She's the only thing keeping you alive. If she dies, there'll be nothing to stop me from coming after you."

Lamech smiles and releases my hair. "You're a logical man. I respect that. And you're right. What have I to gain by such an act? I'm a business man, not a cutthroat. My only desire is to make a meager living so, yes, I'll accept the two pots. See how reasonable I am? I'll return to Achor and wait for you there. You can bring your two sons to help you dig, but no one else. We'll be watching."

Lamech shoves me away, making me stumble into the men behind me. He then pulls an object, about the size of his hand, from his tunic. It is wrapped in a dirty cloth. He throws it down to where Ethan stands and there it lands by the reeds. "In four days we'll come for the coins."

"It will take us nearly two to get to Hyrcania, and who knows how long to find the pots. Do you think Eleazar left a trail in the dirt for us to follow? We need more time."

"Four days. That's all you have." He points to the object by the reeds. "It's a bell. Carry it with you. And listen carefully. This is how it will be. When you've located the treasure, you will ring it, alerting me and my men we are to come and fetch it, and when we do, we will bring your wife with us and make the trade. Your wife for the two pots. But before the exchange, I'll send one of my men to tell you where to meet us. I, not you, will pick the ground. And it will not be where you or your sons can lay a trap."

Lamech's face tightens and his mouth forms an ugly sneer. "You must follow my instructions completely. And don't even think of trying anything foolish. Remember, we'll be watching your every move. Four days, you have four days. After that I'll begin sending your wife back to you in pieces."

Ethan doesn't flinch. He appears so calm and in control that it surely must unnerve Lamech. Only someone who knows him well would know how deeply distressed he is. I watch the fingers of one hand curl into a fist; watch him move his foot slightly as if bracing himself. "I will see you in Hyrcania," he shouts as he picks up the wrapped bell near his feet. Then, after a quick glance at me, he disappears.

The pull of the rope yanks me forward, chafing my neck and the wound Lamech gave me, and nearly causes me to stumble. My hands are tied in front, my neck roped, my tunic torn, my face and body caked with dirt. I could be one of Titus's captives. At the other end of the rope is a thin, sinewy man with a face as pocked as the ground we travel. I suppose he yanks the rope from time to time to see if I'm still there, because he never looks back. I'm only an object to be transported, a burden like the water skins, food, weapons, and other supplies his companions carry in large bags over their shoulders.

I glance upward, past the dusty, barren-looking mountains surrounding us, and see that the sun will soon slide into its resting place for the night. All day we've been traveling at a furious pace, along narrow footpaths and rocky mountain ledges, through ravines and around cliffs. It's obvious Lamech wants to get to Hyrcania before Ethan. To secrete his men in advantageous positions? To prepare a trap? Will a man like Lamech be content with only two pots of silver? It's doubtful. But I saw his face when Ethan entered the pool area. I saw the fear. Perhaps fear will force contentment. But will Ethan even give such holy treasure to a cutthroat and thief like Lamech? Knowing Ethan, it's hard to imagine.

"Faster!" Lamech growls, pushing one of his men forward with his hand. "We must get there before dark. Do you think I want that jackal to outflank us?"

Oh, yes, this madman fears my Ethan. My gentle bear, my love. I'd find it amusing if I wasn't so miserable. I run my dry tongue over parched, crusty lips. My mouth feels as though it's lined with sand. My neck and feet bleed. I'm nearly faint from heat, from having eaten only one small handful of almonds and from having walked for hours without rest. The mountains squeeze me. They rise to the sky like monoliths, taking the air with them. I'm finding it hard to breathe. I've never been to this part of the Judean Desert. How could anything survive here? Still, I'm determined not to appear weak. I must not beg for food or water or rest. As I gather my remaining strength and courage like a poor gleaner who gathers the last kernels in the corners of a field, I remember that I'm in God's hands, not theirs. It will be His decision if I live or die. I take quick shallow breaths trying to fill my starving lungs, and pray.

Oh, Lord be strong in my weakness!

"Wash yourself," Lamech says, pointing to a water skin. "I dislike dirty women." He grins. "I've seen how beautiful you can look." Bending closer, he strokes my loose, tangled hair. "Especially this," he says, letting the strands fall through his dirt caked fingers.

We are in a cave just west of a strange shaped pathway that leads up to a high mountain and the remains of the Hyrcania fortress. We arrived at sunset. After Lamech's men spent time scouting the area for a suitable cave, they chose this one. Already a dozen oil lamps have been lit, flooding our quarters with light and allowing me to see that our cave is modest in size. One of the men unfurls several rush mats, kicks away the strewn rocks littering the floor, smoothes a large area with his foot, then spreads the mats out over the dirt. Another pulls wooden bowls from his sack, still another fills them with dried fruit and nuts, then places them, along with a small stack of flat bread, in front of the now sitting Lamech. Finally, one man pulls a pillow from a large woven bag, and after fluffing it, places it behind Lamech's back for him to lean upon.

If I hadn't seen it with my own eyes, I'd never believe it. This Lamech likes his comfort. I ignore his stares as I shake the dust from my hair, then comb it with my fingers, attempting to smooth out the tangles. Then I rip two small pieces of fabric from the hem of my tunic. Using one, I tie back my hair. The other I wet and begin washing, first the blood from my neck, then the dirt from my face and hands and arms.

"Come, sit here by me," Lamech shouts, though I'm only a few cubits away.

I rise reluctantly, and walk to the rush mats, then take the space across from him. One of the men pours wine from a skin into a wooden cup and hands it to Lamech who downs it without a word, then holds it out for more. The man refills it, then walks away.

"Eat, eat!" Lamech says to me. "You must be hungry." He belches between words. "You took the journey well, without complaint. Not many women would, you know." He grins widely, then lifts his cup for more wine.

His men are gathered in a corner away from us, and have also begun eating their own nuts and fruit and bread, the keeper of the wineskin included. So when he's too slow in rising to fill the cup, Lamech pulls his dagger and nicks him in the leg when he finally strolls over. "Next time I'll hamstring you," he hisses. "Then you'll have reason to move like an old woman."

Lamech drains another cup, smacks his lips, and watches me eat my flatbread and handful of figs. I eat them slowly, my discomfort mounting under his constant gaze. *Oh, God, You are my refuge and strength, a high tower in times of trouble.*

"I'm a man who knows how to live, am I not?" he says, breaking his silence and pointing to the pillow and mats and bowls. Not like your Ethan who would run off to war and leave you to provide for yourself."

In spite of myself I flinch, telling Lamech his barb has hit its mark. He snorts with laughter. "Yet you care for him. I have *seen* how you care." He raises his cup, making the man with the wine skin scramble to his feet and rush over to fill it. When it's filled, Lamech downs it in one gulp.

Oh, God, You are my refuge and strength, a high tower in times of trouble.

The pig belches again and leans toward me, nearly hitting me in the face with his empty cup. "To a man, wine is a necessity of life. It gives him pleasure and comfort. Perhaps before I release you, I'll sample the wine Ethan finds so pleasing." Then he yawns. "But not tonight. I'm worn from the journey." With that he rises to his feet, picks up the beautiful silk pillow, and staggers off to an empty space against the wall, leaving me alone on the mat.

Oh, God, You are *my refuge and strength, a high tower in times of trouble.*

I've lost track of time. We've been here for days, days that seem as endless as the Judean Desert itself. But God has been gracious. No one has molested me, and I've been given all the food and water I want.

I sit against the wall watching Lamech and his men. Their heads are together. Lamech's voice is raised. He's talking to the two men who have just returned from a mission. Did it have something to do with Ethan? I close my eyes trying to recount my time here. Was this the day Ethan was to surrender the treasure? I've slept so much that it's hard to know exactly. Let me think . . . a day and a half to walk here, another one lost to sleep . . . or was that also a day and a half? . . . then another day . . ."

"It seems your husband doesn't care for you as much as I thought."

I open my eyes and see Lamech standing over me, a dagger in his hand. "He's taking too long to find the treasure. He has yet to sound the bell. Is it a trick, do you think? Does he plan to cheat me again? Or maybe he hopes to give his friends at Masada more time to arrive, for surely he has sent the others in your group for help. But all this tells me he doesn't believe me, doesn't believe I will cut you and send the pieces to him, one at a time." He bends closer, his foul stench nearly making me gag. "So now I must show him that I meant what I said." He raises the large ornate dagger into the air. When it catches the light from the cave entrance and glints, I close my eyes and pray.

Ethan

HYRCANIA AND JUDEAN DESERT 70 A.D.

CHAPTER 12

"Father, we've turned the dirt between every building in Hyrcania," Benjamin says, pausing from his labors to look up at me from the hole he is digging. "I think we must concede that the treasure is not between the buildings."

Aaron, who is next to him, continues scooping dirt furiously with his curved stone, showing no sign of conceding anything. We have no shovels with us this time, and that makes the work slower, harder, more tedious.

I wipe sweat from my brow, smearing grit across my forehead. Benjamin was right. We've been digging for three days without success. As Lamech instructed, only my sons and I are here in Hyrcania. I've charged Demas with the care of Esther, along with the other two women, at En Gedi; while Skaris and some of the other captives have gone to Masada for help.

"Our allotted time has run out," Aaron says, tossing another stone-full of dirt over his shoulder. His hands are blistered from using the coarse stone these many days. All our hands are. "Perhaps Lamech never intended to hurt Mama. Perhaps he meant only to frighten you."

"If Lamech has not hurt your mother it's only because *Hashem* has restrained him. But we must find the treasure soon, for I have no wish to test *Hashem's* kindness any further."

Benjamin tosses his digging stone to the ground and climbs out of the hole. "Then we can't afford to waste time. Perhaps you were right all along, Father. Perhaps the word on the scroll meant 'chambers' and not 'buildings' as Aaron and I thought."

We've been digging since dawn. I squint at the overhead sun to determine how much daylight we have left. We must make every moment count. The part of the scroll describing the location is difficult to read. It states that two pots of silver are buried three cubits deep between two . . . what? Buildings? Chambers? Foundations? All were possibilities. I've always favored "chambers," though the past three days I've prayed I was wrong. There were fewer buildings than chambers. And what chambers? Where? The number of rooms and chambers on the summit were endless. Lamech's patience would never hold while we searched between them all. And unlike Aaron, I'm fully persuaded Lamech has every intention of harming Rebekah if I don't deliver the treasure. Skaris should return soon with Josiah. But will it be in time to save my wife?

My heart thumps as I think of Rebekah in that pig's hands. "Yes, it's time to rethink our search," I say to Benjamin, who stands frowning by my side. I know he hears the desperation in my voice. And just as I signal Aaron to stop digging, I see two men approaching in the distance. One carries a basket. When I alert my sons, Aaron quickly scrambles out of the ditch. And by the time the men reach us, our weapons are drawn.

"From Lamech," a tall, nearly toothless man says, dropping the covered basket at my feet. "And he said to tell you that this time tomorrow you'll be getting another basket. In truth, you'll be getting a basket every day until you deliver the treasure."

Aaron raises his dagger and steps forward.

"I wouldn't do that," the toothless man says, out of breath from the climb up the summit, but nervous, too, as he eyes Aaron's weapon. "If anything happens to us, if we don't return safe and whole to Lamech by nightfall, he said he'll kill the woman known as Rebekah."

"Then go! You've delivered your message!" I gesture with my dagger for the men to depart.

"One more thing," the tall, toothless man says, running his tongue nervously over his dry lips, "After you find the treasure and ring the bell, you are to carry it down to the base of the mountain where the crumbling aqueduct intersects the path."

"And how do you expect us to do that? Suppose the pots are large? How can only three of us carry them all the way down that treacherous, steep path?" I squint my eyes with anger, and step closer to the man.

He and his companion back away. "Those are Lamech's orders, not mine. But I'd advise you to do what he says, that is if you want to see that pretty wife of yours again in one piece." Both men continue backing away, and only when they've gone a good distance do they turn their backs on us and run.

My sons and I let them go their way, then stand for some time staring down at the basket, for no one has the courage to look inside. Finally, I square my shoulders, and taking a deep breath, remove the lid. Both Aaron and Benjamin gasp. Had my throat not been nearly closed with fear, my gasp would have joined theirs. Slowly, I lower my bulky frame and squat beside the container, then I reach in and pull out a handful of Rebekah's long, beautiful, auburn hair.

"Father, you can't keep up this pace. It is time for you to rest in the tower and keep an eye on those rogues. That's just as important as our digging."

I ignore Benjamin and continue scraping dirt. We've changed our search. All afternoon we've dug between one chamber after another. There are so many. How are we ever to find the treasure before this time tomorrow? The thought of receiving another basket has made me dig at a furious pace. My sons, too. We have rested little today, having gone to the tower but twice.

"Benjamin is right, Father," Aaron says, scooping dirt like a madman and flinging it over his shoulder, "you're worn out."

"I've worked no harder than the two of you. And I don't need to go to the tower to know what that pig, Lamech, is doing. He's sitting in the cool of his cave, as usual, feeling pleased with himself, pleased and confident that because he has Rebekah, he has won the victory over us."

"Still, you must rest," Benjamin says. "You must spare yourself. It was you who said Lamech will not give up Mama without a fight. We will need your sword."

I continue digging, not even bothering to look up or answer my son. All I can think about is that basket. The next one will be more malevolent. That thought drives me to distraction. How much more must my family suffer for this foolish treasure? And how much more must I lose before it all ends?

What's that? That sound . . . it irritates . . . distresses me. What is it? I try to turn onto my side, but my body is weighted by fatigue and won't move. I am bone weary. I can't even open my eyes. Am I dreaming? I must be. Yes, surely it's a dream. I feel my chest heaving up and down, feel my muscles quiver with pain, feel the fatigue that pins me to the ground like a helpless slug. But that sound! I must . . . make it stop. It is oddly familiar. Where have I heard it before? It almost sounds like . . . a whip . . . a whip being laid against a man's back. I can't bear it. It's sickening. I try to bring my hands to my ears, to stop the sound from filling them, but I can't move my arms.

"Stop . . . no more," I hear myself whisper. But the lashing continues. Over and over. Whisht, wap, whisht, wap. And beneath that sound, I hear a man groan. Again and again the whip is laid to his back. Twelve . . . thirteen. Why am I counting? Sixteen . . . seventeen. I'm splattered with blood. It's on my arms, face, neck. The man's blood is all over me. I see him now bound to a post. The flagrum, with its ox-hide thongs and small knotted lead balls, flashes behind him. Twenty . . . twenty-one. Why doesn't he cry out? Beg for mercy? Twenty-six . . . twenty-seven. My face is drenched. I want to wipe it . . . need to wipe it, but my arms are dead things, useless dead things. Thirty-two . . . thirty-three. They'll kill him for sure. How can any man withstand such scourging and live? I see the lead balls tear bits of his flesh and fling them into the air. And the blood . . . it's everywhere. Why doesn't he just curse his tormentors and die? Thirty-eight . . . thirty-nine . . . oh, at last, it's stopped. That terrible sound has stopped. But the man? Is he still alive? I see him slumped against the post, blood pouring from his wounds. Yes. His chest moves in short, uneven breaths. If only I could wipe his blood from me. I'm drenched. Drenched.

I thrash around, trying to rouse myself, but stop when I hear weeping. Who weeps and wails? I can't see. It's so dark. All around me swirl black clouds. Then through the weeping I hear the sound of a hammer pounding, pounding, pounding. The clouds part slightly and I see that the hammer is pounding nails into the hands and feet of a man, and then into wood. I can watch no more, and with a jolt, force myself awake. My breathing is heavy and ragged. I can hardly pull air into my lungs. Sweat pours down my head and face and neck. Down my arms. My heart thunders. It's been years. Why am I remembering now? I was only a boy, but I can recall every detail.

I glance at my sons who lay sleeping beside me. The night sky still hangs heavy over us and they snore peacefully beneath it. I'm exhausted but my heart is too troubled for sleep. I crave the solace of my sons but dare not wake them. They've worked hard all day, then spent much of the night discussing with me how we might defeat Lamech. We all need every minute of rest we can get.

I turn to my other side, trying to calm myself, trying to forget the dream. But it's still so vivid. It haunts my thoughts. And after I lay there for a long time and can no longer keep my eyes from closing, I once again slip into the foggy world of sleep, and when I do, I hear that sound again: whisht, wap, whisht, wap . . . .

"Father are you sure? If we leave the summit now and dig where you propose . . . and find nothing . . . we won't have time to return here and search among the chambers before Lamech's men come again with another . . . ."

"Don't you think I know that?" I say, clasping Benjamin's shoulder, trying to bolster his confidence and mine. "But it came to me last night when I couldn't sleep. I believe it's where God would have me dig. Don't you see? The two tunnels are two *chambers*. We must dig between them."

Aaron's face twists in thought. "If *Hashem* has favored you with wisdom, Father, let us waste no time. I say we go at once."

Benjamin nods, but I see his agonized reluctance. It is a great risk we take. We have little time. If it's wasted in futile pursuit, Rebekah will pay dearly. Oh, where are Josiah and his men? They should have been here by now. We know the location of Lamech's cave but are too few to execute a rescue. At the first sight of us, Lamech will surely kill Rebekah. My sons and I agree our only option is to find the treasure so we can put our plan into effect, a plan involving only the three of us since we have no one else to count on.

And so, with heavy heart, I lead my sons down the summit, down the steep winding path. It's barely sunrise as we head for the two tunnels located at the base of the mountain, tunnels that lie east of the crumbling aqueduct. We discovered them on our first trip to Hyrcania, and after a brief exploration, found they were nothing but rock-and-dirt littered shafts, and completely blocked within several cubits from their openings.

Aaron is the first to reach the tunnels, and at once paces the ground between them to determine the center, for the scroll tells us that the pots are located midway between the chambers. When he finishes, he begins digging without a word. Benjamin joins him. Then I.

We dig one hole, then another. *Nothing.* Nothing but hard-baked mud and rocks.

"Father, should we try another spot?" Benjamin says, already covered in grit and sweat.

"Yes, move to the right. That's it! Dig there!" I shout. And so we begin digging another hole very near the ones we've already dug. No one speaks. All our energy is spent shifting dirt and rocks. Dust fills the air as we wield our large curved stones like madmen. It powders everything: our hair, our faces, our sweaty arms and legs, our damp tunics. Our hands are bleeding now. Still we dig. Two cubits . . . three cubits . . . and find nothing but more dirt.

"Another spot . . . try another spot!" I shout, unable to keep the desperation from my voice.

Benjamin shakes his head. "The winds are strong here. Look how it carries the dirt back to us. We must consider the possibility that the winds have raised the level of the ground. The scroll said three cubits. But if we assume the earth is thicker now, then we should dig another cubit before giving up."

"We won't have to," Aaron suddenly cries. "I've hit something!"

In a flurry, Benjamin and I dig around the object Aaron has discovered. Our efforts are rewarded when we expose the lids of two clay pots. More digging reveals the pots to be large and round and taller than our waist. When we've completely unearthed one of them, I break Eleazar's seal and remove the top. Though I can plainly see it's full of silver, I plunge in my hand and laugh in jubilation as the coins jingle. Then I pull up a handful and show them to my sons. By then we are all praising *Hashem.*

"Now, to lay our trap," I say, feeling my blood rush, my senses sharpen. "Come, we must hurry! The sun is already climbing."

From the beginning we've known that Lamech and his men were hiding in a nearby cave west of the M-shaped path. For all that pig's boasting about his skills as a general, he has proven himself lazy and careless; so have his men. They made a trail of dust a child could follow, and follow it we did, all the way from En Gedi. Lamech may be competent enough to spy on a group of exhausted, ragged captives, but when it came to his new crop of cutthroats establishing a camp or a proper perimeter or even spying on experienced soldiers, they were hopeless; though the ache in my heart reminds me they were skilled enough to take Rebekah by surprise at the pool in En Gedi.

But we have been busy with our own strategy these past several days. While two of us were always busy digging, one would often rest, and during that time would monitor Lamech's activities from the northwest tower on the Hyrcania summit. And this monitoring paid off. From it we gleaned that Lamech has less than a dozen men, and he has sent no one to spy on us. All his blustering by the pool in En Gedi when he tossed down the bell and said he would be watching, was just that, empty bluster. Not only are we not under his surveillance, Lamech has posted but two men west of here, midway between the aqueduct and his cave. Also, from our tower, we have noticed that Lamech and his men rarely leave the cool interior of their cave.

Even so, we know the danger is real, for surely one of Lamech's men stays near Rebekah, ever ready to plunge his dagger into her throat. This was why we've been careful to follow Lamech's instructions, or at least *appear* to follow it. Lamech had to know I would send to Masada for help. That's why he gave me only four days to find the treasure. He meant to be far away by the time Josiah and his men arrived. It is obvious he wishes to avoid repeating the disaster of his last encounter with us on the summit, by avoiding the summit altogether and insisting Rebekah and the treasure be exchanged at the base of the mountain. It is also obvious that he is supremely confident that since he has Rebekah, we will not move against him. Both his laziness and his hubris we will now use to our advantage.

"Hurry!" I say to Aaron and Benjamin as they cover one of the clay pots with dirt. The other has already been removed from the pit, and stands nearby. We spend time pacing out the spot where the pot remains buried so we can return to it later, then spend more time smoothing the dirt and littering the ground with rocks. Finally, we carry the large pot to the designated meeting place. It's heavy and must be carried on its side and takes all three of us to do it.

By the time we reach the rendezvous point and position the jar in the shadow of the aqueduct, we are panting for air. All around us are the crumbling remains of the fifteen cisterns that once stored rain water. It's a poor spot for a battle. Our backs are against the high walls of the aqueduct, and the ground is littered with trip hazards making aggressive warfare difficult. At least in naming this spot, Lamech has chosen wisely.

"May God go with you," I say, embracing Aaron.

"I won't fail you, Father," Aaron returns, lingering against my chest for a moment before pulling away. His eye patch is caked with dirt, his face glistens with sweat. We are all weary from the morning's labor, though it's not fatigue that mars Aaron's face but a fierceness that makes me shudder.

I watch him scramble so stealthily over rocks and walls that he raises little dust. Then long after he disappears from view, I pull the bell from the pouch at my waist, remove the rag that swaddles the clapper, and ring it.

Even before I see Lamech, I smell him coming. Odors like that of rancid fat and rotting fish fill the air. When I finally see him, there's a grin on his face. His costly blue robe flaps around his legs as he approaches. His large ornate dagger is conspicuously belted at his waist. Behind him are eight men. As expected, Rebekah is not with them.

"So, where is this treasure of yours?" Lamech asks, rubbing the large scar on his cheek and looking around eagerly.

Both Benjamin and I are standing in front of the jar, obscuring it from view. "Where is Rebekah?"

"All in good time, my friend. All in good time." He cranes his neck this way and that, then frowns. "Young Aaron is missing. Laying in ambush, eh? It would not go well for your wife if he tried anything."

"He wouldn't be so foolish. But he's safely away. One of us had to be in case you rewarded our good faith with treachery."

"Hmmmm, no doubt I'd be his first target, eh? Oh, come, come, Ethan, we both know you'd betray me, too, if you could. But fortunately for me, there's a blade at your wife's throat. If harm comes to us, to *any* of us, if the slightest misfortune should befall us, that blade will do its worst."

"This is not our agreement. You were to bring Rebekah while I was to bring the treasure. You have not kept faith with me, Lamech."

The grinning pig bursts out laughing. "Nor you with me! Otherwise you would not have sent young Aaron to . . . what? Attack us from behind? Lay a trap? Follow us back to our hiding place?"

"He's not planning any of these things."

Lamech strokes his bearded chin. "You'd swear to that? You'd give me your word?"

"Why should I give my word to someone who breaks his? You promised me my wife. Where is *she*?"

"And you promised me treasure. Where is *it*?"

I motion for Benjamin to step aside while I do the same, revealing the large clay jar behind us. Lamech's eyes widen, obviously surprised by its great size.

"I see only one jar," he says after regaining his composure. "You promised two."

"And you shall have it, when I have Rebekah. But this time I name the terms." I point to the summit. "The second jar will be waiting for you up there. But not one coin will you get unless Rebekah is with you, and unharmed."

Lamech frowns. "That's your territory, Ethan. It will be easy for you and your sons to set a trap. Your terms are unacceptable."

"You outnumber us three to one. Surely you're not afraid? But before you answer, come see what you are giving up, for this jar is yours, and another like it could be as well." I beckon him to step closer, knowing the draw of treasure would be too difficult for him to resist.

He hesitates, then signals his men to be alert before walking over to the jar. As soon as he removes the top, I know I have him. He rakes the coins with his fingers as though they were a woman's tresses, and I think of what he has done to my Rebekah. My hand moves to the hilt of my dagger. Only the look on Benjamin's face restrains me from using it.

Lamech jingles a few coins in his hand as he studies me out of the corner of his eye. "You will let me take this jar and leave without a fight?"

I nod.

"And if I bring you Rebekah, you'll give me another just like it?"

Again I nod.

"Perhaps we can come to some agreement after all. I will think on it and let you know."

"And in the meantime? Will you give me your word you won't hurt Rebekah?"

Lamech snorts like a pig as he laughs. "If I did, would you believe me? Ah, Ethan, you are soft. No woman should mean that much. It makes you desperate. It makes you *foolish.* I will take this jar, and come back tomorrow for the second. And I will come here, to this spot, and no other; otherwise you'll get your wife back in pieces! The matter is settled. Do not test me in this."

My eyes narrow as I stand looking at this butcher of merchants and women. Lamech's eyes follow my hand as it moves toward my dagger.

"Draw blood and I swear you'll lose what is most precious," Lamech says with a sneer. Then he snorts with laughter. "You should never have let me know your weakness, Ethan. A man with a weakness can be conquered." Lamech motions for his men to pick up the jar. "It would have been better for you to have let your wife perish."

Benjamin and I watch as three of Lamech's men carry away the jar. I still hear Lamech's laughter as he and the rest of his men round the bend. But as soon as he does, Benjamin and I scramble to the top of the aqueduct. Soon, Lamech and his men will be near a patch of rough, sloping terrain where footing is difficult and made worst when carrying a heavy jar of silver. That will leave only six able to react with any speed to an attack. It's the place we have chosen for our face-off.

We move quickly across the top of the aqueduct, scattering a few stones as we go. I fear our noise will alert Lamech, but no, when I look down I see he and his raucous men just ahead, talking and laughing. Once again Lamech's laziness and pride work in our favor, for he has not posted lookouts or ordered his men to be cautious.

With daggers in hand Benjamin and I carefully shadow the cut-throats, and just as they reach the designated spot, we let out a fierce cry and leap upon them as if we were lions. Within minutes, four of them are dead on the ground. Only Lamech and the tall, toothless man remain. The three carrying the jar have dropped it and run. Now it's one on one. Benjamin takes the toothless man while I take on Lamech.

"You dare do this, knowing your wife will die?" Lamech backs away, though he has a dagger in his hand.

"You underestimated my weakness or the length it would drive me," I reply, lunging forward and slicing his upper arm. The blade cuts deep for he can barely hold his weapon. Another cut, and he drops it. Then his face is one of utter surprise as I finish him off. But as he crumbles to the ground I do not feel the satisfaction I anticipated. Rather, I feel relief that such a man will no longer be a scourge to others, and I feel sadness, too, that once again, Jew has slaughtered Jew.

"Father, we must hurry. The three who got away are bound to head for the cave. We must make certain they don't encounter Aaron and Mama."

I nod. Knowing Lamech would never honor his word, it was decided that Aaron would go to the cave and rescue Rebekah, then bring her back. It was doubtful that Lamech would leave more than two men to guard Rebekah, an easy match for Aaron's abilities. But if he was wounded in the process, the three men that just escaped could present a problem.

So we make haste and sprint in the direction of the cave.

The cloud of dust ahead tells me we're not far behind the three jackals we pursue. My only thought is to reach them before they encounter Aaron and Rebekah. My feet fly over the rough terrain. Benjamin keeps pace beside me. And as we scramble over rocks and hard-mud ground, eating dust and dropping sweat, something inside me keeps urging me to run faster. My breathing is heavy, my muscles quiver with fatigue as I close the gap between us. Benjamin is now running ahead, his young body showing little strain.

We're nearing the cave and still there's no sign of Rebekah or Aaron. This troubles me. Surely we didn't pass them on the way? Even if they were hiding, they would have made themselves known to us as we passed. When I hear shouting, then a scream, I quicken my pace, not caring if I raise dust and reveal myself to our enemies. Benjamin also quickens his. As I get closer I see a woman holding a dagger and fending off two men. Nearby, two others lie on the ground, motionless.

"Rebekah!" I shout, racing ahead of Benjamin.

When the two men see me, they turn and run, but I follow. Benjamin is soon beside me, and in no time the last of Lamech's men lay dead at our feet. Then I race back to Rebekah. She's kneeling beside one of the bodies and whispering softly. *Aaron*? Is that Aaron lying in the dirt? I stop. I just stop. Nothing moves, not my feet, my legs, my arms, my hands. I'm as stiff as marble. Even so, from where I stand I can see the blood covering Aaron's tunic. I groan, but it sounds more like the growl of a frightened dog. *Is my son dead*? I fear so. Oh, how can my heart take it? How can I bear any more loss? At that moment I was tempted to curse God and die. It seemed preferable than stepping closer and seeing if what I fear is true.

Benjamin, too, hangs back, breathing heavily and shaking his head in disbelief. I muster all my courage and go to my son. Aaron's face is as white as lime dust. His chest is motionless, his lips look like wax. I hear Rebekah whispering. Prayers? I think so. Slowly, she removes the patch over Aaron's useless eye, then places one hand on the badly scarred lid, the other on his blood-stained tunic. She drops her head, while I drop to my knees and pant silently beside her. She remains like this for a long time then finally lifts her face and *smiles*.

"Our son is brave. He fights like a lion. But he sustained a grievous wound at the cave, and lost much blood. Even so, he managed to bring down this one before collapsing." She gestures with her chin to the body lying nearby. "But he'll live. Not to fight, Ethan. *Not to fight.* God has heard my clanging, and healed Aaron; healed him for *His* service."

As I look at my son's lifeless body, a new fear comes over me. *Has Rebekah lost her mind from grief?* "Rebekah . . . surely you see that life has gone from . . . ."

Suddenly, Aaron's fingers move, then his hand. A sigh escapes his lips. His head turns, his eyes open. Yes, two eyes open. Two perfectly normal eyes; for the eye that was white with scarring is now clear and bright and staring at me! My body trembles. Can this really be true? I bend over my son and lay a shaking hand on his shoulder as I stare into his face.

"Praise *Hashem!*" I say in a quivering voice. "He has restored your sight!" My own eyes fill with tears of gratitude until I look at the blood on his tunic. What good is the healing of an eye when the heart has been ripped in two by a dagger? Yet . . . he breathes normally. Could it be . . . could *Hashem* have healed his chest wound, too? And for the first time in a very long while I dare hope for a miracle.

Aaron looks dazed. His forehead crinkles in confusion as he brings both hands up to his face. He holds them there for some time before blurting, "I can see!" He laughs and turns his hands this way and that, as though viewing them for the first time. Finally, he sits up. "I feel no pain," he says, answering my silent question as he runs his hands over his blood soaked tunic. Then he pokes his chest. "It's gone! The wound is gone!"

When Benjamin and I help him to his feet I notice the joy on Aaron's face, in his eyes. He has the face of an angel, with peace covering him like a *talith*. And he is smiling.

Has God healed the wounds in Aaron's soul as well?

"I can't remember when I've felt so good!" Aaron says, his voice full of wonder and joy. Then he spots the dead men lying on the ground. "Praise God that you came in time, Father. Is Mama hurt?" He looks at Rebekah anxiously.

"Be at peace. No harm has come to me," she says, not looking at Aaron but at me. I see gratitude in her eyes. She fingers her headscarf nervously. "Your father is still formidable."

"You are well, then?" I say, going to her, still dazed and not knowing what to make of all that has happened to Aaron. I try to put my arms around her but she pulls away.

"The only thing hurt is my pride. You might as well see for yourself." Her face reddens with shame as she pulls the scarf from her head revealing short chopped hair. "You might as well see how abhorrent your wife is!"

I take her chin and tilt her face upward as I search her eyes. They will tell me just how much Lamech has taken from her. When I see that unmistakable sparkle I laugh and hug her to my chest. "Oh, Rebekah, you are still as beautiful as ever!"

"As usual, you've left a wake of dead bodies behind," Josiah says with a grin as he walks toward me in full leather armor and a belted sword, and looking disappointed he won't need to use it. A string of over fifty men follow behind, including Skaris. I've been watching their approach for several minutes.

"And you, as *usual*, are late, arriving only after all the hard work is done." I clasp his arm in friendship, glad to see him. "What delayed you?"

"That Thracian, Skaris, and the ragged group of men you sent have never been to Masada, and lost their way. They only arrived late yesterday. We marched part of the night and all morning to get here.

I should have known that you and your sons were more than able to handle things. I only pray your enemy, Lamech, is among those scattered in the dirt."

"He is."

Josiah cocks his head and frowns. "But you do not rejoice?"

"I have better things to rejoice over." I glance at Aaron who is talking to Rebekah and Benjamin. Was it only moments ago that he rose from the dead? I still don't know what to make of it, though years ago I witnessed many of Jesus' miracles, including the raising of Lazarus.

"Yes, I see your wife is safe and well," Josiah says, misunderstanding. "Skaris has told me all. These men," he says, spitting on the ground and gesturing toward the lifeless bodies still sprawled in the dirt, "died too easily. Their clean wounds tell me they suffered little." He signals for his men to collect them. "Robbers and thieves, a disgrace to our race, just like the *sicarii*, those dagger men who live among us and behave like wild beasts. But never mind. I rejoice over your good fortune. *Hashem* has been kind to you. "

I nod. He didn't know the half of it. But how can I explain? Though Josiah saw Jesus' miracles, too, he considers Him a charlatan.

"And *Hashem* has been kind to us as well. I passed the broken jar of silver. Even now my men are preparing it for transport back to Masada."

"There's another like it. I'll show you."

Josiah slaps my back good naturedly. "What luck! If you keep providing us with treasure like this, our fight can go on forever."

His words are like a blade in my heart. *Go on forever . . . on forever . . . forever.*

"And I've heard about Esther. You are twice blessed, my friend. *Hashem* has safely delivered both your wife and daughter into your hands." Josiah frowns. "Still, you cannot be pleased that a Greek has caught Esther's eye." He laughs when he sees the surprise on my face. "I told you Skaris has revealed all. But fear not, once you and your family have moved to Masada, we'll take care of that. There are many worthy young men who would look kindly on your daughter, and they are all *Jews.*"

An uneasiness creeps over me. Is it really wise to separate Esther from Demas now? Especially since he has been the instrument of her healing—at least the beginning of her healing—he and *Hashem,* both? Demas had a way with Esther, and at times was the only one she would talk to. She was still struggling over losing Daniel and over what happened to her at the hands of those two drunken Romans. Demas could draw her out like no other. And he was more than a Greek. He was a follower of The Way. Esther could do worse.

"What is it, my friend?" Josiah says, placing his hand on my shoulder. "With all your blessings why do you look so troubled?"

"I have much to think about," I say, walking away without further explanation.

"I'll not be going to Masada," Aaron says. We're standing by the En Gedi pool where we first made our camp with Titus's captives, and where the women and a small group of men still remain, having been too feeble to make the forced march with Skaris to Masada when he went for help. The dust of Hyrcania has been washed away and we have regained much of our strength, having done little more than sleep and eat for two days. But unlike when we first camped here, we are overcrowded, for Josiah and his men are here too—resting briefly before journeying on to Masada with their heavy bags of silver.

The faithful waterfall still tumbles from the limestone cliffs above and splashes into the large shimmering pool. Some of Josiah's men are in the water, making splashes of their own. The rest are lounging on the rock ledge.

"I'm not going to Masada," Aaron repeats, as if the noise of the water and men had drowned out his original proclamation. "I came to En Gedi only to say goodbye to Esther."

"I know," I hear myself saying. The truth is I've known since the day Aaron rose from the dead. Still . . . I had hoped I was wrong, for his words pain me. Will I ever see him again? "Where will you go?" I say, picking at the large fern by my side.

"To Ephesus, to study under John the Beloved Apostle, and our friend, Zechariah."

At the mention of Zechariah's name, my teeth grind. So . . . that irritant, that man of God, will best me again, this time with my son. Was Zechariah, then, to have the joy and privilege of training Aaron? But training him for what? "I . . . don't understand."

"I was dead, Father. Truly *dead*! You saw . . . you know it's true." Aaron is almost breathless as if experiencing his death for the second time. "And I saw Him—yes I saw *Jesus*. And He spoke to me, He *spoke*! He said I must fulfill my destiny; that I was to be *His* warrior and fight for *His* kingdom, and that my weapons were not to be sword or dagger, but His Word. *His Word!* He showed me that the road will be difficult. That bitter persecution was coming to the followers of The Way, and that I was to help prepare them." His face is tender and eager, but determined, too.

"What of your pledge to Eleazar?" I say, still hoping to deter him. Still hoping to keep him close. "Would you toss it aside as if it were nothing?"

"Little treasure remains hidden that is not under the nose of the Romans. You and I well know that it would take an army to retrieve it. My conscience is clear."

My lips purse. I suddenly feel weary of life, where all is suffering and loss. *How could I bear losing Aaron*? "And your people? Are you content to leave them under Roman bondage? To be sold in the slave markets of the world? Our women raped? Our men crucified? Are you content to live life in Ephesus while such things go on here?" I glance at Aaron. His eyes are so full of tenderness I have to look away or I won't be able to deliver my final blow. "Are you willing to forget how they crucified your *brother*, Abner? How they raped your *sister*?"

Aaron sighs and leans against the rock wall. The large fern partially shades his face. "I haven't forgotten, Father. I pray continually for Esther. She is in God's hands. Even now, He is healing her. I see a great change, and even joy. And Abner? I know how hard his death was on you. But the specter of death has always been a soldier's constant companion, and we all knew that the Romans would punish their captured rebels with crucifixion. But what of that other crucifixion? The one you saw long ago, where One who was innocent was crucified for *our* rebellion. Don't you think His Father looked down and wept, too? Don't you think it broke His heart? I'm going to Ephesus, Father, and nothing you say will change my mind. Please don't try. Rather, give me your blessing."

I shake my head. "I cannot. I'm sorry, Aaron, but I cannot."

"Aaron leaves tomorrow," Rebekah says, dangling her hand in the water beside me.

I notice, with some irritation, that she's the picture of tranquility itself.

"Demas will travel with him as far as Pella," she adds. "It's a comfort to know Aaron will have a companion on the road, at least for part of the way."

I sit glumly by the small pool of our trysting place. This time I know the area is secure having had it thoroughly searched by Josiah's men. Still, I'm ill at ease, restless, and my heart is as heavy as the stone in my hand. I suppose I should take comfort in the fact that Rebekah does not chide me about separating Esther and Demas, even though Esther has done nothing but cry, and Demas walks around like a man lost in a sandstorm.

A soft breeze plays with the strands of Rebekah's cropped hair. She no longer tries to hide it from me, perhaps because it's growing as fast as tamarisk sprouts, and because she knows she's still beautiful, despite professing otherwise. She's lying by the pool's edge and periodically scoops a handful of water, then watches it leak between her fingers. My irritation mounts. How can she be so peaceful?

"You must know that Esther blames you for making Demas return to Pella, even though it was Josiah who told him he was not welcome at Masada." Rebekah rolls onto her back and gazes up at the large reeds that surround us. "But you could remedy that by allowing her to go with him to Pella."

I remain silent. So, I'm to be chided after all.

"I worry about her. She's still fragile. Do you think it wise to separate them?" Rebekah's eyes are on me now.

"I don't know." My mouth is full of agitation and annoyance. "Our world is crumbling, Rebekah. Am I to worry about a young woman's infatuation? In time she'll forget Demas. Someone else will come along. Josiah says there are many eligible men at Masada. And all *Jews*! Surely, you don't want her to align herself with a Greek!" My voice has become loud and defensive.

"He's a believer, Ethan. He follows Messiah. I could wish nothing better for her than to find a man who loves and honors the Lord."

I glare at her. "I suppose you blame me for her unhappiness. As I suppose you blame me for Aaron leaving, and perhaps even for the . . . death of Abner and Joseph? But why stop there? Why not blame me for the destruction of the Temple? Or Jerusalem? And to that, add the slaughter of our people."

She sits up, sweet faced and full of tenderness, looking much like Aaron when he told me he was leaving. Would she leave me too? And go to that irritant, Zachariah? I recoil, fearing her words, then brace myself, not knowing what to expect.

"I love you," she says softly. "And I will accept your decision. If you think Demas is unsuitable for Esther, so be it. I'll not argue for it. But you'll not change Aaron's course. It has been set by God."

I rise to my feet and toss the stone I'm holding into the pond, wishing I could toss my heavy heart in as well. "And Masada? Will you still follow me to Masada?"

She gathers another handful of water and lets it dribble between her fingers. "I'll follow you wherever God leads."

Without another word, I turn and walk away. I find no peace in her answer, for it's really no answer at all, but a question of its own. And what Rebekah was asking was this: where is *God* leading you?

I've been tossing and turning on my pallet for hours. Tomorrow we journey to Masada. I need rest, but the truth is, I'm afraid to sleep. As soon as I drift off, I hear those sounds—the lashing of the whip, the hammer pounding nails, the soft groaning. It's always the same. Even now those sounds seem to fill the night air, like whispers carried on a breeze. Do others hear it? I look over to where my sons lay sleeping nearby. Their snoring tells me they hear nothing.

And Rebekah? I see her slender frame resting peacefully next to our troubled Esther. Oh, to have such peace! I envy my wife. She's told me how God protected her throughout those days and nights in the cave with Lamech, and sustained her with His peace in a new and deeper way. I don't understand it. My heart has not been at peace for years. And I'm weary. So weary . . . I close my eyes, but even before I drift to sleep I hear that whip, that hammer, and jerk myself awake. And for what seems like hours I lay there fighting sleep, not wanting to close my eyes for fear of seeing that blood and hearing those sounds. "Oh, Jesus," I whisper, as I finally roll from my pallet onto my knees, "how far my heart has wandered from you! Help me. Please help me. Tell me what to do. And bring me back to you."

I watch Rebekah and Esther shove the last of the food supplies into several rush baskets, then watch Skaris hoist one onto his broad shoulder. I have never felt such uneasiness. It pricks and pulls and tears at my very soul.

"I'll miss you," Skaris says, coming over to me in long, easy strides, his crop of silky brown hair blowing in the breeze. "I'm grateful for all you've done."

"Take care of them," I say, looking at the two men who have joined my wife and daughter. "Demas is useless with a sword, and I fear Aaron is now loath to use one." I still can't believe Skaris has decided to go to Pella and make his home there with the believers. *Pella.* That name pulsates in my mind. "You should have enough supplies to get you through the worst of the desert." I gesture toward the basket on his shoulder.

"More than enough. I bless God for your generosity."

I clasp his shoulder, trying to ignore the sight of Aaron and Rebekah saying their goodbyes, or Esther, who weeps openly as she clings to Demas. My uneasiness mounts. When I can bear it no more, I leave Skaris and go to their side. Then the three of us watch Aaron, Demas and Skaris descend the path down the mountain. I can hardly breathe. It's as if there's an invisible hand on my throat.

"Be at peace," I hear Rebekah say. And when I look at her sweet, gentle face I realize she's not speaking to Esther, as I supposed, but to me. And I know not how to respond.

"Are you ready?" Josiah says, coming along side me and saving me the trouble of trying. His men are already gathering together to make their descent. He leans closer. "Don't worry, she'll forget," he says, gesturing toward Esther. "They all forget in time. And both she and Rebekah will be proud when they understand that your mission is to gather the rest of the Temple treasure so that we can go on resisting the Romans."

"We'll find little treasure," Benjamin says, joining us. "Most of it lies within enemy territory." His eyes follow Aaron. "My brother has violated no oath by leaving."

Josiah mumbles something about how we all, including Aaron, have done our duty, but I hardly listen. I'm watching Rebekah's scarf slip and expose her hair; watching as she throws back her head and rakes her short wavy locks with her fingers; watching as she sweetly instructs

Esther to gather her things, and I know then and there that the only treasure I'm interested in is that treasure residing within her—that faith and peace and trust and love which only the indwelling Messiah can give—a treasure in earthen vessels. And in that instant, I feel the first bit of peace I've felt in years.

"I'm not going," I hear myself say. "I'm not going to Masada."

"Ethan, you don't mean to abandon the fight now?" Josiah says with a frown. "Every man is needed if we are to defeat the Romans."

"We'll never defeat them." I press my palm against his chest. "In here, you know it's true. Let me go in peace, my friend. You follow your conscience. I must follow mine."

"Even if we don't defeat the Romans, I'd rather die trying than to live under their rule." Josiah looks confused. "I always thought you felt the same way."

"I did . . . once."

"I don't understand, Ethan. What has changed?"

I almost laugh. "Everything."

"What can I say to make you alter your course?"

"Nothing. Just wish me God speed."

Josiah sighs in resignation. "Where will you go?"

"To Pella. To begin a new life." I turn to Benjamin. He's grinning from ear to ear and nods in agreement.

Josiah glances at Rebekah. "Perhaps if I had what you had, I'd be tempted to go, too. *Hashem* has blessed you, and, in truth, we have more treasure than we need. So go, in search of your own."

I'm unable to keep my lips from parting in a smile. "I've already found it, Josiah," I say softly. "I've already found it."

Author's Note

Can we look into the past and see the future? I think so. After all, history is said to repeat itself.

While researching the destruction of Jerusalem by the Romans, my mind kept returning to this one thought: since, according to the Bible, a revived Roman Empire will be the last great empire before Christ's return, are there parallels between the two Roman empires, the old and the revived, and if so, what lessons can be learned?

As I pondered it, I was struck by the power and enormity of the first Roman Empire. It covered much of the known world. It was highly civilized, with paved roads, intricate water systems, a sophisticated government, taxes, pensions and welfare programs. It had theaters and sports arenas. Goods from every corner of the world poured into its marketplace. It was tolerant of all religions except the two that believed in only one God—the Jewish and Christian faiths. These were viewed with suspicion and distrust, and later with hostility. Members of these faiths were openly persecuted, until persecution gave way to outright slaughter.

Rome was also prosperous, advanced, decadent, corrupt and ruthless—so like the one-world government described in Revelation.

The next parallel I saw was between the church of that day and the end-times church of Laodicea. Before the destruction of Jerusalem, Jewish Christians considered themselves part of Judaism and were strongly connected to the Temple. I think of these Christians as the "remnant" and as such they correspond to the body of Christ which will be raptured in the last days before the great tribulation. Indeed, the majority of Christians in Jerusalem escaped the horrors that befell the rest of Jerusalem's population because they fled to a "safe city" such as Pella.

Thus, it is the Temple priesthood and its governing body, the Sanhedrin, which typifies the last day church. To say they were corrupt is an understatement. The High Priest and others associated with the Temple often lined their own pockets at the expense of the people. They cared more for power than obeying and serving God. In league with Rome, they even allowed the Roman government to appoint the High Priests rather than allowing the office to be passed down from the Aaronic line, from father to son, as ordained by God. Consequently, these High Priests were politically motivated. And not only were they part of the corrupt world system, they catered to it, and by doing so left a spiritual vacuum.

This vacuum created confusion among the people, and as a result, countless numbers were deceived by the many "Messiahs" who surfaced during this period. Violence increased as Jewish rebels and bandits roamed the countryside in lawlessness. Seeing the decline of their nation and religious purity, another group, who were zealous for God but moved carnally, believed deliverance from Rome and the return to Holiness would only come by their hand. They employed force and brutality, and ended up becoming as ruthless as the very Jewish bandits and Romans they fought.

Jerusalem can also be seen as a microcosm of the end time world. Starvation, disease, murder, corruption, moral confusion, violence, and infighting (wars and rumors of wars) marred the city, making it ripe for destruction.

Also, during this time, Christians strongly believed that Jesus' return was imminent. So, too, as the end times near, more and more people will begin looking for the return of Christ, for according to the Bible, He will return at the end of the seven year tribulation.

Certainly there are intriguing parallels between the time of the fall of Jerusalem in 70 A.D. and the time of the tribulation period; parallels that can, if we care to look, give us a glimpse into the future. And if we must live through these times, God will give us the grace to do so. But if we are to be raptured beforehand, as some believe (myself included), then let us prepare our hearts now. Let us be ready for the trumpet sound. If you don't know Jesus, now is the time to accept Him as your Lord and Savior. Now is the time to confess your sins and invite Him into your heart. The tribulation could be closer than we think.

"Even so, come Lord Jesus."

Sylvia Bambola

sylviabambola45@gmail.com

website: http://www.sylviabambola.com

FYI for Readers

Here are some facts concerning *Rebekah's Treasure* that may be of interest to readers:

The first Jewish revolt began in 66 A.D. though the tension between Romans and Jews had been building for years. Jerusalem and the Temple were razed in 70 A.D. and the war finally ended in 73 A.D. when Masada fell. The sad part is that thousands of Jews were killed by their own countrymen during the nearly four years the various Jewish factions battled each other for power.

Josephus, the man Ethan describes as a Hasmonean priest and spokesman for Titus, was an actual historical figure. After the destruction of Jerusalem he went to live in Rome, and under the protection and patronage of Vespasian and later Titus, wrote his famous works, among them *Jewish Antiquities* and *The Jewish War*. The latter contains his first-hand account of the destruction of Jerusalem and the Temple.

The cup of the last supper is neither mentioned in scripture after Jesus' death, nor did it hold any significant place in early Church history. Therefore, it is reasonable to assume that the cup was never revered or thought sacred by the apostles or early church. It was only during the late 12th and early 13th centuries that its legend was developed, and when it began showing up in literature and myths.

In the Gentile cities of the Decapolis, the Greeks and Romans worshipped many gods. But while the worship of Isis was popular throughout the Roman Empire, and the facts concerning the worship of Isis are accurately portrayed in the novel, there's no proof that Isis was worshiped in Pella. There was, however, an ancient Canaanite temple there.

In 70 A.D. Israel would have been called *Eretz Yisrael* (Land of Israel) and Qumran would have been called either *Ir-Tzadok B'Succaca* or

Essene Yahad (Essene Community). But since most people are only familiar with the modern names, for reader clarity, I've used those names in the book.

Hezekiah's Tunnel and Solomon's quarries do exist, as do the multiple cisterns and waterways and plastered ashlar stone drainage channels beneath Jerusalem, many of which were indeed used by rebels to move about undetected. However, the tunnel from the Temple to Qumran is not based on fact, though some speculate it did exist and believe it was the very means by which the holy scrolls and temple treasure were evacuated from the city.

The copper scroll is a genuine artifact, and most scholars believe it describes real Temple treasure; a treasure moved sometime before the Romans destroyed the Temple in 70 A.D. The scrolls were found on a shelf in Cave 3, a cave in the limestone cliffs about a mile north of Qumran. Sixty-four treasure locations are mentioned in the scroll.

Scholars cannot agree on the exact location of The Valley of Achor. Some think it is north of Jericho (a common belief of the early Church fathers) while others believe it is the Valley of Hyrcania in the cliffs southwest of Qumran. I have chosen the southwest location as the one I portrayed in the novel, the location John Allegro—the English scholar and member of the original copper scroll-publication team—believed was the site of some treasure mentioned in the copper scrolls: the fortress of John Hyrcania. And where he himself spent considerable time searching for it.

Glossary

abaya: cloak

actio institoria: a claim against a person who placed an institor, or agent, in charge of a business for acts committed by that agent or institor while transacting that busines

Aediles: Market Manager who oversees and regulates all public auctions.

caldarium: Roman hot bath

cubit: 18 to 22 inches, the length from the tip of the middle finger to the elbow

Curule Aedile magistrate who had *imperium*—the power to apply the law within his magistracy

Essene Yahad Essene Community

garum: a popular fish sauce commonly used by Romans over many of their dishes

hyrax: a small, furry, rodent-looking mammal

jus gentium: "Law of Nations". International law that governed the Roman legal system

kaffia: male headscarf

kohl: ancient makeup; a blackening agent used to enhance the eyes

kokh: burial niche

lepta: bronze coin; that and the *prutah* were the smallest denomination of coins; the lepta was probably the widow's mite in Mark's and Luke's Gospel

lictors: Roman civil servant, serving magistrates who had *imperium* (the power to apply the law within their magistracy)

***lex aquilia*:** the law that compensated owners if their property was damaged by another

***mikvah*:** ritual bath, used for spiritual cleansing or purification

***mohar*:** bride price paid by the bridegroom to bride's parents

naturalis

***obligation*:** obligations which may or may not be legally protected but which are prerequisites of all obligations

***palla*:** a cloak worn over the shoulder, somewhat like a toga, by women

***peculium*:** (Roman law) acquisitions/property that are allowed to be held by a son, wife or slave even though technically they belonged to the father, husband or master

praetors: term applied to either an army commander or a magistrate

praetorian law: action introduced by praetors in 149 B.C. by which equity was developed for actions not provided for by Roman law.

***scrip*:** purse

semadi: a headdress with silver coins sewn onto it.

shirwal: pants

stola: a long tunic that usually is worn over another tunic, worn by Greek and Roman women

Sukkot: Feast of Tabernacles

talent: (of silver) There is conflicting information on this. Even several good sources differ, and their claims put the weight of a talent anywhere from 90 to 130 pounds

talith: Jewish prayer shawl

Rebekah's Treasure

Readers Group Questions:

1. There's a lot about treasure in this book. Though we may not think we are treasure seekers, what "Copper Scroll" of treasure do we commonly pursue today?
2. Jesus drank from many cups, including the cup at the last supper. Do you think it would please Him if we made a shrine or idol out of any one of them? Because we are finite and temporal, it's always a temptation to make idols out of what we perceive to be sacred objects. Do you think this is one of the reasons the Bible forbids us to make idols or worship images?
3. Rebekah came from a wealthy family. Her flight to Pella required her to not only leave most of her family behind but required her to adjust to a harsher, poorer way of life, not so unlike those today who must adjust after a natural disaster or a serious economic reversal. What are some of the difficulties and dangers of such an adjustment?
4. The Bible says that Satan is a liar and the father of lies. Argos seems very comfortable with telling lies. He does it so well that he actually seems to believe them himself. In fact, he even accuses Rebekah of doing the very thing he is guilty of. ("You would have the entire city turn against me.") How easy is it to get into the habit of telling lies? Is it easier to tell bigger lies after one becomes comfortable with the "little deceptions" i.e. a mother instructing her kids to, "tell them I'm not home," when someone she doesn't want to talk to calls on the phone?
5. Esther tries to impose her will in her life instead of bowing to God's, and not only makes herself miserable in the process but must face serious consequences. Can you think of a time you

pursued your own will, regardless of what God's might have been? Were you happy? Were there consequences?

6. In chapter seven, though Kyra has heard about Jesus many times at Zechariah's house church, Rebekah thinks she's not interested. Yet, pages later we learn Kyra really was interested, and that Zechariah's words had actually made an impression on her. Have you ever talked about Jesus with someone who seemed disinterested, only to learn later, perhaps years later, that what you said had, in fact, made an impact? Can we ever predict what our witnessing will accomplish? Even if a person seems disinterested, can we really know what's going on inside?
7. In chapter eight, Ethan questions why God would heal the heathen Demas, giving him both physical eyes as well as spiritual ones, and *not* heal his son—a faithful follower of Jesus as well as of Torah and Temple. Have you ever asked this same question? Maybe you have served God many years without seeing a miracle in your life, then a new believer comes along getting a healing or some other wonderful miracle from God, leaving you to feel like that faithful older brother who has labored alongside his father for years but was never as appreciated as that rebellious younger brother who spent so much time in the pigpen? How did it make you feel? Is it fair? Is there a lesson in it? Are we right to feel jealous?
8. In chapter nine, Rebekah feels like she's the only one in the world who has suffered, who is hurting. Have you ever felt like that? How did you overcome it?
9. Both Hannah and Zechariah imagine the worst when they are told to appear before the slave master, right after Judah comes home. How many times have you thought the worst, before praying about it or consulting the Lord or waiting for His guidance or grace? Explain.
10. Rebekah finds out that the Esther in the Market Manager's house is not her daughter, and though she is bitterly disappointed

there is no indication she is angry with God. Have you ever been so disappointed about something that you became angry with God? Even though, like in Rebekah's life, He has already done so many miracles in yours?

11. For years Rebekah had been praying that Aaron, the son who had such a heart for God, would learn more about his faith under the Apostle John. In the end, this prayer is answered. Many times we don't get the answer to our prayers as fast as we would like. Can you recall a prayer that was a long time in coming? What does this say? Should we persevere in prayer even when we see no results? Does God measure time the way we do?